Southern Spitfire!

"You heard me, Yankee. Get out of here," Katie insisted, the barrel of the shotgun pointed directly at Brent's heart.

"Very well, Miss O'Toole, if that's the way you want it!" answered Brent. He made a sudden lunge and wrested the gun from Katie's hands with ease. Lifting her by the waist, he threw her over his shoulder like a sack of grain and swiftly entered the house.

Katie was kicking and scratching, her skirts and hoops swaying. He carried her into the parlor and deposited her squirming form on the high-backed sofa. Then he stood peering down into her flushed and beautiful face. As she sat breathing deeply in an attempt to maintain control, she managed to say, "How dare you! If my father were alive, he would personally horsewhip you! Don't you ever lay your filthy hands on me again, you...you damn Yankee, you!"

The Yankee
And
The Belle

Catherine Creel

LEISURE BOOKS ∞ **NEW YORK CITY**

To Craig, who bought the typewriter

A LEISURE BOOK

Published by

Dorchester Publishing Co., Inc.
6 E. 39th Street
New York City

Printed in the United States of America

Part 1

Corkhaven

One

Katie O'Toole critically surveyed her image reflected in
the tall, ornately carved French mirror. She smiled, for
what she saw there pleased her. Her brilliant red-gold hair
was arranged fashionably atop her head, with a few loose
curls allowed to fall naturally on each side of her beautiful
face. Her creamy complexion was fortunately unflawed
by freckles, and her emerald-green eyes were large and
luminous, fringed by long, curling black lashes. The dress,
which she had just donned over the myriad of underwear
that society dictated women wear, merely served to
accentuate her figure, which was indeed very good. She
possessed a high, full bosom, a small waist, and shapely,
well-rounded hips. The bodice of the dress was cut low,
but not immodestly so, with a rounded neckline, and the
gathered skirt flared gently out over the hoops and
numerous petticoats. The color of the dress was almost
the same shade of green as her eyes, and Katie knew she
looked her best. She always liked to take pains with her
appearance, even if there were not any young men around
these days to notice the effect.

Oh, but how different it had all been before the war,
Katie reflected. She had been the belle of every ball since
the age of sixteen which was when she had finally been
allowed to wear her hair up and remain awake to attend
the dances and parties given with great regularity. She
had attracted men wherever she went, and she had
enjoyed the sense of power her beauty gave her. Of course,
Mama had cautioned her against the vanity that could so

easily surface, but Katie was not actually vain. No, she merely understood that she was unusually attractive. She indulged in innocent flirtations and laughed at the wealth of compliments paid her. She had never fallen in love with any of the young men, although several of them had declared an undying love and devotion for her. She was not hard-hearted; instead, her heart had simply remained untouched. She had become expert at graciously refusing proposals of marriage, although she unfortunately lost control of her temper whenever a beau refused to accept her negative response to his offer. Katie did not lose such control very often, but she became a veritable tigress whenever she did.

"Sarah!" she called across the wide hallway to her maid, "Is Mama ready to leave yet?"

"No, Miss Katie," replied the small black woman as she entered Katie's bedroom, "She ain't downstairs yet, but you better get on down there and see to those brothers of yours." Sarah had been purchased and brought to Corkhaven before Katie's birth, and she frequently spoke with the privilege of a former nurse. Katie loved her, but she dearly wished that Sarah would cease treating her like a child.

Katie, giving a last satisfied pat to her hair, made a face at herself in the mirror. Her two younger brothers were such a bother sometimes. One never knew just what kind of trouble or mischief they would next be into, and Katie and her mother had their hands full with raising the boys. Katie's beloved father had died over a year ago, leaving his wife and children the plantation, but little else.

Corkhaven had obtained its name from Gerald O'Toole's birthplace in Ireland. He had journeyed to America over twenty years ago, when he had been only twenty-five years of age and as handsome an Irish lad that ever set foot off the boat. He had decided to seek his fortune in the South, where he had enough foresight to invest his small inheritance received from his deceased father's will, into the profitable business involving the

6

growing and shipping of the South's precious commodity, cotton. He had married a pretty and well-dowered lady of good breeding, whom he had chanced to meet at a friend's house one afternoon. He had been smitten at first sight with the petite brunette. It had taken him exactly two weeks to convince the lady to marry him, which he had then done with her father's hesitantly given blessing. Gerald had built his dream plantation, and he and his Amelia had settled in and begun a family. After nineteen years of marriage and three children, Gerald O'Toole had died a happy man. Happy, except for the war. He had managed to accumulate quite a sizeable fortune through-out the years, but the war had been responsible for the fact that the fortune dwindled until there was little remaining. Corkhaven, however, survived.

Corkhaven, like almost all of the other plantations in the South at that time, had prospered because of the labor of slaves. Slaves who had been bought on the auction block, who had been carefully selected to maintain the fields and run the house. However, in order to pay several debts owing to the loss of a market for his cotton, Gerald O'Toole had been forced to sell almost all of the slaves he owned, keeping only a few. He had been a kind and just master, but he had been a businessman all the same. Now, Corkhaven no longer produced its crops of cotton and Katie and her mother found it quite difficult to manage at times. There had been a small amount of money left when Gerald died, but it had almost disappeared. They were now barely able to maintain the large house, and some of the land had been sold at quite a loss.

Just when would it all end? Katie asked herself as she began to descend the wide, curving staircase. The war had raged for more than three years now, and the South was suffering monumental losses. In addition to the defeats of the Confederate troops, the plantations and cities of the South were being ravaged by the further encroaching Yankees.

"Damn Yankees!" Katie swore with a decidedly

7

unladylike vehemence. She hated what the enemy was doing to the South. Several of the young men who had been courting her before the war had given their lives to the glorious cause, and more of their friends were being touched by the tragedy of war each day. Thank goodness her two brothers were still so young. She naturally wanted the Confederacy to emerge victorious, but she selfishly rejoiced that her brothers would not be called upon to serve.

Oh, well, she needn't worry, for Corkhaven was still alive, and she, Katie O'Toole, would make sure her family suffered as little as possible because of the war. She loved them all with a fierce devotion, and woe to the intruder who sought to do them harm in any way.

She stepped into the parlour, where her two energetic brothers were wrestling upon the thinning red carpet. Eleven-year-old James appeared to be gaining an easy victory over John, who was seven years old. Katie sometimes wished there were not such an age difference between herself and her brothers. She had turned nineteen just last month. Of course, there had not been much of a birthday celebration, beyond the family and the few remaining slaves presenting her with small, hand-made gifts and congratulations. Her sixteenth birthday had been such a joyous occasion.

Papa had hired a group of the best musicians, who had traveled all the way from Atlanta. The large, white-columned house had been lavishly decorated, and at least a hundred people had been invited to the celebration. Katie's mother had presented her daughter with a stylish new dress and a delicate string of pearls. Sarah had arranged her hair in a mass of shining curls tied up with a yellow satin ribbon to match the new ballgown. She had paraded down the staircase and had been absolutely swamped with admirers petitioning for a dance with the young beauty. She had danced and danced, and Papa had told her how proud he was of his young lady. That had been such a happy time. There were so few happy times at Corkhaven these days.

After her sixteenth birthday, Katie had attended a great many parties, dances, and other sorts of social gatherings. She had very few friends of the same sex, since most of the other young ladies were intensely jealous of the striking girl with the face and figure of a young goddess. But Katie didn't mind, for she enjoyed the conversation and companionship of the opposite sex much more. Now, there were no longer any opportunities to dance or flirt. All her neighbors merely occupied their time with endeavoring to keep their plantations producing enough food for their own needs. Katie assisted her mother in managing Corkhaven, as she had done since her father's death.

Amelia O'Toole, still graceful and attractive, arrived downstairs and entered the parlour. Katie noticed with approval her mother's trim appearance. She always looked nice, and the touches of gray now evident in her dark hair made her petite figure even more distinguished-looking. Amelia was a kind and generous woman, but she did not possess great strength of character, a quality she envied in her beautiful and headstrong daughter.

Amelia demanded that James and John disengage and behave themselves; then she shooed her children outside and up into the waiting carriage. The driver, Old Jonah, cracked his whip and the horses moved forward at a moderate pace.

Today was Sunday and the O'Tooles were going to church. There were no longer very many of their friends or neighbors in attendance, but Amelia O'Toole insisted that her family be present every Sunday.

Katie concentrated her attention on the sights and sounds of the countryside on this early spring morning. The sun was shining upon the land, the trees and flowers were emitting a deliciously fresh aroma, and the birds were singing their songs in sweet unison. Katie did not

9

particularly enjoy attending church anymore; the long-winded sermons were almost exclusively concerned with the war. Always about being thankful that the Lord was on the side of the South, the right side. How they must all have faith that the South would emerge from the battle victorious. Katie believed that the South's cause was indeed righteous, but she wondered just how the minister could predict the Lord's preference as to the outcome of the war. She decided that she could endure almost anything for this once-a-week outing. It was the only time they traveled farther than their own land, except for an occasional visit to a nearby friend or relative of Amelia's.

The carriage arrived outside the small, whitewashed church, and Katie and her family stepped down from the carriage and climbed the steps leading inside. They entered the church and took their seats in the family pew. The service began, and Katie tried unsuccessfully to concentrate on the minister's sermon. She began to daydream, as she was wont to do when bored, and she did not realize that the minister was no longer speaking until her brother, James, nudged her sharply in the side. One of the O'Toole's neighbors, a big, kindly man in his fifties by the name of William Jenkins, was delivering a message to the congregation. He was speaking in a rather hurried and excited manner, but Katie managed to catch the bulk of his speech.

"We have already informed the outlying landowners who are not present today. You should be prepared for this type of invasion. The Yankee troops have been known to steal food, horses, and anything else they think is necessary. You all should go on home and hide anything of value. Instruct your slaves to be on the alert..."

Katie had heard enough. Yankees! Surely they were not so near. Well, they wouldn't get any of the food or horses at Corkhaven! Her mind flew this way and that with thoughts and plans to protect her family and plantation. There were only two grown men left at

Corkhaven, Old Jonah and his one-armed son named Tom. They would not be of much assistance, and she quickly decided that she would have to see to everything herself. They must be prepared for the Yankees, whom Papa had so often referred to as "the scourge of the South."

Two

A week had now passed since Katie and her family had been alerted to the possibility of an invasion by the enemy at Corkhaven. There had been no new reports as to the location of the expected Yankees, and life went on pretty much the same as it had before the startling information.

The O'Toole's had returned home from church that day a week ago, and Katie had immediately instructed the slaves to begin hiding all of the extra food, while she rushed upstairs and gathered up her jewelry. She debated whether or not to hide any of Papa's books, but decided that there would not be enough room in the underground cellar out back of the main house. Besides, she thought with amusement, Yankees probably can't read, anyway!

Everything had been collected and then stored in the cellar, although it now seemed to have been a rather foolish precaution, since there had been no sign of the enemy. Katie mused that the Yankees must have already passed through the area, probably in the dead of night, afraid to show their cowardly, thieving faces.

After returning home from church on this particular day, Amelia permitted her sons to go and play outside, while she and Katie changed from their Sunday dresses and into more practical attire. The dresses they owned were dreadfully outdated, but there was no way to purchase any style books or fabrics without traveling to Atlanta. Katie's ballgowns hung in the wardrobe, unused but not forgotten, while she selected a worn muslin dress

12

and hurried into it. Then, she rejoined her mother in the library, where they began examining the month's accounts. Katie possessed a quick and intelligent mind, and she was grateful that her parents had allowed her to use it. It was true that she had been instructed in the usual social graces deemed necessary for a young lady, but she had also been taught by her father how to read, write, and do bookkeeping for the plantation.

After having labored over the books for almost an hour, Amelia looked up and said to her daughter, "Katie, dear, please go upstairs and fetch one of my bonnets for me. I think I'll go on outside for a while and watch the boys play. It's too beautiful a day to be spending it inside the house."

"All right, Mama. I'll be only too glad to finish this page of figures, anyway." Katie strolled up the stairs and into her mother's bedroom, picked out a bonnet from inside the huge wardrobe in the corner of the room, and then approached the staircase again. Instead of walking down the stairs, she decided to do something she had not done in quite a while. Mama would be simply aghast if she saw her, but Katie lifted her full skirts high, eased a shapely, white-stockinged leg over the bannister, then slid down backwards. Reaching the bottom with a thump, she then climbed down, straightened her skirts, and made sure that the whole procedure had not been observed by anyone else. She then re-entered the library and gave the bonnet to her mother, who tied it on her head and retired to the front lawn. As she was left alone to work, Katie remembered that she had forgotten to give Sarah a petticoat with a small tear in one of the flounces to be mended. She laid aside her work once more and returned upstairs to locate the petticoat before she again forgot.

Entering her bedroom, which was tastefully decorated in various shades of blues and yellows, Katie walked over and opened the doors of her wardrobe. She searched through it for the petticoat, but it was not to be found anywhere within. She then began opening the drawers of the bureau, but was also unable to find what she was seeking there.

Well, since I'm tearing through my clothes, she thought, I might as well straighten things a bit and give Sarah a shock! With that, she began to gather up the articles of clothing she had hastily flung on the floor and neatly folded them, returning them to their correct places.

While Katie was occupied upstairs, two riders had been sighted approaching Corkhaven by James and John, who were playing on the front lawn. After they alerted their mother to the appearance of the horsemen, she grabbed each of them by the hand and pulled them inside the house with her. Although they protested, she sent them upstairs with their nurse, Hannah. Then, she smoothed her wind-blown hair and prepared to meet the two strangers. She walked outside and stood on the front veranda as the two men rode into the front yard.

Amelia's eyes widened suddenly with the realization that the two men were wearing the blue uniform of the enemy. The welcoming smile on her face quickly disappeared, to be replaced by a chilling frown. Yankees at Corkhaven! She inwardly quailed at meeting the two enemy soldiers, but she held her head high and drew herself up to her full height of five feet, two inches. Perhaps if she was cooperative and answered any questions that they might ask of her, they would ride away and leave Corkhaven, untouched, she thought hopefully.

The first man her glance was drawn to, the younger of the two, was a very noticeable person. Over six feet tall, he had light brown hair cut just above the collar of his blue jacket, deep blue eyes, and a rather unconventionally handsome face. Yes, he was attractive, in a rugged sort of way. He couldn't be much above his mid-twenties or so, Amelia calculated. He was smiling at her in a friendly enough manner.

"How do you do, ma'am?" the young stranger asked. The other man, a grubby-looking character of indeterminate age, simply sat astride his horse and seemed occupied

14

with looking over the grounds surrounding the house.

"Sir," Amelia inclined her head cooly toward the Yankee.

"May I please introduce myself and my companion? My name is Brent Morgan, and I am a captain in the Union Army, as you can undoubtedly see. This gentleman beside me is my sergeant, Duffy. We were wondering if we might dismount and come inside for a few words with you?" Again, the Yankee soldier smiled at Amelia in a disarming way.

"Well, I suppose so, Captain Morgan. I am Mrs. Gerald O'Toole, and our property you have just ridden on to is known as Corkhaven. This way, gentlemen." They dismounted and followed Amelia through the front doors and into the parlour, where she instructed one of the slaves to bring them all some tea. The two men courteously waited for Amelia to seat herself, then they sat down upon the high-backed sofa directly across from her.

There are only two of them, she thought. She felt that she might perhaps be able to handle the situation, although she did so wish that Katie would appear. Where was that girl, anyway?

Katie, meanwhile, was still upstairs in her room, pulling her dresses from the wardrobe one by one, and then holding them in front of her to see if anything could be done to alter them and update them in any way. She was completely oblivious to the situation occurring downstairs in the parlour. She had not heard her two brothers being led upstairs by Hannah, as she had closed the door to her room in order to have a few moments of privacy. With those two young scamps around, she thought, it was almost impossible to have any privacy.

Downstairs in the parlour, Captain Morgan was speaking to Amelia.

"Mrs. O'Toole, we have been searching for an estate and house of this size in which to temporarily quarter our men. They number about thirty in all. Corkhaven appears

15

to fit our requirements, so we should like to bring our men here for a few days. I am sorry to put you to such an inconvenience, but we would of course confine ourselves to the downstairs area."

"Oh, sir, I'm afraid that is simply impossible! You see, we barely have enough food for our own needs, and this is quite a busy time of year for us. You will simply have to look elsewhere for the accommodations you need." Amelia had become frightened by the captain's words, but she had also become angry. What in heaven's name made the man believe that she and her family, loyal to the cause, would put themselves out in any way for the enemy? She rose from her chair and was preparing to show the men to the front door, when Captain Morgan again spoke.

"Mrs. O'Toole, I can appreciate your feelings. However, it appears that you are unaware of the importance of such a 'request'. My men need food and rest, and I have chosen this particular plantation. I'm afraid that you will have to comply with our wishes, for I am commandeering this house and estate for as long as I think necessary. Now, will you please inform your family and slaves of the arrangement? Sergeant Duffy and I go now to collect our troops, but we will return in about an hour."

Amelia stared speechlessly at the young soldier. Whatever was she to do? There was no one around at the moment to help her with the situation, and she again wished that Katie would appear. If it weren't for the fact that it might appear cowardly and undignified, she would have gone in search of her daughter that instant.

"But, Captain Morgan, I have already informed you that what you wish is impossible. Be so good as to leave my house and lands this very moment!" Amelia demanded with as much bravado as she could muster. She was nearly in tears by now, but she would not cry in front of the enemy.

"Mrs. O'Toole, I again apologize for the inconvenience, but we will return with our men within the hour. Please see to it that you are prepared for us." With that, he and Sergeant Duffy, who had sat in silence throughout the entire interchange, tipped their hats to Amelia, and left the room. Mounting their horses once more, they quickly rode away.

Devil take the woman, anyway! Brent exclaimed to himself. Didn't she realize that this was war and she had no choice? He didn't particularly relish the thought of moving in on any Southern family, but he had his orders and knew that his men needed rest in order to complete the journey ahead of them. They had already traveled far and had made good time. Now, they deserved a few days' rest.

Katie, finally finished with her labors in her room, descended the stairs once more. Arriving in the library, she thought she heard someone weeping, and she hurried next door to the parlour, where she found her mother standing just inside the doorway with a very distracted look on her face, and tears coursing down her brightened cheeks.

"Mama, whatever is the matter?" she exclaimed as she put her arm around her mother's shoulders and led her over to the sofa.

"Oh, Katie, something dreadful has happened!" Amelia went on to tell her daughter about the impending invasion of Corkhaven.

Katie, considerably distressed by her mother's condition, found herself so angry she could not speak. She inwardly fumed at the audacity of Yankess actually demanding that Corkhaven quarter the enemy! She would be waiting for them when they returned, and she would see to it that they never set foot inside this house again. They would have to deal with her this time, instead of her frightened mother.

Katie persuaded her mother to go upstairs and allow Sarah to put her to bed to rest. Then, she looked in on James and John and found them happily playing games up in their room. She reclosed the door and hurried back down the hall to her bedroom. She began to undress, almost tearing her clothes in her impatience. She flung open the doors of her wardrobe, where she had just finished examining all the dresses contained therein, and she finally decided on a dark blue taffeta dress with a lower than usual neckline. She grabbed up her hoops, which she had earlier thrown on to her bed, and fastened them on, then she drew the dress down over her head and hastily buttoned it up the back. It had cost a pretty penny, but it had by now been let out and altered so many times by Sarah that it was beginning to show the wear. Oh, well, Katie decided, it would just have to do. She couldn't very well appear in front of the Yankees in either her work dresses or her ballgowns. She straightened her wayward curls and pinched color into her cheeks. She applied a small smount of perfume to her earlobes and neck, then she approached the mirror and studied her reflection. Yes, she would do very well, she thought as she tugged the neckline of the dress a bit lower. She would be ready for the Yankees when they returned. She would fight them with charm and courtesy, and if that failed, with Papa's shotgun!

Three

Katie returned to the parlour and settled down in a comfortable chair to await the return of the enemy. After half an hour had passed, her mother reappeared and inquired of her daughter what she was planning to do.

"Mama, you're supposed to be up in your room resting, but, since you asked, I'm going to be as sweet and charming as only a Southern lady knows how. I will simply request of this Captain Morgan that he and his men leave Corkhaven and travel somewhere else for a place to sleep. Don't you worry, Mama," Katie said with a slow, calculating smile, "I'll speak to the odious man this time. You just stay inside. Or better yet, you go on back upstairs and rest some more. If I need you for any reason, I'll call you." She hated seeing her mother so upset, and her anger rose as she watched the dejected figure climb the stairs. She would be in a fine mettle by the time the Yankees returned, that was for certain!

Meanwhile, Brent and Sergeant Duffy had returned to the spot where their men were waiting. Ordering the men to mount their horses, Brent then proceeded to lead them in the direction of Corkhaven, which was a few miles to the east.

Captain Brent Morgan had enlisted in the army over two years ago, when he had completed his education in New York. His parents had been dead set against his decision to fight, and they had protested so loudly that he had left home without a backward glance. He had since fought in several battles, and he had participated in the

Battle of Antietam over a year ago, where he had been superficially wounded in the right leg. He had then been promoted to the rank of captain as a result of his bravery and knowledge of military tactics, and he had since been involved in other battles and small skirmishes. He had received his orders to march what was left of his regiment to Atlanta, where they were to join forces with Sherman's troops. Brent had by now seen enough of pain and suffering, but he would follow any orders he received, and so he and his men were journeying to help lay siege to the city.

Brent again found his thoughts returning to home. He had grown up as the only son of a prosperous banker. He had been sent away to the best schools and academies, when all he had ever really desired was to be educated nearer to home and to spend more time with his parents and three sisters. He had matured to be a handsome and personable young man, and he found that he was able to enjoy quite a success with the ladies.

Brent had known many women in his time, but he had never possessed a desire to marry any of them. He realized that he had broken many hearts, as his mother liked to remind him, but he could certainly not help his feelings. He hadn't yet found the woman who could hold him.

Lost in his thoughts, Brent suddenly realized that they had ridden within sight of Corkhaven. He ordered his men to approach no farther than the front gates, while he would enter and speak with Mrs. O'Toole again. The men did as they were told, and Brent slowly rode up to the front of the house. Contrary to what he had expected, standing there on the veranda was not Mrs. O'Toole, but instead a very lovely young lady.

Brent could hardly believe his eyes. She was absolutely beautiful. And the color of that hair! He surmised that she must be Mrs. O'Toole's daughter. What an unexpected pleasure, he mused. She was tall and graceful, standing there with her pretty head held high.

Katie indeed stood proudly, and she disdainfully

observed the Yankee's appearance. He was attractive, and he also looked like a man used to having his orders obeyed. Yes, he certainly appeared masterful, but he was, after all, only a man, and she had a lot of experience in conversing and charming when it came to young men. She suddenly smiled a slow, innocently seductive smile and spoke to Brent.

"Sir, I suppose that you are Captain Morgan. I am Miss O'Toole."

"Miss O'Toole, this is indeed a pleasure," replied Brent, "May I inquire as to the whereabouts of your mother? We had an earlier conversation and I have come to inform her of my return, along with my men." Brent could still hardly believe his good fortune. Imagine, having a beautiful young lady at the plantation he had randomly chosen.

"Well, Captain Morgan, I do hope you all are not too awfully tired. You see, my mother has already informed me of your request. I'm afraid that we are still unable to offer you our hospitality at this time." Katie spoke smilingly and raised her large, green eyes to his deep, blue ones, "I'm sure that you can find another plantation that would be much more suitable than Corkhaven. We haven't many slaves, and we really do not have the means to quarter your men." She again raised her eyes to his, but she experienced a mild, shocking sensation this time. There was something about the man, she thought, that made her feel that he would see right through her guise of sweetness.

Why, the little devil, thought Brent. She's actually flirting with me! If she thinks that I will change my plans because of her pretty face and charming behavior, she's in for quite a surprise!

"Miss O'Toole, our plans are unfortunately set and cannot be altered. Now, please tell everyone here to make ready for us. I will instruct my men to dismount and stay out here on the front lawn until you have prepared some rooms in the downstairs area. Also, we will be needing some nourishment, so please inform your cook to have ready some sort of meal." Brent could barely conceal his amusement at the young lady's flashing green eyes and abrupt change of attitude. He turned his horse and instructed his men to approach. They rode on to the front lawn, dismounted, and then sat upon the ground to wait.

Brent dismounted, handed the reins of his horse to Sergeant Duffy, instructing him to wait until he motioned for him to bring the men inside, then again approached the front veranda to venture inside and see to it that his orders were being carried out. No sooner had he mounted the first three steps, than Katie reappeared. This time, the charm and courtesy of the Southern lady were gone, and in their place was a very determined air of defiance. The defiance was apparent in the way she held her head, the way she glared at him, and the way she held her father's shotgun, pointed directly at his body.

"No, Captain Morgan, not another step. I will repeat what I have already told you, sir. You will not set foot inside this house, and you will take your men and leave Corkhaven." Katie was stubborn enough to shoot the man if he didn't do as she ordered.

Brent, looking at her and the shotgun she held tightly in her hands, tightened his lips in anger. His blue eyes were glinting with a strange light, and he sought to maintain control over his temper. This young woman was going to be a definite problem!

"Now, Miss O'Toole, you had better lower that gun right this very instant. Because if you don't, I am going to lose my temper. Just what good do you think it would do if you shot me, right here in front of thirty armed men? Don't be a fool, and give me that gun!" Brent reached out to take the gun from her, but she held firmly on to it. She had become a bit frightened by the look in the captain's eyes, but she would hold her ground.

"You heard me, Yankee. Get out of here," she stubbornly insisted. She kept the barrel of the shotgun pointed directly at Brent's heart. It was true that it wouldn't do any good to shoot him with all the other enemy soldiers looking on, but she would show him that she and her family would not give in so easily.

"Very well, Miss O'Toole, if that's the way you want it!" answered Brent. Then, with his men watching the contest with great interest, he made a sudden lunge and wrested the gun from Katie's hands with ease. As she stood glaring at him in surprise and fury, he dropped the gun to the steps with a clatter, and, lifting her by the waist, he threw her over his shoulder like a sack of grain and swiftly entered the house.

Katie was kicking and screeching at the Yankee, her skirts and hoops swaying. He carried her into the parlour and deposited her squirming form on the high-backed sofa. Then, he stood peering down into her flushed and beautiful face. Katie heard the laughter of the men outside and was further incensed by the captain's behavior.

As she sat breathing deeply in an attempt to maintain control, she managed to say to him, "How dare you! If my father were alive, he would personally horsewhip you! Don't you ever lay your filthy hands on me again, you . . . you damn Yankee, you!" She was so furious, she almost burst into tears.

Brent's anger had by now been replaced by amusement as he listened to Katie's outburst. He gazed down into her wide, sparkling eyes and calmly replied, "I regret that I was forced to use such measure on you, Miss O'Toole, but I couldn't allow you to shoot me, especially not in front of my own men! Now, you just sit there and calm down, while I give you time to find your household slaves and instruct them to make preparations for me and my men." He smiled maddeningly at her, and Katie almost kicked him.

"Captain Morgan," she said with more control than before, "you will not bring all of those men into this house! The slaves will not lift a finger unless I tell them to,

23

so you might as well leave. You are not wanted here, and I will do everything in my power to keep you from remaining at Corkhaven!"

"Miss O'Toole, I said that the matter is settled, and I will warn you now against any further interference." He spoke with a sternness that Katie recognized as dangerous to cross. With a last warning glance at her, he strode out of the room and back outside.

Katie, left alone with her turbulent thoughts and emotions, tried vainly to think of something else she could try. Mama and the boys would be of no help, and the blasted man had captured the only gun in the house. Suddenly, she remembered that all of the extra food was stored in the underground cellar out back. Its existence was hidden by some tall grass and weeds. Well, Captain Morgan, she thought triumphantly, let's see how long you stay here without food to feed your men!

She jumped up from the sofa and bounded up the stairs to speak with her mother. She found Amelia still reclining upon her daybed, with a wet cloth covering her forehead.

"Mama, the Yankees have returned. Now, don't get alarmed," she said as her mother attempted to rise, "I can't seem to keep them from coming into the house, but I just recalled that all of the extra food, and quite an abundance of it, is stored out in the cellar. So I don't think they will be staying with us very long, after all," she finished with a satisfied smile.

"Oh, Katie, I'm so glad your father isn't here to see Yankees entering this house. I can hardly stand it, myself. I suppose we will just have to be patient until they leave. By the way, Katie, dear, your brothers are as yet unaware of the circumstances, are they not? What are we going to tell them?"

"Well, I'll simply tell them that the Yankees are just passing through and will only be staying at Corkhaven for a few hours. I think I'll let them come downstairs and see what Yankees actually look like, too. That should keep them quiet for a while. Now, you stay here and relax, while I go find Sarah and Hannah and tell them what's going on. Then, I'll go out to the kitchen and tell Junie to keep quiet about the extra food. The captain will see that Corkhaven is indeed unsuitable for his purposes." And, brushing her mother's cheek with a quick kiss, she went down the hall and into her brother's bedroom. She informed them of the Yankees' presence, and they quickly responded by running downstairs to see the enemy. Then, she found Sarah and Hannah, told them about the Yankees, and instructed them to do nothing unless she gave her approval. She ventured downstairs to the kitchen, where she ordered the cook, Junie, to quickly prepare what little food remained in the huge pantry, and to bring it on out whenever she told her to do so.

Katie returned to the parlour and sat down on the sofa, arranging her skirts and smoothing out any wrinkles. She resolved to sit serenely and calmly and let the captain discover for himself the truth of what she had told him. No slave at Corkhaven would follow any orders unless they were issued by herself.

Brent, who had instructed his men to find the stables and to feed and water their horses, strode back into the house, where he spied Katie sitting in the parlour, looking very cool and lovely.

"Miss O'Toole, I wanted to find out if those orders of mine were by any chance being relayed by you to your slaves, but I see they are not. It appears that you still refuse to cooperate. Very well, where are your household slaves?" He was again becoming incensed by the young woman's open defiance.

"Why, Captain Morgan, the only household slaves we own are our two old nurses, Hannah and Sarah, and the cook, Junie. If you wish to speak with them, I will summon them in here at once." She picked up a small silver bell on the oak table beside the sofa and proceeded to ring it vigorously. After a few moments, the three slave women appeared in the doorway and stood silently staring straight ahead.

"This Yankee soldier has something he wishes to discuss with you," Katie informed them with a knowing smile.

Brent, suspicious of that smile, decided to go ahead and instruct the three women to make the needed preparations.

"Ladies," he politely said, "my men will need some sleeping quarters and bedding for a few days. I think one or two of these downstairs rooms will be sufficient. Please see to it that they are prepared immediately."

Sarah, Hannah, and Junie, receiving silent instruction from Katie's expressive eyes, behaved as if the Yankee had not spoken a word. Brent glanced at Katie, but she sat there in silence.

"Miss O'Toole, will you please tell them to do as I say? My men are getting tired of waiting out in the hot sun, and I am getting tired of your constant refusals to obey my orders." That dangerous glint had returned to his eyes, but Katie refused to be quelled by his look.

"Captain Morgan, I told you that this would happen if you tried to give any orders to our slaves. Now, will you leave?" she demanded with a small smirk of triumph.

"Ladies," he commanded as he turned back to the three slaves, "you will either do as I say this instant, or I will instruct my men to go upstairs and tear the rooms apart to find what we will need. Either you bring some bedding down here and prepare a place for us to sleep right now, or I will carry out my threats."

The three slaves became quite alarmed at the Yankee's words, and hastily giving a last glance at their mistress, they hurried away to do his bidding. They couldn't allow Miss Katie's stubbornness to go too far, and just what would Mrs. O'Toole say if the Yankees came upstairs?

Katie stood up and called to them to return, but it was to no avail. They had believed the captain's threats and still thought of her as a child, anyway. She was once more left alone with Captain Morgan.

"Miss O'Toole, have you instructed the cook to

prepare a meal for us?" he asked. At her abrupt little nod, he went on to say,

"Well, I suggest that you tell her to bring the food out on to the front lawn. I'll send a couple of the men in here to assist her. After the meal, we will enter the house, so please be ready." He strolled out of the room, thinking what a vexing creature the young woman was, but what a face and figure she possessed! She certainly possessed the ability to make him angry, but he was sure she would soon tire of fighting him.

Katie hurried out to the kitchen and began instructing Junie to take the few dishes of food out to the front lawn, when two of the Yankee soldiers arrived to help. She loaded them down with the food, which was not of any great amount. As they carried out their burdens, she retired to the parlour to once again await the appearance of Captain Morgan, whom she knew would shortly be coming in search of her to demand more food for his men.

Brent did indeed notice the small amount of food, which could not possibly satisfy the appetites of thirty hungry men, and he furiously strode into the parlour. This is getting ridiculous, he thought, and Miss O'Toole is becoming quite exasperating!

"Miss O'Toole," he spoke with exaggerated patience, "where is the rest of the food?"

"Why, Captain Morgan," she answered innocently, "that is all the food we have. I told you that Corkhaven would be unable to quarter you and your men, but you refused to listen. There just isn't any more food."

Brent became as angry as he had been in a great while, and he virtually exploded.

"Dammit, woman! You will tell me where you have hidden the rest of your provisions, for I know that you have more than this, or I and my men will conduct a thorough search of the house and grounds. I have had enough of your unwise resistance for one day. Well, what is your answer? Do you tell me, or do I have to find it for myself?" he insisted.

27

"I'll not tell you anything, Yankee!" she almost screamed at him.

At that, Brent turned upon his heel and left the room, returning a few short moments later with ten of his men. He instructed them to comb the house for any possible hiding place where the extra food might be, while he returned to the parlour. There, he sat down directly across from Katie and prepared to wait.

The two of them sat in stony silence, Katie staring toward the doorway, and Brent directing his gaze out the large window. Several minutes had passed when Katie heard her mother calling her. She hurriedly left the room and ran up the stairs to her mother's room. There, she found her mother standing, gazing with horror at the two men searching her wardrobe and under her bed.

"Katie," her mother whispered as her daughter rushed to her side, "what are those Yankees doing upstairs, and in my room?"

"Mama, I refused to tell them where the extra food is hidden," she told her mother in a low voice, "Just lay back down, and everything will be just fine." She persuaded Amelia to do as she entreated, and the two men left the room to go and search elsewhere.

Katie encountered Sarah and Hannah standing in the hallway, and she again orderd them to tell the Yankees nothing. Then she said,

"I'll speak to you two later about your disgraceful behavior earlier. How dare you countermand my wishes!" She returned downstairs and once more entered the parlour, where she found Captain Morgan still sitting.

"You will never find what you seek. There is no reason to upset my mother and the slaves . . ." she began. As she spoke, one of the soldiers came in from outside and informed Captain Morgan that they had located the underground cellar. At Katie's gasp of surprise, Brent took considerable pleasure in saying to her, "You see, Miss O'Toole, I am knowledgeable in the ways of the Southern plantation. I informed my men to search out

28

back of the house, about fifty yards or so, where the underground cellars are sometimes located." He smiled at her, enjoying her mortification.

"Well, you have found the food. But I promise, sir, that ' will not give up. It will take some thinking, but I will find ι way to make you leave Corkhaven sooner than you had ɔriginally planned." She exited the room as gracefully as a ;wan and strolled up the stairs to her bedroom.

James and John came running in from the front lawn and nearly collided with Brent. He smiled at the two young boys, then proceeded outside.

The youngsters ran upstairs and rushed into their sister's bedroom, speaking so fast she could barely understand them.

"Katie," James said, "Sergeant Duffy let us ride his horse, and some of the men told us stories. Those Yankees aren't such bad people." He had been disappointed to find that the Yankees weren't the horned devils he had been led to believe, but his disappointment had turned to delight as the soldiers entertained the two young boys.

John seconded the opinion that the Yankees were not so very bad.

"Katie," he said, "will they be staying very long? I hope they stay a long time. They make this place seem exciting. We never get to have any fun anymore, but if they stayed we sure could!"

Katie observed their happy young faces and couldn't help smiling. At least someone was glad the Yankees had come to Corkhaven!

Four

"Dear Uncle Albert and Aunt Jenny," Katie wrote, "This is to let you know that a troop of Yankees have invaded Corkhaven. Yes, invaded our beloved home. They arrived today and refuse to leave. They tell us that they will only be here for a few days, but I do not believe them. Their leader is a man named Captain Brent Morgan, a perfectly despicable character. I wanted to let you know of the situation, since the Yankees are armed and may decide to do us harm. I am at my wit's end as to what to do about this terrible predicament. Uncle Albert, you have said that you have friends on both sides of this war, so please try to use your influence to have the Yankees ordered to leave. Mama and the boys are doing well, but they are also very upset. Aunt Jenny, I also fear for my virtue, as you can imagine. Please do everything you can to assist us. Your loving niece, Katie."

Downstairs, the troops had been fed, and Brent led them inside the house, instructing them to take extra care and not harm any of the furnishings. Sarah and Hannah had prepared the huge ballroom for the soldiers, where they had brought down all of the extra bedding from upstairs and piled it on the polished floor.

Sergeant Duffy was to sleep in the ballroom with the men, but Captain Morgan was shown into the library by Sarah, who had made up the long sofa for his bed. She seemed pleased by his reaction, and left him in the library while she returned to help Hannah in the ballroom.

Katie had flounced up the stairs as soon as she saw the

30

Yankees entering through the front doors. She had no wish to converse with that hateful Captain Morgan any more for one day, and so she had sauntered into her mother's bedroom to inquire how she was feeling.

"Oh, dear. Not at all well, I'm afraid. I'm sorry I could not be of any assistance to you, Katie. Are James and John safely in their room?"

"Yes, Mama. I told them to stay in their room for the rest of the evening. The Yankees are quartered in the ballroom, and Sarah and Hannah are seeing to everything down there. There doesn't appear to be anything else we can do for the moment, so I suggest you remain in your room for the rest of the evening, also," Katie suggested.

She had then returned down the hall and into her own bedroom, where she had shut her door with rather more force than was actually necessary. She had done her best to uphold the family honor, but a lone woman against thirty Yankees hadn't any real chance from the outset.

She proceeded to undress for the night, and then donned a white nightgown and green velvet robe. She walked over to the small roll-top desk and sat down to ponder the situation. The day had been absolutely exhausting, both physically and mentally. That Captain Morgan was one of the most infuriating men she had ever before encountered! He did not appear to have been swayed by her beauty or charm in the slightest, and this fact certainly added fuel to her dislike of the man.

She had been concentrating on any possible solutions to the problem, and had suddenly hit upon the idea of writing to her father's brother and his wife. Yes, they would certainly do whatever they could for their favorite niece, she was sure. She pulled out a sheet of paper from one of the drawers and dipped the tip of her pen into the black inkpot sitting near the edge of the desk. She quickly decided that she would write a letter informing them of the situation, but that she would embellish it somewhat to impress them a bit more. Maybe they could think of some way to get the Yankees to leave Corkhaven. At least,

Katie thought, they should know. Yes, she had begun to smile with satisfaction at this point, a letter would be just the thing.

After Katie inspected the finished product of her thoughts, she decided that it would do nicely. There, she thought as she laid down her pen, that ought to stir up a hornet's nest! Uncle and Aunt, who lived in Atlanta, would be so worried about her and her family here at Corkhaven, that Uncle Albert would surely do all he could to arrange to have Captain Morgan and his men ordered away.

She rose from her seat at the desk and then sat down upon her bed. She began to wonder just how she would get the letter delivered to Atlanta. After racking her brain for several seconds, she decided that she would sneak away from the house and out to the stables early in the morning, where she would mount her favorite and only remaining horse suitable for riding, Plato. She would then ride to the Jenkins' plantation, where she was confident that William Jenkins would do everything he could to help her. He would see to it that the letter reached Atlanta, she knew. Yes, that was the solution. Maybe the Yankees would be gone in a few more days, after all.

She removed her robe and climbed between the cool sheets of the bed. She would need a good night's sleep if she was going to rise early and be on her way. She sincerely hoped that Captain Morgan and his men passed an extremely uncomfortable night!

Katie awoke at about five o'clock the next morning. Rubbing the sleep from her tired eyes, she jumped out of bed and hastily drew on her underwear and riding habit. Then, grabbing up her hat, she quietly opened her bedroom door and tiptoed softly out into the hallway. She approached the staircase and slowly descended the steps, keeping an eye out for anyone else who might chance to be awake and about at this hour of the morning. Reaching the bottom of the stairs without incident, she quickly walked over to the front doors and carefully eased one of them open. She reclosed it just as carefully and found herself standing out on the front veranda, where she silently gave thanks that she had come this far undetected. She was also glad that there was plenty of moonlight to illuminate her way to the stables, where she now headed to get her horse. Suddenly, she stopped in her tracks, as she had become aware of the presence of a Yankee posted on the front lawn as sentry, sitting beside a big oak tree. She waited breathlessly for a few moments, then cautiously hurried to the stables. The sentry had apparently fallen asleep, too exhausted from his earlier journey to remain awake. She was able to fetch Plato, get him saddled, and then she quickly mounted him and rode slowly across the thick, grassy lawn toward the front gates. She observed that the sentry was still sleeping, so she gave Plato a small slap with her riding quirt, then she silently rode away and through the front gates. Glancing back, she noted with satisfaction that the sentry had remained unawakened. Once at a safe distance from the house, she gave Plato his head and galloped as fast as she could towards the Jenkins place, which was a few miles to the north of Corkhaven. She surmised that she would reach their plantation in about two hours, and she decided to enjoy the freedom the ride gave her.

Brent had passed a comfortable night on the sofa in the library, contrary to Katie's wishes. He awakened much earlier than he had planned, so he arose and dressed, then lit one of the lamps and began to examine the many volumes of books stacked high on the shelves. He suddenly imagined that he had heard some sort of noise, so he returned the book he had been leafing through to the shelf, then he quietly approached the library door and eased it open a mere inch. He peered around it and out into the entrance way, where he saw a figure opening the front door. He gave the figure closer inspection, and discovered it to be none other than the beautiful, headstrong Miss O'Toole! He silently observed her as she went out the door and closed it behind her.

She was obviously hoping to leave the house without discovery. Brent wondered where in the world she would be going at such an early hour of the morning. Could she possibly be running away? No, that couldn't be it, he thought, for she would never leave and abandon her family or plantation to the enemy.

Brent found his thoughts returning once more to their encounter yesterday afternoon. Although he had found her defiance infuriating, he had found himself silently applauding her courage. She was the most unusual and unique young woman he had ever met. He couldn't seem to get her out of his mind.

He waited several minutes before opening the library door and stepping outside to see if he could possibly discover where Katie was going. He stood on the front veranda just as she was galloping away from the front gates. He decided in that instant to follow her, endeavoring to do so without her knowing it, of course.

What did the little idiot think she was doing? he asked himself. Didn't she realize that she might encounter other soldiers while riding alone? He would have to play nursemaid to the young woman, for she was certainly too naive to know what she was doing.

Katie arrived at the Jenkins' plantation and rode up to the front of the house. She dismounted and tied the reins to the hitching post, then climbed the steps and lifted the heavy brass knocker to arouse someone within the house. The pounding of the knocker was soon answered by one of the slaves, who showed Katie into the parlour to await Mr. Jenkins. Katie sat down and pondered what she would say to him.

William Jenkins, aroused from a heavy sleep, slowly descended the stairs and shuffled into the parlour, where he found Katie O'Toole sitting. He managed a "good morning" to her, then plopped down into a chair. Katie realized that it was rather early to be paying social calls on one's friends, but she felt that the urgency of the situation called for such measures.

"Mrs. Jenkins, she is well, I trust?" she began, then, "Mr. Jenkins, I have come to inform you that we have been invaded by Yankees, just as you predicted might happen. I have come to ask you for your kind assistance."

"My dear Katie, I would love to help you in any way I can, but I haven't many slaves and I don't honestly think I can drive the Yankees away for you," he replied sleepily.

"No, no, Mr. Jenkins," she hastily told him, "You see, I merely want you to see that this letter is delivered to my aunt and uncle in Atlanta immediately. My uncle will see to it that the Yankees leave Corkhaven."

"Of course, Katie. I'll have one of the slaves ride for Atlanta at once. He should reach there by tomorrow night, and perhaps you will receive a reply within the week. Now, don't you worry your pretty little head over the matter. You just call on me again if there's anything I can do for you. By the way, are the Yankees treating you well? If not, I suppose you and your family could come and stay here with us for a few days." He sincerely hoped that she would refuse his generous offer, for he was in reality a cowardly man and wanted no part of her troubles with the Yankees.

"No, thank you, Mr. Jenkins. I believe that it would be best if we remained at Corkhaven. If you'll just see to it that my letter is delivered as soon as possible to Atlanta, I will be forever in your debt. Now, I really must get on back home, for I did not notify anyone that I was coming. Thank you again, Mr. Jenkins." She smiled at him gratefully and left the room.

She mounted Plato, who had been impatiently pawing the ground, and quickly rode in the direction of Corkhaven. If she hurried, she might be able to return and get back to her room before any of the others had noticed her absence.

She had not ridden far from the Jenkins' place until she began to have an uneasy feeling. She felt that she was being watched by someone or something. But that's impossible, she told herself, for no one is out riding about at this hour of the morning. Except for me, that is, she mentally corrected herself. She rode on a little further, thinking how glad she was that Mr. Jenkins had not questioned her about just how her uncle would be able to get the troops to leave Corkhaven. She soon became convinced that she was not alone, but she could see no one. She had almost reached a clearing, when she was startled to hear someone address her.

"Miss O'Toole, what a fine morning for a ride, don't you agree?"

She rode a bit further and saw Captain Morgan leaning against a tree, his horse happily grazing in the clearing ahead. Katie became alarmed that he might possibly have discovered the reason she had ridden to the Jenkins', but of course he wouldn't have heard the conversation she had within the house. She attempted to ride on past him, but he reached out and captured the reins before she could jerk them out of his reach.

"Miss O'Toole, I believe that I spoke to you just now. I expect an answer when I have spoken to someone. Where were you riding to this morning, anyway?"

"That is certainly none of your business, Yankee! Now, let go of my horse and allow me to return to my home. I have nothing to say to you."

"Now, Miss O'Toole, don't you realize that you might have been seen by a band of soldiers from either side of this war, and that you might possibly have been harmed? Whatever were you thinking to go gallivanting off alone, young lady?" Brent demanded.

"That is certainly none of your business, Captain Morgan. I told you to let go of my horse!" she responded defiantly.

"Why did you ride to that plantation? What was so important that you had to sneak away from the house?" he insisted.

Katie became alarmed when he mentioned that he had known where she had just ridden. She would have to tell him some hastily composed half-lie to satisfy his curiosity.

"Well, Captain Morgan, since you insist. I rode to see how Mrs. Jenkins was feeling this morning. You see, she has been very ill. I was worried about her, and there was nothing that really required my attention at Corkhaven so early in the morning. There, are you satisfied?" she added spitefully. It was true that Mrs. Jenkins had been ill, and he wouldn't know that she had long since recovered.

"No, I'm not satisfied, Miss O'Toole. I honestly don't believe that you would be paying such a call on a neighbor at this early hour. Suppose you tell me the real reason for your sneaking out of the house and riding miles away to another plantation so early?" Brent spoke with that dangerous glint in his eyes. Katie found herself experiencing a small amount of fear.

"I have already told you. I went to see Mrs. Jenkins. It makes no difference to me whether you believe me or not. In fact, I don't care what you think about anything! Now, for the last time, will you let go of my horse, sir?" She tried to say this with composure.

"Why don't you get down off that horse, Miss O'Toole? I have some further matters that I think we should discuss, since we have the perfect opportunity for speaking in private."

"Get out of my way, you Yankee!" She raised her riding quirt and brought it down with all her might upon his arm. As he swore and dropped the reins of her horse, Katie kicked Plato and galloped away as fast as she could. She glanced behind her and saw the captain mounting his horse and spurring the animal onward after her. She was so occupied with watching his progress, that she was completely unprepared when her own horse suddenly stumbled upon a rock. She lost her balance and could not prevent herself from tumbling from Plato's back.

She lay sprawled upon the ground, her hair and skirts in complete disarray. She sat up and shook her head to

37

clear her senses, but she seemed to be all right. Just a little dizzy, that was all. As she was trying to rise from the ground, Captain Morgan arrived and immediately jumped down from his horse to be of assistance to her. He inquired if she thought she would be able to rise, then he put his arms about her and helped her to stand upright. She was still a bit unsteady and would have fallen, if not for his arms around her. She raised her dirt-streaked face to his and again experienced somewhat of a shocking sensation running throughout her entire body. He was gazing down into her flushed, smudged face, then Katie suddenly found herself being thoroughly kissed by the Yankee!

She remained passive for only a moment, her thoughts in utter confusion. She could only concentrate on the unfamiliar sensations she was experiencing as he moved his lips on hers, then she seemed to awaken and began to struggle. Brent released her as quickly as he had embraced her a few seconds before, but he kept a firm hand on her arm.

"How dare you, sir! Haven't I suffered enough indignities, without you forcing your distasteful, attentions upon me?" she blustered angrily. She could not deny to herself that she had actually begun to enjoy his embrace, and she was furious with herself as well as with him.

"I don't think you found it all that distasteful, Miss O'Toole. However, if you are recovered sufficiently, we will be on our way. I will inspect your horse's leg to see if any damage has been done to him." He walked over to where Plato was standing and raised the animal's right leg, which he was satisfied to see was not broken, merely strained a bit.

He returned to Katie, who merely waited in silence, and said to her, "Miss O'Toole, there has not been much damage done to your horse, but you will nevertheless have to ride with me on my mount, as we do not want to take any chances. Now, are you ready to leave for home?"

38

"I am indeed ready to return to my home, sir, but I refuse to ride upon the same horse with you. However, I will be only too glad to ride your horse, while you walk alongside and lead Plato. I think that is the only gentlemanly thing to do, don't you?" she imperiously demanded.

"I am sorry to disappoint you, Miss O'Toole, but that will not do. We will both ride my horse and your horse will follow. Now, if you are ready to mount?" he replied.

"I do not wish to ride with you, Captain Morgan, as I have just told you. If you will not do as I ask, I suppose I will simply have to wait here until you can send someone back with another mount for me," she stubbornly insisted. She realized that she was being rather silly and childish, but she could not give in.

"All right, I will have to take matters into my own hands, so to speak!" With that, Brent lifted Katie off of the ground with ease, then deposited her roughly upon the back of his waiting horse. Before she could slide to the ground, he had mounted behind her and encircled her with an arm seemingly made of iron. He gently kicked his horse, and they started the ride back to Corkhaven, with Plato obediently following.

They rode the entire distance to Corkhaven in silence, each lost in their own thoughts. Brent was thinking about the kiss they had earlier shared, and how he had been wanting to do that almost from the first moment he saw her. It had been a decidedly pleasant experience, and he sincerely hoped that he could indulge in such an experience again in the near future.

Katie, on the other hand, was still refusing to admit to herself just how much the captain's kiss had meant to her. She would not allow herself to think of a Yankee, an enemy of the South's and of hers, in terms of anything other than the lowest vermin.

When they reached Corkhaven, Katie refused Brent's offer of assistance in dismounting and she jumped down, instructed Tom to see to Plato's leg, then ran into the house. Brent slowly dismounted and told Tom to feed and water the horses. Then, he walked slowly toward the house.

When he had kissed her, he had felt a certain perplexing spark he had never felt before. Could he actually be falling in love with the girl? He sincerely hoped not! He had enough complications in his life right now without Miss O'Toole adding to them. Still, he had better keep a tighter guard on his feelings for the remainder of his stay at Corkhaven.

Katie had immediately gone upstairs and into her room, slammed the door, and then collapsed upon the bed. She had to examine her thoughts and feelings, which were indeed very confused. She had thought that the only feelings she felt toward the Yankee captain were dislike and contempt, but now something else appeared to have crept in. She would not admit, even to herself, that she had actually wanted him to kiss her, had yearned for him to embrace her. No, this was not even a remote possibility, she told herself. She still felt annoyance for the Yankee. Merely annoyance and dislike.

She rose from the bed and ambled over to stand in front of her mirror, where she closely inspected her appearance for the first time since she had returned. Oh my Lord, she thought with dismay, I look an absolute fright! She would have to remedy the situation immediately. Going to the door of her room and calling for Sarah, she began to disrobe and prepared to take a bath. Sarah entered the room and asked her, "Miss Katie, where did you go to this morning? We done looked everywhere for you, and your poor mother has been worried sick. Don't you ever go off like that again! You near scared us to death, young lady! What did you want me for, anyway?" Sarah had just come from Amelia's room, where she had managed to persuade that lady that her daughter would come to no harm, wherever she had run off to.

"Oh, Sarah, stop scolding me and fetch some hot water

for my bath. Have Hannah help you carry it up here. And anyway, what business is it of yours where I go or what I do? Besides, I just needed to get away by myself for a while, that's all. I'll look in on Mama after I've had my bath."

"Well, you look a mess, wherever you been." Sarah always managed to get in the last word.

As Hannah and Sarah carried up the buckets of hot water and filled the elegant bathtub, Katie finished undressing and wrapped a towel around herself to wait until the tub was full. Then, she closed the door securely after the two slaves, and settled down for a long, soothing bath. She reached for the delicately scented bar of soap, allowing the towel to drop to the floor. She eased herself down into the water and began to scrub herself with the sponge. It felt so good that she might just stay there for an hour or so!

Downstairs, Brent was discussing some various military strategy with Sergeant Duffy in the library, where they had locked themselves in with orders to remain undisturbed.

"Look here, Duffy, I'm not much of a Sherman man myself, but we are forced to follow his command. I don't agree with his plan for the siege, either, but there's not a whole lot I can do about it," Brent was saying.

"Captain Morgan, sir, I'm not suggesting that you can change the appointment of Sherman. But, sir, I don't think that our men can hold out for a long siege, if it is indeed going to be a long one," Duffy answered.

"Well, we will be staying here for at least three or four more days, Duffy, and I hope that the rest will renew their fighting spirit."

"Yes, sir. I reckon that a few days' rest sure won't do us all any harm, at that. But, I still think that the men will be unable to hold out long under fire," Duffy insisted.

At this point, a knock sounded upon the library door. Brent strode over to the door and flung it open with impatience.

"Yes, what is it, Williams?" he asked the young soldier who stood at the door.

"Captain Morgan, sir, we can't find any of the women slaves. You see, Private Stewart's knee wound has opened up again and he needs tending to awful bad. But, we can't find any of the slaves to help him. I was wondering, sir, what we should do," the young soldier finished nervously.

"What the hell!" swore Brent, "What has that woman done now?" Brent was certain that Katie must be responsible for the fact that the slaves were unavailable. He instructed Sergeant Duffy and Private Williams to search outside, while he would find Miss O'Toole and see if she knew where the slaves were.

Brent was out of all patience with Katie. She had pushed him too far this time. He would have to teach her a lesson, show her that she could not openly defy him and get away with it. He stalked up the stairs two at a time and went in search of her bedroom. He peered into Mrs. O'Toole's bedroom, but that lady had taken her two sons outside on the front lawns for the day. He looked into a few more rooms, until he finally came to a closed door. He flung open the door, and realized immediately that he had indeed discovered which room belonged to Katie.

There, still lounging in the tub, sat Katie. She had not turned her head when the door had been opened, and, thinking that Sarah had returned for some reason, she said,

"Sarah, will you please hand me my towel? This water is becoming rather cool, so I think I better get out now." She held out her hand, unable to see that it was not Sarah who stood there staring at her entrancing figure in the bathtub.

Brent was thoroughly astounded at the scene he had accidentally walked in on, but he couldn't seem to tear his gaze away from the glimpse he had of Katie's white neck and creamy shoulders, glistening from the water. Her hair was piled loosely on top of her head, and she had never looked more desirable. Of course, from this angle he couldn't quite see the rest of her, but he knew with a certainty that she was equally beautiful from the shoulders down.

With a sudden mischievous urge, he picked up the towel from beside the tub and stretched out his arm to hand it to her. When Katie saw the arm encased in blue cloth, she jerked her head around and discovered, much to her dismay, the presence of Captain Morgan. She hastily covered herself with the towel and sank lower into the water.

"Get out of here, you dreadful man! If you don't get out of here right now, I'll scream the house down!" she threatened. With a last glance at her, Brent smiled a slow and meaningful smile and left the room, shutting the door softly behind him. He had completely forgotten what he had come to say to her. He was sorry that he had been unable to see more of her curvaceous form in the bathtub, but he had seen enough to know that she possessed one of the most exquisite figures he had ever seen. He continued thinking of this most recent encounter with Miss O'Toole, when he realized that he had reached the library again. Sergeant Duffy was waiting to tell him that they had been able to find Sarah and Hannah, who were out in the stables visiting with Old Jonah and Tom. Brent listened to what Sergeant Duffy told him, but he didn't seem very interested. His mind was still upstairs in Katie's bedroom.

Katie, furious that the man had the gall to walk in her bedroom unannounced, and then stand there obviously enjoying the scene he had witnessed, could not keep her thoughts from straying to his handsome face. His look had been so admiring, and she couldn't help savoring a certain feminine pride that he had found her so attractive. Still, he had no right to do what he had done, and she would tell him so in no uncertain terms, just as soon as she again dressed.

She went to her wardrobe and selected a simple but lovely dress of yellow gingham. She put it on and rearranged her hair, then she prepared to venture downstairs and find the captain and confront him with her opinion of just how disgusting and ungentlemanly his behavior had been ever since he had first come to Corkhaven. First, he had treated her so abominably in front of his men that first day, and then today he had followed her and virtually attacked her, and to top it all off, he had burst into her bedroom and had seen her naked in the tub! It was about time that someone made this Captain Morgan realize that he could not treat her so shamefully any longer!

She found Brent reclining upon a sofa in the library, where he was engrossed in a book of her father's. As soon as he observed her presence, he put the book aside and rose to his feet. She gracefully entered the room and closed the door. Then, she was ready to do battle with the Yankee.

"Captain Morgan," she began, "the time has come for me to tell you a few things. First of all, I do not appreciate having enemy soldiers quarter in my home, against my wishes and the wishes of my family. Secondly, I found your attentions quite revolting this morning. Add to that your ungentlemanly conduct upstairs a few minutes ago. Now, sir, I have come to tell you that you are the most disgusting, overbearing, contemptuous, odious man I have ever met. And the sooner you leave this plantation, the better for us all!" Katie delivered her speech with great zeal. She was preparing to leave the room, when Brent's hand closed on her wrist in an uncompromising grip and pulled her back to stand within a few inches of him.

"Very well, Miss O'Toole," he began in a dangerously calm voice, "I believe that it is now my turn. First of all, I had my orders to quarter my men wherever and whenever I thought it necessary, which I did. Secondly, don't try and convince me that you didn't actually enjoy my 'revolting' attentions earlier this morning, for I happen to know that you did enjoy them. I could feel your response, but you refuse to admit that you could respond to a Yankee. And, lastly, Miss O'Toole, I burst in on your

44

happy bath time quite by accident. I was merely searching for you to inquire as to the reason why my men could find no one to help them with a small problem. There, Miss O'Toole, you now have my side of the story. I have had just about enough of your shrewish tongue and willful behavior. I happen to think that it is time that someone, namely me, Miss O'Toole, took your behavior in hand. So, Miss O'Toole," he spoke between clenched teeth, "I am going to take you in hand right now!"

With that, Brent yanked Katie along with him over to the sofa where he had been so comfortably relaxing a moment ago, and sitting down, he drew her face-down across his knees. He then threw up her many skirts and petticoats and proceeded to spank her silk-encased bottom.

"Stop it, you beast! Stop it, Captain Morgan! Stop it this very instant! Unhand me!" Katie demanded indignantly. She tried squirming and twisting away from his punishing hand, but to no avail. He held her down easily and continued to spank her with the palm of his hand several more times, just as hard as he believed necessary. Then, he released her and allowed her to rise and straighten her skirts. She was flushed, tearful, and exceedingly angry, and she could find no words to attack him with at that moment. She flounced from the room and fled up the stairs, where he heard her slam her door with a vengeance.

"My, but I enjoyed that!" he spoke out loud. That young lady had obviously been spoiled for most of her life, and if her father had only done as he had just done, she would not be such a termagant! He rubbed his stinging palm, remembering the feel of her delightfully rounded bottom beneath it.

Katie flung herself across her bed and sobbed out her fury and frustration. She beat her pillow with clenched fists, pretending that it was the captain's head. She had never before in her life been spanked, and it was the most humiliating experience of her life! She was only glad that

Mama and the boys had not witnessed her embarrassment. She hoped more than ever that Uncle Albert would take immediate action when he read her letter. She hoped that he would see to it that Captain Morgan was absented from her life forever!

Five

After having spent most of the remainder of the morning upstairs in her bedroom, where she was actually sulking and trying to think of ways to have her revenge upon the captain, Katie finally ventured down the stairs and escaped outside to the stables. She would see how Plato's leg was doing, and maybe she could avoid meeting Captain Morgan any more for one day.

Katie's mother and her two young brothers were sitting out on the front lawn. Amelia had brought some knitting with her to occupy her time, and James and John were totally engrossed in a story being told them by one of the young Yankees. Katie decided that she would rather not speak with any of her family just yet, as she was still fuming from the terrible humiliation she had suffered, quite literally, at the captain's hand. So, she quickly ran from the house and over to the stables, going out the back way. She went in search of Tom and found him over on the east side of the stables, busy cutting some tall grass and weeds. She inquired about Plato and the extent of his injuries.

"Well, Miss Katie," Tom answered, "Plato, he is doing just fine. Yes, just fine. He don't seem to be hurting none, so I just put him in his stall and rubbed down his leg. I reckon he's a mite anxious for you to come check on him, though."

"Thank you, Tom. Oh, and Tom, please don't let anyone know that I'm out here in the stables, all right? I just want to be left alone with Plato for a while," Katie said. She entered the stables through the back door and approached the stall where Plato was being kept. The horse softly snorted as he became aware of her presence, and Katie began speaking to him in a low, soothing voice.

"There now, Plato. That's a good boy. Yes, poor thing. How is your leg? I'm so sorry that I rode you so hard." She continued soothing and petting the horse.

Outside, Amelia had gathered up her two boys and retired into the house for lunch. The Yankees also entered the house for their meal, leaving only the sentry out on the front lawn. Tom, Old Jonah, Sarah, Hannah, and Junie were occupied with eating their lunch out in the kitchen, so Katie was almost completely alone outside the house.

All of a sudden, the sentry became aware of the sound of approaching riders. He quickly ran for the front veranda, where he hid himself behind one of the large, white columns. From this vantage point, he could easily see anyone who chanced to ride within the front gates of Corkhaven. As he watched, he observed several horsemen top the hill and ride toward the front gates. They rode into the front yard, and the young sentry saw that the seven men wore the gray homespun uniform of the South. He slowly edged inside the house, where he immediately went in search of Captain Morgan to inform him of the enemy soldiers' arrival.

Meanwhile, the Confederate soldiers, who were actually deserters and renegades, dismounted and started to approach the front steps of the house, when their progress was suddenly arrested by the appearance of someone watching them from the front entrance of the stables. They were surprised to notice that the person was a beautiful young woman. The leader of the motley band motioned his men along with him and they all approached the stables where Katie stood.

Katie quickly glanced around and saw that there was apparently no one else outside. Where could they all have gone to? she asked herself. She became frightened and began to pray fervently that someone within the house was aware of the arrival of the men. As they came closer, she noted that their clothes, which were filthy and torn almost beyond recognition, were actually the uniforms of the South's own cause. She felt her fear disappearing and graciously welcomed the men as they arrived to stand before her.

"Gentlemen, how nice to see a bunch of our own boys here at Corkhaven. This is a rare privilege, indeed. My name is Miss O'Toole. What may I do for you, sir?" she addressed their leader, a big, burly man with a scraggly beard. My, she thought, these Confederate soldiers sure do look a fright. Don't they ever bathe?

"Ma'am. Pleased to make your acquaintance. I'm Sergeant Holden, and these here are my men. We've traveled quite a ways today, and we were wondering if you might have any food or horses to spare us?" the man asked with a toothless grin.

"Oh, sir, I am sorry, but we have had an awful lot of our boys stop by, and we do not have any food to spare at the moment. And, as for the horses, why I'm afraid that we have only a few remaining, which are only good for plowing and field work. I suppose, however, that you could water your horses over there at the well, and perhaps you could allow them to graze outside the front gates over yonder." Katie did not want the poor men to approach the house and discover the Yankees within, or worse yet, for the Yankees to gun them down as soon as they were within sight of the house. No, she thought rapidly, I must see to it that these soldiers leave right away.

"Now, young lady. You can't even spare a bit of food for your own boys? We sure would appreciate any kindness you could see fit to do us. We've been through a whole lot of fighting, and we've got some more to go through before we've won this here war," the man insisted. He had made a mental note that the girl appeared

49

to be the only person around, for some unknown reason. Probably weren't any more slaves, except for a few old women inside the house.

"No, Sergeant Holden. I'm afraid that there really is nothing we can spare for you and your men. I suggest that you try one of the other outlying plantations. Perhaps you could find someone who has more than they need. Gentlemen, I'm glad that you stopped by, but I have work to do and I need to get on with it. If you'll please excuse me." She politely smiled at them.

"Now, Missy. I'm still sure that you must have something that you can give us poor soldiers. Suppose we go into the stables and have a look at those old workhorses you spoke of, how about that? And, for good measure, why don't you bring your pretty little self along with us? You're the first young woman we all seen in quite a spell," the leader spoke with a menacing leer at Katie. She became almost terrified at his look, but she resolved to remain outwardly calm. Where was Tom? Or Old Jonah? Where was everyone?

Sergeant Holden suddenly snaked out an arm and encircled Katie's slender waist with his big, hairy arm. Then, with the accompanying laughter and jeers of his men, he took his struggling burden into the stables. His men followed closely after the pair, and they all stopped short at the sight of the horses housed inside.

"Why, Miss, there must be over thirty horses in here. They can't all be workhorses, now, can they? What for did you go and lie to us, little lady? It ain't nice to lie to your own countrymen, is it?" he said in her ear. Katie struggled to free herself from his hateful grip, but she could not escape.

"Sir, these horses belong to some friends of ours. They are not mine, so I cannot let you take them. Now, I'm sure that it is time that you and your men were on your way. I have family within the house who will soon become alarmed at my continued absence. You don't wish to frighten me now, do you? Please release me, sir," she said

50

with composure. She had by now realized that these men couldn't be what they had said, that they must be deserters. She wished they would leave Corkhaven before someone got hurt. She forced herself to speak calmly, when all she really wanted to do was kick and claw at the awful man until he released her.

"Little lady, I think that we will just have to take these here horses, because we all need fresh mounts. Now, you just relax and let old Sergeant Holden look around some more, you hear?" As she began to struggle again, he spun her around and backhanded her hard across her face. Her head snapped back with the force of his blow and she tasted blood from a small cut on her lip. The man was now looking at her with an obvious purpose in his eyes, and she attempted to run from the stables. He caught her easily and spoke to his men,

"Okay, boys. I get first go at her. You all get busy and swap saddles off of those nags of ours and on to these horses here. I'll occupy the girl." He gave a snorting laugh, then suddenly threw Katie into the hay on the floor of the stables. She kicked and clawed at him, but he straddled her with his huge body. He forced her to remain still with his ungentle fingers, then he brought his face close to hers in an attempt to kiss her. She ceased her struggles, thinking that she would let him believe that he had won, then she bit down into his hand as hard as she could.

Sergeant Holden cursed and hit her again. Stunned, Katie lay there trying to regain her senses. Holden ripped her dress, was raising her skirt and petticoats, when a harsh voice sounded from the stable entrance. There, standing just inside the doorway, was Sergeant Duffy and six of his men, with their rifles pointed at the deserters. Sergeant Duffy was the first to speak to the startled audience.

"You men, there, drop your guns. Drop them, I say! Now, line up against that stall there, on the double. Unless you want a hole blowed right through your cowardly bellies."

Sergeant Holden, momentarily taken by surprise at the sight of the seven armed Yankees standing in the doorway, grabbed Katie and pulled her roughly to her feet, putting her body between that of his and the Yankees. He held his pistol pointed at her head.

"Don't move, Yankees. I'll blow her head clean off. Let us ride out of here right now, or I'll kill the fine lady here. You hear me? Move!" He kept a tight hold around Katie's waist, as she frantically tried to think of what she could do to help the situation. Sergeant Duffy and his men were slowly lowering their guns to the ground, when a voice sounded behind Sergeant Holden.

"No, you drop it, you filthy cur! If you don't, I'll shoot you dead before you can pull the trigger!" Captain Morgan threatened. Holden hesitated, appearing to question whether he should attempt something else, but he finally dropped his gun and pushed Katie away. Sergeant Duffy and his men pointed their rifles once more at the Confederate deserters, then rounded them up and led them and their leader outside.

"Take them to the underground cellar and lock them securely in, Sergeant Duffy," Brent instructed. Katie, who had clutched a post for support as Holden had roughly pushed her away, watched the men in the bedraggled uniforms being led away. She was then completely alone with Captain Morgan.

She raised her eyes to his face and could scarcely fathom the depths of emotion she experienced as she looked deep into his eyes. He stood staring into her own eyes and seemed to be waiting for her to make the first move to speak, which she did.

"Captain Morgan, I am grateful to you for rescuing me, sir." She swallowed hard and then continued, "I did not know what to do until you and your men appeared. I thought that those men were loyal Confederates. I didn't realize until a few moments ago that they were in actuality cowardly deserters. Again, sir, I thank you for your help."

She became aware of her torn bodice and proceeded to draw the edges together with dignity.

Brent, who had also experienced a wealth of feeling as he watched her speak, then said to her, "Miss O'Toole, I am only glad that we arrived in time. What were you doing out here all by yourself, though? Don't you know that this sort of thing could happen at any time?"

Captain Morgan, thought Katie at this point, is absolutely the most infuriating man I have ever known! She then replied, "Sir, spare me the lecture, please! I have had quite enough of such scoldings from you. I did not know that I was alone out here, but I would not have been afraid if I had known. This is my home, and I am free to walk about at will!" She glared at him with flashing green eyes.

"Miss O'Toole, I'm sorry for the ordeal you have just been through, but there is no excuse for your taking such chances with your life. If we had not arrived in time, well, you can imagine what would have happened to you. In the future, young woman, I think that you should always remember to inform someone whenever you leave the house, is that understood?" Brent countered. He had been surprised when Private Young, the sentry, had come bursting into the library to inform him of the approaching riders. And then, when he had discovered that Katie was left alone, defenseless, out in the stables, he had experienced a terrible sinking feeling in the depths of his heart. Now, since she was primarily unharmed and the whole incident was over with, he found himself becoming more and more incensed with her.

"I do realize what might have happened to me, Captain. You needn't remind me. However, I should remind you that you are neither my father nor my guardian, and I demand that you stop treating me as if you were! I am no longer a child, in case you hadn't noticed!" She blushed uncomfortably when she realized the import of this last sentence. She wanted to strike him,

53

but she knew that if she did, he would undoubtedly strike her back!

"Stop it, you little fool!" he demanded furiously. He took her by the shoulders and administered a couple of shakes. "When are you going to stop acting like a child? Why must you always be selfishly thinking only of yourself? Don't you realize the hell you put everyone through when you do such harebrained things?" He shook her again, then stopped abruptly. Her beautiful face was becomingly flushed, her lips were slightly parted, and her breath was coming out in little gasps. She stood looking up at him, her brilliant red-gold hair falling down out of its pins, and her bosom rapidly rising and falling beneath her torn bodice. Brent suddenly gave a strangled oath and pulled her into his arms. He brought his mouth roughly down upon hers, and his arms threatened to crush her.

Katie could scarcely breathe, but she did not seem to mind. Instead, she simply melted against his strong, muscular body and enjoyed the pleasant sensations running throughout her entire being. His kiss became more gentle, but just as passionate as before. Katie could not push him away, she could not find the strength or will to struggle.

"Katie," he whispered against her fragrant hair. He kissed her upturned face, her white neck, and then returned his lips once more to her mouth. She kissed him in return, giving back all the passion he gave to her.

His gentle hands caressed her smooth arms and he entwined his fingers in her thick mane of hair. Her body seemed to have a mind all its own. When he slowly pulled the torn, low-cut bodice of her dress even lower, Katie did not resist. He kissed the exposed tops of her well-formed breasts, and she gasped. She couldn't believe the intensity of the searing fire that had shot throughout her body at the first touch of his lips. Where was the capable, determined person she had so prided herself upon being?

Brent's kisses and caresses began to become more

urgent, and Katie seemed to awaken as she became rather frightened by the hunger so evident in his eyes. She now began to struggle and tore her lips away from his to speak.

"Stop! No, please stop. I can't!" she cried. The dumbfounded captain stepped back and noted her disheveled appearance, her wide-eyed expression.

"I don't know what got into me, Captain. I have never done such a thing before," she said. Brent continued staring at her face, trying to fathom the reason she had halted their lovemaking. She became angry at his silent gaze, and she accused him,

"How dare you take advantage of me, sir! You knew that I had been through a terrible, emotional experience. You took advantage of that! You are certainly no gentleman, Captain Morgan!" she informed him. She hastily straightened her clothing, conscious of his eyes upon her shaking fingers. She repinned her hair as best she could atop her head, then she stood a moment looking at Brent.

"Miss O'Toole," he then spoke, "I do not believe that what just occurred between us was one-sided. On the contrary, I believe that you definitely felt something. As you have made the point of telling me, and as I have earlier witnessed for myself, you are no longer a child. I'm sorry that I got so carried away, but your beauty drove me to it, so to speak. And I don't believe that you were either an impartial or unwilling participant!"

"How dare you! I wish that I had never set eyes upon you, you Yankee! If you ever so much as touch me again, I'll claw you to pieces, sir!" Katie spat at him. She was opening the door of the stables when she heard him reply,

"I won't make any promises, Miss O'Toole. I thoroughly enjoyed what we just shared, and I hope that we can share such a thing again. However, I will endeavor to allow you to be the first one to initiate things next time, if that is what you wish!" Brent couldn't help being amused by her outraged dignity. Didn't she know that what she had just felt was normal for a grown woman?

55

But no, here in the South, women were protected and sheltered for most of their lives. And, any unmarried woman was kept virtually in ignorance about the ways between a man and a woman.

"Mark my words, you, you . . . Yankee! You will pay someday for the humiliations you have heaped upon me!" With that, she stormed out of the stables and made for the house.

Brent remained where he stood for a few minutes, then he walked outside and went in search of Sergeant Duffy, to discuss the matter of the prisoners they had locked in the cellar. Yes, Miss O'Toole, he mused as he went, we will have such an encounter again, I can assure you. He had by now admitted to himself that he was indeed falling in love with Katie, an emotion he was completely ignorant about. He only knew that he had almost killed the man in the stables for daring to even lay a finger on her. He knew that it had taken a supreme effort of will to keep from taking her there on the hay a little while ago. He hadn't meant for things to go as far as they had so soon, but he wasn't in the least bit sorry. He began to entertain the notion of visiting the beautiful, headstrong Miss O'Toole again whenever he was finished with this war, but that was where his thoughts reached a halt. For, the war was still being fought, and he did not for one minute believe that she would favorably receive any declarations of love he made her until it had ended. Even then, when the North won the war, it would take quite an amount of persuasion to convince her to accept a Yankee. But, he would keep hoping, and perhaps fate would reunite them again after all.

Katie, whose flight upstairs had been interrupted by her mother, distractedly wondered if she should tell Amelia what had occurred between herself and the captain in the stables, but decided against it. Her mother was not the sort to discuss indelicate subjects with anyone, not even her own daughter. Katie stopped and turned slightly to listen to what her mother was saying.

56

"Katie, dear, Sergeant Duffy told us that he and his men have just captured some Confederate deserters out in the stables, and that they have locked them in the cellar. Thank goodness the dreadful men did not happen upon you while you were outside. To think that you might have been harmed in some way! Oh, dear. Well, why don't you come and have some lunch with us?"

"Mama," Katie lied, "the deserters never saw me, so I could not have come to any harm. I'm going to my room to freshen up a bit, then I'll join you for lunch, all right? You go on back and I'll be down in a minute." Katie watched as her mother entered the dining room, then she quickly fled up the remaining steps and into her room.

She was sorry that she was forced to lie to her own mother, but Amelia would have been in hysterics if she had been told the truth about the incident. She hadn't noticed Katie's torn bodice, as she had taken great pains to hide it with her hands as she entered the house. As for her cut lip, Katie had remembered it beforehand and had wiped the blood from her mouth. She did not want to think about what had happened between herself and Captain Morgan, but her mind refused to obey. She was so ashamed that she had allowed a man to kiss her the way he had. She had always been taught that such things were not proper until a young lady was betrothed, or better yet, married. She was furious with herself, but she directed most of her anger at Brent. Yes, everything had been so peaceful and so nicely arranged until he and his men had arrived at Corkhaven. Now, her thoughts were in utter turmoil, her family was forced to accommodate the enemy soldiers, and she feared that her life was changed forever. No, I will not allow things to change, she insisted to herself. When the Yankees leave, everything will soon become normal again.

She quickly changed her dress and straightened her wayward curls, then she sauntered down the stairs to have lunch with her family. She sincerely hoped that she could avoid Captain Morgan for the remainder of the day, but he seemed to appear from nowhere every time she attempted to avoid him.

She found her mother and her two brothers eating lunch in the dining room. She took her place at the table and began to eat the meal that Junie had prepared for them. Her two brothers were arguing about something, and her mother was forced to raise her voice somewhat in order to be heard above them.

"Katie, I must admit that these Yankees are not nearly the terrible creatures I thought. They have been extremely courteous, don't you think? However, I do realize that they are still the enemy, but it could have been much worse. They have been ever so careful to stay out of the way, and not harm anything."

"Yes, Mama," Katie dutifully answered in a monotone.

"Katie," John said to her, "I like the Yankees. I hope they get to stay longer than Sergeant Duffy says they are going to. Me and James like having men around to talk to, instead of silly old girls!" This he said with a comically wrinkled little noise and a slight giggle.

"Yes, Katie," James added, "those Yankees have been able to tell us so much about the war and the battles they have fought. Maybe they are the enemy, but they don't seem to think of us as their enemy, do they?"

"And I must say that they have almost completely won the hearts of the slaves. Why, they are fairly jumping to please those Yankees," her mother added. Katie could barely stomach the flow of the conversation. She could hardly believe that her own family had seemingly been won over by the Yankees and their deceitful ways. She would never be won over by the enemy, not Katie O'Toole!

"Oh, Katie," her mother thought for a moment and then said, "that Captain Morgan certainly appears to be quite taken with you, doesn't he?"

Six

Katie spent the remainder of the day in her mother's room, where she and Amelia contented themselves with plans for making over some of their better preserved dresses. Katie did not go downstairs for dinner, as she still did not want to meet Captain Morgan. Instead, she remained in her room, where she occupied the evening with finishing the plans to alter a few of her clothes.

After having passed a rather sleepless night, she awoke with a mild headache the next morning. Grimacing slightly with the pain, she wearily climbed from her bed and contemplated on her plans for the day. She resolutely forced her thoughts away from the captain. She was too confused and distraught to examine any feelings she might have toward him. She decided that she would go riding, where she could be completely alone. She needed to be alone, she needed to escape somewhere for a while.

Katie picked up her riding habit from the blue-carpeted floor, where she had carelessly flung it after yesterday's ride. She was glad that Sarah had not chanced to see it there! She hurriedly dressed and left her room. There did not appear to be anyone awake and about yet, so she decided, on a sudden impulse, to repeat the enjoyable escapade she had enacted a few days ago. She gathered her full skirts and climbed on to the bannister, then she effortlessly slid down, her body positioned backwards upon it. She did not see the person who had just walked out of the library and leisurely stood watching her childish prank. She reached the bottom, climbed

59

down again, then turned to leave the house. She instantly gasped and nearly jumped several feet backwards, when she noticed the presence of Captain Morgan directly at the foot of the stairs. He stood looming over her, his face a study in amusement. Katie drew herself up to her full height, which was nearly a foot less than his, and she spoke in the haughtiest tones, "Sir, how very rude of you to stand there watching me. You should have advised me of your presence much sooner."

"I couldn't speak and spoil your obvious pleasure, now, could I? I used to do much the same thing whenever I could chance to get away with it. However, I must admit, I have not attempted it in several years' time now," he said with an unabashed grin.

Katie, who was blushing furiously in embarrassment, merely glared at him once more, then walked to the front doors and quickly stepped outside. Brent, still chuckling in amusement at the enchanting scene he had just witnessed, returned to the library, where he had been involved in reading some more of her father's excellent books.

Katie strolled over to the stables, where she saddled Plato herself, then mounted and cantered away from the front gates, refusing to acknowledge the shouts of the sentry insisting that she halt. This is my home and these are my lands, she thought, and I can damn well ride any time I choose! She did not care if that odious Captain Morgan came after her or not. She would ride to her secret place in the woods ahead, and he would certainly be unable to find her.

Brent, comfortably relaxing in an overstuffed arm chair in the library, suddenly realized that Katie had been dressed in a riding habit. He hadn't really noticed her attire that much, so engrossed had he been in watching her slide down the bannister. He quickly put the book aside and strode outside to the stables. He could see her nowhere within, so he approached the sentry to inquire if he had seen Miss O'Toole that morning. The sentry replied that he had indeed seen her, as she had just that moment ridden away from Corkhaven. The sentry had tried shouting for her to stop, and he was about to come inside with the news of her departure. Brent tightened his lips in anger. When was that spoiled little brat ever going to listen to him? He had specifically commanded her to inform someone whenever she left the house, and he had made it perfectly clear that she was not to go off riding by herself. He would simply have to go after her, and he might possibly have to repeat his admonitions of the day before! He quickly saddled his horse, spurred him onward, and galloped away in the direction Katie had gone.

Katie slowed Plato down a bit when she reached the thickening woods, and she headed for the small, hidden clearing a few yards away. She quickly jumped from Plato's back and led him into the secret hiding place, where she dropped the reins and allowed him to graze upon the thick, sweetly-scented grass. She pulled off her riding boots and plunged her feet into the tiny blue pool in the center of the clearing. It was so very beautiful and peaceful here, she thought with satisfaction, and she could be alone with her thoughts. She removed the jacket of her riding habit and then lounged back against a tree.

Brent, meanwhile, had apparently lost her. He approached the thickly wooded area, but he could see no sign of her. Cursing his luck, he rode on through the trees, until he suddenly heard a horse's soft whinny. She must be in here somewhere, he told himself. He turned his horse slightly to the left and rode a little further. He then thought he heard what sounded like a splash of water. He rode forward a few more yards, and there he saw the clearing. He observed Katie, her feet dangling in the cool water, her jacket removed. Plato was a few feet away, happily grazing.

Brent dismounted and quietly tied his horse to a tree, then stealthily approached the clearing. He stopped before he could be seen and waited a few moments, then stepped through some brush and let Katie discover his presence. She looked up at his movement, observed his progress toward her, then quickly jerked her feet from the water and stood upright, her green eyes flashing sparks at him. She might have known that he would find some way to follow her, for he had the devil's own luck!

"Miss O'Toole, what an extreme pleasure. How is the water? You apparently thought that this little nest was known only to you, but I had little enough trouble in finding it." He came to stand directly before her, towering above her, experiencing great difficulty to refrain from shouting at her.

"Captain, this is an unwarranted intrusion! You could at least allow me a few hours of privacy, sir. I could surely come to no harm such a small distance from Corkhaven, now, could I?" She spoke with annoyance evident in every word.

"Well, since I'm here, I think that it's time we had another little talk. Pray be seated, Miss O'Toole." He motioned to the spot from whence she had just risen. She eyed him suspiciously, then obediently sat upon the grass, tucking her feet up under her skirts.

"I thought I told you not to venture out riding alone. Well, I can see that my words had no effect upon you, did they? In that case, I'm afraid that I will have to give instructions that you are no longer to ride at all, until after we have gone. I can't take a chance on your meeting a troop of Confederate soldiers and alerting them to our existence at Corkhaven. I see by the look in your eyes that I am correct in imagining that you would indeed do just such a thing," he commented dryly as he watched her face. Katie glowered at him in response.

"Well, Miss O'Toole, on to other things. We will be leaving in a couple of days. I know that you will not be overly regretful at our departure, but I want you to know that I have come to care for you much more than I had ever intended. I think that I am not mistaken when I say that you are also not immune to any such feelings for me."

Katie sat up with a gasp, unable to believe the words she had just heard the Yankee utter. Care for her? Her care for him? The man was positively daft!

"Just a moment, Captain Morgan! You are very much mistaken! I do not care for you at all, and as for your feelings toward me, why, you have been nothing but hateful to me ever since you first arrived!" She sat breathing rapidly, trying valiantly to collect her emotions.

"Miss O'Toole, I have not been hateful to you at all. I have merely been following my orders, and endeavoring to see that my own orders are obeyed. However, I can see that you wish no declarations of love from a Yankee, so I will not bore you with my recital of such any longer. Someday, you will admit that you return my regard, of that I am sure. And, I will be returning to Corkhaven after the war, so you will have the chance then to tell me so!" he insisted. He was not nearly so confident and assured as he sounded, but he would not admit defeat. He was certain that Katie felt something for him, and a little time would help to bring those feelings to the surface. He only hoped that the war was over with as soon as he believed it would be.

"Miss O'Toole, I think that it is time we returned to the house. I am truly sorry if I upset you in any way, but I thought it best if you were told how I felt about you."

"Captain Morgan," Katie finally said, "I find your attentions completely unwelcome to me! What in the world makes you think that I could ever return your affection? You, sir, are an enemy soldier, a Yankee, while I am a loyal supporter of the South. How dare you presume that I would even receive your addresses with anything other than complete revulsion?" She was so confused, she did not know quite what to say to him. She would not let him see how much his words had affected her, and she would not allow herself to dwell upon the import of what he had said. She really did feel something for Brent, but her head refused to listen to her heart.

"Well, Miss O'Toole, I can't say that I expected much

more from you. I should have known that you could not behave simply as a woman, but that you are first and foremost a Southerner! It's true that I am a Yankee, but I am first and foremost a man!" He had been telling the truth when he said that he had expected such an outburst from her. He still didn't know what had prompted him to speak, except for the fact that this was the first time he had ever felt this way, and he wanted her to know. He knew that it was idiotic, but he felt hurt by her stinging reply. She stood very still, simply staring at him in anger. He attempted to speak once more, then threw caution to the winds and swept her into his arms. She tried to escape him, but he tightened his arms about her and then began kissing her with urgent desire and passion.

Katie did not want it to happen, but she could not resist his warm embrace. After a first initial struggle, she surrendered. She felt her traitorous body begin to respond to his, and she brought her arms up and wound them around his neck. Her body made a liar out of her, but she did not seem to care at that moment.

Brent slowly lowered her to the soft grass below, and he slipped his hands inside the blouse of her habit and began gently caressing her bare flesh. Then, he unbuttoned the blouse, kissing her all the while. Katie knew that she should stop him, but she could not find the power to do so. She was lost in the delicious sensations engulfing her body. And when his lips traveled downward from her lips and neck to her partially exposed breasts, she almost moaned aloud. He pulled the straps of her chemise off her shoulders, and her beautiful, rounded bosom was then completely bared to his admiring gaze.

He lowered his lips and began kissing her upon her naked breasts. He went lower and took the nipple of one of them into his mouth and caressed it with his tongue, then gently sucked it. Katie gasped and tried to squirm away, but he held her fast and continued arousing her in the most pleasant fashion. He removed his lips from her and slowly undressed her, kissing and caressing her as he went. Then, he removed his own clothing and placed his hard, muscular body over hers. Again, Katie's conscience told her that she should stop, but she could not obey. She was carried away by her newborn sensual feelings.

Brent continued his expert arousal of her, allowing his warm lips to travel an imaginary line from her breasts to her abdomen, then back upwards again. He slipped his hand between her thighs and gently stroked her there, while she became shocked at the fire that swept through her. Oh Lord, she silently prayed, forgive me, but I can't seem to make him stop.

He finally decided that it was time to make her his, so he drew himself up a bit, then gently tried to enter her. Katie's desire quickly vanished, to be replaced by fear. She wasn't exactly sure just what was supposed to happen next, but she knew that this was the most important part of all. He soothed her with gentle words and kisses, then continued with his lovemaking. Katie drew in her breath sharply when he again attempted to enter her. She pulled away from him with a violence and sat upright, her head spinning from the new sensations and pleasant languidness of her mind. She couldn't go any farther, she told herself. She was shocked at what she had almost let herself do. She turned her appalled gaze on Brent, who was now sitting up and staring at her in surprise and confusion.

"I cannot believe what I have just done! You have taken advantage of me once again, and you have come close to stealing my virtue from me!" She spoke as she rose and began hastily drawing on her clothing. She knew that it was unfair to accuse him of any crime, for she had not resisted as much as she knew that she should have. This thought simply made her even more furious with him. He had almost succeeded in seducing her, and she could not forgive him!

"Miss O'Toole," he spoke lazily, still lying on the ground, "I do believe that it took the both of us to have what just occurred. When are you going to stop behaving

65

like some outraged schoolgirl, and admit your true feelings for me? For, I am now more than ever assured that you do care for me, even if you refuse to admit it." He had hoped that their lovemaking would have broken through her icy barriers, but he was disappointed. It would take more time and persuasion before she would ever give in. And, above all else, he hadn't meant to make love to her until they were married, since he knew the moral upbringing she would have had would pose a problem there.

Katie, who had by now finished dressing and pinning up her hair again, glared at him through tear-filled eyes. How like a man to pretend that he was some kind of special gift to a woman, she thought! Well, she hoped that she never set eyes on him again!

"Sir," she said in her iciest voice, "I want nothing further to do with you. I wish to never speak with you again, and I hope that you will oblige me. And, don't you ever dare to tell anyone about what you almost did to me here today, do you hear?" She stalked over to Plato, mounted, and then furiously rode away and out of sight.

Brent finally arose and drew on his clothing, thinking to himself what a muddle he had made of things. He had been completely carried away, a thing he should not have allowed. Now, it would be harder than ever to convince her that she loved him. Well, he would keep trying. He thought over the events of a few minutes ago, savoring the wonderful sensations he still experienced whenever he thought of Katie's voluptuous curves beneath him. He had never had an experience that meant as much to him as this one had, even if he had not completed it. He would never forget her innocent response and passionate surrender. Well, enough of that, he sternly told himself. He mounted his waiting horse and rode out of the clearing after Katie.

Katie reached the front gates of Corkhaven just ahead of him, and he watched as she dismounted, threw the reins to Tom, and ran into the house. Brent slowly rode into the

66

front yard, led his horse over to the stables, where he instructed Tom to see to the animal. Then, he also entered the house.

Katie had gone in search of her mother and brothers to inquire if they were ready to have breakfast with her. She glanced back down the stairs and saw that Captain Morgan had entered the house after her. As she stood there unobserved by him, she resisted the strong urge to scream at him, and instead fled to her mother's bedroom. She found Amelia busily reading a letter she had just received while Katie was out riding.

She looked up at Katie's entrance and said to her,

"Katie, there you are. Dear, this is a letter from your Aunt Jenny. She writes that she has been feeling a trifle ill, but that she and your Uncle Albert are staying very busy. She doesn't really have much else to say. By the way, why are you wearing your riding habit? Are you going out riding this morning?"

"No, Mama, I've decided not to go riding any more while those Yankees are still here. Doesn't Aunt Jenny have any messages for me in her letter?" At her mother's negative response, Katie surmised that, of course, her own letter would not have reached Atlanta by now. She prayed that Mr. Jenkins' slave would be able to get through the lines to deliver it. There were many soldiers in the area around Atlanta, she had heard, Yankees and Confederates alike. She inquired if her mother was ready to go on downstairs to breakfast, and then the two of them walked down the hall to the room shared by James and John, where they found the two youngsters regaling Hannah with some of the escapades told them by the Yankees. They jumped up when they saw their mother and sister, and the four of them happily descended the stairs together for the family meal.

When they reached the bottom of the stairway, Amelia noticed Captain Morgan sitting at the desk in the library, apparently absorbed in a book. She was feeling rather generous, so she called to him to come and join her and her children for some breakfast. He immediately stood upon being addressed, and then listened to what the lady was saying to him. He hesitated just a moment, then decided to accept her kind offer.

"Thank you, Mrs. O'Toole. I appreciate your kindness. I will be only too glad to join you and your family for breakfast. I will escort you to the dining room." He left the library and came out into the entrance way and offered his arm to Amelia. She smiled and accepted it, then the two of them led the way. James and John skipped after them, but Katie held back, wondering whether or not her mother would notice if she were perhaps to run back upstairs. She decided that her mother would indeed notice her absence, so she felt compelled to enter the dining room. She took her place at the table, which she was grateful was at the opposite end from where Brent was sitting. She looked over to where he and her mother were conversing quite animatedly with one another. She found herself scarcely able to breathe, so acute was her embarrassment at sitting at the same table with her would-be seducer. She resolved to remain silent and concentrated on the food Junie served them.

As she was putting a forkful of scrambled eggs into her mouth, her mother suddenly asked her,

"Katie, since you are already dressed for riding, why don't you take Captain Morgan out with you and show him some of the beautiful scenery we have around here?"

Katie almost choked on her food, then she hurriedly answered, "No, Mama, I'm afraid that I do not feel well enough to venture out riding today. And, even if I did," she looked up from her plate and fastened her gaze steadily upon the captain, "I would not deign to ride with any Yankee!"

"Katie," her mother said in reproach, "you will please apologize to this gentleman at once. It's true that he is a Yankee, but for the moment, he is a guest at our table. Sir," she said as she addressed Brent, "I honestly don't know what's gotten into my daughter. She never goes so

68

far as to forget her manners. Katie, apologize to the captain at once!" Her tiny mother spoke with unusual firmness.

Katie opened her mouth to utter a word in rebellion, but she chanced to encounter Brent's eye and decided that she would not lower herself to argue with her mother in front of the enemy. So, she complied with her mother's demands, saying in a barely audible voice, "Captain, I am sorry if I was rude. However," her voice rose again to its usual volume at this point, "I still do not wish to go riding with you." There, thought Katie, Mama cannot force me to go when I have made it so plain to everyone how undesirable I find the prospect of such an excursion.

"All right, Katie, that's enough. No one is going to force you to be hospitable, when you are so obviously set upon being insulting," her mother replied. Amelia was thoroughly embarrassed that her own daughter was displaying such a lack of good, Southern manners.

Brent, who had merely sat silent, taking all of this in, finally spoke.

"Mrs. O'Toole," he said with a twinkle of mischief in his blue eyes, "I thank you for the suggestion, but I think that, instead of going riding, I would like Miss O'Toole to come into the library for a moment with me and show me where her father's books upon any military subjects are located. I seem to be having trouble finding any such books." He directed his amused gaze at Katie, whom he was not surprised to see had bristled considerably at his outrageous suggestion.

"Katie, dear, what do you say?" her mother prompted.

"No, I'm afraid not, Captain. You see, I have already had a very trying morning, so I think that I'll stay in my room and rest for a while, as soon as I have finished my breakfast, of course. I do seem to feel a slight headache coming on, for some reason!" She hoped to make it perfectly clear to the man that she wanted to see him no more. Her mother seemed to accept this answer, so Katie applied herself once more to the meal.

After they had all finished their breakfast, the remaining moments having been silent, Amelia took Brent's arm and led him out to the front veranda, where she wanted to discuss some of the customs of the North with him. She was curious to know what the women were wearing, and just how they managed to run their households without the use of slaves.

James and John kept their seats at the table, where they began to shovel food into their mouths at an alarming rate. Katie demanded that they slow down a bit, which they reluctantly did. She then turned slightly in the direction of the front veranda, and stuck out her tongue. Her two brothers collapsed with boyish laughter, asking her why she had done such a thing. She merely told them to go and play, so they hopped up from the table and bounded outside. She was left alone in the room and she sat in silence as Junie once more entered to begin clearing away the dishes.

Miss Katie sure does look sad, Junie thought as she glanced at Katie's pensive face. Maybe I better fix her up with some of my special herb tea. Junie could not know that no amount of herb tea would help with Katie's problems.

Seven

Two days had now passed since the encounter between
Katie and Brent in the clearing of the woods. Brent had
occupied his time reading the military books he was able
to find in the well-stocked library, and seeing to it that his
men did not weary of their enforced inactivity. They had
become a bit restless, so Brent decided that it was possibly
time they moved on to Atlanta.

Katie had avoided Brent quite successfully the past two
days by remaining either in her own bedroom, in her
mother's room, or out in the kitchen with the slaves. She
did not want to have a chance to speak privately with him
again, as she did not want to be forced to examine her
feelings toward him. She wanted to forget him, and he
would soon be gone if her letter had reached her uncle.

The prisoners remained locked in the underground
cellar, being allowed a few moments a day to emerge
outside and stretch their cramped limbs. They were given
food and water, then once again placed into their small
dungeon.

Katie was sitting at the kitchen table, drinking coffee
and discussing some planting matters with Tom and Old
Jonah, when she heard Sarah calling her from the back
door. She rose from her seat and hurried to the door to see
why she was being called. Standing at the back door was
one of William Jenkins' slaves, a young man by the name
of Peter. She asked him why he had come and he began to
speak, watching all the while for any Yankees that might
approach.

"Miss Katie, I done just got back from Atlanta. I had to sneak through the lines, but I made it in. I got to your uncle's house and I give him your letter. He made me wait for a bit, then he handed this here reply to me to give to you. These Yankee soldiers here, they asked me why I come, but I just told them that Mr. Jenkins sent me over to help out a while. Miss Katie, if it's all right with you, can I come in and have something to eat and drink? I'm powerful hungry, and I been traveling for nigh on to four days now. I'm plumb wore out."

"Of course, Peter. Come on in and I'll have Junie fix you a meal at once. You just sit down and rest, while I read this letter." She returned to the kitchen, telling Junie to prepare some food and drink for Peter, then resumed her seat at the table and hurriedly tore open the seal on the letter from her Uncle Albert.

"Dear Niece Katie," it read, "I received your letter and I am sure that you are suffering an inconvenience. However, I have made inquiries about this Captain Brent Morgan, and it turns out that he is much respected as a soldier, and as a gentleman. So, I do not think that you are in any danger while he and his men remain at Corkhaven. They will indeed be gone sooner than you think, and I have enclosed a message to Captain Morgan from myself, and another message for him from his commanding officer. Do not read them, Katie, for they are not for your eyes. Now, on to more important matters.

"Your Aunt Jenny is very ill. It seems that she has somehow contracted a severe fever, and I do not know what to do for her. The doctor says that she needs complete rest and care, but I am unable to provide her with the attention she requires. Therefore, I am asking you or your mother, whichever the two of you decide, to come to Atlanta and stay with us. Your Aunt Jenny needs you, and I would consider it a great favor for you to come. As for the details of your journey here, please speak to Captain Morgan about that. He will explain after he has read the messages enclosed for him. That is all for now, my beloved niece. Please make arrangements to come right away. Your loving uncle, Albert O'Toole."

Katie was considerably perplexed at the news of Aunt Jenny's illness. She would discuss Uncle Albert's request with her mother at once. However, she could not believe that Uncle Albert had told her not to worry about the Yankees at Corkhaven, that Captain Morgan was an honorable officer and gentleman. Gentleman, my eye! I wonder what Uncle Albert could possibly have to say to him, she thought. She stood up from the table and strolled into the parlour, where she found her mother busily knitting. She would not disclose the full contents of the letter to her mother, but she would simply tell her about Aunt Jenny's illness and the need for one of them to go to Atlanta.

"Mama, I have just received a letter from Uncle Albert. I suppose he wanted to write to me so as not to upset you unduly with the news. It seems that Aunt Jenny is very ill and needs for one of us to come to her in Atlanta. He states that she needs constant care and he wants one of us to come immediately."

"Oh, Katie, how dreadful. Your poor Aunt Jenny. I wonder what kind of illness she has contracted? Oh, dear, I do not know what to do. What do you think, Katie?"

"Well, Mama, I'll leave you to think about which one of us should go for a while, so we can be sure to make the right decision. Why don't you go upstairs and rest a bit? You don't seem to be feeling too well, and I just knew that you would be upset with the news."

"Yes, dear," her mother replied as she gathered her knitting and approached the doorway, "I'll go up and lie down a bit and think on the matter. Katie, if you or your brothers need me, just let me know." Poor mother, thought Katie.

She could no longer contain her natural curiosity about the missives addressed to Brent. She glanced toward the doorway to be sure that she was unobserved, then she hastily tore open the first letter. She scanned its contents, then re-read the words to make sure that she had seen correctly.

"Captain Morgan," it began, "I have gained permission from your commanding officer to request you to escort either my niece or her mother as far as possible near Atlanta. Your superior, whom I will not need to mention herein, tells me that you are bringing your men near the city, and that you should be arriving within the next few days. I realize that the information listed above is considered secretive, but it would be extremely advantageous for you and your men to escort either woman as far as you can on your way. I will expect one of them to arrive within the week. Sincerely, Albert O'Toole."

Katie felt outraged that her uncle could ask a Yankee, her enemy if not her uncle's, to provide an escort for his relative. Uncle Albert, she inwardly raged, how could you do such a thing? Well, she quickly decided, he will not escort either myself or my mother!

She then tore open the other message enclosed, noting right away that it was from the captain's commanding officer. It instructed Captain Morgan to comply with Uncle Albert's request. It also informed him that Albert was a friend of his, so he himself would appreciate the favor.

Katie mentally noted that Brent would be leaving Corkhaven as soon as possible. She decided there and then that she would be the one to go to Atlanta. After all, her two brothers were still young enough to need their mother, and the Yankees would have gone by the time she left. Yes, that was the way of it. She would take Sarah with her and journey to Atlanta. But, she would not be traveling with any Yankees! She would destroy the letters she held in her hand, and Brent would not know of her plans, nor of her Uncle Albert's request. As soon as the Yankees had gone, she and Sarah would leave for Atlanta.

Thank goodness she had discovered that they would be leaving Corkhaven in the next day or so. She had also discovered where the Yankees were planning to go, a fact she knew Brent would not be pleased she had found out. By the time she and Sarah had arrived at her uncle's house, Brent would be somewhere on the outskirts of Atlanta, and she wondered why the Yankees had been ordered so near a Southern city. Oh well, she told herself, don't try to understand, just be glad that the man will be leaving and you will be rid of him at last! Don't worry, Uncle Albert, she thought, I won't disclose to anyone else the information contained in these letters. For, if she did, she would be condemning her uncle to an investigation of treasonable activity against the South. Her uncle had only recently divulged to his family the fact that he was content to remain neutral throughout the war, for he was a shrewd businessman and did not want to lose influence with either side. He was not well-respected for his passive views, but his business, whatever its nature, did continue to prosper. Katie could not respect him, either, but she was very fond of him.

As she stood in the parlour, completely absorbed in her thoughts about her plans to journey to Atlanta, she was unaware of Brent's presence in the doorway of the parlour. He remained still, watching the emotions playing across her beautiful face. He saw that she held some pieces of paper in her hands, and he wondered what she had received and from whom.

"Miss O'Toole," his first words startled her and he waited a second or two before continuing, "I have just been informed by one of my men that a slave from another plantation has just arrived, and was seen approaching the back door by the kitchen. Would you mind telling me what business a visiting slave would have here at Corkhaven?" He pretended that he hadn't noticed her quick movements of hiding the papers behind her back.

"Captain Morgan," she said with the barest civility, "you startled me. The slave has simply been sent over by his master, a friend of ours, to help out a bit with the chores. You see, with this many people around, our own slaves have been much too busy to have any spare time for themselves. We Southerners believe in sharing with one another, didn't you know?" She smiled with a hint of mockery.

Brent found himself becoming angry, a thing he definitely did not want to do at this point. Why is it, he thought, that she always has the power to infuriate me? He controlled his temper and said:

"All right, if that is all you wish to tell me. However, I happened to see you absorbed in what appeared to be a letter as I entered a moment ago. Did the slave by any chance deliver any kind of message to you?"

"I don't know what you are talking about, sir," Katie replied with an uplift of her proud chin. She clutched the crumpled pieces of paper in her right fist behind her back.

"I said that I saw you holding some papers in your hand when I entered the room, Miss O'Toole. Now, who would be sending you a letter? Could it be that you have somehow managed to send word to a Confederate soldier friend of yours, asking him to rescue you from the evil Yankees?" He observed her tightening pose.

"Captain Morgan, even if I did receive a letter of some kind, which I did not, I wouldn't tell you about it. Now, sir, you will please excuse me? I am expected upstairs and have been delayed too long." She continued to clutch the letters in her hand and proceeded to leave the room. Brent blocked her way quite effectively with his tall, muscular body, and Katie could not push past him.

"Let me pass, sir! You are being insufferably rude!" she exclaimed with annoyance.

"No, I will not. Not until you have told me what is contained in the letter you are hiding behind your back!" Katie again tried to push past him, but he grasped her arms and pushed her backwards until the back of her knees made contact with a chair and he forced her into it. She attempted to keep him from taking the letters from her, but he merely yanked her arm from behind her back and forced her small, tightly clenched fist to open. Then, he removed the letters from her hand and stood upright once more.

He scanned the contents of each of the letters, after which he stood staring into Katie's sparkling eyes. He could easily see why the little minx had tried to hide them from him.

"Miss O'Toole, you had no right to read letters addressed to me. However, you did read them and are now aware of some information you should not have known. Why in heaven's name did you write a letter to your uncle?" he demanded angrily. It maddened him that she had written a letter and had somehow managed to have it delivered to Atlanta without his knowledge. Of course, he reminded himself, that early morning ride to the neighboring plantation a few days ago.

"I wrote to my uncle to inform him of your invasion of my home, sir! I asked him for any assistance he could provide to see to it that you were forced to leave as soon as possible! And, as for the contents of the letters, you needn't have any worries on my account. I will not tell anyone what I have read, because it would endanger my uncle if I did. There, are you satisfied?" She was furious that he had caught her reading the letters, but she was angrier still that he now knew what sort of double-dealer her uncle was. She suddenly remembered her uncle's demands that Captain Morgan and his men provide an escort for her or her mother, and she hoped that Brent would refuse.

"I see that your uncle wants me to accompany either your mother or yourself to Atlanta, at least as nearly as I can approach the city. Which one of you illustrious ladies is planning to make the trip?" he asked, almost as if he could read her mind.

"Neither of us would presume to force ourselves upon your generosity, I can assure you!" she replied sarcastically. "My mother and I will wait until you have left here once and for all until we make any plans."

Brent clearly did not believe her; in fact, he believed that he already knew the answer. He felt an ever-growing exuberance that he would be able to spend more time with Katie. Perhaps he could finally break down the staunch barriers she had built around herself.

His thoughts returned to the letters he held in his hand. Damn! Military secrets were certainly no secret any longer, he thought. He did not think he would like his new commanding officer very much at all. And, as for Katie's uncle, he felt disgust that a man would profess loyalty for the South, then have dealings with officers of the enemy.

"Miss O'Toole," he said, "I can see that you do not think I intend to honor your uncle's request. I regret to inform you that I do indeed intend to escort you to Atlanta. You might as well get that fact into your pretty little head right now! You can also forget about refusing, because your uncle must have a very good reason for wanting you to come to Atlanta at this time."

Katie marveled anew at the man's audacity. Didn't he realize that she never wanted to see him again?

"Sir, I told you that I would not think of imposing my presence upon you or your men. I understand that you have orders and are expected somewhere near Atlanta in a few days' time, so I suggest that you leave tomorrow morning and be on your way. What I propose to do after you are gone is none of your business!"

Brent winced when she mentioned his orders, but he replied, "You made it my business when you wrote your uncle that blasted letter!" He almost shouted at her, growing angrier by the minute. "And now, your uncle has made it my business by requesting that I escort you there, which I fully intend to do. I think your suggestion about leaving tomorrow morning a very good one, Miss O'Toole. You see, I have surmised that you, and not your mother, will be the one going to Atlanta. I can see by the expression on your angry little face that I am correct. We will be leaving tomorrow morning, so I suggest that you go upstairs and start packing a few of your belongings right now." He was still incensed with her, but he was beginning to calm down a bit, when she said:

"No! Very well, I am the one who will be going to stay with my aunt and uncle, Captain. However, nothing in the world would induce me to allow you or your men to escort me there. So, you may as well forget this entire conversation. Shall I expect you and your men to depart early in the morning, sir?" She inwardly blanched at the idea of having to travel all the way to Atlanta with the one man she never wanted to set eyes on again. She noted that he had become very angry with her again, and she judged it time to beat a hasty retreat from the parlour. While he merely remained where he stood, looking dangerously calm and collected, she hurried out of the room and up the stairs. She quickly glanced back, but she was not being followed.

Brent sat down in the chair she had just left. It was all he could do to refrain from repeating the measures he had administered in the library the other day! What a tangle everything had become. He would be taking his men and leaving in the morning, just as Katie had suggested. But, he would also be taking along the fiery, stubborn little wench he had come to care for so desperately.

Katie, meanwhile, sought out her mother and related her decision to her.

"Mama, I really do think it best that I be the one to go to Atlanta. James and John will need you, and the Yankees will be leaving in the morning, or so I hope, and there will be no reason why I can't get away for a few days. I won't be staying in Atlanta but two or three weeks, anyway. And, I can take Sarah with me. What do you say?"

"Very well, Katie, if that is what you think best. I must confess that I was dreading the prospect of a trip away from home just now. I have not been feeling my very best, and it will be so nice to have some peace and quiet around here for a change. Oh, I don't mean you, dear, I mean the Yankees. They have been very tolerable houseguests, but

I will honestly be glad when things get back to normal around here, won't you?"

"Yes, Mama, I will be very glad." After discussing a few details about the proposed trip and Aunt Jenny's illness, Katie left her mother and hurried down the hallway to her own room, where she began thinking about what Captain Morgan had threatened. He insisted that she and Sarah travel with them, but she could not possibly do that. I know, she thought, suddenly hitting upon an idea. I'll go tell Sarah to come up here and help me pack. Then, in the morning, I will simply wait until the Yankees have gone and I will leave an hour or so after them. That way, Sarah and I will not catch up with them, and we can travel alone. I'll have Tom prepare Plato and one of the other horses, and Sarah and I can leave tomorrow morning. We can reach Atlanta by the following evening, I'm sure.

She called for Sarah and began choosing which dresses and other garments she would take. Sarah entered the room and Katie sat her down upon the bed to tell her of the plans she had made for them. Sarah didn't like it one bit.

"Now, Miss Katie, what if you and I, two women all by our lonesome, run into some other soldiers or something? Wouldn't it be better to travel with the Yankees, like you just done told me Captain Morgan wants us to? You just said that they was leaving in the morning, and they will be going in the same direction."

"Sarah," Katie cautioned her sternly, "don't you tell another soul what I have told you! Now, you and I will be leaving in the morning after the Yankees have gone. We will ride to Atlanta, and I will see to it that the horses and provisions are ready for us. You go and collect some of your clothes and pack them in a small bag. You hear me, move, Sarah!" Katie gave her an impatient shove toward the door.

After visiting the stables, unknown to Brent, of course, Katie returned upstairs to tell her brothers that she would be leaving in the morning. She also told them that the Yankees would be leaving, and that they and Mama would have Corkhaven all to themselves once again. They were less than delighted.

"Aw, Katie, we were hoping the soldiers could stay for at least another week, weren't we, John? And, why are you going to Atlanta tomorrow, anyway?" asked James.

"Well, honey, Aunt Jenny is sick and I need to go and take care of her, understand? You and John be good boys for Mama and I will see you again in a few weeks." Katie hugged and kissed them both, then walked down the hall and into her mother's bedroom to say goodbye to her.

"Katie, darling, do be careful. I can't say that I like the idea of you and Sarah traveling all that way by yourselves, but I know that your Aunt Jenny needs you. Are you sure that the Yankees will be gone before you go?"

"Yes, Mama, Captain Morgan and I had an earlier discussion in the parlour. He and his men will be leaving before Sarah and I. And, don't worry, for I retrieved Papa's shotgun from the library, where that Yankee thought to hide it behind the desk, so we will at least have some means of protection. Now, I better return to my room and get some sleep. I'll see you again in a few weeks' time, Mama, and I will write to you as often as possible." She kissed her mother warmly and closed the door behind her. She knew that her mother would perk up a bit after the Yankees were gone. The strain of the past few days had been too much for her delicate disposition.

She entered the bedroom and closed the door, then undressed and climbed into bed. She was unable to keep her thoughts from flying in several directions. She hoped that Brent would be gone before she even arose in the morning, but she knew with a certainty that he would delay his departure until he had said goodbye to her.

Why had he said that he cared for her? It was most likely to see how far he could go with his attentions, she thought. She had heard tales from some of her friends that men did things like that. They told a woman that they loved her, expecting those magic words would enable them to make free with their advances.

I don't suppose I'll ever see him again after tomorrow, she reflected as she began to drift off to sleep. He had been a disturbing force in her life these past few days. She didn't precisely despise him, but she didn't think she liked him, either. No, she would have to obliterate him completely from her mind.

As she slept that night, she dreamt of the interlude in the woods. She vividly recalled the touch of his strong hands on her flesh, the gentle and passionate caresses he had bestowed upon her body. She remembered the hunger of his kisses, the fleeting sight of his muscular body. She could almost feel the touch of his warm lips on hers, the admiring look in his eyes. Would she never forget that day? She finally awoke, thinking to herself that it was very good that she would never again see the man who had so incessantly plagued her thoughts.

The next morning, Katie awoke and brought her thoughts into focus. She remembered that she and Sarah were to leave that morning, so she jumped out of bed and quickly donned her riding habit. She picked up her small bag of clothing and Papa's shotgun, then opened the door and crept downstairs to the kitchen, where she found Sarah also ready to leave. Katie instructed her to remain in the kitchen while she looked to see if the Yankees were up and about yet.

She went into the library, but found it to be empty. She then walked outside, where she saw the Yankees saddling their horses and making ready to leave. Brent glanced up from his preparations and saw her standing on the veranda, so he quickly climbed the steps and began speaking to her.

"Miss O'Toole, I see that you are ready to leave. That's good. We're almost ready, so I suggest that you bring out your pack and saddle your mount." He had been startled

82

to see her standing there, and he still couldn't believe that she had for once obeyed him. It was about time, he mused.

Katie, far from obeying him, was reveling in the fact that she would not have to explain her actions to him any longer. Looking at him now, standing in the sunlight with a smile upon his handsome face, she drew in her breath sharply. A tiny voice in the back of her mind asked her if she would really be so glad he was going. She ignored it and said, "Captain Morgan, goodbye. I can't say 'please come again,' you understand." She ignored the hand he offered her.

"What do you mean, Miss O'Toole? Aren't you ready to leave yet?" He wondered just what she would say next.

"No, I am not leaving at all, Captain! I have decided to go to Atlanta later, not at this time, as Mama and the boys need me here. So, I say goodbye to you now." She relished the astonished expression upon his face. So, he actually believed that she would do as he had ordered!

"I thought we had settled that already, but I should have known you would be stubborn to the last moment. All right, where are your things? If you have not packed them yet, you'll simply have to go as you are. Are you going to bring your slave with you? Whatever you wish, please tell me now." Of course, you idiot, he chided himself, you should have known better.

"I am not going! That is final," Katie ground out the words and then turned upon her heel and quickly stalked back into the house. She hurried to the kitchen where she told Sarah that the Yankees were leaving, so the two of them would be able to leave within the hour. As she gleefully smiled at Sarah, she whirled around to find Brent standing in the doorway, idly leaning against the frame and listening to her every word.

"So, that's it. Oh, Sarah, please come outside and bring the bags with you. We are ready to leave right now."

Sarah hesitated, looking at her mistress' surprised expression and then back at the stern, unyielding

83

expression on the captain's face. She made a rapid decision and lifted the two bags and took them outside. Katie was left to face him alone.

"Now, let's go. Come on, I say it's time to leave. I presume that you have already said goodbye to your family. We need to be on our way," he demanded. Katie simply stood staring up into his face, defiantly holding her ground. He was becoming extremely weary of the childish games she had so often played with him, so he picked her up as if she weighed no more than a feather and carried her outside.

Katie kicked and squirmed, trying to free herself, but he held her with one arm around her shoulders and the other under her knees. Her arms were quite effectively pinned at her sides by what seemed to be bands of steel. He took her as far as the stables, where he set her down none too gently. He led out her horse, saddled him, then once more lifted Katie in his arms and placed her upon Plato's back. He returned to his own horse, mounted, and ordered his men to ride. The prisoners, released from the underground cellar, were to ride in the midst of their captors. Brent rode back to where Katie sat astride her horse, unmoving, and told her, "Miss O'Toole, if you don't ride this very instant, I'll tie you on your horse and lead you along! Now, be a good girl and follow!" he threatened in an undertone. The devilish gleam in his eyes was enough to make Katie swallow her pride and spur her horse onward. She certainly possessed no desire to be tied. Sarah followed after her.

Brent led his men, the prisoners, and the two women in the direction of Atlanta. The lives of all of them would be greatly changed in the months ahead.

Part 2

Atlanta

Eight

Katie sullenly rode beside Captain Morgan, keeping her beautiful head held high and her expression one of defiance. She was inwardly plotting various means of bringing the high and mighty captain down from his insufferable manner. She absolutely detested being forced to obey any orders at all, much less orders issued by this particular man. She vowed to herself to be on her guard for the entire trip, a prospect she viewed with less than favor.

Brent glanced speculatively over at the woman riding so haughtily beside him. My, what a vexing female, he thought. She was so damned proud, she would not allow him any chance to show her how much he cared for her. I really do love her, he told himself with a small degree of amazement. After all this time of searching for the one woman who could hold him, he had actually found her upon a plantation in Georgia. He hadn't planned for it to happen, but it had, and he was immensely pleased that he would have two more days to convince her to admit her love for him. It wasn't going to be easy, but nothing worthwhile ever was easy, he reminded himself. He noted with amusement how Katie refused to even glance his way. All right, Miss O'Toole, he silently vowed, two can play at this game. He would be just as stubborn and relentless as she, only in a completely opposite direction, of course.

Suddenly, the two scouts he had sent ahead rode back to inform him of the presence of a large number of Confederate troops advancing over the sloping hill in the near distance. Brent swore with a vehemence, but he quickly determined what was best done about the approaching danger. He ordered everyone into the brush and trees lining the path they were riding along through the thickly-wooded forest.

"But, Captain Morgan, I thought Yankees weren't afraid of anything, especially not of Confederate soldier boys!" Katie mockingly taunted him. She smiled a rather wicked smile and Brent, instead of feeling anger or annoyance at her words, merely smiled in return and repeated his orders for her to quickly dismount and lead her horse into the brush. When she made no move to do as he bid, Brent lifted her down and led her horse along with his into the woods.

"Take your hands off me, sir! I have had enough of your high-handed ways. Let go of me!" Brent ignored her protests and almost roughly threw her down upon the ground, then placed his own body beside hers. She opened her mouth to protest even louder, but he clamped an iron hand over her lips and cautioned her not to speak or utter one sound.

"Miss O'Toole, don't you dare to say a word. Those men out there don't know that we have a fine Southern lady in here with us, so, if you value your own life, you will remain silent. Besides, I cannot allow you to warn the Confederates, as there are too many of them for us to defend ourselves against." He spoke softly and gently into her ear. Katie widened her eyes for an instant, then reluctantly nodded her head in agreement. Brent removed his hand, but continued holding her closely against him as they lay together upon the cool earth.

"You don't have to hold me, sir! I'm not going anywhere, I assure you! Please release me," Katie insisted in a whisper. Brent simply retained his hold upon her and warned her with his eyes to remain silent. Katie complied and forced herself to remain stiff and unyielding beside him.

Within just a few minutes, the Confederate troops

began to pass by their hiding place. Katie noted that the poor boys wore ragged, soiled uniforms. Uniforms, no, not uniforms, she hastily amended; they were what was left of uniforms. Many of the soldiers were barefoot, while others had tied rags about their weary, aching feet. Katie felt a grim foreboding as she watched the tattered army march by. There before her were her own South's men. These were the valiant fighters, the protectors of the cause. She sincerely hoped that these men were not representative of the rest of the Confederate Army.

Brent's men watched in deadly silence as the enemy soldiers marched past. Their lives depended on their ability to remain hidden and quiet. After what seemed like an interminable amount of time, Brent judged it once again safe to emerge from the woods and continue with their journey.

He helped Katie rise from the ground and stood looking down into her green eyes. She drew in her breath sharply, then seemed to recover and hurried toward her horse. He was beside her in an instant to assist her in mounting, and she murmured her thanks almost inaudibly.

Throughout the remainder of the day, the scouts did not see any more of the enemy. Brent led his men along what he judged to be the least-traveled paths.

After they had traveled far into the afternoon, Brent judged it time for them to make camp for the night. The men quickly set up tents in a clearing of the woods. Katie and Sarah slowly and painfully dismounted, saddle-sore and thoroughly weary after the hard riding of the day. They were not used to riding as much as this, and Katie was grateful that they had made camp before nightfall.

As they were making preparations for the approaching darkness, the scouts returned once again to report to their leader that a small detachment of their own soldiers was approaching from the east. Brent strode out of his tent and stood ready to greet the commanding officer of the troops.

Approximately twenty-five Yankee soldiers rode into the camp and, as Katie watched, they dismounted and were greeted by their fellow soldiers in the camp. Brent saluted and then shook hands with their officer, then offered he and his men the hospitality of their camp for the night. There was plenty of food and water for all, so the officer accepted his generous offer.

As they walked toward Brent's tent, the other officer spied Katie and Sarah, sitting upon the ground under a large, shady tree, and asked of Brent:

"Captain Morgan, who is that beautiful young woman sitting over there? How did she come to be out here with you and your men?"

"Sir, that is my wife, and that is her maid with her. They are traveling to Atlanta, where my wife has relatives, neutral of course, and she is going to visit for a spell. I know that this is a dangerous time to be traveling, but she insisted upon making the trip. I saw no harm in it, as long as I and my men were along for protection," Brent lied. He didn't know what had prompted him to tell the blatant lie, but he supposed it was to protect Katie from any of the leers or possible advances from the other soldiers. He knew that she wouldn't like it one bit. No, not one bit.

Katie, sitting well within earshot of the two men, distinctly overheard what Brent had told the major. It was all she could do to keep from jumping up and setting the record straight, but she knew that it would only serve to make her look ridiculous. Oh, she fumed, I'll make you pay for that lie, you Yankee! She continued sitting and striving to listen to what was being said, but the men had by now entered the tent. She glanced around at the soldiers and happened to catch the eye of an older, kindly looking man in civilian clothing standing near the tent that Brent and the major had just entered. She stared at him in confusion, noting the smiling countenance he turned upon her.

After only a few moments' hesitation, the man approached Katie.

"Ma'am," he said with a friendly smile, "I could not

88

help overhearing what the captain told the major. I think it very nice indeed that you and your husband are able to be together during these troubled times. I will pray that you reach your destination safely, Mrs. Morgan."

Katie was shocked by his words. She hadn't realized that anyone else had heard the lie Brent had told. Oh my goodness, she thought, I can't let this go on any longer.

"Sir," she replied sweetly, "I regret to inform you that what Captain Morgan told the other officer is simply not the truth. You see, he wants me to return his regard for me, but I am simply unable to do so. Also, sir, I am a Southern lady, a native of Georgia." She noted the surprised expression on the face of the fatherly man, whom she noticed appeared to be somewhat somberly dressed.

"Ma'am," the man said with an air of confusion, "I don't understand. I do not see any reason for the captain to lie to another officer. By the way, I am the chaplain for this detachment. My name is Father Hanson."

Katie immediately regretted her words to the man. She hadn't realized that he was a Yankee, although she chided herself for such an oversight. Of course, you idiot, she thought, why else would he be traveling with Yankee troops? No Southern gentleman would be associated with them.

"Father Hanson, my name is Katie O'Toole, and what I have told you is the plain truth. Captain Morgan is not to be trusted, as I have discovered for myself. He and his men arrived at my home several days ago and refused to leave. Now, against my will, he is forcing me to travel to Atlanta with him!" There, she thought, that ought to fix the captain's wagon! A man of God would surely understand her dilemma.

During the course of Katie's conversation with Father Hanson, Brent happened to stroll out of his tent and hear what Katie had said. He quickly strode over to the two and began speaking to the chaplain, warning Katie with a frown to keep quiet.

"Father Hanson, I'm Captain Brent Morgan. It is good

to see you here, sir. Have you met my wife yet?" he asked as he placed his arm around her shoulders and drew her close, tightly.

"I am not your wife, you odious Yankee! Let go of me this instant!" Katie cried as she attempted to wrest herself from his embrace. He held on to her just as tightly as before.

"Father Hanson, may I have a few words with you? Katie, dear, you better sit back down and rest for a while. I'll rejoin you in a few minutes," he said as he forced her to sit. She remained upon the ground and glared at him, giving thanks that he was going to be in trouble with the chaplain when Father Hanson informed him that he was now aware of the truth of the matter. Let's see you get out of this one, she challenged him with her flashing green eyes.

Brent led the chaplain over to a tree stump several yards away and motioned for him to sit down, then sat down beside him.

"Father Hanson, this is a sad time, indeed. You see, my wife has been very ill and has begun having these delusions every now and then. Today, the trip has simply been too much for her. She refuses to return to reality when she has these spells, so don't be alarmed by anything she might have told you. She enjoys shocking people whenever she is like this."

"My son, I understand. What an immense burden for you to carry in these times. I greatly admire your stamina, what with your wife's illness and the war. Is there anything I can do to help?" the kindly chaplain said, sympathetically.

"Well, sir, there just might be. If you will please stay here, I'll fetch my wife and maybe if you talk to her along with me, she'll feel better." With that, he left the man and approached the spot where Katie still sat, intently watching his conversation. She hadn't been able to hear what was being said, but she surmised, from the many glances the two of them bestowed her way, that the

90

conversation was centered around her. She stood up as Brent came to stand before her, and she smiled in triumph. I suppose the good chaplain has reprimanded him quite strongly for what he has done, she thought. Her smile faded as she heard what Brent had to say.

"Katie, Father Hanson wishes to speak with you. Will you please come with me?" She eyed him with suspicion, but she allowed herself to be led over to where the chaplain was sitting. She wondered what in the world he could have to say to her, especially with Brent by her side.

"My dear young woman," he began with a patient air, "Brent, your husband, has told me of your illness. Don't worry, my child, you will soon be well again. However, you must face up to reality as soon as possible. Traveling all the way to Atlanta is very dangerous, and you will need all your wits about you when you arrive. Now, would you like to talk about anything? Your husband assures me that his presence will help."

Katie looked in astonishment from one man to another. Just what had Brent told the man now? Well, she would not play his little game, whatever it was!

"Father, I have already told you that I am not married to this man. Why, I would never have married a Yankee, especially this one! Now, I don't know what lies he has been telling you, but I am certainly speaking the truth!" She became alarmed at the disbelief so apparent upon the chaplain's concerned features.

"My child, I understand. Captain, is there anything you would like me to say at this time?" he asked.

"Yes, there is. Since my wife," he said with a quick glance at Katie's outraged expression, "believes that she and I are not legally married, would you perhaps consent to marry us here and now? You see, she claims we have never been legally married. Well, we have lived together as man and wife." He bestowed a knowing look upon Katie's person. She opened her mouth in anger and astonishment, but the chaplain interrupted her denials.

"Captain, if you honestly believe that such a thing

91

would help your wife, of course I will perform the ceremony. You see, no one can have the words said over them too many times. Would that make you happier, Katie?" he asked her.

"Of course not! I have already informed you that I am Miss Katie O'Toole, and I have lived my entire life upon my family's plantation, Corkhaven. I had never even met this man until a few days ago, and I would certainly never consent to marry him!" She could tell by the chaplain's manner that he did not believe a word of what she told him. She turned her wrath upon Brent, who stood with a pitying, knowing expression on his handsome face. She could read the mischief brewing in his blue eyes, and she longed to hit him as hard as she could across his smirking face.

"Captain Morgan, how dare you lie to a man of God! Why, why are you doing such a thing? I have no wish to marry you, so you might as well end this little charade right now!" she said with a heightened pitch to her voice. She was becoming a bit panicky at the great lengths he was so obviously willing to carry his little game.

"Father Hanson," she appealed, "ask any of Captain Morgan's men. Ask my slave. They'll all tell you that I am telling the truth! Go ahead, ask them, I say!"

"Now, now, my child, don't get excited. I should think that you'd want your marriage to be legal. And, as for asking anyone else, why, I'm sorry to say, it's very apparent that you are rather upset and perhaps unbalanced at this time. I expect the war and the trip have been too much for you to handle, my dear. Don't you worry, I'll set everything right. Captain, just allow me a moment to fetch my Bible and book, then I'll return to strengthen the bond." He left Katie and Brent alone as he approached his horse and began rummaging for the books.

"Captain Morgan," Katie hissed in a boiling temper, "I've had enough of this! I will not allow this stupid, idiotic prank to go any farther, do you hear? Now, I am

92

leaving you to explain the truth of the matter to the chaplain." She began to stalk away from him, but he easily captured her wrist and pulled her back.

"Now, Katie, dear, don't you ever listen? The good chaplain is going to marry us, legally. Isn't that what you want? You know that you love me, but you won't admit it. I love you, and I am willing to marry you. Isn't that what you wanted all along?" he asked her with an innocent smile upon his face. His eyes literally danced with mischief and amusement, but also with something else. Katie wondered, could he possibly be telling me the truth? Could he really love me as he says? It doesn't matter, she furiously reminded herself, I will not let this go on any longer!

She struggled, attempting to escape his grip upon her wrist, but he refused to relinquish his hold on her. Father Hanson returned, along with one of the Yankee soldiers to act as witness.

"Now, Captain Morgan, you and your Katie join hands, please. This won't take long at all. Katie, I know you will be very happy to know that your marriage is thoroughly legal," he informed her kindly.

Brent grabbed both of her hands and held them in a crushing grip. Katie gazed in horror at the chaplain, who was now reading the marriage service. This can't be happening to me, she thought. What if I cried out for help, or screamed? She knew with a certainty that no one would pay any heed to her cries, as long as she was safely with the captain. Where was Sarah, she thought frantically. Where could she have disappeared to? What am I going to do?

Katie continued listening to the droning voice of Father Hanson as he read the marriage vows. Brent repeated his vows, then came Katie's turn. She listened abstractedly as her vows were read by the chaplain, then he instructed her to repeat them.

"No, I won't!" she cried in frustration. She wouldn't repeat them, no matter what. And no one could force her to say them!

"All right, my child, it's all right." Father Hanson continued with the service, as if she hadn't refused to repeat her vows at all. When he asked if she would take the man beside her in holy matrimony, she opened her mouth to refuse, but Brent answered quickly for her.

"She takes me, Father. And, I take her. Now, isn't that all there is to it?" Brent asked. The chaplain replied that there was still a bit more, which he quickly read. Then, he happily pronounced them man and wife. He informed Brent that he could now kiss the bride with his blessings.

Katie did not struggle when Brent, her new husband, kissed her. She remained passive and still. She could not believe that she was actually married, and to a Yankee besides. It had all happened so quickly, she hadn't known what to do. She vowed to make Brent sorry, if it was the last thing she ever did! How could he have done such a thing? And, how could Father Hanson have gone along with him?

"Father Hanson, this marriage cannot possibly be legal. Why, I didn't ever agree that I would take this man as my husband, so how can you possibly say that we're married?" she asked with a controlled anger.

"My child, the marriage is definitely legal. You see, once I have pronounced a couple to be man and wife, it is quite irreversible. Now, be happy with your husband and be grateful that he loves you so much," he told her. He had watched the couple kissing and thought it prudent to leave them alone. He and the other Yankee soldier strolled away to rejoin their men in the camp.

"Katie," Brent softly spoke her name, "I'm sorry, but it was the only way to make you see how much I love you. I know that you love me, too, you see. Now, maybe you'll allow yourself to admit it, darling. We're married now, so it's permissible for you to say how you feel. Now, I'm no longer just a Yankee to you, I'm your husband, darling, and I love you very much." He gazed down into her beautiful face with gentle, loving eyes that reflected his innermost feelings.

94

Katie could scarcely breathe as she saw the way he looked at her. No, she declared to herself, I can't give in. I just can't.

"Captain Morgan, I will never forgive you for what you have done to me today. If you truly loved me, how could you do this to me? Oh, I could kill you!" She finally shook off the numbness that had enveloped her throughout the ceremony, and she flung herself at him, flailing at his body with her fists. He caught both of her wrists in his hands with little effort, then pulled her into his arms. She could no longer contain her anger and frustration, and she burst into tears.

Brent continued to hold her until the storm of her temper had passed, at which time she disengaged herself from his embrace and walked across the camp into the tent she was to share with Sarah for the night. Brent did not attempt to stop her. He judged it wise to allow her some time to become used to the idea of being his wife. I pray that I've done the right thing, he told himself. It was done now, and they were legally married. Even if he wanted to relent, it was too late. He only knew that he had felt like a complete and utter cad when he witnessed her tears. Being in love was not an easy thing, he mused.

Katie threw herself down upon her cot and let loose another torrent of weeping. A tiny voice at the back of her mind asked her if she was really all that upset with the way things had turned out, but she squashed it as quickly as it arose. Sarah entered the tent and observed Katie's distress and she knelt beside her former charge.

"Miss Katie, what happened, honey? What has been done to you to make you go and act this way?"

"Oh, Sarah, it's just too awful!" Katie tearfully replied. Then, staunching the flow of tears and hiccupping occasionally, she related to Sarah the story of her wedding. The slave woman listened in grim silence, feeling anger for the captain who had upset her baby so much. However, as she continued listening to Katie's story, she felt her thoughts and emotions undergo a

95

change. Maybe it's for the best, she began to think. Miss Katie has always needed someone like that captain. He's strong enough fo her, and it's obvious that he really does care for her. Yes, maybe it's really for the best. Only thing is, Miss Katie won't see that. She won't open her eyes.

"Now, now, honey, it's not going to be so bad. Here I am to comfort you. Why, at least this way, you don't have to worry none about getting to Atlanta safely. You just know that the captain will do all he can to see that his wife gets there safely," she tried comforting her.

"Oh, Sarah, it's not going to be all right at all! Here I am, married to a Yankee! A man I'd never seen before a few days ago! I'm ruined! I can no longer choose for myself a husband, a man I love and want to marry. What am I going to do? If he so much as comes near me, I'll shoot him!" After this latest outburst, she once more threw herself down upon the cot and cried wrenchingly.

"Miss Katie, begging your pardon, honey, but there ain't been that many men to choose from, now, has there? Anyways, what's done is done, and the faster you get that into your head, the better. Now, don't you worry none, he ain't gonna hurt you. Why, the man must love you an awful lot to marry you. I figure it was the only way he knew to get you for himself, honey. He was afraid of losing you, I figure." She observed that Katie seemed to take an interest in at least some of what she had said, so she felt satisfied. My Miss Katie will be just fine, she thought with pride, she's a fighter. And, she is bound to come to her senses about the captain sooner or later.

Sarah left the tent to go back outside and see if she could help prepare dinner for the men. They had all treated her with respect, a fact that she was most grateful for. Yankees or not, these men were true gentlemen.

After having cried all she possibly could, Katie finally dried her eyes and sat up. She wouldn't think about it any more for right now. She would venture down to the small lake and refresh her tired, aching body with a cool bath. She didn't wish to see her so-called "husband" any more for quite a while.

She gathered up her towel and bar of soap, then she headed for the water, which was only a few hundred yards back into the dense forest, its location she had discovered by overhearing one of the Yankees talking about it. At least she would be unobserved and could have a bath in complete privacy.

However, one of the soldiers had seen her heading away from the camp and had immediately gone in search of Brent to inform him of his wife's absence. Brent told the young soldier that he would return in about an hour, and to tell no one else of Katie's departure. He then grabbed up his gun and headed in the direction Katie had just gone.

When Katie reached the small lake, she marveled at its beauty. It was glistening, blue, and very cool-looking. It was surrounded on all sides by huge trees and piles of brush. She set down her gun, which she had caught up as an afterthought, and proceeded to undress. She hastily peeled off her dress and undergarments, then approached the lake. She slowly eased her naked body into the refreshing coolness of the water and began to wash her hair. She soaped her body all over, then decided to swim for a while and relax.

Suddenly, she heard a twig snap. She stood in the water until her feet touched the sandy bottom, then looked around to see if she could spot anything in the trees. She saw nothing out of the ordinary, so she continued with her swim. After a while, she decided that it was time to go back to camp, as it was beginning to get dark. She emerged dripping from the water and reached for the towel to dry her wet skin. As she bent over to shake out her shining red-gold mass of hair, she heard a voice say:

"Mrs. Morgan, you should not have gone off alone like that. It's a good thing I followed you, to ensure your safety from prying eyes."

Katie jerked her head up and found herself looking into the admiring eyes of her husband. She gave a small squeak, hastily draping the towel around her shivering form.

"How dare you! Can't I have any privacy at all? What do you mean, following me out here? I brought my gun with me, and I assure you that I know how to use it!" She was humiliated by the fact that he had seen her emerging from the pool, stark naked.

"Remember, Katie, I'm your husband now. I have a perfect right to see you without your clothes on. Besides, how could you protect yourself when you were in the water and your gun was up here on the bank?" He smiled in a disarming manner and extended his arm to help her up on to the rocks where her discarded clothing lay. She ignored his arm and climbed up by herself, averting her gaze from his amused face.

"Will you please allow me to get dressed, sir? It is becoming quite cool out here, and it will soon be dark," she asked disdainfully.

"My name is Brent, dear wife. And, yes, I'll allow you to get dressed. Go right ahead," he replied with a lazy smile and a glance at her body in the towel.

"Well, at least turn around, Captain. After what you have done to me, you ought to at least afford me this one small courtesy!" she insisted with a frown. Why didn't he just go away and leave her alone? She was perfectly able to take care of herself. She didn't like the way in which he was eyeing her, either.

"Dear wife, I think it is time that you and I have a discussion about our marital status. I am now your lawful husband, and I have a husband's rights. Katie, stop denying to yourself and to me that you love me. I have felt your response to me, and I have seen in your eyes, when you have left them unguarded, that you do care. Isn't it about time you quit behaving like a child and faced up to your feelings for me?" he asked with a seductive smile. He was trying to control his rising desire, but it was extremely difficult with her standing there, wearing nothing but a thin towel. Didn't she realize how much of her beautiful body was actually revealed? He couldn't stand and banter with her much longer.

Katie felt herself weaken at his words, but she forced herself to turn her emotions aside. She cried out with confusion, anger, and perhaps disgust at herself, then she launched herself at the captain. She kicked him in the shins, pulled his thick hair with a vengeance, and hit at him with her clenched fists. Brent tried to fight her off without hurting her, but he could not. He roughly grabbed her wrists and forced her arms ruthlessly behind her back. Then, he sternly ordered her to behave. As she tossed her head from side to side and struggled to free herself, the towel she was wearing suddenly fell away from her naked body and to the ground. She gasped in dismay and quickly glanced up at her husband's face.

Brent couldn't help looking down at the exquisite charms of his wife so aptly revealed now. As Katie cried out and attempted to run away from him, he ran after her and caught her to him. He clasped her hair in his hands and forced her face up to his. Then, he placed his lips slowly upon hers and kissed her with a controlled passion. Katie tried to struggle once more, but she was trapped by his arms, and by her own emotions. She surrendered her lips to his, parting them with a gasp.

Brent somehow managed to remove his clothing as he continued kissing her and lowered her to the earth below. Katie squirmed as her naked back touched the cool grass, but she could not stop things now. Brent was now entirely naked and he proceeded to finish what had been started that day in the clearing of the woods at Corkhaven.

He slowly and expertly kissed her voluptuous curves, from the top of her head to the tips of her toes. She gave herself up to the marvelous, rapturous sensations coursing through her virgin body. She kissed him back with the passion of her youth and inexperience, and she felt further inflamed by his response. He was guiding her into a new world, initiating her into the ways of love. His kisses left her breathless, and she found herself comparing this time with that day at the other pool. It was much more exciting this time, now that she knew what to do, now that she knew what to expect.

Brent's warm lips traveled sensuously downward from her face, to her beautiful breasts, then once more to her lips. He caressed her in the gentlest, most arousing manner. She opened her thighs and allowed him to place one of his hands at the center of her femininity. She could hardly stand the searing flames she felt at the pit of her stomach. She whispered his name and pleaded for release. He judged it time to finally make her his, and so he slowly removed his hand and began to enter her with great care.

Katie cried out at the first, sharp pain, but she soon found the pain melting away into new sensations. So this is what it's like, she marveled to herself. Brent had now entered her and begun to fulfill their ever-rising passions. She found her body moving rhythmically with his. Finally, he moaned in contentment, at the same moment she gave a small cry of fullfillment.

He removed his body from hers and lay back down beside her, breathing heavily. Katie sought to catch her breath and review what had just passed between them. It had been so deliciously wonderful, she decided. She had never felt this way before. She thought, in her naiveté, that this was to be the only time she would ever be able to feel this way.

Brent glanced over at her face and body. His eyes traveled over her entire form and he could hardly believe that she was so beautiful and perfectly formed. He knew that she had enjoyed their lovemaking as much as he had, and he turned to her to speak the words of love he felt so deeply in his heart.

"Katie, darling. You are wonderful. You are the most beautiful woman in the whole world, and I am glad that you are mine. Can't you say that you love me? Isn't it time now to admit it?" He gazed at her with all the love he felt.

Katie became confused at his demands that she say she loved him. What did he mean? What is love, anyway? she asked herself. True, she had immensely enjoyed their lovemaking, but love? She truly did not know.

"I don't know what love is, Brent. I know that the beautiful thing we just shared was very wonderful, but I don't know if it's love. What right have you to demand my love, anyway? You forced me into this marriage, didn't you? Just what do you expect?" She found herself again growing angry with him. The delights of a moment ago seemed to fade into oblivion as her fury surfaced.

Brent was astonished that she had so quickly turned upon him. He believed that their lovemaking would have finally broken through the barriers, but it appeared he was wrong. It would take more than this to accomplish that, he told himself. It would take more wooing and more time.

"Katie, I did what I had to do. I had to make you mine, you little vixen! I couldn't let you go off to Atlanta and never see you again. I couldn't and wouldn't let any other man have you!" he informed her.

"There is nothing you can say to me to change how I feel about what you did. Now, I think it's time we returned to the camp. I am tired, and I need some sleep," she coldly replied. She arose and turned her back upon him while she quickly drew on her clothing. Brent remained where he sat, watching her dress. He noticed with approval her smooth, creamy skin, her delicately shaped back, her firmly rounded bottom, and her shapely legs. He vowed that he would never give her up.

Katie finished dressing, then began to walk back to the camp, without even so much as a backward glance at her husband. He waited until she had gone, then he too dressed and hurried back to camp. This is my wedding night, he reflected wryly, and my bride and I will be spending it apart.

Nine

Early the next morning, the camp came to life and began its preparations for the activity of the day. The other Yankee soldiers who had joined Brent's men would soon be riding away in another direction.

Katie awoke with a stretching yawn, then hopped out of bed to meet the new day. She glanced over at the sleeping form of Sarah. Poor Sarah, she thought, she must be exhausted. Katie quickly dressed and left the tent to stand outside in the warming sunshine of the early morning.

Suddenly a remembrance of yesterday's events dawned on her. She had completely forgotten the fact that she was now a married woman, in every sense of the term. The smile on her face faded. What am I going to do? she asked herself. She couldn't allow Brent to keep her within the bounds of a conventional marriage. I've got to find some way to remedy the situation, she told herself with determination. She would try speaking to the chaplain again, although she knew that such an action would most likely be of little use.

Father Hanson was busy saddling his horse and packing his bundle for the hard ride of the day. He looked up from his labors as Katie approached and greeted her with a friendly smile.

"Mrs. Morgan, how is the happy bride this morning? I trust that you have recovered somewhat from your little 'spell' of yesterday?"

"Father Hanson, you still may not believe me, but

102

everything I told you was the truth. So, I have come to ask you if there is anything you can possibly do to annul my so-called marriage?" she asked sternly.

"Katie, my child, you are now the lawful wife of Captain Morgan, even if you did not believe that you were such before. There is nothing you can do about breaking your bonds of matrimony. They are forever, my dear. Now, as soon as you are feeling a bit better, you will see that the real world is the best world. And, you need have no more doubts as to the legality of your marriage," he replied patiently.

"Oh, you just refuse to understand, don't you? I can see that it's of no use to talk to you at all. Goodbye, Father Hanson." She whirled around and stalked back in the direction of her tent. As she neared the entrance of the tent, she saw Brent walk out of his own tent and call to the chaplain. I wonder what he could possibly have to say to him, now? she wondered.

As she continued watching the conversation between the two men, she noted that they looked her way several times. It was all she could do to keep from grimacing at them.

Brent, who had observed Katie's watchful presence, had a particular favor to ask of the chaplain.

"Since I and my men are going to join Sherman's forces to the northwest of Atlanta, I was wondering if you might be persuaded to escort my wife and her maid into the city. I realize that you are not my troop's chaplain, but I don't honestly know how to get my wife into the city safely. I, as a Union officer, cannot approach too near to the city. But, I thought, since you are a chaplain, you might be able to get them in with little or no trouble."

"Captain Morgan," replied the chaplain, "I would be honored to escort your wife and her maid into Atlanta. You see, I was preparing to ride there myself. I have decided to visit the church there and speak with a few of my colleagues before I rejoin the troops. And, my son, I am everyone's chaplain, not just a certain detachment's."

"Thank you, sir, I really do appreciate this very much. Now, I won't have to worry about the two women having to cross the lines alone. Although, I must say, my wife is a very persuasive person. I realize that she would probably encounter little difficulty in charming her way into the city! Again, thank you. I will go now and inform her of the plans." He tipped his hat to the chaplain and moved Katie's way. She eyed him warily as he strolled over to stand before her.

"Darling wife, good morning. I trust you spent a restful night? I missed you, Katie," he said with an earnest expression.

Katie ignored this last bit and responded to his greeting.

"Good morning, Captain Morgan. What do you have to say to me, sir? I just saw you talking with Father Hanson, and it was most obvious that you were speaking about me," she said with no small degree of annoyance.

"Well, Katie, I have successfully persuaded the good Father to escort you and Sarah into Atlanta today. My men and I will not be able to see you safely within its limits, so he has kindly granted my request to see you there himself. You will be much safer with a man along, especially a chaplain, than you would be with only Sarah as your chaperone. And, your safety is of major importance to me, dear wife," he told her.

"I see no objection to such a plan, Captain. Except that I will have to listen to his prattle about my good and holy marriage for the entire trip!" she said comically.

"Katie, quit fighting it. We are married now, and for good. Cheer up, you may even be a widow within a few days. Or hadn't you realized that your loving husband would be going back to the war and the battle?" he asked her mockingly.

"Of course I knew that you would be participating in some battle eventually, you oaf! I just happen to think it for the best that we never see each other again, that's all. And, I don't mean that I wish for you to be killed! I just mean that I will try to have our marriage annulled somehow."

"Katie, there is no way. Darling, after what passed between us yesterday evening, we are no longer eligible for an annullment. We have spent a time together as man and wife, and that is what we will remain. Don't tell me, by the way, that you actually do not wish to see me dead?" he inquired sarcastically.

"Oh, you idiot! Quit taunting me and leave me alone. And, as I said, I probably will never see you again after this day. Marriage or not, the next time you hear from me, it will be in a letter to inform you of our divorce!" she said with growing exasperation.

"No, Katie," Brent cut in with growing anger, "I will never go along with any divorce! I will most definitely be seeing you again. I will find some way to see you while you are in Atlanta, my dear. I will find some way to be with you again before this war is ended, mark my words!" He furiously strode away and into his tent.

Katie remained standing very still, surprised by his sudden outburst. He wasn't going to let her go without a fight, that was for certain. She felt drained by their encounter, and she wearily trudged into her tent to awaken Sarah.

"Sarah, it's time to get up. Everyone is making ready to leave, so you had best hurry up about it. Come on, sit up. You have got to be the only slave I know of that is allowed to sleep after her mistress is already up and about!" Sarah obeyed and sleepily climbed out of her warm bed. She slowly dressed and then the two of them once more packed their small bags and went outside to sit and wait.

Within the half hour, the entire camp was dismantled and the men were ready to leave. The troops under command of the major said their goodbyes and rode away. Brent ordered his own men to mount, then he approached Katie and Sarah.

"Ladies, it is time for us to be on our way. Sarah, would you please allow me a few moments to have a word with

105

Katie in private?" he asked politely. Sarah willingly complied and left the two of them alone.

"Katie, I don't think I'll be having much of a chance to speak with you alone before we separate later today. I just want you to know that I love you, and that the days I have spent with you were the most exciting and wonderful days I have ever had. I want you to remember what I said, too—I will never let you go. You are my wife and my wife you will stay. So, you might as well get any notion about an annullment or divorce clean out of your scheming little head right now! Come and kiss me goodbye, dear wife. I doubt if you will want to do so later, with all my men looking on," he told her.

Katie hesitated for a moment, searching for words, but Brent took no notice of her hesitation. He swept her into his arms and kissed her hungrily. She endeavored to keep herself from responding, but she could not. When he finally released her, she stood breathing rapidly.

"Now, Katie, it is time for us to go. I will send word to you somehow in Atlanta. Can't you tell me that you love me, too? Surely you don't want to send your brave husband into battle without those precious words, now, do you?" he said with a small twinkle of mischief.

"Oh, Brent, you are impossible!" she exclaimed as she marched away from him and toward Plato. Brent was beside her in an instant and helped her to mount, allowing his hand to rest upon her leg a moment longer than was necessary. Katie turned away in confusion, and he left her to mount his own horse. Then, giving the order, the whole group began the final leg of their journey toward Atlanta.

As she rode, Katie reflected upon everything Brent had said to her before they left. Did he really mean it when he said he would never let her go? She still did not understand his feelings for her, much less her own feelings for him. It was all so complicated. She would endeavor to forget him when she reached Atlanta. She knew that she must try to do so. Her subconscious, however, disagreed about her success. It told her that she would never be able to forget Captain Brent Morgan, no matter how insistently she tried.

They rode the rest of the day without halting to rest, only stopping momentarily a few times to water the horses. Katie and Sarah were bone-weary and extremely tired of traveling, but they rode uncomplainingly.

Toward late afternoon, they were finally within a few miles of Atlanta. They had managed to avoid any enemy troops for the entire day, thanks to the careful observance of the two scouts. Brent ordered his men to halt and dismount for a few minutes' rest. Sarah and Katie also dismounted and stretched their cramped limbs. Brent approached Katie and asked her to speak to the chaplain with him. She reluctantly agreed, not quite sure of what would be said.

"Father Hanson," Brent began, "I thank you again for escorting my wife and Sarah into the city. I need not worry about them while they are in your good and capable hands. Katie, dear, I want you to do everything he tells you to, is that understood?" Katie did not like the manner in which he asked her the question, but she did not want to add any more fuel to the chaplain's opinion that she was a creature given to delusions.

"I will of course give heed to any advice you give me, sir," she replied to the chaplain in a monotone, unable to resist a defiant glance in her husband's direction.

"Don't worry, Captain, I'll see them safely to the house of your wife's relative," the chaplain said reassuringly.

"Thank you. Goodbye, Father. I appreciate all you have done for us," he said as he shook hands with the man. Then, taking Katie's arm in a firm grip, he led her a few yards away from the others.

"Goodbye, dear wife Katie. Remember all I have told you. I will manage to receive reports about your visit in Atlanta, never fear. I will expect you to be a good and dutiful wife, patiently waiting for the return of her husband from the war!" he stated with a wicked smile.

"Goodbye, Captain Morgan," she replied composedly.

She would hold herself aloof, no matter what he said. She suddenly found herself upon the verge of tears, for some absurd reason. She angrily shook them away and extended her hand to her husband. He looked at it in disgust, then pulled her into his embrace and passionately kissed her goodbye, as if he were really going to be killed the very next day. Katie felt several conflicting emotions assailing her and she found herself a bit disappointed when he suddenly released her.

"I love you, Katie. Goodbye," he said simply. Then, with another wave at Father Hanson and a word to Sarah to take good care of his wife, he mounted and ordered his men to to the same. He waved to Katie and then turned his horse and led his men and their prisoners away.

Katie stood very still, watching as her husband rode out of sight. She felt a sadness descend upon her, a sadness she could not seem to shake, an emptiness.

"Miss Katie, we got to get ourselves into that city before it gets too dark to see in front of our noses. Come on, child," Sarah said to her. Katie awakened from her thoughts and allowed Father Hanson to help her mount. The three of them rode in the direction of Atlanta.

Ten

As Katie rode alongside Sarah and Father Hanson, she viewed the nearing city with a certain awe. So, this was Atlanta! This big, beautiful city in the nearing distance. She marveled at the tall buildings she saw outlined against the horizon. She had not been to Atlanta since she was a child. As they rode a little further, they encountered a small troop of Confederate soldiers stationed at the city's western limits.

"Howdy, folks!" the young soldier at the forefront called. "Ya'll going into Atlanta?"

"Of course we are, young man," answered Father Hanson. "Is it all right for us to pass?"

"Sure, sir, come on through. That is, if you all ain't Yankee spies or nothing," he said with a grin.

"Young man," Katie said imperiously, "we are loyal citizens of Georgia. We have private business in the city, which is none of your affair. May we pass now?"

"Surely, ma'am," the young soldier said as he gulped in surprise at the vision sitting upon the horse before him. He had just now noticed how beautiful she was. She was the prettiest thing he had ever seen!

"Thank you," Katie replied sweetly as she spurred her horse onward and instructed Sarah and the chaplain to follow. The three of them then rode on into the city.

"Father Hanson, I am truly sorry that I had to lie about your being a loyal citizen of this state. I keep forgetting, I suppose, that you are a Yankee," Katie said.

"That's perfectly all right, Mrs. Morgan. I'm sure that

what you told the young man was much better than to admit to him that I am indeed a Yankee. However, I am a man of God, and I belong to all of the people even if my own personal opinion about this war is in sympathy with the Union. Now, my dear, do you happen to know in which direction your relative lives?"

"Well, he has written us that he lives near the hospital. Suppose we ride a bit further into the city and then inquire of some resident the whereabouts of the hospital?"

They did as she suggested and eventually were directed to her uncle's house. As they dismounted in front of it, Katie took the time to view the house and surrounding area. My, but it's certainly a grand house, she thought. And, the other houses around it were equally as nice. Uncle Albert has certainly done all right for himself, she mused. Of course, when one has rather shady dealings with both sides of a war, one can expect to acquire a certain amount of wealth, she judged.

"Father," she said to the chaplain, "won't you come inside and meet my uncle? My aunt is ill, but I'm sure Uncle Albert would welcome you into his home." Yes, she thought in amusement, Uncle Albert would certainly welcome a Yankee into his home.

"No, thank you, Mrs. Morgan," he declined politely, "I have to get to the church before it gets too dark. I have enjoyed knowing you and Sarah. May God be with you both. I will pray that you and your husband are reunited safely some day soon, Mrs. Morgan. Good evening, ladies." He remounted his dusty horse and rode down the tree-lined street toward the center of the city.

"Well, Miss Katie, are we gonna stand out here in the street all night? Come on, child, let's go inside and let your folks know we're finally here," Sarah said. Katie tied the reins of her horse to the hitching post located near the front gate of the white picket fence. She opened the gate and she and Sarah approached the front of the house and climbed the porch steps. Katie lifted the heavy knocker and let it fall.

The door was opened by Uncle Albert himself, who just happened to be home from his office for the evening.

"Katie, dear! How very nice to see you! Sarah, how are you? Please, please come inside this instant!" he said excitedly. He was so relieved that they had arrived at long last.

"Uncle Albert," Katie began as she stepped inside and hugged him tightly, "how is Aunt Jenny? She is better, I hope? What has the doctor said about her condition? Where is she now?"

"Whoa, whoa, Katie. No, my dear niece, I'm afraid that she is not doing that much better at all," he said as he held her at arm's length. She noticed how much older and how haggard he was looking. The portliness she had expected to see was gone; he had lost a considerable amount of weight since she had last seen him several months ago.

"Now, Katie, your aunt is resting upstairs in her room. The doctor says he doesn't know precisely what her illness is. She is much weaker, and she asks me daily when you will come to her. I informed her of your impending arrival and she was much cheered by the news. However, I'll have Esther fix you something to eat before I take you up to see her. You must be famished after your long journey." Esther was the only remaining slave; all of the other household slaves had long since departed. Things were much worse in Atlanta than Katie had ever expected. Runaway slaves were becoming more and more common.

"Esther!" he called. The large, friendly black woman rounded the corner from the kitchen and greeted Sarah and Katie warmly. She led them into the kitchen, where she set about preparing them a meal. Uncle Albert returned upstairs to his wife to inform her that Katie would soon be up to see her. Thank the Lord she has come, he thought. He was completely at his wit's end.

"Esther," remarked Katie, "this coffee is delicious. And, so are these eggs and biscuits. Why, Sarah, maybe we ought to have Junie take lessons from her!"

"Thank you, Miss Katie," replied Esther with pleasure.

"Sarah," said Katie as she laid down her fork and cup, "I'm going upstairs to see Aunt Jenny now. You stay here and help Esther clean up." With that, she rose from the table and hurriedly mounted the stairs. She heard her uncle speaking, so she approached the direction from whence she had heard his deep voice. As soon as she had stepped through the doorway, she almost gasped at the sight of the pale, sickly face peering at her from under the covers.

"Katie," her aunt's weak voice said, "dear, how good of you to come. I have missed you so much, honey. Come over here and sit down on the bed beside me."

Katie hurried to do as her aunt bid, and she took her aunt's frail, cool hand into hers.

"Aunt Jenny, I know that you are going to get well. It's about time you were up and about! I'm going to see to it that you are out of bed and on your feet in no time at all, you hear?" she said encouragingly.

After spending a quarter of an hour with her aunt, she left the room to view the bedroom she would be occupying throughout her visit. Uncle Albert said he had some business matters to attend to at his office, so he left the house, vowing to return before long.

Katie set about unpacking her bag. The dresses and other garments were exceedingly wrinkled and a little dusty, but she would soon have Sarah set them to rights again. She was so very tired. She decided to retire to bed early that night. She walked out into the hallway and called for Sarah.

"Sarah!"

Sarah came out from the kitchen and stood at the foot of the stairs.

"I'm going to go on to bed now. I don't want to be disturbed before nine o'clock tomorrow morning, unless, of course, Aunt Jenny needs me. Good night." She went back into her bedroom and closed the door. She wearily undressed and climbed into the big, four-poster bed. She was too exhausted to notice the finery of the room. She was too tired to think about her husband. In only a few moments' time, she was soundly asleep.

Sarah did as Katie had told her and didn't awaken her mistress until nine o'clock the next morning.

"Miss Katie," she said as she drew back the covers of the bed, "it's time to get up now, honey. Your Aunt Jenny been asking for you. She says that she has got a lot of talking to catch up on. Come on, get up."

"All right, Sarah," Katie replied sleepily. She slowly arose from the bed and shuffled over to the washstand to perform her morning toilette. With that completed, she was ready to see her aunt.

"Good morning, Aunt Jenny! How are you feeling today?" she asked cheerily.

"Oh, Katie, dear, I'm so glad that you've come. I feel better already. Come and sit down and chat with me for a while. I have so much to tell you and so many questions to ask you," her aunt replied with a weak smile. She does look a trifle better this morning, thought Katie.

The two of them talked for almost an hour, at which time Katie said she did not want her aunt to overdo it, so she bid her goodbye for the moment and left the room, shutting the door behind her. She then went in search of Sarah, whom she found sitting in the kitchen with Esther.

"Sarah, may I have a word with you? Come on out into the parlour," she told her.

Sarah followed her into the parlour, where Katie took a seat upon the finely-upholstered velvet sofa. She spoke sternly to her slave.

"Sarah, you mustn't tell anyone about my marriage to Captain Morgan. Is that clear? I mean it, Sarah, not a word to anyone. No one must know about the disgraceful affair. Especially not my aunt or uncle. I am still Miss Katie O'Toole, is that understood?"

"Miss Katie, if that's the way you want it, that's the way it'll be. I don't know why you want to go and make me keep it a secret, though. Seems to me like you got yourself

113

a pretty good man, honey. I'd be proud if he was mine," she replied decisively.

"I didn't ask for your opinion, Sarah! Just do as I tell you, understand? And besides," she relented, "I can't let anyone know for a very good reason. Captain Morgan is a Yankee, an enemy soldier, and I am a Southern lady in a Southern city. There, does that satisfy you, now?"

"Yes, Miss Katie, I suppose so. Is there anything you want me for right now? I thought I'd go back out and help Esther start cleaning this here big house. They surely ain't got any slaves to help out around here, but we're sure gonna do our best," Sarah said.

"All right, Sarah, you may go now. I think I'll go out and take a walk about the city, anyway. I didn't have much of a chance to look things over when we rode in yesterday."

"All by yourself, Miss Katie? Don't you think it would be better if I was to go with you?" Sarah asked with concern.

"No, I want to look things over by myself. I'll see you later, Sarah," she said as she dismissed her with a wave of her hand. Sarah left the room, and Katie ran up the stairs to fetch her bonnet and purse. She quietly peeped in on Aunt Jenny, but that lady was sleeping exhaustedly. Uncle Albert had left the house early that morning, so Katie decided that she would be able to have a few hours to herself. Sarah would see to it that Aunt Jenny was taken care of.

As she tied her bonnet strings and walked out of the house, she noticed the bustle of activity throughout the streets of the city. She sauntered down the stone walkway and through the gate, then she prepared to do an afternoon of sight-seeing and window-shopping. She strolled down the boardwalks, noting with interest every shop and building. She made a mental note of the women's dresses, as she was planning to have Sarah help her alter a few of her own. She was so completely absorbed in her observations, she did not notice a young

Confederate officer standing on the boardwalk before her. She bumped into him with full force.

"Oh, I'm so sorry, sir! I wasn't paying any attention to where I was going, I'm afraid!" she said breathlessly.

"That's quite all right, ma'am," replied the nice-looking young officer. He removed the hand he had extended to help steady her balance. Then, he removed his hat and introduced himself.

"I know that this is a bit forward, but I'd like to introduce myself. My name is Ben Adamson, and I am a lieutenant in the Confederate Army. I haven't seen you in this area of the city before, ma'am," he said courteously.

"Oh, I'm new to Atlanta, Lieutenant Adamson. And, I don't think you're too forward at all. I'm Miss Katie O'Toole, and my uncle lives here in Atlanta. Where is your home, Lieutenant?" she asked in a friendly tone.

"Why, Miss O'Toole, I'm from Richmond, Virginia, originally. I've been stationed around and about all over the South, though, ever since this war began. Are you a native of Georgia, ma'am?"

"Yes, I am. My family owns a plantation to the west of Atlanta," she replied. The young officer was very nice and attractive, and he was obviously a gentleman. How nice to carry on a conversation with a gentleman, for a change, she thought. No, she caught herself, I won't think about Brent. I won't compare.

Lieutenant Adamson stood nervously fingering his hat. He appeared to gather courage and said, "Miss O'Toole, would it be too presumptious of me to come calling on you at your uncle's house? You see, I don't know too many people here in Atlanta. I'm stationed here in the city. I don't know exactly when I'll receive my orders to leave, but I'd sure like to further our acquaintance, ma'am. Oh, but there I've gone and been too forward again, haven't I?" he said.

"No, not at all, Lieutenant. I would be delighted to have you come and call on us. I live at the end of Julep Street, the last house on the right. My uncle's name is

Albert O'Toole. You may come calling any time you like, as I will usually be present at the house. You see, my aunt is very ill and I have come to stay until she is better," she informed him. He was such a personable young man, it would be pleasant to have him in attendance on her.

"Thank you, Miss O'Toole. I will come to your uncle's house tomorrow evening at six, if that is convenient? I will look forward to seeing you again then, ma'am. Good day for now," he said as he bowed slightly to her and then resumed his walk down the boardwalk.

"Good day, Lieutenant Adamson. And, I will see you tomorrow evening," Katie called in return. My goodness, he's so very shy, she thought. Well, I suppose it's time for me to head back and check on Aunt Jenny. She had toyed with the idea of going to the church that Father Hanson had spoken of, but she decided against it. She really had no wish to see him again, to be reminded of what had occurred the day before yesterday. I think I will like Atlanta just fine, she mused. She had already attracted one nice young man, and she knew that there would be others coming to call as soon as Aunt Jenny was able to entertain again.

When she returned to the house once again, she immediately went upstairs to speak with her aunt. She slowly edged open the door, and seeing that her aunt was awake, she entered the room.

"Oh, Aunt Jenny, how are you? I have just been out walking around this lovely city of yours. It is so large! And, there are so very many people! By the way, I happened to run into a young Confederate officer by the name of Lieutenant Ben Adamson. He asked if he might come to call on us tomorrow evening. Is that proper, Aunt Jenny? I told him that he could, but I wouldn't want to have him come against your wishes," she said in a rush.

"No, Katie, it's all right. Of course you may have any of your friends to call on us. I only wish I could be downstairs to meet him myself. Oh, Katie, are you by any chance involved with some young man back home?" she inquired innocently.

"No, Aunt Jenny, there is no one back home for me. I never fell in love with any of the beaux I had before the war. Heaven knows I tried, but it just never happened. And, this young officer coming to call tomorrow is not very forward at all, so I doubt if he would have enough courage to so much as kiss my hand!" she said laughingly. When her aunt had asked her the question, she had momentarily frozen. No, there was certainly no one back home. She felt so guilty at having to deceive her aunt about her marriage to Brent. Aunt Jenny would never understand, she thought in excuse.

"Well, I'll leave you for a while now, Aunt Jenny. Has Sarah been taking good care of you?" she asked.

"Yes, my dear, she and Esther have been very solicitious. The doctor is coming to examine my condition tomorrow. I really do feel better since you came, dear." Katie left her aunt and went down the hallway and into her own bedroom. She noticed for the first time how tastefully decorated the room was. The carpet, a deep green, appeared to be very expensive, as did the flocked green wallpaper and lighter green upholstery and curtains. Uncle Albert had always declared that green was the color that suited her most. She knew that they thought of her almost as a daughter, since they had no children of their own.

She went over to sit in the window, which overlooked a small back street below. Atlanta is so lovely, she thought. She hoped that nothing would ever change its beauty. The war had already destroyed so many landmarks of the South, she had heard. She prayed that Atlanta would remain untouched.

Eleven

While Katie was enjoying her visit in Atlanta, Brent and his men were riding to join Sherman's troops to the northwest of Atlanta. They finally encountered his great army near Dallas, Georgia. Brent reported to his new commanding officer and was informed of the army's past battles and future plans.

"You see, Captain Morgan," the officer told him, "we are preparing to advance upon and lay siege to the city of Atlanta. It has been deemed necessary to Sherman's campaign, so it will be captured. We have already skirmished with Johnston's army earlier in the month, at Rocky Face Ridge, at Resaca, and now we are preparing to do battle here. You will be assigned to the cavalry division, of course, and you will instruct your men to prepare for battle. Sherman has now acquired a total of nearly 113,000 men, Captain, and we will desperately need every one of you for this campaign. That is all for now," the officer said as he stood and saluted. Brent left the tent and went in search of his men to brief them for the upcoming battle.

A battle already, he thought. We have only just arrived, and it seems we are in time for a battle that is set to begin at any moment. Damn, he swore silently. He wasn't a coward by any means, but he had hoped to have a while longer before engaging in any serious confrontations. He had never liked the business of killing his fellow man, but he would follow any orders he received.

In late May of 1864, the battle began at New Hope

Church, about four miles north of Dallas. Brent and his men participated in the incessant fighting. The two great armies of Sherman and his opponent, Johnston, stretched out for a distance of nearly ten miles. The fighting was made more difficult by the fact that the countryside was composed of a continuous succession of hills which were covered with dense forests. The battle lasted for ten days.

Brent was fortunate enough to escape injury during the battle. He and his men were beside Hood's division when it attacked the Confederates under the leadership of Stewart on that first day. The Union soldiers held out for nearly two hours against sixteen field-pieces and a total of 5,000 infantry who were stationed at close range. The Federalist soldiers quite accurately dubbed the spot "Hell Hole" after that day.

Brent, after the fierce battle, relaxed as he sat upon the ground, thinking of Katie. He wondered what she was doing, whether or not any of her thoughts were of him, and just when he would get to see her again. He knew good and well that she had not forgotten him, of that he was sure. Oh, Katie, he fervently appealed, will you ever give in? Not that he wanted her tamed; no, he loved and admired her wild spirit, her fierce determination, her stubborn Irish pride. He would never want to change her in any way, except for her admission that she loved him. He knew that she would always be difficult to handle, but he relished the prospect of being the one to take her in hand.

During the next few days, Brent participated in several other skirmishes. He always managed to escape any serious injury, although several of his men were either killed or wounded. Finally, by the last day of fighting, the Confederates were repulsed with serious losses. There had been a total of 2,400 losses on the Union side, while the Confederates had lost even more.

Meanwhile, Katie was making new friends and helping her aunt to recover. Aunt Jenny was now able to leave her bed for a few hours at a time, which the doctor said could do her no harm. Whatever her illness had been, she was now fast upon the road to recovery. Katie continued her walks about the city every day. She had been introduced by Lieutenant Adamson to several of his fellow officers, and her aunt had promised to give a ball as soon as she was up and about for good.

Lieutenant Adamson was obviously becoming quite infatuated with Katie. He had come to call with great regularity almost every evening for the past two weeks. And, although Katie enjoyed his visits and liked talking to the attractive young soldier, she began to weary of his ever-increasing protestations of love.

One evening, she decided that she could no longer listen to his declarations, and she judged it time to set things straight for good.

"Ben, I'm afraid that I can never love you the way you love me. I seem to be incapable of that kind of devotion. I'm sorry, but there is absolutely no hope for you and it would be unkind of me to allow you to think so. Now, please, please cease with your proposals of marriage! Ben, I do not want to hear another word on the subject from you, do you hear?" she declared. She was genuinely fond of the tall, blond officer, but she certainly didn't love him. She knew no other way to convince him of such, beyond telling him the way she just had.

"Miss Katie, I suppose I will always love you, but I can't hold it against you because you don't feel the same for me. May I still come to see you, Katie? May we still be friends? I just don't know what I'd do if you wouldn't let me see you any more," he replied dejectedly. He was earnestly heartbroken over her refusal to marry him, but he could not give in to despair. Even though she had declared there was no hope for him, he would nonetheless continue to hope.

"Of course we can still be friends, Ben," she replied gently. "Now, tell me more about your home. I've never been to Richmond."

Later, after Ben had left, Katie slowly climbed the

120

stairs to her room and plopped down on her bed. Unbidden thoughts of Brent kept coming into her head. She wondered if he was safe, if he was thinking of her. Oh, for land's sake, she told herself, quit thinking about that man! However, she still found her thoughts returning to her husband. She could not seem to help herself. Before she retired to bed for the night, she even went so far as to pray for his safety, a thing she would most certainly have never done a few days ago. I'm just tired, I guess, she excused herself.

Aunt Jenny was much better the next day and declared herself ready to give Katie a ball in her honor.

"Aunt Jenny, are you sure you'll be well enough by Friday? Why, that's only five days away and the doctor said that you still need plenty of rest," Katie replied.

"Of course I'll be all right by then, Katie. Besides, I think it will do me a world of good to have some company. I have already begun thinking about whom I shall invite, and your Uncle Albert has given me free license with the planning. Now, sit down here and let's discuss the decorations and the food."

A ball in her honor! It had been so long since she had been to a ball, she found herself becoming as excited as a giddy schoolgirl! She would wear the green dress that Sarah had helped her alter only last week. She would wear her hair piled high upon her head and filled with flowers and she would dance all night! Oh, coming to Atlanta was the best thing that had happened to her in so long, she decided. Suddenly, she remembered Ben. Oh, drat, she thought, he'll probably expect me to save quite a few dances for him. Well, I won't! This is going to be my ball, and I want to dance with every handsome young soldier that Uncle Albert and Aunt Jenny invite!

Throughout the week before the ball, Katie was kept busy with helping her aunt address and mail out invitations and with helping Sarah and Esther decorate the ballroom and plan the refreshments. Uncle Albert was usually absent and so was of little help. Once Katie and

Sarah had arrived to take care of his wife, he had devoted more and more of his time to his business. Katie could never seem to pin him down on exactly what sort of business he was engaged in, as he always blustered an unintelligible reply and rapidly changed the subject. Oh, Uncle Albert, she warned him silently, be careful.

The day of the ball finally dawned bright and clear. The weather was warm and mild, there were only a few clouds dotting the blue of the sky, and there was still much to be done before that evening. Aunt Jenny was now able to walk about on her own and she was pleased and excited at the prospect of a ball.

"Katie, dear, I know there is still a lot to see to, but isn't this exciting? I do declare, it almost seems as if it's my first ball again. I do so hope Albert will be able to arrive on time today, don't you?" she asked her niece.

"He will, Aunt Jenny. Now, suppose you rest for a while, and I'll go downstairs and see to some of those last-minute preparations," she said with a smile. Aunt Jenny is the sweetest, most generous person I've ever known, she thought. It was really too bad her uncle didn't appreciate his wife as he should. "I'll come back upstairs in an hour or so to help you dress."

Katie, true to her word, returned to her aunt's room in little over an hour. The two of them managed to get Aunt Jenny dressed, her hair arranged atop her head, and her jewelry placed just so. Katie then left her to go to her own room to dress. Sarah was waiting for her.

"Miss Katie, I'm so happy for you, child. Imagine, a ball given for you in this time of war. Your mama and brothers would surely like to be here, I know," she said.

"Yes, Sarah. This is going to be one of the happiest nights of my life! Already, I am reminded of the last ball we had at Corkhaven before Papa died. Oh, well, here help me get this dress on over my head."

Sarah assisted her in drawing the dress down and arranging it in place upon her figure. The emerald-green satin was shimmering in the light. The bodice was fashionably low-cut, allowing the swell of her young, well-formed breasts to show. The waistline of the dress had been cinched in, while the flared skirt was fuller than usual. The hoops Katie wore added to that fullness. Sarah had arranged her red-gold curls in a loose style atop her head, then placed a few fragrant flowers in the curls. Katie fastened the string of pearls given to her by her mother around her neck, then she faced her reflection in the mirror. Yes, I am going to dance all night! She was pleased with her appearance. She would certainly not be ashamed of her dress tonight, even though it had been altered and made over.

She flew down the hallway, where she showed her aunt the result. Her aunt declared her to be most breathtaking, then she hurried downstairs to give a last inspection to the decorations and refreshments. She was satisfied and so hurried back upstairs, by now out of breath, to await the arrival of the first guests. She wanted to make her appearance at just the right moment!

When Katie heard the musicians strike up the first notes of music, she judged it the precisely correct moment to descend the curving staircase. She knew her aunt and uncle would be in the entrance foyer, greeting the guests as they arrived through the front doors. She gave a final pat to her brilliant curls, flicked an imaginary speck of dust from her skirt, then left the room and headed for the staircase. She paused at the top of the stairs for effect, then gracefully and slowly descended the steps. She noted with approval the several heads turned in her direction, the glances of the various guests. The men's were admiring, the women's were jealous. She reached the bottom of the stairs and Uncle Albert immediately moved to offer her his arm. Then, he swept her into the ballroom with him and proceeded to whirl her around in the dance.

"Uncle Albert, this is so wonderful! Why, you are a very good dancer. I had better warn Aunt Jenny to keep an eye on you tonight, you old devil!" she said teasingly.

She looked around at the many guests as she was whirled into a waltz. There were several handsome and dashing young officers, along with other men in civilian dress. There were few young women present, she noticed, probably because her aunt and uncle did not know that many young ladies. Or, she mused, because they wanted the young men to pay attention to no one else but their beloved niece! That's perfectly all right with me, she thought with satisfaction.

The dance finally ended, and Uncle Albert stepped aside to allow the young men a chance to petition the young beauty for a dance. Katie was deluged with offers and her dance card was quickly filled. She had saved the second dance for Lieutenant Adamson, for whom she still felt a bit sorry. He was obviously pleased with the honor, and she smiled at him as they danced around the crowded ballroom. She continued dancing with different partners for the entire evening.

Ben led her over to a chair so she could sit and rest for a moment, when another Confederate officer approached them. Katie observed his presence and studied his appearance. He was quite different from any of the other young men at the ball. He was in his upper twenties, with dark, almost blue-black hair, and a hawkish expression. His long, aristocratic nose bespoke him to be well-born. She extended her hand gracefully for the darkly handsome man to kiss.

"Miss O'Toole," said Lieutenant Adamson, "this is a friend of mine, Captain Richard Collins. Captain Collins, this is Miss Katie O'Toole, of Corkhaven, Georgia."

"Charmed, Miss O'Toole," said the captain. "I have been observing your beauty from afar this entire evening, and I have been endeavoring for quite some time to gain an introduction to such a fair young lady. Will you be staying in Atlanta very long, Miss O'Toole?" he asked. Katie felt an uneasy feeling creep up into the back of her mind at his words. She wasn't at all sure that she liked this Captain Collins.

"Sir, I do not know exactly how long I will be visiting with my relatives. However, it will not be for any extended length of time, I presume." She removed her hand from his grasp, feeling a slight chill at the touch of his cool lips upon it.

"Miss O'Toole, may I have the honor of this next dance? You don't mind my taking her away for a few minutes, do you, Ben?" he asked with supreme confidence.

"No, I'm afraid not, Captain Collins," Katie cut in, "I have already promised this dance to Lieutenant Adamson. Some other time, perhaps," she then replied with a lift of her proud nose. She didn't much like this man's attitude at all.

"Oh, I'm sure that he will understand, won't you, Lieutenant?" Captain Collins said assuredly. Without waiting for an answer, he placed his hands upon Katie's small waist and drew her up in front of him, then placed his arm around her and swept her into the dance.

"Captain Collins, you had no right, sir!" she fumed indignantly.

"Miss O'Toole, I had to have a chance to speak with you. You were clearly not going to allow me a dance, so I had to make the most of my opportunities. Now, when can I see you again?" he demanded. He had been smitten with the first sight of the beautiful young stranger. She was quite different from any other woman he had ever met before. There was a certain something about her that seemed to draw him toward her. He would pursue her until he had discovered what the certain something was.

"Captain Collins, I do not wish to dance any more for now. Please release me and allow me to return to Lieutenant Adamson. Please, sir, I demand that you release me at once!" her voice rose alarmingly. She was endeavoring to keep a tight control over her fiery temper, but this man was making it exceedingly difficult! She felt a small amount of fear surface in her mind, but she would not back down.

"Miss O'Toole, that young puppy is not for you. You, young woman, require a real man. Someone like me, if I may be so bold to suggest?" he said imperturbably.

"I'll thank you to keep such opinions to yourself, Captain! Now, please let go of me. I have no further wish to either dance or converse with you!"

"Miss O'Toole, you are ravishing when you are angry! May I suggest that we go out on to the back terrace for a stroll in the evening breeze? Doesn't that sound agreeable to you, my dear?" he suggested with a wicked grin. Instead of complying with her demands that he release her, he maneuvered her out on to the back terrace, knowing full well that she would not want to cause a scene in front of so many guests.

"Captain Collins, you are insufferable! I have nothing further to say to you. Good night, sir!" she declared as she attempted to hurry back inside the French doors leading into the ballroom. He caught her around the waist and roughly pulled her back and into his tightening arms.

"Miss O'Toole, I told you that I have been watching you. I find myself irresistibly drawn to you. What is there about you that makes you much more exciting than other women? What certain spark is there about you?" he asked as he held her. Katie struggled to free her arms, but he held them pinned at her sides. Suddenly, without warning, he lowered his head and imprisoned her lips with his own. His mouth bruised her tender flesh and she tried to keep from fainting at the brutal assault of his lips. She struggled and was finally able to lift her knee and manage a well-aimed kick at his body. He instantly released her and doubled over in extreme pain.

"There, Captain Collins! I told you that I have nothing further to say to you. Now, I will expect you to leave my uncle's house at once!" She hastily re-entered the ballroom and went in search of Lieutenant Adamson. She would of course not breathe a word of what had occurred to anyone, but she would feel safer if she kept close to either Ben or her uncle for the remainder of the ball.

Sometime later, she noted the departure of Captain Collins. She happened to catch the look upon his face as he was leaving. She felt a chill run down her spine. The expression in his cold eyes seemed to be saying, I'll not give up so easily. I'll see you again soon.

She forced herself to concentrate on the conversation she was having with several of the young officers. She suddenly found herself wishing that Brent were in the city. She knew that she was being silly, but, somehow, she knew that she would feel safer if he were near. Don't be an idiot, she chided herself, you don't need him. You can take care of yourself.

When the last guests had finally departed, Katie wearily bade her aunt and uncle goodnight and slowly climbed the stairs to her room. She undressed without waiting for Sarah and flung herself down upon the bed. The ball had been such fun, and, except for the disagreeable incident with Captain Collins, she had enjoyed herself immensely. Many of the officers had requested her permission to come calling, which she had wholeheartedly given. After all, she reminded herself, she wanted to wipe out the memory of her husband once and for all. And, what better way to accomplish that? She would force herself to be charming and courteous to all the young men, even those who always seemed to bore her. She would force herself to accept their attentions, their compliments.

As she lay in the large bed all alone, she found herself remembering the time in the woods with Brent. She would find it extremely difficult to forget what had occurred between them there. She found her traitorous body yearning for his touch, for his sweet kisses. She sternly ordered her body to go to sleep. Her body finally concurred with this demand, and she was soon fast asleep.

While Katie was occupied with her social obligations in Atlanta, Brent and his men had been involved in another major battle, this one at Kenesaw Mountain. He had seen two more of his men killed in the fighting, fatally injured by a single cannon blast. This particular battle raged even longer than the previous one. It lasted for nearly the entire month of June.

Again, after a day of fierce fighting, Brent would retire to think of Katie. He loved her more each day, and he prayed that the war would end soon. If Sherman were successful and they were actually able to capture the city of Atlanta, the war would most certainly swing even more in their favor. Atlanta, he thought, the city where my wife sleeps tonight. He knew that Katie's aunt and uncle would see to it that she was sent home at the first sign of danger, so he tried not to worry himself on that score. He missed her, however, and he was terribly concerned about her. Dammit, he swore silently, when will it all end? When will we be able to live as a united people once again?

Twelve

The week following the successful ball was almost totally occupied with shopping and sewing. Uncle Albert had finally noticed the scant condition of Katie's wardrobe and had generously instructed her to purchase new dress goods during her stay in Atlanta. Katie was overwhelmed at the prospect of actually being able to have new clothes.

"Aunt Jenny, are you going shopping with me today?" she asked, as she put the finishing touches on her attire for the day and turned toward her aunt.

"No, dear, I'm feeling a little tired. Oh, no, nothing to worry about, though," she reassured her niece.

"Very well, but I would much prefer your second opinion on anything I may find. I'll only stay gone for two hours today, I promise. And, I can't tell you how very grateful I am for yours and Uncle Albert's generosity. Why, this week alone, I've ordered fabrics for at least half a dozen new dresses and two new ballgowns!"

"Katie, we want you to get whatever you want. Now, you scat and pick out something lovely today. I'll just stay home and do some knitting or something. Good day, dear," said her aunt. Katie kissed her cool cheek and donned her bonnet. She stepped out into the warm sunshine and proceeded down the boardwalk and into the main artery of the city.

As she was passing the hospital, she slowed her brisk walk. She had never paid much attention to the large building. She had seen many soldiers carried in and out of the doors of the red brick structure. Something at that moment prompted her to venture inside, and she strolled through the heavy doors and paused a second until her eyes adjusted to the new darkness.

The sight that greeted her was completely unexpected. She had never before been inside a hospital and she was surprised at the great amount of activity. There were people hurrying everywhere, patients crammed into small spaces, and a decidedly unpleasant stench. Good gracious, she exclaimed inwardly, I would have thought this place would be much roomier and more cheerful than this. No wonder so many people cringe at the thought of going to a hospital.

One of the nurses scurrying about, an older, graying woman, touched Katie on the arm and demanded in stern tones:

"Miss, are you here to visit someone?"

"No," Katie replied, "I just wanted to look around. You see, I've never been inside a hospital before, and this is my first visit. I thought I'd come in and find out what a hospital is actually like."

"I see," replied the nurse in an unapproving tone. "So many ladies are curious about hospitals, but, when it comes to volunteering their precious time to help these poor boys recover, they simply do not have the time. Well, I'm sorry, young lady, but this is not a sideshow attraction. If you really wanted to do something useful, you could roll up your dainty sleeves and help out. Good day to you." With that, she marched away to tend to a patient. Katie noted that there were so few nurses compared to the number of occupied beds. The place was so crowded and the moans of the dying and wounded were heartwrenching.

Katie whirled around and exited through the doors she had entered a few minutes ago. Dear God, she silently prayed, help those poor men suffering in there. So many of the wounded had to wait hours before a doctor or nurse could tend to them. She couldn't shake the thoughts turning in her mind about what she had witnessed at the hospital, so she decided to return home instead of completing her shopping excursion.

As soon as she returned to the house, she went in search of her aunt, whom she found sitting in the parlour.

"Aunt Jenny," she remarked casually, "I happened to go inside the hospital today."

"Oh, dear, whatever for, Katie?" her aunt replied in shocked tones.

"Well, it wasn't that awful, Aunt. They simply need more help and more supplies, I'm sure. I haven't been able to get it out of mind, so I was wondering if I might volunteer my services a few days a week. You know, I could help the nurses, write letters for the men, and generally try to cheer up the place. What do you think?"

"Oh, Katie, I don't know. Are you sure you know what you'd be letting yourself in for? I've heard that place smells positively ghastly, and sometimes the volunteers are required to put in some awfully long hours. Maybe you should wait and speak to your Uncle Albert about it," she suggested.

"No, I think I've already made up my mind, Aunt Jenny. A nurse who happened to speak to me while I was there told me that most young ladies would not help, but I most certainly will. She somehow made me realize just how little use I have been during this terrible conflict. At Corkhaven, there was really no chance to help, but there is a chance for me to do something worthwhile now. I would feel like I was helping with the cause if I could help the wounded soldiers at the hospital. And, you are recovered now, anyway. I think I'll go back over to the hospital right now and talk to that nurse about it. She will most certainly be surprised to see me again! I'll see you later," she said as she was leaving. Her aunt simply sat and stared at her departure, not at all sure what to think about her niece's scheme. She knew that certain of her friends had volunteered their services at the hospital occasionally, but she couldn't see why. Didn't they have more qualified women to do such things?

So began Katie's sojourn at the hospital. She left the house immediately after breakfast the next morning and briskly strolled to the hospital. She was there instructed to see a particular nurse, Mrs. Walker. She was given an apron to tie on over her dress, and a cap to fit in place upon her head. Then, she was told to begin visiting with the various patients in one of the wards and to inquire if there were anything she could either get them or do for them.

Lieutenant Adamson continued to call on her quite frequently in the evenings, along with other young officers. She grew more and more fond of Ben, treating him like an older brother. She would be sorry when he was ordered away from the city, which she hoped would not be soon. In this she was disappointed.

"Katie," Ben began one evening after dinner, "I have received my new orders. I'm to join the troops somewhere north of Atlanta. I will surely regret leaving here, but only because of you. I will miss you, Katie, very much." He looked so very forlorn, so Katie tried to comfort him.

"Ben, don't be upset. You can still write to me, and perhaps you'll be able to return to Atlanta before too long. I'll write to you, and I'll pray for you every night. You have been a great friend to me, the best I could ever have."

"I know, Katie," he answered. His eyes held a sadness she could not erase.

Lieutenant Adamson left Atlanta the next day, and Katie prayed he would be safe. She was still occupied with her work at the hospital, work she was becoming accustomed to more each day. She enjoyed speaking with the young soldiers, hearing about their families and homes. She was always friendly and helpful, endeavoring to brighten the dismal atmosphere as much as she possibly could.

One day, she received an unexpected letter. She had just returned home from a trying day at the hospital when Sarah brought it to her, telling her it had arrived a few minutes earlier.

"Who's it from, Miss Katie? Is it from your mama? Are she and the boys doing all right?" asked Sarah nervously.

"No, it's not from Mama, Sarah, it's private. I'll take it up to my room to read," Katie replied impatiently. She had instantly stiffened when she read the signature at the bottom of the page. She always read the signature first, so she would be more adequately prepared for any bad news the letter might contain. She waved away the remainder of Sarah's anxious questions and quickly mounted the stairs to her bedroom. She closed the door securely behind her and went over to sit upon the bed.

"Dear wife Katie," it began. "This is to let you know that your beloved husband is still alive at this writing. I have been in several fierce skirmishes, but I have fortunately emerged unscathed. A few of my men have been killed or injured, although Sergeant Duffy remains at my side.

"Katie, I have missed you greatly. Do you ever think of me, darling? Do you ever wonder where I am? I love you and I hope that by now you have come to the realization that you return my regard.

"It is going to be difficult to get this letter to you, but I am entrusting it into the hands of someone who will try his utmost. I do not know when I will be able to send you word again. I will manage to receive a report of you in return, though.

"I must go now, for the battle is set to begin again. Love me, Katie, for that's all I ask. Your loving husband, Brent."

Katie dropped the letter upon the satin coverlet on the bed. She sat staring out the window of the room, trying valiantly not to cry. Why did he have to go and write me a letter? she asked herself. I was trying to forget him, not to be reminded of his danger.

He had said again that he loved her. Perhaps he truly did. Perhaps he had been honest with her from the very beginning. I will probably never know, she thought. And what did she feel for him now? Was it dislike and contempt, as she had thought? Or was it something far deeper than either like or dislike?

She hastily refolded the letter and hurried over to place it under a pile of clothing in one of the bureau drawers. She would not think about any of it now, for she had been asked to return to the hospital that evening for some extra work. She did not like venturing out after dark, but they had stated that they desperately needed her assistance that evening, so she had agreed to come. It was barely dusk now, so she hurried down the stairs once more and informed Sarah of her plans.

"Sarah, I know Aunt Jenny is resting and Uncle Albert isn't home yet. I am returning to the hospital. I don't think I will be home for at least two hours, so please tell my aunt and uncle where I have gone. Also, tell them not to worry, for I'll have one of the doctors walk home with me afterwards, if one of them is available."

"Miss Katie, I don't like the idea of you being out by yourself here in this big city after dark, and I think maybe I better come along with you and wait till you're ready to come home," Sarah protested.

"No, that's not necessary, Sarah. I'll be perfectly fine. Just do as I say! I'll be home later." She picked up her bonnet and hurried outside and down the street toward the hospital.

She decided, once she was there, to use the side entrance to the building for a change. It was the one most used by the other volunteers and nurses. Darkness was falling rather swiftly, so she was forced to focus more intently on where she was going. As she approached the side door, she suddenly heard a scuffling noise behind her. She quickly turned around, but saw nothing in the darkness. As she reached out to grasp the handle of the door, she was grabbed roughly from behind, and an iron hand clamped over her mouth. The assailant dragged her over behind the hospital to a deserted back street, with Katie kicking and trying to free her mouth to scream all the while. She could not twist around, and she could not see who her attacker was. Suddenly, she was released, and she whirled around to stare into the amused eyes of none other than Captain Richard Collins.

"Captain Collins! Why ever did you do such a thing? You nearly frightened me half to death, sir!" she exclaimed breathlessly. She still did not know whether to stay and speak with him, or to scream and run for help.

"Miss O'Toole, I'm sorry for the scare I gave you. I wanted to talk with you, and I knew that you would not come along willingly. I have been watching you for quite some time. You are quite a creature of habit, it seems," he said with a wicked smile.

Katie could not fathom just why he had thought it necessary and urgent to speak with her, and she was becoming frightened again. The man was sinister-looking and seemed to exude evil for some reason. Oh, but I'm being ridiculous, she sternly scolded herself. He wouldn't dare try to harm me out here where I can scream for help at any moment.

"Captain, I am expected inside the hospital at this moment. If you have anything to say to me, please do so at once!" she demanded.

His eyes flashed dangerously at her command, but he suavely answered:

"Miss O'Toole, I did not appreciate your actions at the ball I attended in your honor. I have been wanting to reprimand you for your behavior ever since that night. I told you that I was quite taken with you, and I now think you should heed my advice. Don't shun me, Katie, for I am a dangerous man to cross. I want you to appreciate what I can do for you, what I can make you feel. It is

135

about time you had a real man to show you what life is all about. I have desired you from the first moment I saw you."

Katie's eyes widened at his words. Why, the man was insane!

"Sir," she informed him rigidly, "you disgrace me with such ungentlemanly talk! And, as for my actions at the ball, you deserved just that and much more! Now, let me pass, for I must get inside." She attempted to walk toward the door, but he captured her and proceeded to drag her struggling form back into the side street, then he picked her up and carried her quickly into the trees and bushes behind the hospital.

"Let me go, or I'll scream, you distasteful creature!" she cried, trying to claw at his face.

"Go ahead and fight me, Katie, for I will enjoy it just that much more! You little wildcat! I think it's time someone tamed you, honey!" He clamped a hand over her mouth once more and threatened to crush her jaw if she tried to scream again. Her eyes told him of her immense contempt for him, but he was completely undaunted.

Finally, he set his struggling burden down upon the ground and threw his own body on top of hers. He removed his hand on her mouth and replaced it with his bruising lips. Katie tried ineffectually to push him off her, but he was much too strong for her to fight. As he began pushing her skirts and petticoats above her knees and up to her thighs, she panicked and began to squirm even more.

Oh, Dear God, she prayed, don't let him rape me. Don't let his foulness penetrate me. Help me to be strong and fight him.

He suddenly ripped the delicate bodice of her dress from her body, exposing her ripe, naked breasts to his cruel gaze. With an oath of admiration, he lowered his lips savagely to her bosom and let slip his hand's crushing grip on her lower jaw. She took a deep breath and managed to scream. He immediately covered her mouth again and tore at her clothing once more.

Just as she thought she could no longer take any more of his vicious abuse, Katie heard someone approaching through the brush. She discerned a pale stream of light from a lantern and heard someone call out.

"Hey, in there! Who's that making such a ruckus?"

Captain Collins released his hold upon her and quickly scrambled to his feet, adjusting his disheveled clothing. Then, with a last lustful gaze at her exposed flesh, he turned and ran from her and out of sight into the thick darkness. The man with the lantern stumbled upon Katie where she had managed to sit up, trying to hold the shreds of her bodice up around her bosom.

"Oh, sir, I'm so glad you heard me!" she told the astonished man. He looked to be some sort of common laborer, but his kind expression and sympathetic eyes told her she was safe with him. She felt bruised and dirty, and she was grateful for his helping arms. He supported her weight as she slowly made it to the hospital, then she thanked him once again and entered the building. She couldn't go home looking as she did, so she borrowed a cloak she found hanging inside the doorway and put it on over the torn and tattered dress. Then, she went in search of Mrs. Walker to tell her that she didn't feel well and so would not be working that night.

As she trudged home in the darkness, peering back over her shoulder repeatedly to observe any approaching figure in the night, she reflected upon the ugly incident.

She did not want to tell anyone about the attempted rape. She would hope that Captain Collins was soon ordered away from the city, and, in the meantime, she would never journey out alone after dark again.

If only Ben were here, she thought. But no, Ben would be no match for Richard Collins. And, besides, the two of them were friends and Richard was Ben's superior in rank. No, it would be better to say nothing and to be on her guard. She was much too ashamed to say anything to either her aunt or Sarah.

When she arrived home, she immediately flew up the stairs and into her room, thankful that she had not chanced to encounter anyone on the way. She closed the door and then began to remove every stitch of her clothing. She examined her naked body in the tall mirror, noting the bruises now appearing on her arms and legs. She felt her muscles becoming very sore. Oh, well, she could at least cover the bruises. The scars inside her mind would take longer to heal.

She wearily donned a nightgown and climbed into the softness of the bed. She remembered the letter she had received from Brent. He, at least, had never attempted to rape her. He had always been gentle with her. And, he was a Yankee. Captain Collins, a Southern gentleman, had attacked her. She had always believed that a Yankee was capable of such an attack, but surely not one of the South's own boys. She was beginning to become aware of a certain truth that night, a truth that had come with a hard lesson.

Oh, Brent, she told him silently, I do think of you. I still don't know exactly what I feel for you, but I certainly do think of you. As much as I try not to. Dear Lord, please keep him safe.

She rolled over painfully and attempted to sleep, trying not to think about the evil Captain Richard Collins any more for one night. She knew, however, that he would haunt her in nightmares for quite a while.

Thirteen

Brent stood upon the hill and surveyed the death and destruction displayed in the grisly sight before him. The Battle of Chattahoochee River had been yet another swath cut into the Georgia countryside by Sherman's invading armies.

Brent had received word that his letter had successfully reached Katie in Atlanta. It had taken several weeks, but the courier reported back that she was doing well and entertaining quite frequently. A woman as beautiful and spirited as Katie would always have admirers. And, of course she had informed no one of her marriage to a Union officer.

If only I could reach Atlanta now, he was thinking, I could make her realize just how married she really is! The Union troops were slowly advancing upon Atlanta, but Brent did not know exactly when or if he would be seeing his wife once they reached the city. At least she was enjoying her stay, he mused. That was fine with him, just so long as she didn't take any of it too seriously. He forced down the rising jealousy at such an idea. He would see her again and see to it that she then realized a thing or two!

In the latter part of the month of July, the Battle of Atlanta finally began. There were thousands of losses suffered by both sides, and the Confederates were forced to recuperate within the defenses of Atlanta.

"Aunt Jenny," Katie breathlessly called as she rushed into the parlour, "our boys have been forced to retreat into the city! I heard that Sherman and his army are within a few miles of here, but I have been assured that our own army can keep them out of Atlanta. You should have seen the hundreds being brought to the hospital. There isn't anything anyone can do for most of those poor souls, for we are quickly running out of proper medicine and drugs. Oh, Aunt Jenny, don't look so alarmed, dear!" Katie hurried over to her aunt and placed a supportive arm about her shoulders.

"Katie, this is the end, isn't it? Your Uncle Albert has told me a bit of what has been happening, and he has been preparing to leave the city. Oh, I know you did not know of his plans for leaving, dear, but he wanted to keep silent about it until it was necessary to tell you."

"Aunt Jenny, you mean to tell me that Uncle Albert knew that Sherman and his invaders would be advancing on Atlanta right now?" she asked incredulously. It seemed that she had forgotten her uncle had friends in the Union camp.

"Yes, dear, he knew something about it, although he did not tell me very much. He only said to be prepared to leave the city within the next few weeks. Oh, Katie, I will hate leaving our home. I suppose we will be going to stay at Corkhaven for a while."

"I, for one, do not intend to retreat before those Yankee scum! I am going to stay right here in Atlanta until they absolutely force me to leave! You and Uncle Albert do what you think best, but I'm going to stay. I am sorely needed at the hospital right this very moment, so I will speak to you more about your plans later. Don't worry, those Yankees haven't broken through the lines yet, and they very well may never get through!" She said goodbye to her aunt and hurried back down the street to the hospital, taking care to avoid being trampled by the Confederate soldiers marching or riding into the city.

Little did Katie know that the actual siege of Atlanta was yet to begin. She walked inside the hospital and began scurrying about to fetch supplies and to make the injured outside of the hospital as comfortable as possible. There were no eager volunteers to help the many soldiers who were forced to lie in the streets, waiting for some kind of relief from their agony.

As Katie made the rounds behind the nurses, she suddenly halted in her tracks. There, lying upon a pallet placed near the door was Lieutenant Ben Adamson. His head was heavily bandaged, one of his legs was badly mangled and shredded, and he appeared to be struggling to maintain his precious hold on life. He had lost a great deal of weight since Katie had bid him goodbye, and she peered intently at him for a moment to assure herself that it was indeed her good friend.

"Ben," she whispered as she knelt beside him, "Ben, can you hear me? This is Katie. Katie. Ben, open your eyes."

He awoke, slowly opened his eyes and focused upon her face bending down before him. He reached out a bony hand as far as he was able and Katie took into her own strong grip. She felt the weak pulse and fought down the growing urge to cry.

"Katie," he managed to croak, "Katie, my darling. You are really here. Katie, I'm going to die, dear. I want you to know how much I love you. I always have. Katie, are you still there?" He had lost most of his sight and he was fading fast.

"Yes, Ben, I'm still here, my dear. I won't leave you. Lie still and try to hang on. I'll call for a doctor or nurse to attend you. You just keep quiet and preserve your strength." She turned her head from him and called to a passing nurse.

"Nurse, over here! Could you come over here, please? This young man needs your help desperately. He's a dear friend of mine," she told her tearfully.

"Sorry, miss, I've got many young men to care for at this moment. We'll get to your friend as soon as possible. There are so many seriously wounded, we just can't attend to them all at once."

Katie turned back to Ben and tightened her hold on his hand. She tenderly stroked his forehead and bent to speak

141

gently to him once more.

"Ben, hang on, dear. I'll stay here with you until one of the nurses comes. Don't be afraid, Ben. Just hold on to my hand."

"Katie," he whispered with obvious difficulty, "Katie, please see to it that my folks know how I died. I know you can do it somehow. You are so strong, Katie, so strong and good and beautiful. I'm not afraid . . ." With that last whispered sentence, he gave a sudden gasp and peacefully died. Katie continued to hold his hand a moment longer, then she carefully laid it by his side and closed his eyelids. She could not cry at that time, she would cry later. He had been very dear to her, and she would sorely miss him. He had gone on to a much better world, a world with no pain and war and dying. He looked so serene and happy now, she couldn't be sorry for him.

She continued assisting the doctors and nurses for the remainder of the day, then wearily trudged home before darkness fell. She ignored the voices of her aunt and uncle and climbed the stairs to her room, where she collapsed upon the bed. She was too utterly exhausted to undress, and she drifted off to sleep. Sarah peeked in on her later and gently removed her dress and shoes, then covered her sleeping form with a light coverlet and tiptoed from the room.

Downstairs, her uncle and aunt were having a discussion in the parlour.

"Jenny, we must do as I say. Suffice it to say that Sherman and his army will be invading Atlanta, and we must not be here when they do. I do have friends among their ranks, but the majority of the men will not be interested in whose property they are vandalizing, only in plundering and destruction. Now, have you done as I told you? Do you have the necessary clothing and articles assembled?"

"Yes, Albert," she replied obediently, "but, dearest, what about your business? Are you simply going to run off and let the Yankees have everything?"

"No, of course not, Jenny. Don't be absurd. I will be taking all the essential papers and money with me when we leave. I will still have my contacts and I can continue to prosper once we have gone. Now, please inform Katie to be ready to leave at a moment's notice. I don't know exactly when we will be evacuating the city, but it will be soon, I'm sure. Is all of this understood?" he asked his wife sternly.

"Yes, Albert. I'll tell Katie to have most of her things ready to leave this week. She may not leave, though, dear. She told me earlier that she intends to stay until she is driven out. What am I going to do if she refuses to leave with us?" she asked him.

"Well, she is a young woman now, Jenny, but she's also our niece, our flesh and blood. I'll see to it that she comes with us, never fear. Now, I'm going to the office. There is a lot to be done if we have to leave soon. Good night, dear." He gave her a quick kiss and strolled out the door. She sighed heavily and then went on up to her room and to bed.

When Katie awoke the next morning, she remembered Ben's death and finally allowed herself the luxury of tears. He had been so good and kind to her, loving her with an unfailing devotion.

Her thoughts again turned to her husband. He would naturally be with Sherman's army at this very moment, preparing to attack and invade the city. Her heart tumultuously pounded at the thought of actually seeing him again, and she wondered anew at the depth of her feelings for him. She only knew that she had to see him again, she had to be with him in order to know precisely what changes, if any, her feelings had undergone since he had bid her goodbye. It had seemed like such a long space of time since that day in the woods after their 'wedding.' She still awoke in the middle of the night, restless and yearning for something intangible, something she could not discern.

She climbed from the bed and quickly dressed, aware

143

that she was expected to arrive at the hospital earlier than usual this particular day. She would have to miss breakfast and be on her way. There were so many men to take care of, so many wounded to comfort.

Late in July, the actual siege of Atlanta began. It would have been impossible for Sherman to either assault the Confederate forces behind their almost impregnable barricade, or for him to surround the city with his numbers. He finally determined to strike at General Hood's supply line. On that day, a fierce battle ensued at Ezra Church, which was located on the west side of Atlanta, and the Confederates were again defeated with heavy losses resulting. And, so the siege continued.

Katie returned home completely exhausted every evening. There were scores of wounded and dying soldiers arriving at the hospital by the hour. She cursed the fact that they were unable to get further medicine and needed supplies for the hospital. She felt utterly useless and frustrated as she watched the men suffer.

Katie would follow the nurses on their rounds, helping to hold a poor soldier's head as he was given water, holding the limp and almost lifeless hands of the dying, writing letters for the doomed who would never again see their homes or their families. She was forced to harden her thoughts against the emotional onslaught of watching these men daily. She was no longer entertaining in the evenings, as there were no longer any dances or parties to attend, nor any desire for such.

For one endless month, Sherman was virtually unable to accomplish much toward his final goal of conquering Atlanta. Until, one humid day late in August, he ordered his men to destroy the Macon and Western Railroad. It had been the only remaining line of supplies to the Confederate Army.

Uncle Albert had waited as long as he thought he possibly could to leave the city, but now it was absolutely imperative that he get away. He instructed his wife to be ready to leave the next morning, after he had learned

144

about the destruction of the important railroad.

"Jenny, the time has come for us to journey to Corkhaven. We will leave the first thing tomorrow morning, so you had better go on up and tell Katie about our plans. Tell her to have Sarah prepare everything she needs and have it ready. We can't tarry any longer in this city, for it is fated for destruction."

"But, Albert," his wife replied, "Katie has repeatedly told me that she will not leave. She says that there is too much to be done at the hospital, and that she furthermore refuses to retreat from any Yankee scum. What am I supposed to do if she refuses to come with us?"

"If that happens, just let me know. I'll find some way to persuade her. Now, do as I say and make your preparations for the trip." With that, he strode out of the house to gather up some more papers and articles at his office.

Jenny went upstairs as her husband had bid to consult with her niece.

"Katie, dear, your uncle has instructed me that we will be leaving for Corkhaven early tomorrow morning. I know, my dear, that you do not really want to leave, but he said that it is absolutely necessary for us to go before Sherman and his army invade our city," she told her. Katie, who was sitting upon the bed, composing a letter to her family at that moment, raised her head and looked her aunt directly in the eye.

"No, Aunt Jenny, I will not leave. I feel I am more needed here than at home. And, Uncle Albert cannot know for sure that Sherman will be able to break through into the city. Even if the Yankees do come, I'll manage to take care of things, don't you worry! Oh, I can't go at this time, Aunt, for someone has to try and help those poor, wretched souls at the hospital. That is my final word on the subject. I will be sorry to see you go, but Sarah can stay here with me and I'll look after your house while you are away. I'll send you word as often as I can." She would not budge, no matter what Uncle Albert said.

"Oh, Katie, your uncle will be very disappointed in you. Why, you'll be all alone with only one slave in this big old house. What will all of our friends say if we go off and leave you here for the Yankees? They could surely do you a great deal of harm if they do get into the city. I can't bear to think what might happen to you if they find you here all alone!" she said tearfully.

"Don't worry. I will be able to take care of myself, Aunt Jenny. Now, you go on and get your things ready for the morning. I'm so tired, I think I'll go ahead and go on to sleep. Please tell Sarah not to disturb me until at least eight o'clock, will you? Oh, that's right, you said you were leaving early, didn't you? Well, go ahead and wake me before you leave then, all right? Good night, dear. I will miss you both, but I really must stay. Please deliver this letter to Mama for me, and tell her and my brothers that I love them. Be careful, Aunt Jenny, for I sometimes wonder if Uncle Albert really knows what he is doing." She finished with a yawn and closed her heavy-lidded eyes. Her aunt stood peering closely at her, then quietly left the room. She would have to tell her husband about Katie's decision, and he would not like it at all. She didn't see what he could do about it, though. Katie was no longer a child. No, for some reason, she had appeared much more mature lately than when she had first arrived.

As Esther and Aunt Jenny were making their final preparations to depart the doomed city the next morning, Uncle Albert knocked upon Katie's door and was told to enter. He found her already dressed and apparently waiting for him.

"Katie, you must see reason. We can't go off and leave you here all alone. Why, my dear, the Yankees will be invading the city any time soon, and you simply must not be here. It will be very dangerous for anyone to remain in the city once they have broken through the lines. Now, you must see that your mother would want you to come with us. I'm sure that she is anxious to see you again. I know for a fact that she had no idea you would be staying

146

this long," he finished smugly. Surely she could not withstand such a reasonable argument.

"Uncle Albert, I have already told Aunt Jenny that I will not leave. Now, that's enough of that. I must stay here and continue to help out at the hospital, for whatever that is worth. I will keep Sarah here with me and we will leave whenever we think it is necessary. I promise you that we will leave before there is any real danger to us. Now, you better get on downstairs and get ready to leave," she insisted. No one could outdo her for stubbornness when she had her mind set!

"No, Katie, I can't go without you. If you want me and your aunt to remain here in a city about to be overrun with the enemy, well, all right. You will be the reason we stay, and you will be the cause if anything bad happens to your poor aunt! Now, you either come with us, or we will be forced to stay!" He did not actually intend to stay in Atlanta, but he thought it would make a good bluff. However, he had underestimated his niece's perception.

"Very well, Uncle, stay if you want to. Now, I really must get to the hospital. I'll go on downstairs and say goodbye to Aunt Jenny. Goodbye, Uncle Albert. I'm sure I'll be seeing you at Corkhaven if the Yankees do get into the city, and, if not, I'll be seeing you again when you return here." She gave her startled uncle a quick kiss and retired downstairs. He remained stockstill, realizing how deftly she had managed to call his bluff. He would now either have to remain, or go on without her. He pondered his decision for only a moment, but he knew that he would go. He could not stay here and risk everything for his obstinate and headstrong niece, no matter how beloved she was to him.

Katie found her aunt out in the kitchen with Esther and quickly said her goodbyes. Then, giving her tearful aunt a last hug and kiss, she hurried toward the hospital. She didn't look back.

They would all be gone when she returned home that evening, everyone except for Sarah. She experienced a sudden pang of homesickness, but she knew that she must not waver. She was desperately needed here in the city, while she knew that her mother and brothers would be safe at Corkhaven. And, as for the Yankees, why, she wouldn't worry about them just yet. There was still a slim hope that they would not be able to break through the Confederate lines.

Her thoughts rested upon her husband. He, if he were still alive, would be among those now laying siege to the city. He could even have been among those enemy that destroyed the railroad, the only avenue by which Atlanta could have received the needed supplies. However, she was unable to associate such destruction with Brent, for some unknown reason. Her mind continually returned to the evening of their wedding, and to the time he had said goodbye to her within sight of Atlanta. She experienced a longing to see his face again, to hear his deep and resonant voice issuing commands. Oh, dear, she told herself, why can't you get that man out of your mind? Perhaps, answered a tiny voice inside her, because he is also in your heart.

She shook off her thoughts and entered the hospital. She was forced to step over many wounded soldiers lying on the hard surface of the floor. She donned her apron and cap and went to work, soothing the suffering men and trying to reassure them that someone would soon tend to their wounds. She forced down a lump in her throat as she again surveyed the hundreds of men in obvious agony. Yes, she thought, I did the right thing in staying. They need me, they need so much.

She thought about the day Lieutenant Adamson had died in her arms. He had been so young, so kind and generous. So many of these soldiers were even younger, their families unaware of the horrendous conditions their loved ones were enduring.

Brent was not among those who had been ordered to destroy the railroad. He was not among those who had killed so many Confederates at Ezra Church. He and his

148

men were forced to simply bide their time, fighting an occasional skirmish now and then. The men were all anxious to be done with the waiting; they wished to enter the city as Sherman had promised them they would.

"Sergeant Duffy, I do believe that this siege is about ended. I have been informed that the Confederates can no longer hold out without the supplies they so desperately need, so that, in consequence, means that we will indeed be the conquering invaders within the next few days. It's been a hard campaign, Duffy. I'm proud of you and the other men. You have served well," Brent told him.

"Thank you, Captain. Yes, sir, I think we will be seeing Atlanta before too much longer. I hear Sherman is mighty anxious to add it to his successes. By the way, Captain, isn't your wife in Atlanta right now?" he asked, knowing the answer beforehand.

"Yes, Sergeant," replied Brent with an amused smile, "She is, I suppose. I mean, she may very well be back home at Corkhaven by now. If it's up to her relatives, I'm sure she is at home. But, she has a decided ability to obtain her own way, as I'm sure you have observed. Duffy, I don't know about you, but I'm very ready for this war to end."

"Yes, Captain, I sure do know what you mean. I've seen an awful lot of bloodshed since I joined up. I'm about ready to settle down and do some farming," his friend replied with a sigh.

"Anyway," said Brent, "I will try and locate the house of my wife's uncle as soon as we enter the city. I only pray that she is not still in the city when we do."

Fourteen

When Katie returned home from the hospital that same evening, she found that Esther had remained behind.

"Miss Katie," she said, "I couldn't go off and leave the two of you here all by yourselves. I had to stay and help out. Your Aunt Jenny said it was all right with her if I was to wait to come with you whenever you gets ready. Now, how about some nice, hot supper, honey?"

"Yes, thank you, Esther. Oh, and thank you for staying. That was very thoughtful of you. I am so tired," she said with a heavy sigh. "Maybe you better wait on that supper, Esther. I seem to be feeling a little faint or something. Oh...I..." Before she could finish the sentence, she slowly slumped to the floor. Esther caught her in her big and capable hands and called for Sarah. The two of them carefully carried her upstairs and placed her on the bed.

Sarah set about removing her clothing, while Esther returned downstairs for some cold cloths and smelling salts. They finally managed to revive Katie and then instructed her to lie quiet.

"Oh, I've never before fainted in my life. I guess I'm sort of wore out," she commented as she returned to consciousness.

"Yes, honey, you are most certainly all wore out. You are gonna stay here in this bed for a couple of days and rest up. We're gonna take care of you, so you just lie back and rest. Those there people at the hospital will just have to do without you for a while, and that's that!" Sarah informed her. She was worried about her Miss Katie; the poor child looked so worn and colorless.

"Very well, Sarah. I'm just too weak to argue with you right now. I guess I'll go on to sleep now. I can't seem to keep my eyes open any longer."

Sarah and Esther quietly left the room and stood out in the hallway. The two of them exchanged worried glances and began to descend the stairs.

"Esther, I know Miss Katie done told me not to tell anyone about this, but I just got to now. You see, that child is married! Yes, and what's more, she's married to a Yankee captain!"

"Oh, Sarah," replied the surprised Esther, "you don't mean it! Our Miss Katie married to one of the enemy? I just can't believe she would go and do a thing like that!"

"Well, she did. And, I sure am afraid that she's not just tired! I'm getting worried that she may be expecting a baby!"

Esther turned an even more startled gaze upon her friend and remarked:

"No, are you sure? How come Miss Katie done gone and married a Yankee? It's not what I would ever think that young lady would do! Has she said anything to you about missing her monthly courses?"

"Well, no, not yet. Miss Katie is married to the same Yankee that come to Corkhaven with his men a while back. He really loves that child, Esther, but she just ain't sure that she loves him back. But, she does. Oh, yes, you mark my words. And, she ain't too knowing in the ways of life, that's for sure. She hasn't said anything about it, but that don't mean nothing. She probably believes she's just tired out or something. But I'm gonna have a talk with her first thing in the morning!"

"Oh, Sarah, what if those Yankees really do come into the city? What are we gonna do if they come here to this house?"

"Well," Sarah thought a moment and then replied, "Miss Katie told me that we're gonna stay until they make us go. I'm certain she's got some kind of plan in her mind. Miss Katie always has some kind of plan in her mind. She's got a plan for everything, for sure!"

Katie awoke with a headache the next morning, then remembered that she would be unable to go to the hospital that day. She cursed her weakness. Oh, drat! Here we all are with the Yankees right at our front door, and I'm stuck in bed like a baby! She was so badly needed at the hospital, too.

"Sarah, where are you? Come on up here and talk with me, you hear?" she called out. She attempted to rise, but found herself unable to lift her head much farther than the pillow.

Sarah materialized in the doorway and swiftly hurried over to press Katie down into the bed once more.

"Honey, we told you to lie back and rest. You ain't going anywhere for at least another day or two. Now, how about some breakfast? You know you gotta keep your strength up if you want to get better," Sarah said as she fussed over her patient.

"All right, Sarah. I can see that I will have to follow your strict orders if I'm ever going to be allowed out of this bed!" Katie replied with a twinkle.

"Yes, Miss Katie, that's right. Now, there's something I got to ask you," Sarah said and then paused, "Well, you haven't missed any of your monthly courses, have you, honey? Tell the truth to old Sarah, child."

"No, Sarah, I haven't. Why do you ask?" Katie replied in confusion.

"Well, I was just wondering if maybe you might be expecting. A baby, that is. I thought that Yankee husband of yours might have got you with child. Honey, if there ever was a man that looked like he could get a woman with child the first time out, he is certainly the one!" Sarah commented with an amused chuckle. She glanced at Katie's face and ceased her teasing. Her mistress' face had gone beet-red and Katie looked rather distressed.

"Oh, now, honey, don't pay me no never mind. You

know I was just joshing you. Now, at least we know that you ain't gonna have a baby. I'll go get your breakfast right now." Sarah hurried from the room, sensing that Katie needed to be alone.

Katie dwelt upon what Sarah had said. Expecting a child? Did she want a child? Would she want the child of Brent? Her mind conjured up the image of a small boy, his hair as dark as his father's, his eyes the same deep blue. No, it could never be. He was a Yankee, an enemy, even if he was her husband. However, the delightful image returned to her mind throughout the remainder of the day.

For the next two days, Katie stayed in bed and rested. She occupied her time with reading books and sleeping. Brent came to her mind quite frequently, and she wondered if she would see him again as he had promised.

Oh, Brent, why can't I forget you? Why must I yearn for your kisses, your touch? I can't seem to think straight about anything whenever you come to mind. During the nearly four months she had now spent in Atlanta, she had become aware of an apparent softening toward her husband. For the first time in weeks, she truly examined her feelings for him.

Yes, it was true that she disliked the truly reprehensible manner in which he had forced her to marry him. She had found herself wanting to defy him in anything he ordered. She had found her stubborn pride surfacing whenever she encountered the man. Then, how come I can't stop thinking about him, she asked herself. Why can't I forget him and go on with my life as before? She knew that she would have no easy answers to her questions. She knew that it was imperative that she see him again, speak with him once more. Well, if things keep progressing the way they have so far, she mused, I may very well be seeing him within the next few days! She had heard that the Confederate soldiers were becoming quite alarmed at the progress Sherman's siege was making. There had been talk already of the Southern troops actually abandoning

153

Atlanta to the Yankees. That just can't happen, she thought fiercely, they can't leave this city to the Yankees and to that creature named Sherman.

The first of September, General Hood sent General Hardee and his men to attack the Federals, while he and his own men tried to find an opportunity to attack Sherman's right flank. However, Hardee's attack failed miserably and Hood finally realized the necessity of evacuating Atlanta.

Katie had risen from her bed that morning and dressed to go to the hospital. Before she had gone any further than the front porch, she spied Esther hurrying toward her from the direction of the center of the city.

"Miss Katie, our boys are leaving! Yes, honey, they are gonna leave Atlanta to the Yankees! We got to hurry up and get ready to leave here ourselves! Come on inside, Miss Katie, we got to hurry," she said excitedly. Katie went inside with her and summoned Sarah to the parlour.

"Sarah, Esther has just told me the horrible news. The Yankees will be entering the city before too much longer. We must prepare to evacuate at once. You go on upstairs and gather up our clothes, while I help Esther barricade the windows and doors. Go on, now. Esther, you come with me."

Sarah did as she was ordered, while Katie took Esther with her to the shed at the back of the house. There, gathering up the reins of the three remaining horses, she led them around to the front of the house and tied them to the hitching post. Then, she and Esther rushed back inside and began closing all of the windows and drawing the shutters tight. They barricaded the back door with the kitchen table and gathered a small supply of food and provisions for the trip. Sarah returned downstairs with a small bag, full to overflowing with Katie's new dresses and other garments. She and Esther bundled together their own clothing and the three of them sat down to rest for a moment before they would begin the journey to Corkhaven.

Outside, in the city, the Confederate troops were making ready to evacuate their forces. They were instructed to blow up their magazines and destroy any supplies they could not carry with them.

Many of the residents of the city were also preparing to leave Atlanta. Like Katie and her slaves, they were gathering up a few of their belongings and piling them into wagons or on to horses. They would leave before the Yankees came; they would not be here to see the triumphant enemy pollute their beloved city with their hateful presence.

Katie peered out the front window from the parlour, which she had kept unshuttered to watch the activity in the streets. She viewed the retreating soldiers, the fleeing citizens. This is so damned unfair, she thought with clenched teeth. All of these people being forced to leave their homes, and for what? Where would they all go and how would they manage to survive?

"All right, I think it's time to leave now," she told the two slaves. "The last of the troops appears to be going. There are only a few people remaining out in the street. Come on, let's lock up and get out of here before the Yankees arrive."

Many of the city's residents would remain. They would not abandon their homes, but, instead, they would stay and hope that the Yankees would leave them unharmed and their homes and businesses untouched.

As Katie walked outside to place their bundles on the horses' backs, she stopped in surprise. The horses were gone! Someone had stolen them while she and the slaves were preparing to leave. She had apparently missed the occurrence when she left her post at the window. Oh, why didn't I think of that, she chided herself furiously. Now, how would they be able to leave? Would they be able to get horses anywhere now? She concentrated upon their predicament, but was unable to come up with any solutions. Maybe there are other horses left in the city, she told herself hopefully, but she knew this was not a possibility. No, the fleeing people would have taken every horse they could lay their hands on, she now realized. She again cursed her thoughtlessness and returned inside to inform Sarah and Esther that they would all have to remain inside the house when the Yankees came.

I'll be ready with the gun, she planned. We'll barricade the front door and keep the windows secure. Maybe the Yankees will pass us by, maybe they will not bother to approach the house at all.

"Sarah, Esther, you may as well stop hurrying. The horses have been stolen. We are forced to remain here. Don't worry, I still have Papa's gun, and we have enough food and water to last us for quite a while. We may as well go and sit in the parlour and wait for the thieving Yankees," she wearily informed the two women. They entered the parlour and sank down into chairs to await the arrival of the enemy.

Katie continued to try and think of some way to get out of the city before they came. She knew it would be useless to try and walk very far. They would be swiftly overtaken for sure that way. No, we will have to stay and hope for the best. Uncle Albert, she thought with ironic amusement, you were right. It seems as if we should have gone with you to Corkhaven after all.

General Hood and his army headed toward Andersonville, the Confederate prison camp which held approximately thirty-four thousand Union prisoners at that time. Since the prison camp had been left virtually unprotected, Hood decided to place himself and his forces between Andersonville and Sherman.

Sherman and his army, receiving the reports that the Confederates had indeed evacuated Atlanta, began their march into the city. When they entered, they would find many of the residents gone, although many of the injured soldiers had been, of necessity, left behind at the hospital. The doctors and nurses had also refused to abandon their patients, and so they all waited for the enemy with dread expectancy.

Katie and the other citizens remaining within the limits of the city waited through the night for the sight of the Yankees. Early the next morning, the Yankees began marching within the city's earthen walls. Since May, the Union ranks had been depleted by nearly 28,000 killed or wounded, while almost 4,000 of them had fallen as prisoners into the Confederates' hands.

As Katie peered through a crack in the shutter of the front window in the parlour, she observed the enemy marching along the streets of Atlanta. She instructed Sarah and Esther to remain perfectly still and quiet. She grasped the gun in her hands and tightened her hold upon it, praying that she would not be forced to use it. Suddenly, she watched as a small band of Yankees broke away from the ranks and approached the house. They laughingly strode up the walkway to the front porch, smashing down the gate of the white picket fence as they came. They began to pound on the heavy front door with the ends of their rifles, jeering and exulting at their victory.

"Yes, you Southern gentlemen, here we are! Let us in! What's the matter, it get too hot for you in this here city of yours? Hey, Paul," the lead man called to one of the others, "let's break down the door and see what a fine Southern home really looks like, what do you say?" Paul and the other four companions quickly agreed and started to pound on the door in earnest.

Katie gasped and momentarily panicked. What was she to do? She decided to stand her ground and face the Yankees. It would most likely do no good to hide. She motioned Sarah and Esther to stand behind her. The two of them were ready to attack with a fire poker in one hand and a meat cleaver in the other. Katie raised the barrel of the shotgun and pointed it directly at the center of the front door.

The Yankees broke through the door in a matter of minutes and managed to swing it open. They stopped in their tracks as they entered the house, falling silent as they peered into the face of a beautiful young woman pointing a shotgun at their bodies.

"You Yankees can very well leave the same way you came in. Out, I say! Get out of this house right now, or I'll blow your thieving heads right off your cowardly bodies! Sarah, Esther, get ready to move when I say to," she said with the light of battle in her brilliant green eyes.

"Ma'am," said the soldier in the front of the group, a young man with a slight squint and a decidedly evil gleam in his eyes, "we don't mean you no harm. Now, you just lower that gun and we'll be on our way. We didn't have no idea there was one of those Southern belles right here in this house! All right, honey, we're going right now. Just take it easy and give us a chance to turn around and leave," he coaxed.

"No, you back out that door, Yankee! Keep your hands up where I can see them and back out that door and down those steps. Don't make a move for those guns you're holding at your sides, or you're dead men where you stand. I mean it, you filthy vermin, move!" she told them unwaveringly. They judged it wise to obey this young goddess of battle, so they began to slowly and stealthily back away and out the front door. Once outside, they turned and fled as fast as they could to rejoin their advancing troops. They had been disobeying strict orders when they had broken rank, and they had no wish to be discovered in the house.

Katie heaved a sigh of relief and approached what remained of the front door. She handed the gun to Sarah and instructed Esther to help her try and close the door once more. They managed to right the damaged door and push it back into place. Katie threw the bolt once more and surveyed the damage. There were several splintered holes in the door, but she decided that it would offer enough protection as long as it was guarded.

"Now, you two, sit down right there on that floor, and let's be ready for any other Yankees who might decide to come and gloat. It's been a long night, but we can't rest just yet. We must maintain our vigilance until I think of some way to leave the city," she told them. She sank down on the cool tiles of the entrance foyer and cradled the shotgun in her lap. She closed her eyes for a second and prayed that they could remain awake.

Captain Brent Morgan, following the directions of the courier he had once sent to deliver the letter to Katie, rode down the street and toward the house. He checked the name displayed on the white picket fence and dismounted. He noticed the destruction of the gate and thought, surely she is not still here. However, I better have a closer look. He approached the front door of the house and halted. He saw the gashes which had previously been pounded into the door and frowned at the thought of what he might find within. He discovered that his heart was beating at an alarming rate of speed, and he raised his fist to knock upon the dilapidated door.

"Hey, is there anyone in there? I'm Captain Brent Morgan, and I have come to inquire about a Miss Katie O'Toole. Is anyone there?" he called out in his deep voice.

Inside, Katie was jarred awake by his knock and the sound of his voice. Brent! Here in Atlanta! He had somehow found her. She roused Sarah and Esther and flew to open the door.

"I'm coming, Brent! Push on the door. It doesn't seem to want to open," she shouted in her excitement. He pushed and she pulled, then she stood back as the door creaked upon its hinges and swung open. She stood facing her husband, whom she had not seen for four long months, whom she had dreamed of and yearned for. He also stood, simply gazing at her, drinking in the sight of her flushed and beautiful features.

"Katie, darling, what are you still doing in Atlanta? Why haven't you gone?" he asked her with an air of command. He was forcing himself to refrain from crushing her in his arms.

Katie was flustered by his scrutiny and answered him tartly, "Uncle Albert and Aunt Jenny have already left the city, but I refused to leave! I was needed to help out at the hospital, and by the time we were going to leave, the horses had been stolen by someone. There, that does answer your question, doesn't it?" She was sorely hurt and disappointed by his manner. Where was the love and tenderness he had professed for her?

"Well, young lady, you can't stay here. Oh, Katie, you little fool! Why didn't you go with your aunt and uncle in the first place?" he demanded angrily. He was immensely relieved at seeing her safe and sound, but he was unable to fight down the growing fury he felt inside of him. Leave it to her to refuse to obey anything that was for her own good!

"Well, I like that! Here you are, among the conquering enemy, and you start in right away questioning me! Well, it's none of your blasted affair what I decide, you Yankee! Who asked you to come here in the first place? Who asked you to come back into my life, anyway?" she cried, fighting down the rising tears. Why didn't he even behave as if he was glad to see her? He must have been lying all along; he didn't love her at all.

"Katie, darling, don't cry. I'm just so relieved to see you unharmed, even if I am not particularly glad to see that you're still in Atlanta! Of course, I am absolutely delighted at this chance to see you again!" Finally, he ignored his cautious instincts and caught her to him in a hungry and passionate embrace. He kissed her long and lingeringly and threatened to crush her beneath his powerful arms.

"Oh, Katie, I've missed you so much! I've dreamed about you, remembered your voice and face and touch. I still can't believe that you're actually here in my arms. Oh, Katie, I love you," he murmured against the softness of her hair. She gave herself up to his embrace and nestled her head comfortably against his muscular chest. Suddenly, she thought, I feel so safe and secure. I feel as if a great weight has been lifted off my shoulders.

"Brent, I doubted if I would ever see you again. I really

did mean to leave the city before you Yankees came, but it was just too late. What am I going to do now? Where are we going to go?" she asked him distractedly.

"Well, dear wife, I will have to think about that. I can't think too clearly with such a delightful little baggage in my arms! Sarah, you and your friend there go and fix me something to eat. I have to be getting back to my outfit before too long. I don't think anyone will be coming here to the house just yet." He led his wife into the parlour and gently pushed her down into the soft cushions of the sofa.

"Katie, I told you I would see you again before this war had ended. I only wish I knew what to do with you now! I happen to know that Sherman intends to order the complete evacuation of the entire city, allowing no one to remain, for any reason. My darling wife, what am I going to do with you?" he asked her with a small light of mischief in his tender eyes.

"Well, sir, I don't rightly know! If you could manage to get up some horses, I suppose we could go on to Corkhaven. Oh, Brent, I was becoming so very frightened before you came! We had been watching all night for any soldiers to return."

"What, my fiery Katie actually frightened? Don't tell me that! I have a feeling that you are about the most capable and determined female there ever was, my dear! Anyway, I thank the Lord that I have found you again. And, I'll see what I can do about some horses. Getting you some mounts is not the problem. The problem is getting you safely out of the city. Funny, once I was concerned with getting you safely into the city! By the way, who broke down the door?" he asked her sternly.

Katie related to him the incident of the Yankee soldiers. Afterwards, he sat grimly staring into space, feeling very murderous toward the men, whoever they might be. His Katie had been placed in danger, and that was something he could not endure. He turned to her and bestowed a tender and loving glance on her.

Katie felt a warm glow come alive inside of her again, a

glow she could not define. She did not know exactly what to say to him now, for she was feeling unaccountably shy at that moment. She only knew that she was very glad to see him again, very desirous of feeling herself safe within his loving and strong arms.

"Katie, you know what I've waited so long to hear from your lips," he softly told her as he continued to gaze down at her. "Tell me that you love me, Katie. Tell me that you care for me as I care for you. I want, I need to hear it now." He waited for her to speak, afraid to press her further at that time.

"Oh, Brent, I'm still so confused. I know that I am happy to see you again, to be near you once more. I know that I have prayed for your safety and dreamt of you. I have longed to see you again so that I could examine my feelings for you. Only, now, I'm still confused. Give me time, and I'll honestly try to give you an answer. For now, just hold me and make me feel loved and secure," she replied. Do I love him? she asked herself.

"All right, honey. I won't demand any more from you right now. Come on, I must eat and get on back to my troops. I will come again as soon as I can manage to get away, and I'll see about those horses for you." He lifted her high in his arms and brought his head slowly level with hers. He gently kissed her and then released her before he could no longer maintain control over his desires. He led her into the kitchen and proceeded to devour the meal Esther had grudgingly prepared for him.

Throughout the meal, Katie sat and watched his face, his motions, his eyes. Oh, why couldn't you be on our side, she silently asked him. Why did you have to be a Yankee? For, if you were a Confederate officer, it would be so much simpler. I could love you without any restraint, without these traitorous feelings I experience every time I admit to enjoying your embraces and kisses. I could be proud to be your wife.

After the meal, Brent rose from the table and once more escorted his wife back into the entrance foyer. He drew her into his arms and said:

"Katie, I must go back now. You stay here and barricade this door with something, you understand? Keep your gun handy and don't let anyone in. I'll be back as soon as I can, but that probably won't be until late this afternoon. I will count the minutes until I see you again, dear wife. I love you." With that, he kissed her passionately once more and then abruptly tore himself away from her and strode out the door. He turned and waved before he rode away.

For some unknown reason, it dawned upon Katie at that precise moment that she had the answer to her long-asked question. I love him! She discovered to her amazement that she had loved him for quite some time, that she had refused to admit her love for him because he was a Yankee. She had wanted to deny those feelings, but she no longer could.

I love him! she exultantly repeated to herself. I really do love him. It was such a startling realization, she sat down on the floor and sought to regain her breath. He had been so patient for so long, when he had known all along that she loved him. He had been able to see that from the early days at Corkhaven. He had known long before she had known herself. Oh, why couldn't I have discovered this sooner, she lamented. We could have had more time together, instead of my acting like a child and avoiding him. Why, he didn't even know yet that she loved him! She could hardly contain her excitement when she thought of telling him that very afternoon when he returned. He would be deliriously happy! She would enjoy watching his handsome face when he received his long-awaited avowal of love.

Katie happily hugged herself, gleefully chuckling as she savored her wonderful secret. Love had come to her at last. And, it had come in the form of the handsome, domineering, stubborn, loving Yankee captain! Suddenly, she remembered the war. Oh, yes, the awful war. What are we going to do? she wondered. When would they ever be able to live together as man and wife? I can't worry about that just yet, she admonished herself, I must take one day at a time. I must simply be happy with the discovery of my love for Brent, and with the knowledge of his love for me.

Katie, Esther, and Sarah waited several more hours before they again heard Brent's voice at the front door. Katie told Sarah and Esther to retreat into the kitchen, while she hurried to let her husband in. When her eyes lit upon his face, she smiled seductively and threw her arms around his neck.

"Well, what's this, dear wife? I knew that you were glad to see me, but this appears to be completely out of character for you! What on earth has happened while I was away?" he asked with amusement.

"Brent, come into the parlour. I have something to say to you that is very important," she replied seriously. He frowned in thought and followed her into the room. She motioned for him to be seated, then she came to stand directly before him.

"First of all, Brent, I've been a fool. Yes, an absolute fool. I have loved you, my darling, almost from the first moment I saw you that day so long ago at home. I discovered it for the first time today, and I regret that I did not know sooner. Oh, Brent, I love you so much!" Before she could say any more, he had pulled her down into his lap and entwined his arms about her. He smiled a bewitching smile and brought his lips demandingly down upon her own. After several minutes thus, Katie raised her shining face and said to him:

"Oh, Brent, I can hardly believe all this is happening to me! Why, I thought that when I saw you come through that door today, I would positively faint from joy! I was never so glad to see anyone in my entire life."

"Katie, honey, I don't mean to doubt you, but I have to be sure. Are you certain that you don't merely feel gratitude for my arrival? I mean, you were frightened and about at your wit's end. Are you sure that what you feel for me is really love?"

164

"Yes, darling, it really is love. Oh, it's taken me so long to know myself! I've never had to search my heart and soul like I have these past few months. I again apologize for all the mean and childish things I have said to you, but that's all behind us now. The question is, what are we going to do about it? What are we going to do about this war?"

"Well, there isn't much either of us can do about the war, Katie. I don't exactly know how long we will be staying in Atlanta, but that's beside the point. The point is, dear wife, that you and your slaves have got to go to Corkhaven, where you will be safe. I can't bear the thought of anything happening to you, especially not now that we have really found each other. When the war is ended, I will come to you, Katie, darling. I don't think that day is so very far away. Anyway, I came to tell you that I was able to smuggle out three horses for you. I want you to leave first thing in the morning, you understand? I will escort you as far as the city's western limits, but then you will have to manage on your own. I hate to see you go like this, but Sherman is ordering the complete evacuation of the city. You must get to safety, Katie, because I can't bear the thought of anything happening to you. It continually amazes me how I could let myself fall in love with a spoiled, headstrong, willful, stubborn little vixen such as you, but it has most certainly happened!"

Katie playfully punched him in the stomach, then she settled back on his lap and whispered into his ear,

"Brent, can you stay the night? We could go on upstairs and talk some more, make some more plans, couldn't we?" she asked with a strange gleam in her luminous eyes.

"Yes, darling, I can stay the night. But, understand, you are to leave first thing in the morning. We will have to rise early and get you on your way before sunup. We haven't much time together, Katie, but we can make it seem like a lifetime."

Brent lifted her high in his arms and slowly climbed the stairs to her bedroom, which she directed him to. He carried her into the room, closing the door behind him with his booted foot. He deposited her on the four-poster bed and placed himself lovingly beside her. They proceeded to express their deep love for one another, not caring what would come tomorrow, not daring to think about anything beyond the present and each other.

They quickly undressed and then again drew together. Brent kissed her and caressed her until she could no longer control the tumultuous feelings she felt rising within her very being. The two of them joined together in the age-old expression of love, giving and receiving.

Katie never imagined anything could be as wonderful as the fiery explosion assailing her every nerve, every fiber of her being. She had thought never again to experience the feelings she had felt on her wedding day, but her senses were afire with the ecstasy.

"Brent, oh darling, I love you so much," she whispered as they both reached the climax of their intense lovemaking.

Brent would never have believed he could ever feel as he did this moment. Mutual love between a man and wife, expressed in this sexual response, was truly made in heaven. He held Katie tightly in his arms and told her how much he loved her and how terribly he had missed her these past months.

They talked and planned for their future, laughing with joy at each other's suggestions. In a short while, they again expressed their all-consuming love and passion for each other.

Much, much later, they nestled against one another and drifted off to sleep, happy and contented.

Fifteen

Katie awoke to the morning with the comforting feel of Brent's arm stretched lazily across her warm body. She smiled and kissed him gently upon his cheek, whereupon he awakened and returned her morning greeting.

"Dear wife, good morning to you. I trust you spent a restful night?" he asked wickedly.

"Oh, of course. I always remain awake for most of the night, making love to a man! Oh, Brent," she said as she sobered, "it was so wonderful. I hate to think that it will be such a long time until I see you again. I don't think I can stand being apart from you, darling."

"Katie, honey, I hate it, too, but there isn't anything we can do about it. Now, it appears that dawn is not too far away, so we've got to rise and be on our way," he replied. "I love you, and I will cherish the memory of last night. Darling, I don't think this war will last that much longer, so don't worry. I have no intention of getting myself killed! Now, come on, up you go."

Katie grumbled good-naturedly as he rose from the bed, stretched, then drew her up beside him. He gave her a playful smack on her bare bottom, then set about drawing on his discarded clothing. Soon, they were both dressed and ready to leave.

"Katie, I will send word to you somehow. I want you to ride like the wind to Corkhaven, where I have hopes that you will stay! You will most likely encounter other refugees from Atlanta once you are outside the city, so be careful. This is the last time we will have a chance to say

167

goodbye in private. I will miss you terribly and think about you constantly. You will, of course, do the same, I trust?"

"Brent," she barely choked out through her rising tears, "I don't think I can stand saying goodbye to you! Hold me! Hold me like you'll never release me!" she said as she clutched at him.

He drew her into his arms and cradled her head against his strong shoulder. He held her tightly for a few moments, then kissed her once more. They clung to one another until he broke the spell by drawing away and taking her firmly by the hand to lead her downstairs.

Esther and Sarah had apparently been awake for some time, for they had already prepared provisions for the journey. Brent bid them both a good morning on his way out to the shed where he had tied the horses and bolted the door. Katie remained in the kitchen with the two slaves.

"Miss Katie," began Esther haltingly, "honey, how come you done got married to a Yankee?"

"Oh, Esther, it's a long story. By the way," she suddenly remarked, "how did you know we were married, anyway?" She glanced meaningfully at Sarah.

"Miss Katie," Sarah quickly explained, "I had to tell her. When you got sick, we was worried about you and what might be the matter with you. Besides, honey, you wouldn't want Esther here to go and think you done spent the night with a man you ain't married to, now would you?"

Katie could not keep a straight face and began to chuckle at Sarah's words. She turned once more to Esther.

"Esther, I can see that you don't approve of my marriage. Well, it doesn't really matter to me what you or anyone else thinks. I expect you to be civil to my husband, and to obey his orders, even if he is a Yankee. Now, you and Sarah take these bundles out back to the horses. I'm going to finish closing up the house."

Finally, the four of them were ready to begin their

departure. The three women gave a last glance at the beautiful white house, before riding away at a swift pace set by Brent. Katie constantly gazed over at her husband, savoring the rapture they had earlier shared.

My husband, she thought proudly. He is the handsomest man I have ever seen. He's also strong and courageous. It's really too bad we aren't on the same side of this war. I still believe in the South's cause, as I suppose he still believes in what he is fighting for. Oh, well, I love him too much to bicker about politics right now. Perhaps, after this war is ended, we can discuss it more thoroughly. Now, all I want to do during our brief time together is simply enjoy his presence, his affection.

As Brent led them along through the city, Katie noted the disturbing presence of hundreds of Union soldiers. She ignored their admiring looks and whistles and kept her head proudly erect. Thank goodness it was still so early; not too many of them were awake yet. Finally, the four of them reached the western limits of Atlanta. Brent dismounted and strode over to lift his wife down from her mount. Sarah and Esther remained on their horses and discreetly averted their gazes from the young couple.

"Katie, I can't go any further with you. I have to report back in a few minutes. Dawn is here now. Honey, I love you so much. I want you to go on home and stay put, do you hear? That is an order, Mrs. Morgan!"

"Well, I don't know about that, sir!" she responded, pretending annoyance at his tone, "I'll have to think about it, Mr. Morgan! Oh, Brent, take care. I'll pray for you constantly, darling. I love you so very much. I feel in my heart and soul that we will be together again. Send me word when you can. I'll anxiously await any message from you."

The two of them stood gazing deep into the eyes of one another. They embraced for one last time and tenderly, yet hungrily, kissed each other goodbye. Brent then led Katie back to her horse and lifted her upon its back. He swung up on his horse and began to ride away, waving one last time as he began to disappear into the distance.

Katie swept away her tears, sighed heavily, and tried violently not to break down and weep openly. She ordered the two slaves to follow as she rode toward the west, toward Corkhaven. She spared no glance for the city she had come to love, the city now occupied by the enemy, now awaiting destruction at Sherman's hands.

Before they had ridden far from the city, they came upon a small troop of Confederate soldiers and civilian refugees. As they rode through the center of the group, Katie glanced to and fro to see if she could spot anyone she might recognize. Finding no one she knew, she spurred her horse onward and continued upon the journey.

They rode throughout the morning and afternoon, stopping now and then to rest or water the tired horses. The day was hot and muggy, and they found it increasingly difficult to breathe as they rode. They encountered several other groups of people, but they merely rode onward and concentrated their energies upon reaching Corkhaven. As darkness began to draw near, Katie judged it time to make camp for the night. They rode into the same dense forest she had remembered from the earlier trip to Atlanta, and she spotted another troop of Confederates and refugees. She dismounted and instructed the two slaves to do the same.

"I think we'll camp here with the other people for the night, Sarah. Esther, you help her unload the horses while I find the commanding officer. I think I'll ask him if we can help out in any way." She left the slaves and strode through the camp until she came to a tent which appeared to be somewhat larger than the others surrounding it. She was stopped from entering by the sentry guarding the tent.

"Halt! What do you want here, ma'am?" he asked.

"I would like to see your commanding officer, soldier, I am on my way home, after leaving Atlanta. I wish to speak with him about your wounded, to see if there is anything I might do to help." The young man lowered his rifle and stood aside for her to enter the tent, saying:

"Ma'am, begging your pardon, but we ain't got no wounded with us. You can go on in and speak to the colonel, though."

Katie started to question him as to why they had no wounded, but she decided to speak to the commanding officer on the subject instead.

Inside, she found an older, stooped man bending over some papers. She noted the weary lines creasing his tired face. Surely this man had been further aged by the war.

"Sir, I am Katie O'Too...I am Katie Morgan. We, that is, I and my two slaves, wish to camp here behind your lines for the night, and I was wondering if I might be of any assistance with your wounded. I have had some experience, for I was a volunteer at the hospital in Atlanta. The sentry outside your tent informed me that you had no wounded, but I find that hard to believe."

The man turned around as she began speaking and ominously surveyed her. He impatiently listened to what she had to say, then he gruffly replied, "Miss Morgan, we have hundreds of refugees camped around and about our troops. You can do as you wish. As for tending the wounded, why, we have no wounded with us, just as the sentry informed you. We were forced to leave them behind in Atlanta as we evacuated."

"You left them behind to Sherman and his army?" she asked him incredulously.

"Yes, ma'am, that is what we had to do. Now, if you have nothing further to say to me, I am very tired and need to finish going over these papers before I can rest. We are marching quite a ways tomorrow. Good evening, ma'am," he said as he abruptly turned his back to her and once more resumed his scrutiny of the papers spread upon a makeshift table.

Katie hesitated for a moment, before she flounced angrily from the tent. What a sour old goat, she thought. Imagine, leaving his own wounded behind to be captured, or worse, by the enemy. As she stepped out of the tent, deep in thought, she almost collided with a soldier. He stepped back and slightly bowed as he allowed her to pass. Suddenly, Katie felt her arm held in a vise-like grip and jerked her head upward.

"Katie! Katie, what are you doing here?" a familiar voice demanded of her. She widened her eyes in absolute dismay. It was none other than Captain Richard Collins holding her arm so tightly.

"You! You unhand me right this moment, you fiend! I told you to never come near me again! Let go of my arm, or I'll scream!" she whispered furiously. He slowly complied with her demands, but he began to follow her as she made her way back to the horses and the slaves.

"Katie, I have been extremely worried about you, you little wildcat! I was afraid you had already gone home to your plantation. And, after our last little 'meeting,' I wondered if I would ever see you again. If I hadn't been ordered away from the city, I assure you that we would have completed our unfinished business," he told her with a lecherous grin upon his hawkish features.

"We have nothing whatsoever to say to one another, Captain Collins. After the shabby and disgusting way you treated me, I could kill you! In fact, I will kill you if you ever so much as touch me again!" she shouted at him in rising fury. She had reached the spot where the horses were tied, but there was no sign of either Sarah or Esther.

"Very well, go ahead and play coy, honey. I'll get you in the end, Katie," he laughed. "You see, I feel like we were meant for one another. You will be mine soon, you can mark my words on that. How long are you staying here?"

"That's none of your business! Now, go away before I call for help! I despise you, I loathe you! I never want to see your face again!" she cried as she stood glaring up into his hateful face.

He smiled a slow, secretive smile, before turning on his booted heel and strolling away toward the tent she had just exited. Katie remained where she stood, watching him as he went, noting the jaunty and self-assured way he had of walking. Oh, what a horrible creature! After he had nearly brutally raped her, he had the nerve to behave as if it had been a pleasant pasttime for her! She again longed for her husband, for his comforting arms about her. No, I can't dwell on him just yet, she firmly told herself, for, if I do, I won't be able to go home at all. I'll just have to turn right around and go on back to Atlanta and face everything with him, no matter what Sherman orders!

Sarah and Esther returned from a small pond in the woods, where they had gone to wash some of the journey's dust from their tired and aching bodies. They set about finding a secluded place to sleep for the night, while Katie informed them that she would also visit the pond and wash up after the long ride of the day.

"You two go on ahead and start supper. I won't be gone long. I simply must wash some of this dust off of me!" She picked up her gun and headed into the trees and underbrush. Once at the small, sparkling pond, she decided to plunge her weary feet into the water and sit for a while to rest. She removed her riding boots and stockings and lowered her feet into the coolness of the pool. She then removed the pins from her hair and shook it out, running her fingers through its thick masses to comb out any tangles.

She sat for several more minutes, then decided it was time to return to camp. She drew her feet up out of the water, dried them with the edge of her skirt, and put on her stockings and boots once more. She was pinning up her hair when she thought she heard someone approaching. Before she had the time to pick up her gun and aim it, she was grabbed by someone and the gun knocked from her reach.

"Katie, I told you I would have you. Now, do you come peacefully, or do I have to drag you along by your beautiful hair?" Captain Collins whispered menacingly in her ear.

Katie opened her mouth to scream, but only managed a small squeak before he had covered her mouth with his brutal hand. He lifted her off the ground and carried her along with him to the spot he had left his horse waiting. He threw her up on to the horse's back, and she had a moment to scream, which she proceeded to do as loud as she possibly could. He climbed up behind her and once more covered her mouth, then kicked his mount and began to ride away through the thick forest. His powerful arm was nearly cutting off her breath, so tightly he had placed it around her mid-section. He laughed into her ear as they rode, rejoicing in his triumph.

"You see, I told you that you would be mine, Katie. I knew that I only had to bide my time. I decided that this was the only way after you reacted the way you did back there in camp. I'll bet you thought I had forgotten you since that night in Atlanta, didn't you? Well, I could never forget you, Katie. You are my woman, and I expect that you will come to enjoy your new position in a very short time. We really are two of a kind, you know."

As they galloped along at a breakneck pace, Katie managed to free the upper part of her mouth and bit down with all her might into his hand. He cursed in pain, and she said, "You despicable worm! Are you also a deserter? I thought you were at least a Confederate soldier, even if you are obviously not a Southern gentleman!" she hissed.

"What does it matter to you, Katie? I'm your man now, honey. Besides, the South is doomed," he replied nonchalantly, "That's right, it's doomed for sure. If I had stayed with my outfit, I would have most likely ended up in some Union prison camp somewhere, or dead. No, from now on, it's just you and me. I think I'll head on towards the northwest, where we can make a new life for ourselves. Wouldn't you like that, honey?" he asked her with a touch of malice.

"I don't want to go anywhere with you! Can't you see that I despise you? It won't do you any good to keep me with you, for I will find some way to escape. I will never be your woman, no matter what you say or do!" she cried. He simply chuckled in return and kicked his horse onward.

Sarah and Esther had heard the scream Katie had managed as she was being abducted. They both ran to the small pond in hectic unison, arriving to find only Katie's gun to give evidence that she had been there. They looked at one another in growing alarm, and Sarah put into words her suspicion.

"I think somebody done carried our Miss Katie off, Esther! What we gonna do?"

"Well, let's go see if we can get some of these here soldiers to listen to us. Maybe one of them can help find her," Esther replied hopefully. They hurried back through the trees and approached the tent of the commanding officer.

The sentry stopped them at the entrance. They were so upset and excited that their speech was barely intelligible, but he managed to decipher the main gist of their story.

"Boy, we got to see your officer! Our Miss Katie done been carried off by someone or something! We got to tell him to go after her and bring our baby back!" Sarah babbled tearfully.

"Just a minute. I'll ask him if he'll see you. You two slaves wait right here." He disappeared inside the tent and emerged a moment later with permission for them to enter. They ducked inside at once and began to relate their story to the colonel.

"Sir, we beg your pardon, but our Miss Katie has done been carried off! We went to the pond where she was bathing, but there was only her gun there. We heard her scream one time, then no more. What are you gonna do about it? You just got to go after her and bring her back to us! You just got to! That poor child!" Esther told him in distress.

"Now, hold on, you two. Try and calm down so I can make some sense out of what you're trying to say to me. You there," he said as he nodded toward Sarah, "you tell me what happened, and tell me quickly. I'm a very busy man, and I haven't any time to listen to your incredible concoctions!"

"It ain't no concoction, sir!" Sarah replied with more spirit. "It's the truth! Miss Katie went on down to this here small pond out there in the woods, and we heard her scream a while back. We done ran on down there to see what was the matter, but she was gone. Only her gun was there. Someone has made off with our Miss Katie, and you just got to go and get her back!" She wouldn't back down from the man, even if he was a Confederate officer and she was just a mere slave.

"Oh, damn it! I can't spare anyone to go out and look for your wayward mistress! She's just probably gone off in the woods with some man she met here! Now, get out of here and leave me in peace. She'll turn up in a couple of hours. Private Stone, get these two slaves out of my tent!" he called to the sentry. "And, see that I'm not bothered any more tonight!" The sentry entered and forcibly ushered the two women outside and told them to go on back where they belonged.

"What we gonna do, Esther? What a mean thing for that man to say about our Miss Katie! She ain't gone off in the woods with no man, you and I both know that for sure! Who's gonna help our Miss Katie now?" Sarah asked, wringing her hands in despair.

"I don't rightly know, Sarah, honey. Maybe there's someone else here abouts who would help us. I don't think so, though. Ain't no one going to listen to two slaves, it appears."

Before they had gone very far from the tent, they observed a soldier hurrying inside to speak with the colonel. The sentry allowed him to enter, so it must be urgent. They crept in closer to hear what was being said. It just might concern their Miss Katie.

"Sir," the young soldier said, "Sir, it has been brought to my attention that Captain Richard Collins is missing! He has been gone for well over an hour, and no one seems to know where he has gone to! Should we send out a patrol to search for him, sir?"

"Blast it, man! Can't you see that I'm busy? I've got enough troubles without worrying about some officer that may have gone gallivanting around the countryside! No, you will not send out a patrol to search for him. Either he turns up or he doesn't. We will be marching again early in the morning, and I have scads of details to work out in the meantime. Now, get out of here and leave me to my work! This war isn't going too well, in case you hadn't noticed," he said sarcastically, "and I've got to try and do what I can to salvage our honor. That is all, soldier!" he barked. The young soldier saluted and left the tent.

Esther and Sarah had been able to hear almost every word uttered inside the tent. So, there was a soldier missing, too! He must be the one responsible for the disappearance of their Miss Katie! It was apparent that the colonel would offer no assistance. They would have to go on to Corkhaven and inform Katie's uncle of her abduction. He'd see that Miss Katie was recovered. What could two old slave women do, anyhow? Yes, that was the way of it, they would have to ride swiftly to Corkhaven and tell Uncle Albert.

Meanwhile, Katie was being forcibly held upon the back of a swiftly galloping horse. Captain Collins had uttered no further words to her, and her anxiety and fear were growing. What did he intend to do with her? Would he attempt to rape her again? Where could he be taking her? Surely the Confederate Army would hunt down a deserter. Oh, Brent, she thought, I'm glad you don't know what is happening to me right now. For, if you did, you would certainly desert, also, and come looking for us. Whatever happens to me, I'll always love you, no matter what this vile man may do to me. He will never touch my heart, even if he does violate my body. Oh, I can't stand the thought of being raped by him! The mere idea made her violently shudder.

After traveling far into the night, Captain Collins finally slowed his mount to a halt and jumped down. He reached his powerful arms upward and bodily lifted Katie from the saddle. She twisted, squirmed, and kicked, but he held her fast and carried her to a small clump of trees where he intended for them to camp for the remainder of the moonlit night.

"Put me down! I'll escape, you know. I won't stay with you. Oh, if I only had my gun, I could very well shoot you right this moment!" she told him as she struggled. He merely laughed and replied, "Go ahead and fight, my temperamental Katie! I thoroughly enjoy a woman who possesses the courage and spirit you have so frequently shown me. And, I intend to enjoy you in a different way, tonight, my dear! Now, I suppose I'll have to tie you to this tree in order to keep an eye on you while I make camp." He deposited her roughly on the ground and drew out some leather thongs. He wrapped the ends of them around each of her wrists and securely tied them to the tree. Katie could not move further than a foot or so. She sat glaring at him and began to try and reason with him.

"Captain, you are a Confederate officer. You will most assuredly be missed back at your camp. They will come looking for the two of us. Wouldn't it be wise to let me go? I will only slow you down as you run from them. Can't you see that?"

"Katie O'Toole, I admire your intelligence. However, I have already told you that I will never let you go. Until perhaps I tire of you, of course. That is for me to decide, though. I really don't believe that my commanding officer will send even one soldier out to look for us. He's much too busy planning his useless strategy to try and salvage some dignity in this war for the South. I'm smarter than you think, Katie—I already know that the war is lost. I think we'll go south to Mexico, instead of up to the northwest. They won't be able to find me there, even if they do ever hunt for me. What do you say to that, honey? How does Mexico sound to you?"

"You know how it sounds to me, you cowardly deserter! I will never stay with you! You would do better to go ahead and release me now. I'll escape the first chance I get. You can't keep me tied up forever!" she shouted at him.

"Oh, no?" he replied with a devious laugh. "I'll keep you tied up until you come to realize your good fortune, honey. In the meantime, you just sit back and relax. I'll see about rustling up some grub." He turned his back upon her and began to gather up wood for a fire. She decided to take his advice and relax. She would need all her strength to escape when she saw a chance to do so.

That same night, back in Atlanta, Brent was trying to sleep. He could not stop thinking of his wife, nor of their last night together. Sherman would indeed be ordering the complete evacuation of the city, so at least he was glad he had managed to get her out when he did. She would be halfway to Corkhaven by now. He only hoped that she had encountered no difficulty on the way. But, with both Sarah and Esther to look after her, he felt pretty sure she would be all right. She also had her gun. He knew full well how handy she could be with a gun! His mind traveled back to that first meeting with Katie, and he soon gave himself up to dreams of her.

The next morning, the remaining people of Atlanta would be forced from their homes. Sherman would allow absolutely no one to stay, not even the aged or wounded. He spared no compassion for any of the residents; they were merely a hindrance and a nuisance to his plans. His troops settled down now for a brief rest, while the cavalry protected their flanks and rear.

Captain Collins had successfully built a small fire and prepared a simple meal for himself and Katie. She took the plate he offered her, resolving anew to save her strength for the battle ahead. After they had finished eating, he re-tied her wrists and began to remove his clothing.

"What are you doing?" she asked him in alarm.

"Why, my dear, what does it look like I'm doing? I'm getting ready for bed. I thought we might get better acquainted tonight, seeing as how you will soon be my wife," he replied suavely and confidently.

"Your wife!" she exploded. "I will never be your wife, sir! For your information, I happen to be the wife of someone else!" She gasped as soon as she had uttered the words; she hadn't meant to tell him of her marriage. It might serve to enrage him and prove to further endanger her.

"So, you are already married, eh?" he asked as he narrowed his eyes, "And when was this so-called marriage supposed to have taken place? When I attended your ball, you were still being introduced as Miss Katie O'Toole."

"Well, it happened after I last saw you. Anyway, I am the lawful wife of a man, so I cannot marry you. You may as well release me now. As you can see, your evil dreams can never be realized."

"It makes no difference to me, honey. Oh, of course, I would have liked to have been the first man to taste your womanly delights, but I suppose I'll just have to settle for being the second, won't I? As for our marriage, well, you will just have to become my mistress instead of my wife. At least you know that I was willing to do the 'honorable' thing by you!" he said with a purposeful gleam in his dark eyes.

Katie widened her eyes in fright as he began to stride toward her. He had stripped down to wearing nothing but his trousers now, and he eyed her own clothing meaningfully and expectantly.

"What say you take off some of that finery, pretty Katie? Here, I suppose I ought to untie your wrists so you can enjoy it all the more. You can't run away from me, anyway, for we are the only ones around for miles and miles. You can scream now all you want to, for there will be no intruder to rescue you this time." He untied the leather thongs and sat back upon his haunches as she rubbed her painful wrists.

"I won't give in willingly, you foul creature! If you touch me, I'll mark your evil face for life!" she threatened with as much bravado as she could muster.

"All right, fight me. Go ahead and fight me all you like. It makes no difference to me, honey, for I mean to have you tonight! I've waited too long already!" he replied as he lunged for her. The force of his embrace knocked her backwards to the ground. He placed his own body over hers and began running his hands roughly up and down her soft curves.

Katie struggled as much as she was able, until he grabbed both of her wrists in one of his strong hands and proceeded to draw up her skirts with the other hand. She screamed again and again, knowing it was entirely to no avail. She searched her mind for some way to ward off his attack, and she finally managed to free one of her hands from his bruising grasp. She felt around on the ground for any kind of weapon she could use, and her hand suddenly seized upon a rock. She grasped the rock and drew it upward, holding tightly on to it.

By this time, he had managed to draw her skirts up around her waist and he was busy trying to free himself from his trousers. She brought her arm downward and struck him on the back of the head with the sharp rock. He had been so occupied with his cruel caresses, he did not notice her movements. She hit him with all her might and then watched in horrid fascination as his eyes rolled upward and his body slumped heavily upon hers.

"Oh, my Lord!" she exclaimed aloud. She eased her body painfully from beneath his unconscious form and knelt beside him to inspect the damage she had wrought with the rock. She observed the deep gash the rock had made in the back of his head, but she felt for his pulse and found it to be faint but still in evidence.

"Thank the Lord I haven't killed him!" she breathed in relief. She didn't want the blood of this man on her hands, no matter how evil he was or how much she detested him. She straightened her torn and disheveled clothing and hurried toward the horse. She gathered up the supplies and then mounted. Giving one last glance at the man who had so cruelly abused her, she kicked the horse and rode swiftly from the campsite.

As she rode, not knowing precisely in which direction, she reflected upon her relative good fortune. She had now twice escaped rape at the hands of Captain Collins. She had managed to survive his attacks with little more than a few cuts and bruises. She had no idea where she would now ride; she did not know in which direction Corkhaven would be. She only knew that she had to get as far away from her abductor as she possibly could. She gave the horse his lead and settled down for the remainder of the ride through the night. She would ride until the horse slowed, and she would leave her destination to fate.

Part 3

Dixie

Sixteen

While several of Sherman's troops remained behind in Atlanta to guard its walls and provisions, Sherman and the rest of his numbers followed the army of General Hood. For weeks, he pursued the Confederate leader in vain. Finally, he decided to return to Atlanta.

It was at this time that he conceived the idea of his infamous march to the sea. Brent and the other officers were then given orders for the destruction of Atlanta, being told to see to it that their men tore down the fine buildings of Atlanta; the machine-shops, the great depot, the round-house, and numerous other landmarks were destroyed. There were enormous heaps of rubbish covering the sites of buildings every where, and the torch was applied to the vast debris. Sherman's army was then prepared to march. Atlanta lay in ruins.

Brent was called in to appear before his commanding officer some days before the march was to get underway. He entered the building and stood at attention.

"Captain Morgan," the officer said, "your orders have been changed. It seems now that you are needed in our intelligence force. You are to ride to Savannah and contact our man there; his name and location are written upon this piece of paper. Memorize it and then destroy it. I do not need to remind you that all of this is top secret. It seems that our intelligence men find your particular qualifications necessary, although I cannot see why. Anyway, you will mount up and ride out tomorrow morning. You will be furnished with civilian clothing. Are there any questions, Captain?"

"Yes, sir," answered Brent, "what about my men, sir? Whose command will they be placed under after I'm gone? You see, sir, we have been riding together during the course of this entire war, and I hate to be parted from them at such a crucial moment."

"They will be assigned to someone else, Captain, and it need not concern you whose command it will be. If that is all, you are hereby dismissed." The officer saluted and turned his back. Brent controlled his anger at the man's obviously disapproving attitude and strode from the tent.

Damn! Ordered to Savannah, the intelligence force there. What possible qualifications could the man have been talking about? Well, there was nothing for it, he would have to follow orders. He hated leaving his men, just as they were about to embark on the great march. Sergeant Duffy would see that they received fair treatment, however, of that he was sure.

Oh, Katie, he thought, when will I ever get to see you again? Savannah was on the eastern seaboard, quite a few days away from Corkhaven. It wouldn't matter, for he wouldn't get any leave until he was either wounded again or the war ended. My dear wife, he entreated her silently across the miles that separated them, I want you to be patient. I'll send you word somehow about my change in plans. He didn't even know if he would be staying in Savannah, or assigned elsewhere. Perhaps he could get a letter to her from Savannah.

Meanwhile, Katie had ridden without much pause throughout the night, her horse now beginning to show signs of complete exhaustion. She had to find some place to ask directions. She searched the countryside for any farms or plantations but she observed nothing, except for a few charred ruins. She gently urged the poor horse onward, but he refused to budge. She wearily dismounted and led him to a stream for watering. She would have to allow him to rest and graze for a while before she could hope to ride him again.

Where in the world am I? she wondered. She hoped

that Captain Collins had now recovered. He would be without a horse, and so would be slowed down considerably and certainly unable to follow her right away. Perhaps he would be able to return to his camp. But, no, they would most likely be gone by now. She hoped that Sarah and Esther had gone on to Corkhaven without her.

Sarah and Esther. She had completely forgotten about them until just now! They must be frantic about her disappearance. Surely they would have sense enough to go on home. With a bit of luck, she herself would be able to emerge at Corkhaven within a few days.

As she sat down upon a rock, thoughts of Captain Collins and her husband occupying her confused and disjointed mind, she suddenly heard the sound of hoofbeats approaching. She jumped up in alarm and hurried to hide behind some underbrush near the stream where her horse was thirstily drinking. She waited and peered through the tall bushes so that she could see who or what was coming her way.

Two men on horseback were riding beside a wagon, which was being driven by two women. Oh, thank goodness, she breathed in relief, for they appeared to be other refugees from Atlanta, judging from the way they had piled belongings into the wagon. She judged it safe to hail them and she stood up to call.

"Hey! Hey, you over there! I'm lost! Could you please help me?" she shouted across the grassy land.

The two men halted and sighted her, standing and waving her arms. They turned their horses and began to ride toward her, while the women driving the wagon flicked the reins and turned the wagon to follow. They reached her in a matter of just a few moments.

"Howdy there, young lady. What in tarnation are you doing out here all by yourself?" the man directly in front of her asked. The two men had by now dismounted and the women were climbing down from their perch upon the wagon seat.

"Hello. I'm lost. I became separated from my party and have been wandering all night. Could you please give me some directions?" she asked smilingly. She was vastly relieved to see them, and she almost hugged the friendly man.

"Well, missy, you're about ten miles north of Atlanta. You do know where Atlanta is, don't you?" he asked.

"Yes, of course, I have just come from Atlanta. I mean, before I got lost yesterday evening. You see, we were leaving the city and traveling west, toward my family's plantation. It seems that I have traveled much farther than I expected!"

"Honey, you do look plum tuckered out, at that!" said one of the women. She was an attractive woman of about thirty years of age, while the other woman appeared to be about five years younger and less comely, but equally as kind.

"Yes, why don't you let us introduce ourselves? I'm Miranda, and this here is Julie, and these two men are Jake and Robert. What's your name, honey?" the younger of the two women inquired.

"I'm Katie Morgan. I'm very pleased to meet all of you," she replied. She supposed that the two couples were all related in some way. But then, the woman hadn't introduced the men as their husbands. And, these certainly didn't seem like the sort of woman she had heard about, the kind that would latch on to a man for a while, for so-called protection and security.

Miranda sensed her confusion as she peered into Katie's face and laughingly said, "Katie, we ain't living together or nothing like that. These two gentlemen have kindly offered to escort us to our destination, that's all. You see, we're also fleeing Atlanta. Now, why don't you have a meal with us? We've got plenty, I assure you."

"Why, thank you very much. I'm absolutely famished at that!" she replied gratefully.

Jake and Robert led their horses to the stream and then returned to unhitch the horses pulling the wagon.

Miranda and Julie drew out their provisions and utensils and began preparing the meal. Katie offered to help, but they wouldn't hear of it.

"Miranda, you didn't tell me any of your last names. I'm sorry that I ever thought that you and Julie were anything less than honorable women, but I didn't know what else to think," Katie said by way of apology.

"That's all right, honey. Anyway, I'll tell you now. I'm Miranda Archer, Julie's last name is Banyon, and that's Jake Teller and Robert Duran," she informed her, then changed the subject and asked, "Are you from Atlanta, Katie?"

"No, as I told you, I was traveling to my family's plantation when I became lost. I was in Atlanta visiting relatives when Sherman came. My husband is away fighting, and he and I happened to see one another in Atlanta, before Sherman came. What about you all? Where are you from, and what were you doing in Atlanta?" Katie asked curiously.

"Well, we're all from different places," she quickly answered. She paused a moment, then asked, "Katie, are you a loyal supporter of the South?"

"Why, of course I am, Miranda! I was born and raised right here in Georgia, and I would do anything I could to help the cause. What ever gave you the idea I wasn't?" she replied staunchly.

"Nothing at all. I just thought I'd ask. You can't be too careful who you talk to these days. Julie," she said, turning to her companion, "do you think Jake and Robert would mind if I explained to Katie?" Katie wondered what she was referring to, but she remained silent.

"I don't know, Miranda. Maybe we better ask them first. I'll go on over and speak with them. I know what they're going to say, though, and that's that we shouldn't rush things." She stood up from the fire and strolled over to the two men. Katie observed their glances toward her as they conversed, and she was becoming terribly curious about what could be so important to explain.

Julie returned momentarily and nodded to Miranda, who then said, "Katie, what I'm about to tell you is very secret. You mustn't reveal any of this to anyone. Do you promise?" she demanded sternly. Katie nodded in agreement, marveling at the quick change in the woman's speech. Why, she has a very cultured voice, she thought. A moment ago, she sounded as if she was straight off a backwoods farm.

"Well, you see, we aren't just ordinary citizens fleeing from Sherman and the Yankees. We work for the Confederacy. That's right, Julie and I help smuggle medicine to our troops, while Jake and Robert act as our escorts. We travel together, but Jake and Robert are married, while Julie and I are both army widows. We had to do something to help the poor men who were suffering without so much as a drop of ether. There is a great shortage of any kind of medicine throughout the South."

Katie listened to her story, hesitated for a moment, then replied, "I wish I could do what you two are doing. I greatly admire you and the men, and I am thankful there are people like you to help the cause. I worked at the hospital in Atlanta, and I know what a shortage of medicine can do. I saw the hundreds of men in agony, the doctors and nurses frustrated by the lack of something to ease the pain of their patients. Why, though, did you trust me enough to tell me all of this? You just met me a few minutes ago."

"Well, because out here, there is no one for you to tell if you are indeed a Yankee spy. Secondly, because I trusted you from the first moment I saw you, as I guess the others did also. Jack and Robert gave their permission so it must be all right."

"Those two don't trust too readily." Julie stepped in to say. Katie smiled at her in return and replied:

"Very well, thank you for your confidence in me. Where are you all from, anyway? And, what were you doing in Atlanta? You surely weren't able to smuggle medicine into the city, and there simply wasn't any for you to smuggle out."

"We were in Atlanta on 'business' and we had to leave rather abruptly. We had delivered a shipment of medicine there, but that was back before the siege began. We couldn't leave after that, because it became too dangerous for us to cross the lines. It seems that they broke our cover somehow, and there were warrants issued by one of Sherman's top-ranking officials for our arrest and imprisonment. You see, Katie, even though all we smuggle is medicine, we are considered to be Confederate spies. Anyway, I am from Nashville, while Julie here is from Richmond. Jake and Robert are both from Alabama. We've traveled all over the South, though, since we started this over two years ago," Miranda said.

Katie sat in silence, pondering what the amazing young woman had just revealed to her. So, there were actually people trying to help the wounded. There were people courageous enough to risk imprisonment to smuggle a few bottles of precious medicines. She wondered what Brent would think of such people. He would most certainly admire their bravery, she concluded. What would he say if I were to undertake such a task, she then wondered. He wouldn't like it at all, but he wouldn't even know about it. And, as long as he didn't know about it, he couldn't be angry with her or worry about her. Perhaps she was meant to be abducted, perhaps she was meant to encounter these four people. She had always wanted to do more than just help out at the hospital, she had always wanted to help the suffering in more ways than merely talking to them and holding their hands. This was surely a way she could be used. What good would it do to go on back to Corkhaven and sit and wait? She would send word to her mother that she was safe and unharmed.

"Miranda," she began haltingly, "what would you say if I wanted to come along with you and help? I can do it, I know I can. I'm not really needed at home, and I'll manage to send them word about my whereabouts. As for my husband," here she paused, her breath quickening at the thought of him, "he is away fighting and won't be home until this war is ended. What would you think if I traveled with you and became a medicine smuggler such as yourself and Julie?"

Julie and Miranda looked at one another in satisfaction and approval, then Julie nodded to her friend and jumped up again to fetch Jake and Robert. Finally, they all assembled around the fire and discussed Katie's proposition.

"Katie," Jake began patiently, "you really don't know what you are saying, honey. I don't think you're aware of the dangers involved. If you are captured, you will be imprisoned, maybe even shot! We need you, that I can't deny, but you mustn't get into this venture with your eyes closed."

"And," Robert added, "what would your husband say if he knew? Julie told us he was away fighting, but what if he should arrive home looking for you?"

"He won't," Katie insisted. "He told me himself that I won't see him again until the war is ended. And, as for the dangers, I understand completely. I know it will be hazardous, but I want to do it. I've sat at home for the majority of this conflict, and I want to continue trying to help in some way, the way I tried to do in Atlanta. If you need me, why won't you just agree?"

"All right, honey, welcome to our 'family.' Do you think it wise, though, to use your real name?" Julie asked.

"Well, I don't really know. Aren't you all using your real names?" she asked.

"No, we aren't, and we don't have the right to divulge our real names. When we undertook this assignment, we were told never to tell anyone our real names, for fear of reprisal upon our families. Of course, our families don't know about what we're doing. You can't tell your family, either, so you'll have to make up a story about why you aren't coming home," Robert answered.

"Very well, I'll change my name then. How about," she said as she racked her brain for a suitable alias, "how about Katie Brent?" Oh, Brent, it's the least I can do, she thought with amusement. This way, no one would connect her with her husband, nor with her family.

"That's fine. Now, how about some breakfast? We'll explain some of the other details afterwards," Julie suggested.

The five of them sat around the campfire and began to eat, discussing all the while the various details of the venture Katie was about to undertake. She listened with utmost attention, resolving to be one of the best medicine smugglers they had ever seen. A sudden picture of Brent crept unbidden into her thoughts; the picture of him totally outraged at what she was about to do, instead of staying home safe and sound as he had ordered. Oh, Brent, she again thought, I can't sit idly at home waiting for you. This way, the time will pass much more quickly for me as well as for you. And, as for the danger involved, why, I'll be more careful than I have to be. Uncle Albert wouldn't like it one bit, either, but he would just have to accept it. At least he was at Corkhaven to look after her mother and brothers. She began to become excited at the prospect of the new adventure she was sure lay ahead.

Captain Collins had awakened to the bright sunshine of the morning with a severe pain in the back of his head. He managed to rise and now stood looking around for any sight of Katie or his horse.

Damn the red-haired vixen! he cursed silently. She had nearly killed him, and now she had run off with his horse! What was he to do now? He couldn't return to camp, even if he was able to find it again. Where would he head now? He bathed his aching head gently in the cool stream and sat down to think about his predicament. He finally decided to begin walking toward the north. He would find a horse somewhere, and he would find Katie. She would pay dearly for the injury she had dealt him, for the theft of his horse. He would have her yet, but he would make her suffer first.

Brent dressed in the civilian clothes he had been provided with the previous evening, following his talk with the commanding officer. He was now ready to begin the journey to Savannah. It felt strange to be out of uniform, the first time he had been such since he had enlisted. If only Katie could see me now, he mused, she would see quite a difference without the sight of the familiar blue uniform. I no longer look like a "Yankee," I look like a gentleman farmer. He had already taken leave of his men and Sergeant Duffy. It had been a painful farewell for them all, but he must put the thought behind him and be on his way. He left the building and mounted his horse, turning it toward the east. He could reach Savannah within a week and a half, providing he wasn't stopped and questioned by any troops along the way. He now appeared to belong to neither side, a prospect he viewed with less than favor. However, he had his orders and must follow them to the letter. He pulled the slip of paper from inside his coat and read again the name of the man he was to contact, then tore it to bits and let the pieces flutter away on the wind. He shouldn't be too difficult to find, thought Brent, but I still wonder what sort of business they need me for. Spying wasn't exactly what he had joined up to do.

"Where are we headed for, anyway?" Katie asked of Miranda as the five of them continued on their way.

"We're going to Nashville first, Katie. We are to receive the medicine there and then head on to Savannah. It entails an awful lot of traveling, but we can't travel so that anyone can track us, you understand. As I already explained, you will hide the medicine in the special pockets we will sew into your petticoats. Why, you can carry hundreds of bottles that way. We've carried quite a number in the two years we've been smuggling," Miranda said proudly.

The three women rode upon the wagon seat, with Jake and Robert riding escort alongside of them. They traveled quickly throughout that first day and it took them another week before they finally spotted Nashville in the distance. During that time, they had acquainted Katie with the details and dangers of the smuggling operation, and she was instructed exactly how to carry the medicine, and what to do if she was ever detained and questioned.

"Don't ever let on that you are anything other than a simple Southern lady. Try and speak as if you are royalty or something, Katie," Julie told her. "You are the only one of us who can carry it off. Miranda and I will have to continue speaking as if we are farm wives because no one would believe us if we said we were fine Southern ladies. You, though, certainly have the look of a duchess!"

"Oh, Julie, I don't know what you're talking about. Why, it's quite obvious that you and Miranda are educated. Why can't you just act like yourselves?" Katie responded.

"Because, we have to say that Jake and Robert are our husbands sometimes, and they certainly don't appear cultured! Anyway, you will be known as our rich, widowed cousin."

Katie spent hours sewing many pockets into the multitude of petticoats she would be wearing. She was shown how to place the bottles carefully into the pockets and how to walk as if she had nothing to hide. Julie and Miranda loaned her a few of their finer dresses and showed her how to conceal the bulges the medicine bottles sometimes made in the dresses.

As they rode into the city of Nashville, Katie looked around in wonder. Surely, this city was even finer than Atlanta! She observed the many people occupying the boardwalks and streets, hoping anew that there would be no one there from Atlanta or from home who would recognize her. She now had a new identity; Katie Brent, a wealthy widowed lady from Georgia.

They put up in a rather shabby hotel for the night,

resolving to save their funds for any emergencies that might arise on the trip to Savannah. Julie and Miranda took Katie with them when they went to see their contact, a man by the name of Frederick Varney. Jake and Robert remained outside.

"Frederick, this is Katie Brent. We met her on the way here. She has expressed a desire to help us out in our cause. We've already questioned her and warned her about the dangers involved, but she is still willing to continue," Miranda told the small, stocky man wearing the thick glasses. He was seated behind a desk in an old storeroom near the hotel where they were staying.

"Katie, welcome. Since you already know all about us, suppose you tell me something about yourself. Are you married? Won't your family question you about your activities? What will you tell them? What makes you think you are in any way qualified for such a dangerous mission?" He questioned her rapidly.

"Well, Mr. Varney, I am married, but my husband is away fighting. As for my family, I intend sending them a letter telling them that I am safe, but I will not tell them of my destination, nor of my new business. They will be unable to reach me, so you needn't worry about them. They are in Georgia, and they won't be able to question me," she answered calmly. She knew full well that the man was trying to make her nervous, but she wouldn't give in to his badgering.

"Yes, well, what about those qualifications I asked about? Young lady, just who are you? Are you sure you aren't a Yankee spy? Are you sure you can keep your mouth shut about our operations?" he insisted.

"I am not a Yankee spy! I am a true and loyal subject of the South, of the state of Georgia. I was born and raised on my family's plantation. I am a Southern lady, and I know how to keep a secret! I resent your implications that I am any less!" she said as she began to raise her voice. She tried to control her temper.

Frederick Varney studied her intently for a few moments, then said, "Very well, Katie Brent. That will be all for now. Will you please wait outside that door there? I want to speak with your two friends here in private."

Katie did as she was bid and slipped quietly out the door and stood waiting. A few minutes later, Miranda and Julie called for her to enter once more and she was addressed by Mr. Varney.

"Katie, you are assigned to assist Julie and Miranda as they take the medicine to Savannah. You will be traveling through enemy lines, and you must not waver. If you think you will have any doubts or apprehensions, now is the time to get out and never look back."

"I'm well prepared, Mr. Varney," Katie answered with a proud lift of her head in answer to his challenge. "I already know what to do, as I have had very adequate teachers in these two. Now, when do we start?"

Mr. Varney looked at Julie and Miranda and then suddenly smiled with satisfaction.

"You are very anxious, my dear, but that will wear off, I assure you. You will leave Nashville the day after tomorrow, and I advise you all to rest up before you begin the long and dangerous journey. Julie, please tell Jake and Robert to come and see me now. You may return to your hotel. That is all, ladies. Good luck and may God be with you." Katie smiled at him in return and the three of them returned to the hotel.

"He certainly is a hard task master, isn't he?" she commented to Miranda.

"Yes, but he is a kind person, and he knows his business well. He only had to treat you that way to be sure you would qualify, Katie. Now, you are duly approved and recorded. Come on, let's go on up to the room and get some rest. Julie, are you coming?"

"No, you two go on ahead. I'll be up later," she replied.

"All right. Katie, I don't know about you, but I'm thoroughly exhausted!"

However, when they were in the room and undressed for bed, Katie began to question Miranda about her life and her late husband.

"Well, I was born and raised right here in Nashville, but my family no longer lives here. My father is dead, and my mother and brothers have all moved away. Mr. Varney enlisted my aid over two years ago. I met him through a mutual acquaintance here in the city. As for my late husband, he was killed nearly three years ago. We had no children. What about you, Katie, where's your husband now? Where did you meet him?"

"I met him at my home in Georgia. Its name is Corkhaven, for my late father was a grand Irishman! Anyway, I've only been married for a few months, and my husband and I haven't been able to spend much time together. The last I heard, he was near Atlanta, but I don't know where he is now. What about Julie, what about her family and husband?" she asked as she steered the conversation away from herself.

"Oh, Julie is very secretive, you'll find. Her husband was an officer and I'm not exactly sure where or when he was killed. They had a little boy, but he died of diphtheria when he was only two. Julie doesn't talk about either of them a great deal, but I feel she carries a heavy sadness in her heart. I don't know anything about her family, for she never mentions them. Katie, you're so lucky your husband is alive. I only hope he remains so until this war is won," she said as she yawned and climbed into bed. Katie nodded in agreement and then snuggled down into the covers to sleep.

Yes, dear Lord, keep him safe and alive. If only Julie and Miranda knew the truth about his identity. But, they need never find out, for I will keep it a secret. Brent, where are you tonight? My darling, I love you. Wouldn't it be a strange coincidence if we were to meet along the way to Savannah? No, you wouldn't like that at all, would you? Katie finally drifted off to sleep.

The next morning, she and Miranda and Julie decided

to explore the sights of the city. Since Miranda had been raised in Nashville, she had several places she wished to show her friends. They would spend the day in rest and relaxation.

Miranda took them on a complete tour of the city, meeting several of her friends along the way. She never offered to introduce her two friends, but they didn't seem to mind. Katie marveled at the size of the city, being completely unused to what she considered to be a large metropolis. Atlanta had also been large, but Nashville appeared more so. Then again, Atlanta had been preparing for a siege when she had first seen it.

Katie wrote a quick letter to her mother and had it posted. It would take many days to reach Corkhaven, but at least her family would know she was safe. As for Captain Collins, she never expected to see him again. Perhaps he had died where she left him. No, he had still been alive, and had most likely recovered and found his way to a farmhouse or somewhere for help by now.

Brent was still riding swiftly toward Savannah at that moment, having spent a restless night hidden in a small grove of trees. He had now turned toward the southeast, heading straightaway for the coast and Savannah. Sherman would be approaching along the same route. But, of course, he would be arriving long after Brent. With an army numbering near sixty thousand, the progress would be slow indeed. However, Sherman had divided his army into two immense wings and they were to march by four roads, keeping as nearly parallel as possible. Soldiers were forbidden to enter private homes along the way, but this rule was not strictly enforced. The foraging parties were to take everything they deemed necessary; horses, wagons, etc.

Katie, Miranda, Julie, Jake, and Robert left Nashville early the next day. They would travel by a little-known route to Savannah, trying to avoid any confrontations with Yankees. Katie was to be known as Miranda's cousin, who was to be known as Jake's wife. Julie and

Robert were also paired. Katie was dressed in much finer attire than the other two women, as she was to be introduced to anyone as a wealthy widow, a genteel lady of Georgia.

They traveled throughout the morning, encountering no other people. Later on in the afternoon, after they had already taken a brief rest for lunch, they came upon a camp of Federal soldiers. They were immediately halted by the sentry.

"Halt! Who are you people? What are you doing here?" the young Yankee soldier asked them as they approached. There were tents erected everywhere, and the soldiers appeared to be sitting idle.

"Hello there, young fella. We're farmers, and we've been driven from our homes by this here war. We're on our way to join up with some relatives of ours in a small town near Atlanta. This here is my brother and his wife, and this is my wife. Yonder sits her cousin," answered Jake respectfully.

The sentry eyed him warily and then demanded:

"You got any extra provisions in that wagon, mister? Especially any salt or sugar?"

"No, I'm afraid not, soldier. You see, like I done told you, we was driven from our home, and we was barely able to escape with our lives and a few sticks of our furniture. Now, is it all right if we go along on our way? My wife there ain't feeling too well, and it'll be near nightfall soon."

"All right, go on," said the Yankee. He had orders to not accost any civilians, but he had toyed with the idea of seizing the wagon and making a thorough search of its contents. However, it would mean his hide if the commanding officer got wind of it. Jake and Robert spurred their horses and Julie flicked the reins once more. They continued on their way.

"Why did they stop us?" Katie asked. "What could we possibly have that they would want?"

"Honey, those soldiers are a long way from home, and

198

they most probably thought we might have something they could use. It doesn't matter, you'll have to get used to that sort of treatment. The thing is, just behave normally and don't act suspiciously. Even our own troops will make us stop, and sometimes they'll even demand to search the wagon. However, no one yet has thought of searching under a lady's petticoats to find what they're looking for!" Miranda remarked as she chuckled at the thought. "We haven't had anyone yet try and search me or Julie, although they have done so to the men."

"Well, I'd like to see them try and search me!" Katie commented decisively.

They camped for the night and Katie gladly stepped out of her petticoats. She had carefully wrapped each individual bottle of precious medicine and secured them in the pockets, but she was still happy to remove them from her and be able to relax for a while. One had to be so careful not to break any of the bottles, and the petticoats were so heavy.

They traveled for more than three weeks and came across several more camps of soldiers along the way. There were no other incidents to speak of, for they were quickly allowed to pass at each station, and they soon began to near their destination. The night before they were to enter Savannah, Julie and Miranda discussed the plans with Katie once more.

"Now, you are to take your cargo to the hospital there, while Julie and I will enter after you. We can't be seen entering together, so we'll go in one at a time. There are Yankee spies and informers everywhere, and we can't take any chances, even in a Southern city."

"I understand," replied Katie. "But, why such secrecy? I mean, why would anyone suspect us in the first place?"

"Well, word has gotten around," Julie answered, "and there are people who know our faces. We've covered most of the major cities in the South during the past two years. We've been stopped quite a few times, but they couldn't find any evidence to hold us, even though they suspected what we were doing. We had already delivered the medicine, thank goodness. We've also had some traitors in the ranks, too, and you have to be careful."

"Very well, what do we do after we've delivered the medicine to the hospital?" Katie asked.

"Well, we stroll on out and return to the hotel room. Then, we have to find our contact and receive our next orders. Sometimes, we're assigned to remain in the city for a while and smuggle medicine to some of the surrounding camps. There are Yankees everywhere now, so there are times it is necessary for the organization to use us near the city."

"I see. Well, I for one am not too very frightened about tomorrow. In fact, I'm rather looking forward to the whole thing. It will mean that I've succeeded on my first assignment!"

"We've been lucky this time," cautioned Miranda, "for we haven't even been searched, which is very fortunate. Like we told you, they never search our persons, but we've had the wagon searched quite a number of times. And, we're not in Savannah yet, so anything could still happen. The toughest part is still to come; the area around the city is thickly infested with Yankees."

They ceased their conversation and retired for the night. Katie was unable to sleep very well, so excited was she at the thought that she had actually become a successful medicine smuggler for the South. She knew that Brent would disapprove, but he would admire her for it just the same. She hoped that he would be able to send word to Corkhaven. Sarah would see to it that the letter was kept safe until her return. She didn't know precisely how long she expected to continue with this adventure, but she wanted to be home before the war ended, of course. How, though, could anyone know when it would end?

Seventeen

Brent slowly rode along the streets of Savannah, grateful again for his civilian disguise. He could imagine only too well how he would have been greeted had he been wearing his blue uniform. Now, he thought, I've got to find the Nugget Livery Stables and find a Mr. Watson. He's supposed to be my contact, and I only hope that he is aware of my new assignment to him. Brent continued along his way, stopping once to ask the way. He arrived at the stables and dismounted to go in search of the mysterious Mr. Watson. He entered and found a man bending over an anvil, hard at work pounding upon a red-hot horseshoe.

"Excuse me, mister. I'm looking for a man named Watson. Could you please tell me where I might find him?" he asked the man.

The blacksmith looked up from his labors and said:

"Out back there, mister. He's the tall fella wearing the red shirt. You can't miss him." He then resumed his pounding and Brent walked in the direction he had indicated by a nod of his head. He found a tall man wearing a red shirt and approached him.

"Mr. Watson?" he inquired.

"Yes, what is it?" the man answered.

"My name is Brent Morgan, and I was told to contact you by..."

"Quiet, man! You want someone to hear you?" the man cautioned. "Come on inside and we'll talk there." Brent followed him as he entered the stables and ducked into a vacant stall.

"Mr. Morgan, hasn't anyone ever told you about our agency's policy of secrecy? Don't ever approach anyone like that again, you understand? You have to be a bit suspicious of everyone, no matter what they tell you. Now, I'm Colonel Frank Watson. You, I presume, are the young captain they promised me. How do you do, Captain?" The two of them shook hands as if nothing out of the ordinary was taking place.

"Colonel..." Brent began.

"Call me either Frank or Mr. Watson from here on out, never Colonel," he broke in.

"All right, Mr. Watson," Brent amended, "why have I been assigned to your organization? I was told that I possessed specific qualifications that you thought necessary, but, I must confess, I am completely ignorant as to what those qualifications might be. I was told absolutely nothing, only to come to Savannah and contact you."

"Mr. Morgan, you were not told so that you could not divulge anything should you have been discovered on your way here. I had not had the chance to speak with you yet, and we thought it necessary that you remain ignorant about any details. Your qualifications are simple, but very necessary. You, as I have been informed, are married to a Southerner, a native of Georgia."

Brent widened his blue eyes in surprise. How could the man know of such a thing? Who could have told him, when he was so far away from Atlanta and Corkhaven?

"I can see that my words have rather astonished you, Mr. Morgan. Let us deem it sufficient to say that I have my sources of information. Anyway, you are familiar with the Southern people, are you not? You spent some time on a Southern plantation, and you have traveled extensively throughout the South during the course of this war. I need a man like you. I need someone who knows their customs and habits, their ways of speech. Does that answer your question?"

"Mostly, sir. Say that I do have the qualifications you need; why do I have orders to join the intelligence force?

202

What is my particular assignment to be?"

'Well, you have been highly recommended to us by a high-ranking official within our organization. You have therefore been assigned to us upon request. Your orders, for the time being, are to gather information, any kind of information, that we might find useful. To do such a thing, you have to be able to travel freely throughout the South. Perhaps your wife could be of assistance to you there?" he inquired hopefully.

"No, sir, my wife is at home at her plantation. She, although I suppose you already know, is a loyal supporter of the Confederacy. Now, where do I go from here?"

"First off, you must check into the Baker Hotel. You will familiarize yourself with the city for the next day or so, then come and see me again. Keep your eyes and ears open for anything you may overhear in the meantime. Needless to say, you are to discuss what has been said here with absolutely no one. We have other agents throughout the city, and they will be contacting you. One other thing, Mr. Morgan," he added, "we have received word that there are medicine smugglers due here in the next few days. Keep an eye out for anything that might look suspicious. The other agents will also be watching. Now, if there are no more questions, you may go."

"Thank you, sir. I'll see you again soon." Brent sauntered out of the stables and mounted to ride to the hotel. So, they know all about me, he thought. They know all about Katie, too, evidently. He wasn't at all sure he would like this new assignment of his. He didn't much like the idea of spying. Thank goodness Katie wasn't here in the city, he thought, for they'd try and involve her, too. She wouldn't like it if she knew about his new orders. No, not at all. He'd have to send her word somehow about his change in orders. Of course, he couldn't say anything about his change in great detail, but he could simply tell her he had been ordered elsewhere, away from Atlanta, away from Sherman's army. She'd have been home for a few days by now, and he liked to think of her at the beautiful spot in the woods, where he had followed her so long ago.

Katie, contrary to Brent's thoughts of her, was not at home. She and her four companions were riding near the city at that moment. They had been halted by a Confederate troop as soon as they were within sight of Savannah, but nothing untoward had occurred. They were now approaching the western limits of the city, and Katie again felt supreme satisfaction at the success of their adventure.

"Miranda, when do we go to the hospital?" she asked.

"Well, we'll let you off near the hospital as soon as we get into the city, honey. We'll wait for you across the street. Julie and I will then go in a few minutes later on. You seem rather excited about it, don't you?" she asked Katie with a small amount of amusement.

"Well, yes, I suppose I am. I've never done anything like this before! How long do you think we'll be staying in Savannah?"

"Katie, don't ask so many questions," Julie admonished her. "You'll find out soon enough. One thing you learn in this business, you have to have patience."

Jake and Robert had begun riding ahead of the wagon by now, so as to avoid any congestion in the narrow street they were traveling on. They were nearing the center of the city, where Katie knew the hospital would most probably be located. Sure enough, they drew up across the street from it in a matter of minutes.

"Now, remember, Katie, don't tell anyone why you're here. Just ask to see Dr. Morrow. He'll take care of everything," Robert whispered as she jumped down. She nodded without turning and strolled across the street, forcing herself to remain outwardly calm and casual.

She entered the hospital and asked a passing nurse for the whereabouts of Dr. Morrow.

"He's down the hall to your right, young lady."

"Thank you," Katie replied as she continued on her way. She knocked on the doctor's office door and was told to enter by a deep voice within. She opened the door and then closed it behind her.

"Dr. Morrow?" she inquired tentatively.

"Yes? What is it, young woman?" the middle-aged doctor asked.

"I'm Katie Brent, sir, and I've come to you by courtesy of Frederick Varney."

"Well, well, come in, child, come on in. Here, sit down for a moment while I fetch one of the nurses." He left her then to call a nurse, and returned to stand directly before her.

"Miss Brent, you're new to this, aren't you? Yes, I can see that you are. Well, it will all be over with in just a moment. You have done very well your first time out. Oh, Nurse Freeman," he said as she entered the room, "do come in. Miss Brent has just come to deliver our medicine. I'll leave you two for a moment, since I know you will have to remove the petticoats." He left the office and stood guard outside in the hallway, keeping a sharp eye out for anyone approaching.

"Come on, honey, we haven't got all day!" the nurse snapped impatiently. Katie closed her mouth tightly, endeavoring to swallow a tart reply to the woman's abruptness. She raised her voluminous skirts and removed the many petticoats from underneath them. She and the nurse then removed the bottles from their secure pouches and placed them upon the desk.

"That does it, Miss Brent. You may go now. The doctor and I will see to everything else," the nurse told her with authority.

"Oh, you're quite welcome, too," Katie couldn't refrain from replying, noting that the woman hadn't even had the courtesy to offer any thanks for the risk she had run. Outside, the doctor thanked her and she left the hospital to rejoin her friends. However, when she arrived out in the street, she found no trace of them. They were not where she had left them, and she frantically searched the streets near the hospital for any sign of them.

She was becoming rather frightened that they may have gone off and deserted her, although she couldn't understand why they would go and do such a thing. No, there must be a reasonable explanation, she told herself firmly. They must have had to move along for some particular reason.

As she began to walk toward the hotel she had earlier heard Miranda mention, Katie forced herself to slow her walk and then glanced speculatively about to see if she could spot any of her previous companions. Unknown by her, she herself was being carefully observed from around the corner of a building along the same street.

Katie! Here in Savannah! How in blue blazes did she come to be here? Brent asked himself angrily. He was more than angry; he was totally furious and astonished at finding his wife so far away from the home he had thought she would now be occupying. He knew that he must speak with her at once, without drawing undue suspicion to himself. He left his observation point and began to approach her from the rear. She obviously appeared to be searching for someone or something. He still couldn't believe it—his own wife, here in the same city as himself! Enough of that for now, he sternly ordered himself, first I've got to find out what she's doing here, and just why she chose to disobey my orders to return to Corkhaven.

Katie continued nonchalantly upon her walk, telling herself that she would soon have to stop and ask someone where the hotel was located, since she had evidently forgotten its precise location. She had almost panicked when she had come out of the hospital back there, but she knew that she was under control now. Where could they be? Before she knew what was happening, she found her waist firmly encircled by a strong arm and she was being propelled down a side street. She glanced at the person forcing her along, and found herself utterly speechless. Brent! It was her own dear husband who was holding her so commandingly and forcing her into a secluded area of the city. How in the world did he come to be in Savannah?

She almost wept with joy and relief at seeing his beloved face, until she realized that he didn't seem as equally happy to see her own.

"Katie O'Toole Morgan! Woman, what are you doing in Savannah? Why aren't you back at Corkhaven, as I told you?" he demanded in a furious undertone. He tightened his hold upon her waist and glared down into her green eyes and upturned face.

"Brent, don't be so angry! Aren't you even glad to see me, darling? And, besides, what are you doing in Savannah, must less me?" she retorted.

"Katie, I swear, I could shake you until your brains rattle! I ought to turn you over my knee right here and now and spank you until you can no longer sit! I told you to go home and stay there. It appears that you have complete disregard for my wishes, doesn't it?" he ground out between clenched teeth.

"Well, Brent, it's a long story. You aren't even giving me a chance to explain, are you? And, don't you dare threaten me, Brent Morgan, for I'll scream as loud as I can if you so much as give me one shake! Now, what are you doing in Savannah? And, what are you doing out of uniform?" she asked him with more spirit. She was becoming rather frightened and apprehensive at his tone.

"Katie, you have a lot of explaining to do, and this just isn't the place. As for my being in Savannah, I'll explain that to you later. Now, where are you staying?" he asked her with a quiet, yet still deadly tone.

"I don't know, Brent. I've become separated from my friends. They mentioned a certain hotel earlier, the Hotel Savannah. I was on my way there when I was so rudely accosted by you! You look as if you're about to explode!" she told him teasingly, which did nothing whatsoever to ease his boiling temper. He growled out a curse and clamped an iron hand on her upper arm to lead her along the way. Several minutes later, they arrived at the hotel and Katie stepped up to the desk to request a room. She also inquired if anyone had left a message for her, which the desk clerk answered in the affirmative. It seemed that a Mrs. Archer had requested that Miss Brent meet her in the hotel lobby at three o'clock that very afternoon. Katie thanked the man and turned back to Brent.

"What's this about your name being Katie Brent?" he demanded.

"Brent, let's go on up to the room and talk."

"You're damn right we're going to go on up to the room and talk!" He took her arm in the firm grip once more and led her unyieldingly up the stairs to the room. She unlocked the door with the key and walked inside. Brent entered and slammed the door behind him. Katie almost quaked in the face of such a white hot anger. Never had she seen him so angry before! But, she was certainly not a coward and so would face up to him squarely.

"All right, Katie, sit down on the bed there and start explaining. Go on, sit down!" When she hesitated, he forced her roughly down upon the bed and then pulled up a chair in front of her. She gulped and then began speaking.

"Brent, please calm down and try to control your temper. It wasn't my fault, I assure you! Well, at least it wasn't my fault that I was waylaid from going on home. You see, I was abducted from the camp that first night after we left Atlanta." She went on to relate to him the story of her abduction by Captain Collins and the story of her subsequent escape.

"And then, I met up with the four people I mentioned earlier. They told me where they were going, and I decided to go along with them," and here she paused and gathered courage, "and, Brent, here comes the part you will like the least of all. They told me that they were medicine smugglers for the Confederacy, and I decided to join them!"

"Smugglers! Katie, are you out of your mind? Don't you know how dangerous smuggling medicine for the Confederacy is?" he shouted at her. At least this last part she had confessed had turned his mind away from his murderous anger toward the fiend who had assaulted her.

"Please, Brent, lower your voice! Yes, I was told that there was a certain element of danger involved. But, as I told you, I decided that I would help them. I became separated from them just before you found me. It seems, though, that they will be meeting me downstairs at three o'clock, so that is settled."

"Is that what all this is to you, Katie, an adventure? Don't you know that you could be arrested and imprisoned for spying? Katie, you can't possibly know what you have become involved in! It doesn't matter now, for you are going home, even if I have to drag you all the way back to Corkhaven myself!"

"Brent," Katie answered him defiantly, "you haven't yet told me just what you yourself are doing in Savannah. Don't you think you owe me an explanation, also?"

"Katie, I can't tell you precisely what I'm doing here. All I can say is that I have been re-assigned to another division. These civilian clothes are a necessity. I don't know how long I'll be here in Savannah. I was planning to write to you and tell you that I had been ordered away from Sherman's army. However, that is not the main concern just now. You do realize, that as a Union officer, I should report your activities to my superiors here, don't you?" he asked her sternly.

"Yes, certainly. And, you do realize, don't you, that, as a loyal citizen of the South, I should report the presence of a known Union officer to the authorities, don't you?" she retorted with spirit.

Brent looked so thunderous, she almost backed down. He appeared as if he were indeed going to carry out his earlier threat of beating her, but she faced him defiantly and then smiled seductively.

"Oh, Brent, darling, enough of this quarreling. I know that you're really glad to see me, even if I have disobeyed your orders. Can't we cease this discussion for a while and be happy with our time together? I have to meet with my friends in a couple of hours."

"Katie, you are the most exasperating, infuriating . . ." he paused and took a deep breath. "Of course I'm glad to see you! You are the only one who has ever been able to make me as totally angry as you have today, but you are still the most lovable woman in the world! I'm still angry with you, but I guess you're right. There's no sense in us wasting our time together, is there?" he said as he smiled meaningfully. Katie opened her arms to him and he quickly joined her on the bed. They had two hours in which to overcome his anger, in which to renew their love for one another. Katie surrendered her waiting lips to his, and entwined her arms about his neck. He kissed her long and passionately, feeling the familiar stir of desire he always experienced whenever he was near her. He slowly and expertly began to undress both himself and her, and they finally lay naked to each other's loving gaze.

Katie sighed deeply and said, "Oh, Brent, it seems like ages since you've held me like this."

"And who knows when it will be again, Katie? Now, shut up and concentrate on your husband!" he demanded teasingly.

Katie sighed again and gave herself up to the marvelous sensations assailing her body. Brent continued to kiss her slowly and hungrily, traveling from her lips to her neck and then to her swelling breasts. Katie moaned in ecstasy and arched her body beneath his. Brent taught her even more about the delights of love, and he was certainly an able teacher, while she was assuredly an apt pupil.

Finally, when their energy was spent, they lay back and snuggled closely together. Katie felt the love and contentment she always experienced after their lovemaking, and she closed her eyes in peace.

Two hours later, after resting and then resuming their passionate embrace, Brent rose from the soft comfort of the bed and his wife's loving arms and began to dress. Katie threw back the covers and began to follow suit, hurrying because it was nearing three o'clock.

"Brent, what am I going to tell them?" she asked him again.

"Katie, I positively forbid you to go on any longer with this escapade of yours! You are to tell them that you have to go home, that you have seen your husband and he has ordered you to do so. It's the truth, and you had better do as I say if you know what's good for you. I'll have to find some way to get you back to Corkhaven safely."

"Oh, Brent, can't I stay with them a bit longer? I mean, after all, I told them that I would help them. I've only been on one assignment. I can't see that it would hurt to stay with them until they travel closer to Corkhaven."

"Absolutely not! Now, enough of this, woman! You are to tell them you are leaving for home, and that's that. I'll meet you back here in your room sometime this evening, understand?"

"I understand, Brent," she replied with a sigh. "By the way, can't you even tell me a little about why you're here in Savannah?"

"No, not at this time, darling. I'll explain to you someday, but not now. I don't think I'll be in Savannah that much longer, anyway. I'll send you word once you are at home. And, I do mean at home!"

"Brent, can I at least remain here with you for a few days? I don't see how you're going to get me safely home, anyway. I'm all by myself now, what with Esther and Sarah already at Corkhaven," she suggested.

"Well, I suppose I'll have to send word to your uncle. He'll have to come and fetch you, you little baggage! That will take at least two weeks, so you'll have to be with me as long as I remain here in the city. There, does that satisfy you?" he asked her. She came over to put her arms around his neck and then kissed him gently and lovingly.

"Yes, that satisfies me, Captain Morgan," she purred.

"Not 'captain' for now, darling—Mr. Morgan. That's something else you'll have to keep quiet about. I've got to go on to my own hotel now. I'll see you later on this evening. Try and see if you can stay out of trouble until

211

then!" He kissed her once more and then left the room.

Katie watched him go and, in a few minutes, left the room herself, making sure to lock the door behind her. She descended the stairs and entered the downstairs hotel lobby to search for any sign of her friends. She found Miranda and Julie seated on a sofa and hurried over to them.

"Miranda, Julie, where in the world did you all go to?" she asked.

"Katie, we're so sorry about that! You see, we saw a Federalist agent we know. Actually, he works for both sides. He's here in Savannah under cover, but he knows about our operation. We can't reveal his identity, for he would then reveal ours. And, his Yankee superiors would see to it that we were captured right away. As it is now, he is biding his time and watching us like a hawk. We had to leave rather quickly. I knew that you had heard me mention this hotel, so I came here to leave a message for you. Julie and I have already been to the hospital to deliver the goods. What have you been up to for the past few hours, Katie?" her friend asked her as she peered closely at Katie's glowing features.

"Oh, Miranda, the most wonderful thing has happened! My husband is here in Savannah, and we happened to find one another while I was out looking for you all. And," here Katie paused, "he has ordered me to return home. He has forbidden me to have anything further to do with you and the others. I'm very sorry, but there isn't much I can do about it. I never dreamed that I would run across him here in Savannah! The last I saw of him, he was in Atlanta."

"In Atlanta?" Julie questioned her as she had a sudden thought. "I thought you said that he was stationed near Atlanta. Sherman's troops occupied Atlanta before you left, didn't they?"

"Oh, that's what I meant. He was stationed near Atlanta, but the last I saw of him, he was in Atlanta, before Sherman arrived. Anyway, I'm dreadfully sorry. I

212

did so want to help you. I dare not cross him again. He was exceedingly angry that I was not at home!" she told them confidentially.

Miranda glanced at her and then said, "Katie, you could go ahead and help us, you know. What would your husband know about it if you did? He won't be home until after the war. The chances of you two running into one another again are very unlikely. What do you say? We do so need your help. You have been an invaluable accomplice to us, you know."

"Oh, I only wish I could. I'll try and persuade him to change his mind. I'll be in Savannah for at least another two weeks or so, at least until my uncle can arrive to take me home. I don't think I'll be successful, but I'll try. The only thing is, will you all be staying in Savannah for that long?"

"I really don't know, Katie. I'll keep in contact with you, though. Julie and I are staying on the third floor, in room 345. Please let us know if you need anything. Jake and Robert are staying next door to us. Like I said, I'll contact you again. Meanwhile, take care, Katie Brent. Thank you for the help you have given us, even if you are unable to continue." With that, Miranda and Julie arose and walked up the stairs. Katie watched them as they went, not at all sure that Julie wasn't a bit suspicious about the while thing.

There must be some way I can go on and help smuggle medicine, she thought. Suddenly, she hit upon what she thought would be an excellent plan. She could pick up the medicine that Miranda and Julie would be receiving from Nashville, and she could smuggle it with her when she left Savannah with Uncle Albert. She'd ask Miranda about it, for she wasn't sure if they would actually be receiving any more medicine for a while.

Yes, thought Katie with satisfaction, she could at least do this one last thing. Brent would never know. She would simply ask Uncle Albert if she could visit a Confederate medical station, saying that she wanted to see how a particular friend had fared. At least she could do this one last thing for the South, before she was relegated to spending the remainder of the war sitting at home, waiting for her husband to return.

Katie smiled to herself as she climbed the stairs to her room. Brent would be arriving back here within a few hours, and they might even have as much as two weeks together before he was again ordered away. She suspected what his new assignment might be, but she would not attempt to discuss it with him. It was obvious that he had received strict orders not to reveal his plans to anyone, not even his own wife. She needn't worry, for she would find out in her own good time.

Eighteen

Captain Richard Collins rode silently along the busy, winding streets of Savannah. He had traveled far and fast; all the way from Nashville in the matter of less than three weeks. He was weary, but he was determined. He would find Katie O'Toole if it was the last thing he did upon this earth.

"She'll regret the rebuttals she dealt me. Damn her vixen hide!" he spoke aloud. Several people gazed curiously at the Confederate officer as he rode, speaking furiously to himself. However, in these times of war, they were quite accustomed to seeing peculiar or strange sights, so they thought nothing much of the stranger.

He had tracked her as far as Nashville, then had temporarily lost her, afraid that it would be forever. He had chanced upon a man at the hotel where Katie had stayed, and the man distinctly remembered overhearing the ladies discussing some sort of trip to Savannah. So, Collins mounted up and rode with vengeful haste toward that city. He would find her yet, and he would make her suffer.

Brent returned to Katie's hotel room early in the evening. He knocked and called out to her, and she quickly flew to open the door to her husband. He had some rather unfortunate news to impart to her, and the sooner he got it over with, the better.

"Katie, honey, sit down. I've got something to tell you that neither of us is going to like. It seems that I've been ordered out of the city for a couple of weeks, maybe even

215

longer. But, I'll be right back after that. I've still got to send that message to your uncle. I'm sorry, darling, but it can't be helped. Orders are orders."

"Oh, Brent, this is getting ridiculous! During the entirety of our married life together so far, we've only been able to spend two whole nights together! I suppose you can't tell me what's so all-fired important for you to leave just now?" she complained. Torn apart again!

"No," he replied calmly, "I can't tell you anything about it. You know that I can't. Anyway, I'll only be away for a couple of weeks, and then we may have the remainder of the time it takes for your uncle to get here. Katie, I'm truly sorry. You don't know how much I looked forward to spending some time with you. I know you can't want it any more than I do."

"Brent, it's just that I'm so tired of always having to bid you goodbye! I'm your wife, for heaven's sake, but I feel more like a once-in-a-while fling!" she angrily retorted. She was becoming teary-eyed now, and he didn't seem to care at all.

"Katie, I hate it as much as you do. Now, be a good girl and don't cry. I've got to leave in a few minutes." He attempted to pull her into his embrace, but she struggled free.

"In a few minutes! Why, I thought you could at least wait until morning!" she exclaimed.

"No, I've got to leave now. Katie, come on and don't be angry with me. There isn't just a whole lot I can do about the situation. I'll be back before you're gone, and then we'll spend several days together. Come on now and kiss me, dear wife. This is war, Katie, and we all have to make sacrifices. Why, there are many wives who never get to see their husbands at all," he reminded her. He truly did detest being separated from her again, but he had to maintain control over his emotions, or he'd certainly never be able to go.

Katie pondered thoughtfully his words for a moment, then said, "Oh, Brent, you're right. I'm acting like a child.

I do so love you! I'll miss you terribly, that's all. What am I going to do without you the next several days?"

"You're going to behave yourself and not get into any more trouble, Katie Morgan! You can look around the city, do some shopping. Things like that. I've got some money here that I'll leave for you, as I'm sure you're running low on funds at the moment. Now, I've really got to get going. I love you, darling. Come on and kiss me goodbye."

Katie clasped him tightly and kissed him very thoroughly. He returned her embrace with fervor, before pulling himself away with determination. He placed his hand lovingly upon her cheek, then strode to the door and flung it open. He left without looking back again, knowing full well that it would only weaken his resolve.

It was at times like this that made him sorry he had ever become involved in this hateful war! Here he had a wife he never got to see, a new assignment he knew very little about, and a uniform he was no longer allowed to wear. Morrow had given him his new instructions this afternoon, after Brent had left Katie at her hotel room.

"Mr. Morgan, we've received word of some Confederate intelligence activities near Charleston. You and one of the other agents are hereby assigned to travel there and find out all you can about their operations. You are to leave immediately. The other agent's name is William Woodson. He'll get in touch with you at your hotel room as soon as you leave here. He'll also explain your assignment more fully to you. Are there any questions?" the colonel asked.

"No, sir. That is, if this Mr. Woodson will be explaining everything to me in more detail. How long do you think I'll be gone, sir?" he ventured to inquire.

"Oh, not more than two or three weeks, I'm sure. I need you both back here by then. This is sort of a trial run for you, Brent. Of course, it is an actual assignment, but it's certainly not the most important mission you will be given. We'll see how you do with this one."

"Thank you, sir. If that's all for now, I have some business to attend to before I leave." Brent left as he was given permission and hurried to inform Katie of his altered plans. He was fully aware that Colonel Morrow must know about his seeing Katie, but the man would probably not be aware of the fact that she was Brent's wife.

Now, he and the other agent were riding swiftly toward Charleston. They wouldn't be entering the city, just scouting around its southern edges. Brent sincerely hoped that his fellow agent knew what he was doing. If they were caught, it could mean hanging.

Meanwhile, Katie sat forlornly on the bed in her room, reflecting anew upon the ill fortune that had constantly beset her brief marriage. She couldn't sit around and fume or sulk the whole time, so she had best get herself up and see about some dinner. She suddenly realized that she hadn't eaten a thing since early that morning. Perhaps Julie or Miranda would want to take dinner with her. She couldn't see the harm in just eating with them, even if Brent didn't want her to see them again.

She got up and straightened her crumpled dress, then quietly left the room and climbed the remaining steps up to the third floor of the hotel. She knocked on the door, but, receiving no answer, she decided that she would surely have a chance to talk with them later. She descended the stairs and walked out of the hotel to stand outside in the cool evening air. It was beginning to become quite chilly in the evenings now. She would have to keep her shawl drawn closely about her body. She stepped down on to the boardwalk and began leisurely strolling across the dusty street to the restaurant she had earlier noted.

Captain Collins crept slowly out of the shadows of the hotel, where he had been waiting for Katie since late afternoon. He had successfully traced her to the hotel, having received information from a contact he had looked up here in Savannah. His contact was a rather wily

218

character, a double agent of sorts. He had been questioned by Collins and had definitely remembered the beautiful young woman with the red-gold hair. She had been traveling with some acquaintances of his own.

So, this was finally it. He had her, entirely defenseless and all alone at last. She wouldn't be able to escape so easily this time, he'd make sure of that. First, though, he'd put a little scare into her, make her squirm a bit. He sauntered across the street and entered the restaurant a few minutes behind her. He glanced about the room and noted her presence at a table far in the corner. She hadn't yet seen him; that was good. He approached her table, then turned his back and seated himself at the table only a few feet from her own. He sat down comfortably and awaited her observation of him. His gaze swept over her body, her lovely appearance. Yes, this was going to be the best revenge he had ever taken. Afterwards, he supposed that he might just have to go ahead and kill her; some women were such a damned nuisance after a man had had his way with them.

Katie studied the menu before her, grateful that Brent had been thoughtful enough to provide her with money. She finally decided on a small steak and potatoes, then lowered the menu and started to drink the water the waiter had set before her. Before she had swallowed, she saw the Confederate officer seated across from her at the other table. He was looking directly at her. She quickly set down the glass and hastily arose from the table, almost upsetting the other chairs as she stumbled.

Captain Collins merely remained where he sat and evilly leered at her as she watched him. He wouldn't make his move yet; no, she had seen him and knew that he would be coming for her. That was enough for now. He'd go on up to her room in a few minutes and have his pleasure of her. On second thought, he decided, perhaps he'd just go ahead and eat his dinner first. She'd have more time to contemplate the fate that lay in store for her that way.

219

Katie rushed back across the street and frantically climbed the stairs to her room. How in the world had that man found her? He must have known someone who had seen her and her companions. Perhaps he had been watching her all along, perhaps he had even been in Nashville. She shivered at the thought of that creature watching her, waiting to reach out and envelop her with his wickedness. She had to think about what to do now. She had to think of some way to get out of town safely. With Brent absent for some time, she had no protection whatsoever. No one would believe her if she told them she was being ruthlessly stalked by a Confederate officer.

She returned to the third floor and pounded on her friends' door once again. This time, Julie answered the knock and stood back as Katie rushed into the room. Miranda was seated upon a chair, and it appeared as if the two women had been preparing to go out. Katie took a deep breath and said:

"Miranda, Julie, I need your help. Remember my telling you about that Confederate officer who abducted me and attempted to rape me? Well, he's here in Savannah. In fact, I was across the street in that restaurant, and he came in and took the table next to mine! He didn't say anything at all, he just sat there cool as you please and smiled at me. What am I going to do? My husband is away for a while, and I don't know where else to turn." She attempted to gain control over her thumping heart and labored breathing.

"Katie," began Miranda, "there's only one thing you can do." Here she paused and looked to Julie for confirmation. Julie nodded.

"You've got to come with us. We've received orders to travel right away to Charleston and there receive a shipment to take to Richmond. You might as well come with us, because it looks as if there isn't any other way. Your husband will just have to understand. I'm sure he would want you to be safe with us, instead of waiting around here for that villain to find."

"And, Katie," said Julie, "we do still need your help so desperately. This is an awfully large amount of medicine we're to pick up in Charleston. It will take all three of us to transport it all. Now, I don't see as if you have any other choice but to come with us, do you?"

Katie thought long and hard about their suggestion. Brent would be terribly hurt and angry that she had once again disobeyed him. But, once again, she had to get away from Captain Collins. She couldn't stay here and wait for him to pounce upon her. Oh, dear, she thought, I don't know what to do. She was grateful for the silence of her two friends. They were giving her a chance to consider all the possibilities. Finally, she swallowed hard and made her decision, resolving to leave Brent a long letter, explaining everything and telling him where she would be going.

"All right, I'll go with you. When do we leave?"

"We leave first thing in the morning, Katie. You can sleep here with us for tonight. He won't know where to find you that way. Now, why don't we hurry on down to your room and gather up your things? You can leave your husband some sort of message, deleting our exact destination, of course. Then, you can leave your room and move in here with us for the night. Come on, we'd better hurry before he comes," suggested Miranda.

The three of them hurried down to Katie's room and collected all of her belongings and then locked the door behind them. Katie went downstairs to the desk and quickly scrawled a message to Brent, ignoring Miranda's warning that she not mention their destination. Of course she would tell him that, in case he wanted to come after her. After all, he wouldn't inform on his own wife! Miranda and Julie wouldn't understand, though, especially if they knew her husband was really a Yankee. They still believed he was a Confederate officer. Strange, she mused, that they would mind my telling a Confederate soldier of our plans. I guess they must have to insist on absolute secrecy.

She handed the sealed letter to the desk clerk and returned upstairs to the third floor. She reported that she had not seen Captain Collins, but that he would surely be coming soon.

"We'd best go out and get some food and bring some back for you, Katie. I'm sure you're absolutely famished. Come on, Julie, let's go on so we can hurry back," said Miranda. The two of them left the room, instructing Katie to keep the door locked and to open it for no one but themselves.

An hour later, they returned with a covered plate of food for Katie. After she had eaten, they turned out the lamps and retired for the night. Julie had contacted Jake and Robert regarding the quick change in plans when they had left for dinner.

Captain Collins decided to wait until late that night to go to Katie's room. He had asked the desk clerk for the room number of Katie O'Toole, but there had only been a Katie Brent listed in the register. Collins surmised that this was probably his Katie, for she would most likely be using her married name by now. He supposed that Katie must certainly be even more frightened of him than he had previously believed.

He crept up the stairs to her room and tried the door, only to find it securely locked. He considered breaking it down, but he knew that such an action would arouse someone else within the hotel. He decided to leave, vowing silently to return early in the morning. She couldn't leave before then, for her friends were still in town. And, from what he'd heard, they'd be staying a while.

Before sunrise the next morning, Katie and her friends arose and dressed. They packed their bags and went next door to meet with Jake and Robert, who were impatiently awaiting the arrival of the women. The five of them tiptoed down the stairs and hurried across the street to the livery stable where they had boarded the horses and wagon. Katie's gaze swept the deserted streets, but she saw no sign of Captain Collins. It appeared as if she would be able to leave town without his knowledge after all.

Jake and Robert hitched up the wagon horses and then mounted their own. Katie and the two women climbed aboard the wagon seat and they all started on their way. With luck, they would be in Charleston within the week. There, they would stop over for a few days and then collect the medicine to begin the long journey to Richmond.

Katie's apprehensions lessened as they rode further away from Savannah. She knew with a certainty that they had left the city undetected. Captain Collins would surely be unable to trace her this time. Her companions had told no one they were leaving, merely paying for another day in advance at the hotel, so that it would appear that they would be staying that extra day.

She again thought of Brent and of his dismay when he returned to find her gone. The letter she had left for him would explain everything, but she still knew that he would be angered at the recent turn of events. He had made it all too clear to her that he thoroughly disapproved of what she and her friends were doing. However, she wasn't the slightest bit afraid of being caught; she didn't even give it a second thought. No one would ever suspect a young and beautiful Southern lady of smuggling medicine.

She wondered once more about Brent's new assignment. She knew that it must involve some sort of intelligence work, but she didn't really know that much about such movements. She had heard about them, and she knew that Brent's life would be in danger. Oh, dear Lord, keep him safe. Someday, I want us to live together as a man and wife should, to raise a family.

Brent and Woodson had ridden throughout the night. They were now stopping to rest, to allow their tired mounts a chance to drink and graze for a while. Brent wondered what Katie would be doing right now. She would be mighty lonesome for the next several days, but he knew she would find something to occupy her time.

223

She had a decided knack for finding ways to occupy her time! Anyway, they would be back in Savannah soon and he would show her how much he had missed her. He still hadn't sent that message to her uncle. He supposed it was because he didn't really want her to go home at all. As long as he was stationed in the city, he wanted her there with him. Oh well, he'd have to send the message sooner or later. She needed to be back at Corkhaven, where he wouldn't have to worry about her so much.

Captain Collins hurried to the hotel just before dawn and knocked once again on Katie's door. There was still no response from within, so he went back downstairs to check with the desk clerk.

"Is there still a Miss Katie Brent in Room 202?"

"No, sir, I have a note here saying that she's checked out. That's all it says, it don't say where she was going or anything. She did leave a message here for someone. What's your name, mister?"

"I'm Captain Richard Collins, an officer in the Confederate Army. Did she leave any clue as to her destination? What about those friends of hers, the other two women?"

"I ain't got no idea where that little lady has gone, just like I said. As for her friends, why, they're still here. They've even paid me for another day in advance."

Collins turned his back on the clerk and strode angrily out of the hotel. Damn! He'd apparently lost track of her again. Where could she have gone to this time, especially since her friends were still here in the hotel? She surely wasn't with them, or so he believed. If she were up in their room, he'd find her tonight. He wouldn't care about causing a disturbance; he had to find her, for he'd had her right here in the palm of his hand, and she had somehow managed to disappear! Somehow, though, that just seemed to make the prospect of finding her even more delightful. She was a wily little cat and he would have to show her who her master was.

Katie and her friends reached Charleston with no

224

incident. They put up in one of the hotels for the night to get a good night's rest. They'd collect the medicine the next morning, but they wouldn't have to leave for Richmond for a couple of days. Katie was to stay in the same room as Julie and Miranda, for she was still too frightened that Captain Collins might have found some way of following her.

They had received their orders; they were to smuggle the medicine through the lines, into the city of Richmond. They had previously planned to drop off their cargo to a contact outside of the city, but that had all changed. It would be a long trip, wrought with more risks than they had previously had to take. It might even take as long as four or more weeks to reach the city, and Katie felt uneasy qualms about the extended length of time it would be before she would be returning home. She knew that Brent would like it even less, but he would most likely never know. That is, unless he had received permission to follow her, which she seriously doubted. Well, she'd already committed herself for this assignment, and she couldn't go back on her word now.

Several days later, Brent returned to Savannah. Instead of finding himself being welcomed by his loving and hopefully obedient wife, he found a message waiting for him at the desk at the hotel. He tore open the seal and began to scan its contents, a wave of different emotions playing across his handsome face as he discovered the contents of the letter.

She's done it again! was his first thought. As he read further, he reflected on the reason she had given for leaving without waiting for him to return. So, that same Confederate captain had tracked her to the city, had seen her. Poor Katie, she must have been scared stiff at seeing that scoundrel here in Savannah. No wonder she hadn't waited for him to return. She was gone now, but what was worse, she had resumed her involvement with those medicine smugglers. No telling what else they were. From what he had heard, they weren't merely smuggling medicines. Katie was enmeshed in something she didn't know anything about.

Brent thanked the desk clerk for the message and then left the hotel. He'd already reported back to Colonel Morrow, but he'd now have to go and speak with him again. He simply had to gain his permission to travel to Charleston. At least Katie had enough foresight to reveal where she was going. If he could only reach the city before she had again disappeared, he would see to it personally that she was returned home to Corkhaven! He didn't know exactly how he could wrangle it, but he'd do it, come hell or high water!

Several hours later, Brent returned to the hotel and asked to see the room his wife had occupied. The clerk was dubious about the whole thing, but he finally relented. After all, the room hadn't been rented out again, so it couldn't do any harm. Brent took the key and climbed the stairs. He unlocked the door and began to search the room for anything Katie might have left behind. He was hoping that he might find another letter or message for him within the room, but he found nothing. He didn't know exactly why he had wanted to see the room, it was simply a feeling he had. As he straightened from searching under the bed, the door was suddenly flung open and Brent just had enough time to duck down by the side of the bed.

Captain Collins surveyed the room, but it appeared empty. He'd returned to this room every day since Katie had disappeared, but to no avail. It had cost him plenty to keep that clerk quiet about this. It seemed that Katie's friends had now gone, also. He kept hoping that she'd return here, but it appeared that his hunch was mistaken. As long as he was in the room, he might as well make another search of it. If she had left some clue, anything, it would satisfy him for the time being.

Brent watched as the stranger entered the room, trying to keep his breath low and steady. Maybe this was the same man who had been so intent on terrorizing Katie. I it was indeed that villain, heaven help him. For he, Katie's husband, would see to it that the man never bothered her again.

Brent stood up quite suddenly and threw Collins completely off guard. Before he had time to reach for the gun at his belt, Brent had covered the short distance between them and had knocked the other man to the floor. The Confederate officer managed to gasp:

"Who the hell are you? What's going on here?"

"You know damn good and well what's going on! Your name is Collins, isn't it?" Brent ground out in return. He kept the man effectively pinned to the floor.

"Yes, but who are you? I don't know who you are, but you've got to be crazy or something! I only came here looking for a friend of mine."

"Yeah, and I know which 'friend' you're talking about, you coward! Katie just happens to be my wife! Come on, stand up and fight like a man, even if you aren't one!" Brent stood and allowed the other man to rise, then brought his fist up into Collins' face as hard as he could. Collins shook his head as if to clear it, then returned the punch. Although he was heavier and an inch taller than Brent, Brent was more agile upon his feet.

The two of them grappled for several minutes, Collins beginning to yell obscenities about Katie at Brent. Brent was taking a beating, but it was nothing compared to the one he was administering to the other man. Suddenly, Collins lost his footing and fell back toward the closed window of the room. Brent yelled a warning at him, but it was too late. He crashed through the glass and went hurtling to his death, down to the dusty street below.

Brent hurried to the window and peered out through the broken pane. Sure enough, down below, there lay Captain Richard Collins, sprawled grotesquely in the dirt. He was quite obviously dead.

Brent gingerly rubbed his bruised knuckles and wiped the blood from his nose. He walked slowly to the door, opened it once more, and locked it behind him. He climbed down the stairs and handed the key to the desk clerk, who had already heard the commotion out in the street. He took the key with a startled expression upon his face, but Brent simply ignored him and left the hotel. He didn't bother to approach the dead man lying in the street. He mounted his horse and rode away.

He hadn't meant for the man to die, but it was perhaps better this way. After all he'd done to Katie, and attempted to do, the man didn't deserve to live. Now that he had received permission from the colonel to travel to Charleston, he'd best be on his way. He wouldn't spare any more time or thoughts for the cowardly Captain Collins.

He'd had a devil of a time convincing the colonel to let him go off to Charleston, but he'd finally persuaded him with the argument that he could gather loads of information within the city, and, if need be, he could travel elsewhere. Things were slowing down quite a bit here in Savannah. His job certainly wouldn't be neglected. He would send word through the list of agents he had been given. Colonel Morrow had been reluctant, but he had finally agreed. Brent suspected that he already knew at least something about Katie, that she had traveled the same way.

This last job he had been sent on had worked out well indeed. Perhaps that was why the colonel had given his consent for the trip to Charleston. Well, it didn't matter what the reasons were, he was going, and he was going alone. He had to find Katie, he had to see that she was returned home. He had enough to worry about, without his darling wife leading him a merry chase all over the South. Oh, he loved her more than life itself, but he couldn't tolerate much more of this!

Nineteen

Katie, Miranda and Julie had already collected their supply of medicines and were now on their way back to the hotel to prepare to leave Charleston. It was still relatively early in the day, so they decided that it would probably be safest if they were to be on their way as soon as possible.

Katie hated to leave Charleston; she kept hoping that, somehow, Brent would be able to follow her. However, the wish he would appear and claim her appeared to be ungranted. They had now been in Charleston for five days. When they had first arrived to collect the medicines, they were informed that the shipment had not yet been delivered. So, they were consequently forced to wait patiently for another four days until it finally did appear.

Oh, Brent, I hope I did the right thing in leaving Savannah, Katie thought again. I was just so afraid of Captain Collins doing me harm. Katie O'Toole Morgan had been afraid of very little in the course of her young life, but she had found herself very much afraid when she had faced that man across the tables in the crowded restaurant. She had experienced a feeling of complete helplessness and defenselessness.

As they finally departed from Charleston, Katie took one last look at the city, willing her husband to miraculously appear out of its depths. She sighed heavily and turned back around on the wagon seat. She supposed that she now wouldn't see him again until she was home at Corkhaven and the war had ended. She might as well make the best of her time before that occurred.

She adjusted her petticoats and skirts as she sat upon the hard wagon seat. Miranda and Julie seemed much more at ease with their cargo than she did. She reflected that this journey would probably be just like all the others; they would be stopped a few times for questioning, then allowed to pass. There were always some who insisted on searching the wagon, but there was nothing there for them to find. It would take several weeks for them to reach Richmond. She almost hoped that something would indeed happen to alleviate the boredom of the trip! Miranda and Julie were certainly not very conversant while they were traveling, and Jake and Robert never rode close enough for Katie to speak with. It wasn't exactly that they were not friendly; they simply appeared to dislike too much idle chatter as they were traveling.

Brent arrived in Charleston the week after Katie and the others had left the city, but he had been unable to find a trace of her. He had immediately contacted one of the other agents upon his arrival, but nothing had been heard of Katie or her companions. He checked at the various hotels, but none of them had a Katie Brent listed in their registers, nor did they recall seeing a beautiful young redhead fitting her description.

Maybe she didn't register this time, he thought. Maybe she simply roomed with those friends of hers and didn't go out too much. Damn! He hadn't ever thought to inquire about their names from Katie. Now, he'd have even more trouble in finding her.

After spending two days in Charleston, Brent was called in to see one of the agents, a man he had never before met. The man was seated at a desk in an old, abandoned building located on the east side of the city. Brent entered the darkened room and stood waiting at attention.

"Mr. Morgan, please be seated. I am Mr. Hardwick. Mr. Morrow has granted me permission to use you for an important assignment that has just come up. Now, let me explain. We have received word of some very wily and competent Confederate spies that have been traveling throughout the South for the past two years or so. They have successfully delivered many secret missives to their Confederate superiors. They have also successfully avoided getting caught at it. It seems that they have never even been questioned about their activities, which reflects somewhat poorly upon our agency. Now, Mr. Morgan, your assignment will be to find them."

"Yes, sir. But, how am I going to know where to search for them?" Brent asked politely. Of course, he would have to manage to combine his two missions somehow. He couldn't let this put a damper on his search for Katie.

"Well, let me continue, Mr. Morgan. It seems that there are four of them—two men and two women. We do not know by which names they are known at the moment. However, I have here a recent physical description of them and some background of their various 'accomplishments.' It has been reported to us that they were last seen here in this city, probably headed for Richmond. We would have picked them up when they were here within our grasp, but we received some final information too late. Now, you are to head toward Richmond, or wherever you think necessary, and see what you can discover about them. We have agents now in most of the cities along the way; you are to contact them when you are able and discover if we have sent along any further information. As I stated earlier, I have the consent of your superior to order you on this assignment. Are there any further questions?"

"Yes, sir. Seeing as how you know what these spies look like and something about their whereabouts, how come they haven't been apprehended before now?"

"Well, you see, we've known about them a long time, but it wasn't until a certain source of ours gave us some further information that we knew the full details of their operation. Suffice it to say that our source has contacts

231

among both sides. If that is all..."

"Mr. Hardwick, supposing that I do not find them? What then?" Brent broke in to ask.

"Well, then you will receive other orders. Don't worry, man, we'll be keeping up with your progress. You ought to know by now that there are quite a lot of things in this business that none of us know. Only a select few know everything. If that is all, you can go now, Mr. Morgan. Let me say that we have chosen you for this task for a particular reason; you seem to work well on your own, and you know the South and its people. We received reports that you and Mr. Woodson did very well a few days ago, but that you kept to yourself and did your work alone. Anyway, that is all. Don't leave Charleston until tomorrow morning. That way, no one will become too suspicious about your hurried departure."

"Yes, sir. Goodbye, Mr. Hardwick." Brent tipped his civilian hat and strode out of the dilapidated old building and out into the warming sunshine.

So, these spies were headed for Richmond, most likely. He had a feeling that Katie and her companions were also headed for that city. He hated the knowledge that his beloved wife was endangered at this very moment. She certainly didn't realize the full implications of what she had involved herself in. Why, if someone were to discover all those bottles in her petticoats, they wouldn't just stop with that evidence. She would be arrested as a spy, not simply as a medicine smuggler. He knew too well what happened to spies after they were captured.

Katie shouldn't be all that difficult to track, if she were indeed traveling to Richmond. There didn't seem to be any reason for them to travel elsewhere; the medicine would be distributed most easily from that particular location. Oh well, he'd pray that he caught up with her before she neared the city. It would be extremely hazardous for her once she was close to Richmond; he knew for a fact that there were hundreds of his own troops surrounding it and several agents within its limits. Richmond was the most important city of the South that still remained unconquered by the Union forces; it was the capital of the Confederacy.

Katie's letter had finally been received by her family back home at Corkhaven. A courier had arrived that day, stating that he had ridden quite a few miles through enemy lines to deliver it. He was invited into the kitchen, where Esther and Junie set about fixing him a hearty meal.

"Could it be from Katie, do you think, Albert?" Amelia asked anxiously. They had not heard a word from her since she had disappeared so long ago. They hadn't given up hope for her safety, but they were beginning to become a bit discouraged. Albert had made several inquiries into her disappearance, but nothing had turned up yet.

"Just a minute, Amelia, let me open the blasted thing!" replied her brother-in-law impatiently. He tore open the seal and scanned the letter's contents with a quick sweep of his eyes. He handed the letter to Amelia, saying, "It's from Katie. Why don't you come into the parlour and sit down to read it? You don't look at all well. Come on, Jenny, let's all go into the parlour with Amelia and she can read the letter for us." He ushered the two women to the sofa and then seated himself opposite them.

"Oh, Jenny, I'm so very excited! Why, I do declare, I can't read a single little word! Here, you read it for us." She thrust the paper at Jenny, who drew out and adjusted her reading glasses and began to read.

"Dear Mama, James and John, Aunt Jenny, and Uncle Albert: This is to let you all know that I am alive and well. As I'm sure Esther and Sarah (I do hope that they have come on home) told you, I was abducted by a horrible man, a Confederate officer. He forced me to go along with him for several miles, but I managed to escape. I met up with some very nice people who were also fleeing Atlanta, and they invited me to travel along with them. I'm sorry, Mama, that I did not come on home at that time, but I had been lost and couldn't seem to think very straight at the time.

"Anyway, I traveled with them here to Nashville. They

are very nice people, two men and two women. They are taking very good care of me; they loaned me some clothes and are paying for my room and board. You would like them, I'm sure. Don't worry, Mama, for the men are married to other women and are simply providing an escort for my two friends until they reach their destination.

"It doesn't look as if I'll be coming home for a while yet. I can't tell you exactly why. Just believe me when I say that I have something important to do. Don't worry about me, for I am well and happy. I expect to be home in a couple of months or so. I'll send you further word whenever I am able to do so. I know that this letter won't reach you for a few weeks. That's all I can say at the moment. Take care and please don't worry about me. I love you all. Katie."

"Oh, Jenny, whatever can she be talking about? What could be so important that she can't come on home? And what with this war, why, I can't bear the thought of my precious daughter right in the middle of it!" Amelia exclaimed, very upset by Katie's news.

"Now, now, Amelia, you know Katie. Why, I told you how she refused to leave Atlanta with us. She's got a mind of her own, but I'm sure she can take care of herself. From what Esther and Sarah have told us, she certainly took care of them all when those Yankees broke into our house! Don't you worry your head about it, she'll come on home when she's good and ready," Jenny soothed her.

"That's right, Amelia, Katie's certainly got a mind of her own! She was perfectly all right when she sent us that letter, so there's no reason to believe that she isn't so now. We'll just have to wait for her to come home. That young lady has always needed a stronger hand! Haven't I always told you that? I tried telling you and Gerald that the whole time she was growing up, and now it's too late," Albert expostulated. He was silenced by a disapproving glance from his usually docile wife.

Amelia nodded tearfully and then Jenny offered to

help her upstairs. Albert sighed at the foolishness of women and strolled into the library to finish some more paperwork. He had carried on his business from Corkhaven since he had first arrived from Atlanta. The business was still proceeding very well, being operated by way of messengers sent back and forth between Corkhaven and Albert's various contacts.

There were always those who would profit from such unfortunate circumstances as a war, and Albert O'Toole was certainly one of those enterprising individuals. He had been involved in this particular business since the war had first begun, and he certainly had no intention of ceasing his lucrative practices now. Of course, he had run a much higher risk since coming here to Corkhaven, but he hadn't been caught yet, and he didn't intend to be. His wife knew very little of what he did and his somewhat silly sister-in-law knew nothing at all. He preferred to keep them in ignorance; that way, they couldn't go wagging their tongues and spill the beans.

Esther and Sarah hurried back to the kitchen as Jenny and Amelia emerged from the parlour. They had been curious to hear what all the uproar was about. It was a good thing they had listened in. So, their Miss Katie was safe, but she wasn't coming home!

"Esther, thank the good Lord for that child's safety. I don't know what I would've done if she hadn't been all right," Sarah muttered with relief.

"Yes, Sarah. I wonder what she found so important for her to do that she couldn't come on home where she belongs? Do you suppose it's got something to do with that Yankee husband of hers?"

"Well, I don't rightly know. I guess it could have, maybe. Anyway, we don't got no business letting her secret out. She done told us to not tell anyone about her marriage. You know that, Esther," Sarah admonished her.

Esther merely looked a trifle smug and replied:

"Yes, I know. But, I think maybe it's better if her mama

235

knows about it, don't you? I mean, that poor lady's gonna cry her eyes out with worry for her child. If we tell her why Miss Katie ain't coming home right now, she'll feel better for the knowing."

"No, Esther. Woman, Miss Katie said not to tell! You're gonna get it good if she ever finds out you even thought such a thing. You can't go and tell her mama. It might upset her even more," Sarah said reprovingly.

Esther said no more, merely slipping away a few minutes later and climbing the stairs to Amelia's bedroom. She'd better hurry before that Sarah came looking for her. She knocked on the door and was told to enter.

"Miss Amelia, begging your pardon, ma'am, but I got something real important to tell you."

"Esther, what in the world are you doing up here? Can't you see that Miss Amelia is upset at the moment? Now, you get on back downstairs and help Junie and Sarah," Jenny ordered her sternly, but not unkindly.

"Miss Jenny, I got something Miss Amelia has got to hear. It can't keep. I'm mighty sorry, but somebody should have done told you a long time before. You see, Miss Amelia, your daughter is married. And, what's more, she's married to a Yankee!"

Jenny and Amelia gazed at each other in absolute confusion and astonishment.

"Esther, whatever are you saying? Why would you tell us such a dreadful thing?" Amelia demanded.

"Miss Amelia, it's like I done told you. Miss Katie done up and married with that Yankee captian, Captain Morgan, what was here a few months back. They been married since right after they left here to go to Atlanta. Sarah told me all about it. And, he come and visited Miss Katie in Atlanta, after Miss Jenny and Mister Albert gone. They done spent the night together and all, and Miss Katie herself told me they was married. I only thought you should know, because I think that's the real reason she ain't coming home yet."

"Esther, are you certain what you're saying is the absolute truth?" Jenny demanded.

"Yes, ma'am. It's the truth all right. You can ask Sarah for yourself. She was there. Anyways, that's all I got to say, except that I still don't see how Miss Katie could go and marry a Yankee!" With that, she turned around and hurried from the room, leaving two startled women in her wake.

"Jenny, I can't believe it! I simply can't believe it! Why, Katie and Captain Morgan didn't get along at all! I had to call her down for being very uncivil to the man. She didn't even like him, although he seemed to regard her a bit differently. I just can't believe that they're married. No wonder Katie won't come home to us. She's out running around all over the countryside with her Yankee husband!" Amelia finished.

"Now, Amelia, we can't be sure that what Esther told you is the whole truth of the matter. Why don't you let me call Sarah up here to explain the full details?" Amelia agreed and Sarah was called. She soon arrived at the doorstep, appearing very nervous.

"Sarah, Esther had just told us a piece of surprising and almost unbelievable information. Is it true that Katie is married to a Yankee, Captain Morgan? If so, why didn't you tell us about this sooner? When did it happen?" Amelia asked.

Sarah went on to explain the full details of the journey to Atlanta, of Katie's rather hurried wedding to Brent, of his subsequent visit to her in Atlanta. Amelia and Jenny were both now fully convinced that the story was true.

"Thank you, Sarah. I only wish you had told me sooner, but I understand your devotion to my daughter. Your loyalty is touching. That is all, you may go," replied Amelia.

Sarah rushed back downstairs and prepared herself to admonish Esther for revealing Miss Katie's secret. Why, that meddlesome old slave woman had no right to go and tell on her Miss Katie!

Jenny and Amelia discussed the news they had just received. To think that Amelia O'Toole's daughter was now a married woman, and to an enemy soldier besides! They didn't doubt it any longer, for it did indeed sound like just such a thing the Katie they knew so well would do. They both realized how headstrong she could be, how completely unpredictable. Well, since she was married to a Yankee, they couldn't expect her home at least until the war ended. Not knowing that wives weren't allowed to remain with their husbands on their military campaigns, they were ignorant as to the fact that Katie would not be with Brent. They believed that she was now safely with her husband.

Several days out of Charleston, Katie and her friends were again stopped by a sentry belonging to a troop of Union soldiers. Jake and Robert jumped down from their horses, while the three women remained seated.

"Young man, we're just simple folk on our way to live with some relatives of ours a few days north of here. We ain't got nothing of importance," Jake said amiably.

"Sir, will you and the women please come this way?" the young soldier responded politely.

Katie and her friends climbed down from the wagon seat and followed Jake and Robert as they were led along by the soldier. They were all shown into the tent of the commanding officer.

"Young ladies, gentlemen, please excuse this delay. It seems that there have been an awful lot of smugglers and Confederate spies getting through the lines, so we are forced to search and question quite a number of you people every day. Your wagon is being searched at this moment. Ladies, you may step aside and wait over there. Gentlemen, please come with me. I must ask you to submit yourselves to a thorough search," he said. Jake and Robert willingly followed the officer outside the tent.

"Why are they doing this? Do you think they suspect us of anything?" Katie whispered to Miranda.

"I don't know. Sometimes, like I told you before, they

238

just like to search the men and the wagon as a matter of routine procedure. They're always on the lookout for spies. Don't worry, Katie, they won't bother us. We'll be out of here in just a few minutes."

Sure enough, Jake and Robert returned shortly and they were allowed to go on their way. The women hadn't even been questioned, and Katie was thankful for the respite. She didn't like having to lie to anyone. She couldn't see why a few bottles of medicine was so all-fired important to the entire Union Army, anyway. All she and the others were doing was helping ease the pain and suffering of a few men.

Brent was several days behind Katie by now. He had ridden fast and hard, trying to find a trace of her and her companions. So far, he had found very little. No one remembered seeing the two men, three women, and the wagon. No one recalled seeing a beautiful young woman with flashing red-gold hair and the face of an angel, albeit a mischievious one.

Oh, Katie, I only hope I find you before something terrible happens to you. I don't trust those so-called friends of yours one little bit. I doubt very seriously if you really know them at all.

Finally, he came upon a troop of Union soldiers a few days outside of Charleston. The sentry halted him, and Brent asked to be shown to the commanding officer's tent, stating that he had important business to discuss with him. The young soldier eyed the man in civilian clothing warily, then reluctantly agreed. He escorted him to the tent and Brent thanked him as he ducked inside the flaps.

"Sir," he spoke to the man sitting at the makeshift desk, "I'm seeking information on some folks who might have traveled this way. There were three women, one of them very pretty with red-gold hair, and two men. Have you seen anything of them, and when?"

"Young man, by what right do you come busting in here asking me questions?" the officer blustered.

"Sir, I am Captain Brent Morgan. Here are my papers.

I'm a special agent for the intelligence force. I need to find these people as soon as possible."

"Very well, Captain. Your papers appear to be in order. Yes, to answer your question, I did see such a group a few days ago. We searched their wagon and then searched both of the men. One of the women was just as you described. May I ask why you are looking for them, Captain? They had no contraband of any kind, and they appeared to be just what they claimed—a group of settlers relocating."

"Sir, I can't tell you precisely why I'm looking for them, but it is very important to me. I can only say that I've got to catch up with them soon. If you see or hear any more of them, please pass on the information. By the way," Brent said as he thought, "I'm also looking for some Confederate spies who are supposedly traveling to Richmond. There are only two women and two men. Here is a list of their physical descriptions. Have you by any chance seen anything of people fitting these descriptions?" he asked as he handed the officer the paper.

The officer studied the words written on the piece of paper, then turned once again to Brent, saying:

"Captain Morgan, I can't believe it. It just so happens that these are the same people we stopped, the very same ones you just questioned me about. Of course, the beautiful redhead isn't on this list, but this perfectly fits the other women and the two men."

Brent widened his eyes in surprise. Of course! It all fit into place now. Why hadn't he connected the two before?

"You're sure, sir?" he asked. At the man's nod, he said:

"Very well. Thank you very much, sir. I appreciate your help. Please don't say anything about this matter to anyone else. I've got to catch up with them before they reach Richmond. I don't want anyone else trying to follow them. Thank you again. Good day." Brent saluted and left the tent, striding quickly to his horse and mounting once more. He kicked his mount into a fast gallop, wanting to ride like the wind and think about what he had just discovered.

So, she really is mixed up with more than medicine smugglers. What the devil was he going to do now? He'd have to ride almost non-stop in the hopes of catching them, provided he was able to follow their tracks. Maybe he'd get lucky and would find someone else who'd seen them. Oh, Katie, this is what I was afraid of all along. You're too trusting, and these scoundrels can easily take advantage of that misplaced trust. He knew with a certainty that she was unaware of the people's true vocation; if she had known, he knew she wouldn't have gone with them willingly. She thought medicine smuggling a noble cause, but he knew for a fact how she regarded spying and anything associated with it.

Katie removed her petticoats slowly, glad once more to be rid of their cumbersome bulkiness. She didn't know why Miranda and Julie weren't around, but she supposed they must have had something they wanted to discuss with the men, some detail or other. She didn't much care if they didn't come around for a while; she hadn't had much privacy for the past few weeks.

It was getting much colder in the evenings now, the winter fast approaching. She donned her long-sleeved white flannel nightgown and wrapped her velvet dressing robe tightly around her shivering body. She decided to go to the creek to fetch some more water with which to bathe her face. While she was there, she would wash out a few items of clothing, also. She picked up the articles and headed for the creek she knew lay behind a large clump of trees several yards away. As she approached the water, she heard the voices of her friends carrying through the trees. They appeared to be speaking in such low tones, but she could hear some of their words. She couldn't make out every sentence, but she was able to hear the bulk of their conversation. She stopped and listened carefully.

"Jake, Katie doesn't suspect a thing. I don't know why we can't tell her, though. She's done real well so far. She's making a good cover for us, too. Nobody would suspect a fine Southern lady such as her. You know that everyone's going to be on the lookout for two men and two women, but not for two men and three women," Miranda was saying.

"Yeah, I guess you're right. Miranda, honey, I don't want her to become suspicious and start digging into things. You and Julie tell her that this is our last job. I think we ought to go on our own once we reach Richmond," replied Jake.

"But, Jake, what's she going to do then? How will she get back home?" Julie asked.

"Well, it don't matter none to us what she does then. I only agreed to take her on because we needed some extra cover, and I thought it sort of fate or something that we came upon her there in the country outside of Atlanta. It's up to her what she does after we get rid of her. Anyways, I'll give her a few dollars to get home on. If I don't, she'll start raising a ruckus about us, and that we can't have. You know that someone's been watching for us, and we can't be none too careful right now. Why, my heart nearly jumped in my throat when they stopped us last week!" Jake commented.

"Don't worry about her, Miranda. I know you're kind of soft on that girl, but she'll get along all right. Why, she did all right when she was abducted by that Confederate officer, didn't she? You have to be harder in this business. For now, we've just got to keep her from guessing the truth. It's a good thing she doesn't suspect anything so far. Once we deliver the medicine and letters to Richmond, we'll go and lay low for a few weeks," Robert suggested.

Katie suddenly stumbled upon a twig and it snapped loudly. The four people speaking to each other near the stream ceased their talking and began to wander back to camp. Katie remained stock-still, trying hard not to make any further noise and give herself away.

What in the world could they have been talking about? she wondered. What was there for her to become suspicious about? She wouldn't say anything about what she had heard just yet, for she didn't want them to know that she had been eavesdropping on their conversation.

As for them leaving her in Richmond, stranded, well, she'd just see about that! If they had more assignments to complete, she couldn't see why she couldn't go along and help them. What was that last bit about some letters' they had to deliver to Richmond? This was all becoming mighty suspicious, and she meant to get to the bottom of things immediately.

She walked nonchalantly back to camp, stopping at the stream to wet the clothing she had intended to wash.

"Oh, Katie, there you are. Did you go to the stream?" Miranda asked her, eyeing the wet clothing.

"Yes. It felt so good to have such clean water to wash my face with. I decided to go ahead and wash out a few things while I was there. I looked everywhere for you and Julie. Where have you all been, anyway?" she asked innocently.

"Why, we just had a few details to discuss with Jake and Robert, that's all. It wasn't anything that you need concern yourself with. Now, how about us turning in for the night? I'm really bushed," Miranda responded. Katie nodded and walked over to her bed in the wagon, but her thoughts continued racing for some time afterwards.

Maybe Brent was right, she began to think, maybe I shouldn't have become mixed up with these people. Oh, they had been very nice to her and had included her in their small family, but she began to wonder now why they had said those things down by the stream. Surely they weren't delivering secret messages to the Confederacy, not spying? Surely they weren't spies? At such a thought, she drew in her breath sharply.

Oh, my goodness, if they were spies, then she was a spy, also. She had never intended to become involved in spying, though. No one would ever believe her innocence. Maybe these letters they mentioned were personal letters and not military secrets. Maybe she was just jumping to conclusions.

Well, whatever they had been talking about, she'd find out as soon as possible. She had no intention of staying with them if they were indeed Confederate spies. Wait a minute, she cautioned herself at a sudden, new thought. What if they are in actuality Yankee spies? What if I have been helping to work against my own side? She'd have to get some answers, and soon. It was obvious that neither Miranda nor Julie would volunteer any information on the subject.

Enough for now, she sternly told herself. I've got to get some sleep so I'll be ready to face tomorrow, be ready to find out what's been going on all this time. She yawned and pulled the covers more closely over her body. Her last thoughts before she drifted off into a troubled sleep were of Brent and his numerous warnings against her present companions.

Twenty

Brent shifted in the saddle and cursed his bad luck. He
had been unable to overtake Katie and her companions,
even though he had been traveling for more than two
weeks now. He had continually lost and then recovered
their trail. They must be in quite a hurry, he told himself;
they must be traveling with great haste in order to deliver
those messages and bottles of medicine, if there is indeed
medicine in those bottles.

It was nearing Christmas now and Brent hoped more
than ever that he and Katie would be able to spend this,
their very first Christmas since their marriage, together. If
only she isn't captured. I've got to find her, no matter
what. As he followed their trail, he stopped on several
occasions to inquire of various Union troops if they had
seen anyone fitting the description he offered them of
Katie and her friends. So far, no one had remembered
seeing them pass that way.

Brent reined in his horse and slowly dismounted. He
had been halted momentarily by the guard outside the
tent of the camp's commanding officer, but he stated his
business and was then allowed to enter. He saluted the
officer, saying, "Sir, I need to ask you a few questions.
Have you seen two men and three women traveling
through here lately, with a wagon? Here is a list of their
descriptions, all except that of the third lady, whom I
happen to know about. I'd appreciate any information
you're able to give me about these people."

The officer read the papers and the list, then replied:

"Captain Morgan, I was hoping you'd stop by here. You see, one of your agents is here within my camp at this moment. He brought several messages, one of them concerning the spies you are chasing. It seems that the third lady has now been added to their list, plus a description of her appearance. If you already know about her, then you must know that she has red hair and a very pretty face, not to mention a genteel upbringing and manner of speech. But no, they haven't been through here, at least not yet. I'm sure the other agent will wish to speak with you. Just a moment, please, I'll have him sent to you." He rose from his seat and began to leave the tent. Brent watched him for a moment, then said, "Sir, you say that he has brought word of this third woman spy. How long ago did he bring such information? Did he say how long they have known about her?"

"Well, he arrived here just yesterday, so I suppose he must have received the information prior to his departure from Charleston, but not just because of this particular matter. He's got some sort of business nearby, and he's simply bunking in here with us for the time being. Does that answer your question? If so, I'll have him summoned now."

"Thank you, yes, sir. If you don't mind, I really haven't got the time to stay and chat with him at the moment. Simply tell him that I know where they're headed and that I'm on their trail. I'll send word to my superiors when the time comes." Before the officer could protest, Brent had saluted and hurriedly left the tent. He returned to his horse, mounted, and galloped away with haste.

I can't let that other agent, whoever he may be, find out what I know about them, he told himself. I can't let them know that I'm so close to catching up with them. Katie's got to be protected. I've got to get her away from them before they're apprehended. I could most certainly get into a lot of trouble for this, but she's my wife, for heaven's sakes! As soon as I find her and pry her loose from their grasp, I'll send word about their whereabouts and then someone else can have the honor of picking them up. That way, Katie will never be identified as their accomplice. I'll have to invent some sort of excuse for not being the one to arrest them.

Katie rode in silence on the wagon seat. Miranda and Julie appeared to be somewhat sullen today. Katie hadn't mentioned the enlightening conversation she'd overheard between all of them that night in the woods. She had tried learning small bits of information from Miranda, but, so far, she still didn't know what it was they were trying so hard to keep her from discovering. She still suspected that it had something to do with smuggling military secrets as well as medicine, but she had no concrete evidence to support this suspicion as of yet. She'd kept to herself more than usual since then, but the others hadn't appeared to notice anything out of the ordinary in her behavior.

When they stopped to camp for the night, Katie jumped down and told them she'd like to go and wash up before the temperature dropped too much more. They nodded their heads in silent agreement and she went off to have a few moments' privacy for herself. She had an enormous amount of thinking and planning to do, and she had to be alone to do it.

After she had disappeared into the trees and brush, Miranda and Julie began speaking to one another in rather low undertones, afraid that Katie still might be within hearing range of their voices.

"She's been acting rather strange lately, don't you think so? You don't think she's heard anything, do you?" Julie asked her friend.

"Well, I don't know. I mean, she's been quieter than usual, but that could be for a variety of reasons. After all, I suppose she still thinks about having to leave Savannah without waiting for her husband to return. I wouldn't know what that's like, but it appears that it could be that, from what she's said before," Miranda replied caustically.

"Shhh. Don't ever say that; do you want her to know that you've never been married before? I declare,

Miranda, you haven't got the brains of a goose sometimes! I know she isn't around at the moment, but, I swear, I think that girl's got the eyes and ears of a hawk!" she remarked cuttingly.

"Oh, don't be silly. Besides, 'Widow Julie,' you must admit that you envy her somewhat. Jake and Robert sure ain't ever going to marry either one of us, and you darn well know it! As soon as we've won this war, they'll be off in another direction so fast you won't even have time to say goodbye. Come on, we've got to get the camp set up." The two of them began to unload the provisions from the wagon.

Jake came by at that moment, just as they had finished setting the heavy cooking pot over the fire. He grabbed Miranda by the hand, and, heedless to Julie's warnings about Katie seeing them, he dragged her along with him into the woods. Miranda laughed delightedly and chided him with mock sternness.

"Jake! You want Katie to see us? What's got into you, man?"

"I don't give a damn about her seeing us any longer! We've had to be so damned careful because of that silly little gal, I ain't even got to hold you for several days now! Come on, honey, give me a kiss and act like you're glad I made you come into these woods with me!" He yanked her to him and proceeded to bestow on her a long and passionate kiss.

"Jake, I do declare, you are an absolute monster! I've got to get on back and help Julie with supper, and you know it. Katie'll be back soon and she might become suspicious," she finally was able to say as he released her for a brief moment.

"I told you, I don't give a damn! I've waited too long for you now, woman! Come on, you're coming in here with me and we're going to get 'reacquainted.' They won't miss you for a while, anyhow. I don't really care if they do. This don't make any difference to the rest of our plans about the girl. It won't hurt none if she does find out the truth about you and me, as well as Julie and Robert. I said I don't care what she thinks, and I think it's about time you quit worrying about it!" With that speech, he lowered her to the soft ground and threw himself on top of her. She giggled and entwined her arms about him, as he proceeded to slip his hand up under her skirts.

Meanwhile, Katie had finished her bath in the cold water and was returning to camp. She spotted a squirrel gathering nuts for the winter ahead and she smiled. She sat upon a rock to watch it for a while, to sit and enjoy the quiet peace of the deserted forest. She thought she heard voices from across the stream, but ignored the sounds.

After a few moments, she knew that she definitely was hearing a woman's laughter. She decided to go ahead and investigate the noises, hoping that maybe she'd be able to overhear something else connected with her companions' secret. She carefully picked her way through the trees and then paused to watch in astonishment the scene being enacted a few yards away.

There, before her very own startled eyes, lay Jake and Miranda. They were quite obviously involved in making love. Katie stood still, completely aghast at the sight. So, they had lied about that, too. Making her believe that Jake and Robert were married men who were graciously escorting them all about the countryside! She bet they weren't married at all, and, even if they were, the relationship she had thought so innocent wasn't innocent at all!

Well, she'd had just about enough of their deception and secrecy. She'd go back to camp right now and confront Julie with her discovery right this very moment. This little game had gone on long enough. They must think her an absolute fool to lie to her about such a thing. They must be having a good laugh quite often at her expense.

She whirled and stomped off through the forest and emerged back at camp, still fuming and shocked at what she had witnessed. She strode up to face Julie and demanded, "Julie, is it the truth that Jake and Robert are married to other women? Is it the truth that they are married at all? And, what about you and Miranda? Are you two really widows? I want some answers right now, for I'm tired of being lied to! I'm not as stupid as you all seem to believe. I'm only sorry that I didn't discover the truth before now. Why did you have to lie to me about this? If you only had told me the truth to begin with, I might have understood!"

Julie gazed at her in awe. So, Katie must have seen Jake having his way with Miranda in the woods. I told them not to do it with her around, she thought. Now, Katie had discovered them for sure. Oh, well, why should she hide it from the silly fool any longer? After all, it wasn't like telling her any great secret. If she'd only opened her eyes before now, she'd have realized the truth. Why, even Robert and I haven't been as careful as we should have been.

"Katie, sit down. Go on, sit down. I'm afraid you aren't going to like what I'm about to tell you, but it won't hurt you any to know the truth about this. No, Jake and Robert aren't married men, not at all. Miranda and I aren't widows, either. I've got a husband, but I left him nigh on to three years ago now. As for Miranda, she's never been married. She came to us from a traveling actor's troupe. She joined our organization after she left them in Richmond. There, does that satisfy you? We had to lie to you, because that's our cover story, too, and we just didn't want you to think real bad about us, that's all. We knew you'd get on your high horse if you knew the truth. Robert and I have a 'relationship' also, so you might as well know that now. The four of us joined up together more than two years ago. Now, are your ladylike ears so very shocked at our wickedness?" Julie demanded sarcastically. She didn't know why in the world she was going to such trouble to explain personal matters to this insignificant child. Why, Katie'd been nothing but trouble

250

from the beginning. She'd only been nice to her because Miranda had asked her to.

"Yes, Julie, I see. Well, I think I better tell you now that I intend leaving you once we reach Richmond. I don't think that, under the circumstances, we can ever have a working relationship again. I'm sorry for all this, but that's just the way I've been brought up. I can't ever approve of what you're all doing. Now, I think I'll skip supper for tonight and turn in early. Thanks for telling me the truth, finally. If you'd only told me from the beginning, but..." She turned her back on the older woman and stalked off to her bed. Julie glared after her, not at all sure how she could ever have come close to liking the girl. Why, the little hypocrite, she told herself. Holier-than-thou little ninny!

Katie nestled down under the covers and smiled with satisfaction. She'd been wanting an excuse to tell them she wouldn't stay with them any longer, and now she had been conveniently provided with one! Julie had certainly appeared to be furious when she'd acted that way, and that was all for the best. Miranda wouldn't like the way she had taken it, either, not after all her kindness. Now, though, she wouldn't have to worry about making them suspicious if she chose not to stay with them. They had been good to her and she was grateful to them. She didn't want to leave them with any bad feelings, but that was simply impossible. No, it was better this way.

Brent, if only we can make it to Richmond without getting caught. I'll wait for you there, she silently informed him. She'd stay there as long as possible, for she still had most of the money he had left behind for her in Savannah. She would wait for a while and see if he showed up, if he had indeed been able to follow her. After her money started to run out, she would have to either find a job or try and return home to Corkhaven.

She knew what Brent would say when he saw her and she told him about her suspicions of her friends. He would tell her that he'd warned her about them to begin with, not to trust them. He'd tell her that he knew she would become disenchanted with her little adventure, that she'd eventually give up. Oh, Brent, I don't care how much you may scold me, I only want to see you again, to feel safe within the loving circle of your strong arms. Some bride I am; I haven't even been with you enough since our marriage to know you at all.

Meanwhile, Miranda and Jake had returned from their loving interlude in the woods. They and the others were discussing the latest developments around the campfire.

"So, she knows about us being lovers. So what? That doesn't change anything about our plans. She's still going to stay with us until we get to Richmond. This way, she'll be out of our way after we finish the job. We won't have to worry about her leaving us after this is done," Robert was saying.

"Oh, Robert, she's so upset about us. She's evidently been raised in a closet! She didn't even suspect a thing before she saw Jake and Miranda in the woods tonight!" Julie commented impatiently.

"Well, it can't be helped now. If she's going to get so damned emotional over such a natural part of life, then good riddance to her. In fact, I'm beginning to be afraid that the little lady's going to blow the whole thing with her prejudice against us now. Maybe it'll be less trouble in the long run if we get rid of her now. Maybe it'll be for the best," Jake suggested.

"What do you mean, 'get rid of her'?" Miranda demanded.

"I only mean, we'll just go off and leave her here with the wagon. We'll sneak away before dawn and go on our way. That way, we won't be bothered with the damn thing any more and we'll be rid of her. She won't be able to follow without a horse. We'll just be free and easy, able to ride much faster without the burden of pulling that wagon," he said.

"But, we were instructed to have the wagon with us to

252

give evidence that we're ordinary folk going to live with our kin," Miranda reminded him.

"Well, I'm hereby changing the orders, and I'm the one who's in charge here! You all heard what I said, we'll go off and leave her before dawn in the morning. Now, let's get on to bed and get some sleep. She won't know anything if we're careful not to wake her. We'll pack our grub and bedding behind us on the horses in the morning."

"Jake, I don't know. It don't seem right to abandon her without a horse or any way of getting to a town. I mean, after all, she has helped us out a lot," Miranda remarked as she considered his plan.

"I don't want to hear any more about it, Miranda! She'll manage, I'm sure of that! All she's got to do is turn those big green eyes on some soldier, wiggle her shapely tail, and she'll most likely get to Richmond before we do!" He laughed at his own summation of her character and shuffled off to get some sleep. Miranda and Julie, being women and somewhat more soft-hearted than their male counterparts, felt uneasy about the whole situation. Maybe Jake would change his mind. They couldn't hold their breath for that, though. Even Julie didn't want to leave her stranded, much as she now thoroughly disliked Katie.

Before dawn the next morning, Katie awoke and turned over on her side. She soon discovered, much to her dismay, that Miranda and Julie were not in their beds. She threw back the covers and grabbed for her dressing robe. She rushed outside to the wagon and found Miranda and her friends preparing to ride. Jake and Robert had just finished saddling the horses.

"What in the world are you people doing? Why didn't you wake me?" she asked in confusion.

"Katie!" Miranda whispered as she saw her. She looked to Jake, who said, "Katie, we're in an awful hurry. We decided that it's best if we part company here and now, instead of waiting until we get to Richmond. You've already voiced your opinion of us, and that you intended to leave us once we reached the city. Well, we're going to go on now. So, you'll just stay here. Someone will be along before too long to take you where you want to go."

"Why, you simply can't do this to me! I'm sorry for what I said last night," she said, affecting a tearful and apologetic attitude. So, they were going to just abandon me, leave me here stranded! I'll show them that they'll have to take me along.

"Katie, please don't go to pieces now. You'll be all right. We're leaving the wagon, and you've got your gun. Don't worry, you'll find a man to help you, what with your high and mighty way," Julie told her spitefully.

"Oh, Jake, Robert, please don't do this to me. I truly am sorry for the terrible way I behaved last night. You see," here she paused to turn her luminous green eyes on the two men, "I was raised so strictly, I had such a sheltered life. I know better now, I know that such things happen all the time. I just didn't know how to take it last night. I was so shocked and all, finding Jake and Miranda there together in the woods. I'm a married woman, but I was shocked all the same. Please forgive me for threatening to leave you all. I know you still need my help, and I really do want to continue upon this assignment with you all. I won't cause you any trouble, I give you my word," she said as she ended her convincing speech and then waited for them to announce their verdict. If this doesn't work, she schemed, I'll threaten to inform on them or something!

"Jake, I think she really is sorry. Can't we go ahead and let her finish the job?" Miranda asked, rather moved by Katie's tears and apparently sincere regret.

"Well, I don't know..."

"Jake, it might not work out if we let her stay. She'd forever be looking down her nose at us," Julie put in. She had just lost any soft feelings she might have felt for the girl. She'd caught Robert gazing at Katie with admiration and something else in his brown eyes.

254

"All right, Katie," Jake agreed after thinking it over for a few minutes, "you can stay with us as far as Richmond, where we'll deliver the medicine. Then, you'll have to find some way to get back home on your own. Come on now, get yourself dressed and let's get moving." Katie smiled at him in gratitude and rushed back into the wagon to draw on her clothing.

So, they believed her story! She could have screamed, so disgusted was she at the idea of having to give in, at least outwardly, to those scum! They were going to leave her here all alone in the woods, where anything in the world might have happened to her. She'd let them think she was happy to be with them, at least until they neared Richmond. Then, the first chance she got, she'd leave the medicine in the wagon and head on into the city on her own!

Two days outside of Richmond, the smugglers came upon a large troop of Yankee soldiers. They had passed several Confederate troops, but they were seldom, if ever, halted or questioned by their own side. At the Union camp they were now slowly approaching, there were many tents erected and many soldiers bustling about in various activities. The sentry who stood at the outermost edge of the camp shouted his warning to them.

"Halt! Who goes there? What are you doing here?" he demanded.

"Howdy, young fella. We're traveling to Richmond to settle in with some family of ours. This here's my brother and his wife, my wife, and my wife's cousin. We ain't got nothing of value within the wagon, because we was burned out by the war," Jake told him voluntarily.

"Well, get on down from those horses and follow me. Ladies, you please climb down and come with us, also. I'm afraid that you've all got to be questioned by my commanding officer. He's requested that we stop anyone fitting your descriptions. This way, please."

Katie, Miranda, and Julie all glanced at one another in dreaded silence. Jake and Robert complied with the soldier's demands and began to follow as he led the way toward the camp, which was located several yards down the hill. The three women followed closely behind the men, each one of them feeling a growing fear and apprehension at what was to follow.

Katie wondered what the sentry had meant about them fitting some kind of a description. A description of two men and three women with a wagon? Could someone know about our smuggling activities? she wondered. What am I going to do if they question me? She then sternly ordered herself, you're going to answer them boldly and directly, but untruthfully! Don't be afraid, just face up to them as if you had nothing to hide.

Jake and Robert whispered to one another as they followed along a few feet behind the sentry. They were discussing the possibility of an escape. It seemed that they had been discovered, and they couldn't take any chances. Perhaps they should make a break for it right now. They'd manage to signal to Miranda and Julie. As for Katie, well, they'd let her fend for herself. Come to think of it, they'd let her stay behind and occupy the soldiers while they made a break for it. Even if she were captured and questioned, or even searched, they knew she couldn't reveal anything to the Yankees about the letters.

Jake edged close to Miranda and grasped her arm tightly, explaining in the barest whisper their drastic plan for escape. Robert did the same to Julie. Suddenly, at Jake's signal, which he gave by coughing loudly, the four of them rushed the sentry and knocked him to the ground, hitting him over the head. Then, they turned on their heels and ran as fast as they were able back toward their horses waiting upon the hill. The sentry finally struggled to his feet, dazedly picked his gun from off the ground, and raised the barrel to take aim and shoot. He called out for assistance before he pulled the trigger.

"The prisoners have escaped! Somebody come quick! The prisoners are getting away!" He pulled the trigger then and managed to shoot Jake in the shoulder before he could mount his horse. Julie and Miranda had already ridden away and were traveling at a swift pace, back through the trees and away across the countryside. Robert helped Jake on to his horse and the two of them followed after the women.

The sentry continued shooting in their direction several more times, but they were moving too quickly to hit. Finally, some other armed soldiers arrived to help. It was too late, however, for they hadn't been prepared.

"Quick, get to your horses! You've got to go after them! You've got to get them and bring them back! I'll go and tell the colonel of their escape. Go on, hurry!" the sentry shouted at the soldiers.

Throughout the entire incident, Katie had remained standing beside the sentry, an avid observer of the events. Jake and Robert must've had it all planned, she surmised. They didn't even try to take me along with them. She knew that it would have been impossible for her to try and follow them, for, by the time she had realized what was going on, the sentry had already risen to his feet and was firing at her fleeing companions. Former companions, she thought wryly. Anyway, she was the sole remaining prisoner of the Yankees now. They would probably question her about the others, but they wouldn't dare think of searching her, she was certain. The sentry turned to her and mumbled, "Ma'am, please come with me. I don't know why your friends left you behind, but you're certainly left holding the bag, so to speak. Come on, let's go." He grasped her by the arm and forced her along with him, none too gently. He was very angry at the outcome of the events. He ushered her into the colonel's tent and said, "Sir, this is the only prisoner we were able to apprehend. The others managed to escape, but some of the men are going after them at this moment." He saluted briskly and left the tent, after being gruffly dismissed. Katie stood very still, holding her head proudly.

The man seated behind the makeshift desk, a gruff-looking man of some fifty-odd years, stood and demanded in a booming voice:

"Young woman, do you know what sort of trouble you're in? I don't think you really do. You see, I happen to know all about you and your friends. We were alerted to the fact that you might be passing by here on your way to Richmond. We were watching for you. Now, you've got a lot of explaining to do. Come over here and sit down." He motioned her to a campstool and she gratefully sank down upon it. She didn't like what he had said, about having information about them and having been notified ahead of time of their arrival. Who could have known about her and her companions?

"All right, first off, please tell me your name. Where do you come from? How long have you known those comrades of yours? What have you been doing during this entire war?" He continued shooting questions at her, being convinced that she knew more than she was willing to admit. She endeavored to answer the questions as truthfully as possible, for she knew that trying to tell the truth would work to her best advantage. She had to bend the truth now and then, of course, but she could honestly say to him that she was not a Confederate spy.

"I don't know why you keep asking me these questions. I've already told you that I am not now, nor ever have been, a Confederate or Yankee spy! And, I don't know anything about any letters! I am simply a Southern lady on my way to Richmond to visit some relatives. My cousin and her family must have been frightened away from here for some reason. They probably believed I was right behind them. Anyway, I don't see why you insist on keeping me here. I've done nothing wrong, and I really must get to my relatives in Richmond!" She answered all of his questions with a decisiveness, but he didn't appear to be convinced.

"Very well, Miss Brent, it appears as if you're not going to volunteer any information. I'm going to call in one of our special agents and see what he can discover about your little game." He left the tent, only to return a minute later with another man, a tall, rather attractive man in his late thirties. However, his attractiveness ended at his eyes, which were a cold, steely grey. There was no warmth within their icy depths.

"Miss Brent, I have asked Colonel Denison to remain in the tent with us, as I'll need a witness. Now, will you please stand?" Katie remained stubbornly seated and looked up into his eyes defiantly. Surely the man couldn't be suggesting that she submit her person to a search?

"Miss Brent, I've come all the way from North Carolina to find you and your accomplices, and I am running out of patience with you! If you don't get up this very moment, I'll be forced to remove you from that stool myself. Now, please rise. This won't hurt a bit, I promise; only your pride, I'm sure." At the expression in those hard eyes, Katie slowly and tremulously rose to her full height. She stood very still, waiting to strike at him at his first touch upon her body.

"Colonel Denison, please witness what I am about to do. I mean no personal harm to the lady, I only need to search her clothing for any contraband. Miss Brent, don't be alarmed, I only want to see if you have anything hidden within the folds of your petticoats." He reached out and attempted to lay hold of her skirt, but she viciously slapped at his hands and backed off into the far corner of the tent.

"Don't you dare lay one finger on me, you Yankee! I am a Southern lady, and I certainly expect to be afforded the courtesy of being treated as one! A gentleman would never dare think of asking a lady to submit herself to such indecent treatment! Now, I have nothing to hide, as I have already said, and I insist that you stop this insane nonsense this very moment! You'll just have to take my word that I am not a spy!" she insistently said as she breathed deeply in her fury. She was becoming very angry and more than a bit frightened by now. She couldn't fathom what the man would attempt to do next, so she waited and watched him with wary eyes as he approached her once more.

"Miss Brent, now, I don't want to hurt you. Colonel Denison, please give me some assistance with her."

"I say, Mr. Stephens, I don't think you should treat a lady like that, even if she is a spy. Miss Brent, why don't you comply with his wishes and simply remove your petticoats for us?" he suggested helpfully.

"I won't, sir! I won't disrobe one little bit in front of you two disgusting men! Now, you keep your filthy hands off me, or I'll scream as loud as I can! I'll mark your face something awful if you touch me!" she threatened to the advancing agent.

"Go ahead and scream, Miss Brent, for I'm going to search those petticoats. You see, being a special agent, I know all about you Southern ladies and the way you hide things in those petticoats, how you sew several pockets into their folds and conceal anything you desire. Now, Colonel Denison, I must insist that you give me some assistance. The quicker we get it over with, the quicker we can tell Miss Brent what her fate will be." He reached for her again and she struggled against his iron grip. Colonel Denison hurried over to take her into his grasp, while Mr. Stephens fought off her striking feet and flaying legs. He managed to reach up under her skirt and untie the strings of one petticoat and then drew it off her squirming, twisting body.

"Unhand me, you beast! I'll report this conduct to my husband! He'll see that you are severely reprimanded for this conduct, you Yankee! Let go of me!" she cried imperiously, but to no avail.

Finally, the colonel released her arms and Mr. Stephens stood searching through the pockets of the petticoat he had managed to remove from her. He reached inside one of the pockets and removed a bottle of what appeared to be medicine.

"So, you had nothing to hide, eh, Miss Brent? What is this, may I ask? Are there any others hidden in the other petticoats? It appears that there are quite a number of bottles in this one. Now, take off those other petticoats, or we'll be forced to enact the amusing little scene again," he sneered at her. She glared at him in return and turned her back on the two men. She untied the strings of the remaining petticoats, letting them drop to the dirt.

"Well, Colonel Denison, there truly is medicine in this particular bottle, anyway. However, we will want to search through every last one of them and see if there are any messages contained in them. Miss Brent, you are under arrest for medicine smuggling, and maybe for more than that. We'll see about any other charges later. Colonel, please see that she is placed under heavy guard. I'll look through the rest of these now. Miss Brent, I'll come and speak with you later. Perhaps you'll be a bit more willing to cooperate by then, do you think?" he smirked. She glowered at him in her fury and humiliation, making no secret of the fact that she detested his odious, insinuating manner.

"Miss Brent, will you please come with me?" the colonel asked her politely. He hated this business of treating a lady such as had just been done, but he could see now why Stephens had been so eager to search her clothing. He had seen a lot of women who would have fainted at what this one had just been through, but she seemed even prouder and more disdainful than before.

As she was led to a tent and placed under guard, Katie tried gathering her jumbled thoughts about her. So, they knew now that she smuggled medicine. Surely that wasn't such a great crime. She felt humiliation at the way she had been treated. She didn't think, though, that they would do anything very bad to her for trying to help the suffering, even if those she was helping were Confederate soldiers.

The scene in the colonel's tent flashed through her mind again. She hadn't meant to blurt out that threat of telling her husband, it had just slipped out. Anyway, the Yankees hadn't appeared to notice anything untoward in her words. She would surely be released within a few days. After all, these were times of war, and they couldn't afford to waste time and soldiers on guarding a lone woman, could they? She prayed that she was right in her assumption.

Twenty One

Katie sank down upon the single stool in the drafty tent. She drew her warm cloak about herself, endeavoring to keep some of the cold away from her body. As the sun set, the temperature began to drop considerably. Soon, soon they would surely have to summon her once again. She couldn't take this waiting much longer.

She reflected on her former companions as she waited. They had left her to the mercy of the enemy. She hadn't believed that they would actually do such a thing to her, but they most certainly had. Surely they could have just as easily taken her along with them when they had escaped. But no, they wouldn't want to be bothered with someone as insignificant as she.

I hope Brent comes this way. I hope he can find me soon. Maybe he wasn't able to come after me at all. Maybe he hasn't been able to follow us. Dear Lord, don't let that be the case. Let him be somewhere out there right now. He must come this way.

Mr. Stephens entered the tent without warning, startling Katie as she was lost in her own thoughts. She immediately rose and faced him proudly.

"Miss Brent, I'm sorry to inform you that there were indeed several messages contained in those bottles. I don't know for sure yet if you knew about them or not, but I intend to find out. The information, as you may already be aware, are very important secrets. They are secrets the Confederate administration in Richmond would have been very glad to receive. Tell me, Miss Brent, did you know about their existence, that they were hidden in those bottles?" he inquired suspiciously.

"No, of course I didn't! I'll admit to smuggling medicine, yes, but I am certainly no spy! I only meant to help alleviate the unnecessary suffering of a few of our men, that's all. I never had any intention or inclination for spying for the Confederacy. My former companions must have placed those particular bottles in my petticoats. I'm sure they wouldn't have gone off and deserted me if they had remembered that I still carried them. I am sure, you see, that they were placed with my bottles by mistake. Anyway, sir, I am innocent," she cooly insisted. She closely observed his sardonic face for any sign that he believed her innocence, but there was none.

"That is a most interesting story. However, you have failed to convince me. Whether you knew about the missives in those bottles or not doesn't really make any difference. The fact is, you were willingly smuggling contraband across the lines and you were, willingly or not, carrying secret military information upon your person. I can't say that I expected you to do anything other than deny it, though. Now, the problem is, what do I do with you?" He smiled then, apparently delighted at her discomfiture.

"I am not a spy! You have no right to treat me as such! I know that smuggling a few bottles of medicine is considered by you Yankees to be a crime, but I don't consider it such. I'm completely innocent of the charge of spying or carrying military secrets! I tell you, sir, that those messages were placed on my person without my knowledge or consent," she nearly shouted. Oh, what a hateful man he was! He wouldn't believe her, no matter what she told him or how much she pleaded her innocence. She realized that he was actually enjoying this little game with her. He enjoyed the spectacle of her vehement denials.

"That is quite enough of your little dramatics now, young lady. By the way, what is your real name? I know it isn't Brent, surely. I think I'll just call you by your first name, Katie. You can call me Mr. Stephens!" He chuckled at his own humor, while Katie fumed in response. She quite obviously didn't know what to do now, and he decided to make her squirm a bit more.

He slowly and insolently eyed her figure, his gaze traveling downward from her head, across her ample charms so apparent under the clinging dress. Even her efforts to hide herself from him by drawing the cloak about her didn't hamper his observations.

"Sir, you are insulting! I demand that I be shown into Colonel Denison's tent at once. I have something I wish to speak with him about. Now, will you please step aside and have the guards escort me to him," she demanded, much more calmly than she felt. She'd show this egotistical Yankee that Southerners were made of stronger stuff than he apparently imagined!

"No, I'm afraid not, Katie, for he's already retired for the night. You are now in my custody, not his. I can do whatever I wish with you, did you know that?" he asked her, a certain cruel glint now appearing in his steel-grey eyes.

"You are the lowest vermin, sir! If you lay one hateful finger on me again, I'll make such a racket that someone will surely come to my rescue. Now, you stay away from me. Simply because I am under arrest and perhaps in your custody gives you absolutely no right to speak so to me!" she spat at him in growing fury and alarm.

"I am in command as far as you are concerned, Katie, and no one would dare interfere. However, I think I'll leave you to think about everything I've said. I'll decide what to do with you later. I'll most likely take you to my headquarters, back to North Carolina. I don't really know yet. But, whatever I decide to do with you, we'll have a nice, long time to spend together, you can count on that. Good night, you Confederate whore!" he sneered. He tipped the brim of his hat mockingly and left the tent.

"Oh! You Yankee..." she yelled after him. She

couldn't think of any appropriate words with which to finish the sentence.

She'd have to find some way to escape from him. She couldn't trust him to behave like a gentleman. He'd just made that very clear. Calling her a whore! Oh, Brent, why can't you come right this minute? I need your help so desperately! I think I've finally gotten myself into something I can't get out of! She sat down on the stool once more and contemplated the situation. Perhaps she could bribe one of the guards. But, what could she use? She only had a few dollars remaining from the amount Brent had so generously given her. She remembered that she was wearing a necklace, the pearl necklace her mother had given her on her sixteenth birthday. She thought she would save it and give it to her daughter some day. But now, she pushed such thoughts aside. Yes, maybe this will do the trick, she thought as she removed it from around her slender neck. She held it out in front of her, trying to see it more clearly in the darkening twilight.

Yes, maybe it would appear to be valuable enough to barter with. She'd add the money to it, though, just in case. Now, to approach the guard on duty and try and bargain with him for her freedom.

"Hey, young man, you out there!" she called softly through the tent. She heard a rustle and he stuck his head in the entrance of the tent.

"Sir, could you please help me? You see, I'm not really a spy. I'm just an innocent little Southern girl who's been falsely accused," she simpered as she looked up into his surprised face. She sniffed pathetically and blinked her big, green eyes, fluttering the long and curly eyelashes. She moved her body seductively toward him as she spoke.

"Ma'am, what are you talking about? I can't help you, you know that. Why, if I was just seen talking to you right now, I'd get skinned alive!" the young Yankee muttered as he gulped nervously.

"Oh, please. Please, kind sir, please help me get away. Here, I've got a few dollars here and a very valuable

266

necklace I'll give you as soon as you just turn your head and let me sneak out of camp. You won't have to do anything but just ignore me as I leave. You can do that, can't you?" she pleaded with him as she edged closer.

"No, ma'am," the Yankee replied, moving backwards a step, "I can't do that. I'm real sorry for you, but I don't think I can help. That would be treasonable to let you get away when I knew about it. Now, ma'am, could I get you something to eat or drink?" He backed out of the tent, but Katie followed and came to stand in the entrance of the tent.

"Please! I'll even make it look like I knocked you out with the stool. No one will have to know that you knew anything. Here, take the money and the necklace and hide them in your coat. Just stand there real still, and I'll take this little old stool and bump you over the head with it just a little. You can fall down and pretend that I've knocked you out. There isn't anyone else about just now to notice, anyway. Come on, you will do it for me, won't you? What's to become of me if you refuse?" she continued to plead. She slipped her hand out the entrance and gently laid it upon his arm.

The young man gulped even harder, beginning to become a bit panicky by now. He just couldn't do as she suggested, he just couldn't! But, she looked so darn sad and helpless. And, she was the prettiest little thing he'd ever laid eyes on. Maybe he could do it. He could sure use the money. And, he could sell the necklace once he got back home. He peered around the camp, then slowly began to turn around and tell her that he'd agreed to her plan after all. Suddenly a deep voice startled him.

"Nice try, Katie! Private," Mr. Stephens commented to the young guard, "don't ever let me hear you conversing with my prisoner again, do you understand? I'll have the colonel place you under arrest if you do." He waved the guard aside and stepped inside the tent to confront the angry, disappointed Katie.

"Katie, don't try to bribe anyone again, do you hear? It

won't work, for I'm on to your little schemes. Are you sure you haven't worked as an actress before? Or possibly you really have worked as a whore? How many other men have you coerced with your beauty?" he asked her softly as he raised a finger to her soft cheek.

"You damn Yankee! Get out of here and leave me alone! And, I'm neither a whore nor an actress. I am a lady, which you wouldn't understand, since I'm sure you haven't known many!" she hissed as she slapped his hand away.

He merely chortled at her anger and nonchalantly walked out of the tent. The young guard stood at attention, fully intending to heed the agent's warning.

I almost had him agreeing, Katie told herself in frustration. He had almost given in and said he'd go along with my plan. Oh, that dreadful Mr. Stephens! Now, I'll have to wait for another opportunity, another guard. I don't intend to let that disgusting Yankee get the upper hand!

The next morning, Brent arose early and continued on his way. He would find her today, he just knew it. He'd had this feeling since last night, a feeling that she was near by.

Along about dusk, Brent rode into the Union camp and dismounted. He strode to the commanding officer's tent and requested admittance of the guard outside. He produced his papers and only then was he allowed to enter. As he ducked his head to avoid the tent flaps, he observed that the colonel was occupied with another man, a man in civilian clothing.

"Sir, please excuse my intrusion. I'm Captain Brent Morgan, and I'm on assignment for the intelligence organization. I need to ask you a few questions, if you don't mind," Brent told him.

"Ah, yes, Captain Morgan. I've had word that you'd be coming this way. Why, it just so happens that this gentleman here is also an agent with your organization. Morgan, this is Mr. Stephens."

Stephens stood upon being introduced and shook hands with Brent. Brent felt an immediate dislike for the man. There was something about him that made him compare the man to a snake. Brent continued with his request.

"Colonel, I really do need to ask you a few questions. They concern a group of suspected Confederate spies I have been pursuing ever since I left Charleston. There were two men and three women. They were traveling together, with a wagon, and they were supposedly headed for Richmond. I have here a list of their various descriptions. Have you by any chance seen anything of them? Has anyone passed through here that might fit these descriptions?"

Stephens and Colonel Denison both glanced at the list and then back at each other. Colonel Denison nodded and Stephens replied, "Captain Morgan, these people have indeed passed by here. The two men and two of the women managed to escape, unfortunately. However, we do have one of the spies here under guard in this camp right now. She's the one so adequately described as being young and beautiful, and as having red hair. I've already placed her under arrest and she is now my prisoner. You may question her, though, if you like."

Brent controlled his turbulent emotions on hearing his dear wife discussed and accused as a Confederate spy. So, Katie had been captured and was here in this camp right now. The worst had come to pass, just as he'd feared; she'd been caught before he could get her away from the others. But, why had she been the only one they had managed to apprehend?

"Mr. Stephens, why was this particular young woman the only one the men were able to capture? And, what makes you so sure she actually is a Confederate spy?" he inquired casually.

"Why, the men tried to catch the others, but they rode away before the colonel's men had a chance to apprehend them. This woman was left behind by the others. It seems

269

that she wasn't all that important to them. Either that, or she became confused about their escape plans. She has not volunteered any information, as I'm sure you can understand. As for knowing that she is indeed a spy, why, we found several bottles of medicine concealed within pockets that had been sewn into her petticoats. Hidden within several of the bottles were pieces of military information she was obviously delivering to the Confederate administration in Richmond. Would you like to see her for yourself and question her? Perhaps she'll answer some questions, but I seriously doubt it."

"Yes, I'd like to see her. Thank you, Stephens. Just tell me where to find her and I'll go by myself. I'd like to speak with her alone, if you don't mind. Perhaps I can get her to tell me a bit more about her business. Colonel, thank you for the information. I'll see you both later." He waited until Mr. Stephens had given him the directions, then he casually strolled from the tent and out into the December evening.

Damn that pompous Stephens! He'd behaved as if the whole thing had been his own accomplishment, as if he'd captured Katie single-handedly. He shuddered to think of that oily creature questioning his wife, interrogating her relentlessly. He controlled his rising temper at his thoughts and approached the tent the man had described. Yes, this was certainly the right one. There were two guards outside, holding their guns upright and standing at rigid attention.

"Halt! Sir, no one is allowed to see the prisoner!" the one on the right said.

"Private, I have permission from Colonel Denison and Mr. Stephens to speak with the prisoner. I'm Captain Morgan. Here are my papers." He drew out the papers, which the guard quickly scrutinized, before he was allowed to enter.

Katie was seated forlornly upon the stool, her chin held despondently in her hands as she sat scheming for ways to escape. She didn't look up as Brent came into the tent.

270

thinking it was either one of the guards bringing her supper, or that horrible Mr. Stephens returning to bully her and call her despicable names, or worse.

"Katie," Brent whispered, barely audibly. She jerked her head upright and bounded off of the stool as soon as she recognized his beloved form standing there before her very own eyes.

"Brent," she almost shouted, then remembered to lower her voice, "what in heaven's name are you doing here? Oh, Brent, how did you find me? Oh, my darling, I've been praying for you to come! Ever since we left Savannah, I've hoped that you'd come after me!"

"Katie, it seems that you're in a bit of a mess, doesn't it?" he demanded of her sternly, after he had kissed her most thoroughly and hungrily.

"But, Brent, this isn't my fault. I know it's my fault that I'm smuggling medicine in the first place, but this last bit about the military information contained in some of those bottles has nothing to do with me! They put those in my petticoat pockets without my knowing it. You do know what I'm talking about, don't you?" she asked as he nodded. "Anyway, I have suspected those people of being spies for some time now." She went on to relate to him the details of the incidents that had occurred to convince her of her former companions' guilt. Brent listened in stony silence, trying valiantly not to blow his temper at the shabby and deceitful way they had treated his wife. He listened to her story, then replied:

"Katie, you poor little idiot! You should have known what was going on all along, since you had so much evidence there before your eyes. Well, that won't serve you any good now, will it? Now, dear wife, we've got to think of a way to extricate you from the clutches of that Stephens fellow. I assume you've been trying to think of ways in which to escape upon your own." At her smile and nod, he continued. "Well, I'll just have to get you out of this tent and out of the camp somehow. I'll ride away with you then and we'll go on to Richmond. I have a feeling that it's the last place they would expect us to go. I suppose I could first try and convince Mr. Stephens that I should be the one to take you in. I don't think he will agree, but I may as well try. Katie, I'll be back later. It may be a while, but don't worry, I'll see that you get safely out of this. And, once you are out of this, I'm going to wring your pretty little neck! Give me one more kiss, darling, for luck." He pulled her up beside him and tilted her face upwards toward his own. He brought his warm and caressing lips down upon hers and clung to her for a few moments, then set her aside and left the tent.

Katie dreamily smiled after him, still tingling from his expert kiss. So, her prayers had been answered, her husband had come to rescue her once again. She had thought she would faint from supreme joy and relief when he had walked into the tent a few minutes ago. She had complete faith and trust in his ability to extricate her from this situation. He'd get her away and make sure she was safe.

Brent found his way back through the camp to Colonel Denison's tent and entered without waiting for permission. He approached Mr. Stephens, who was delivering a discourse to the colonel upon the activities of several Confederate spies he'd encountered. Brent interrupted him and said:

"Mr. Stephens, you were right about one thing. She certainly isn't willing to volunteer any information to us, is she? Well, I wanted to ask a favor of you. You see, I was specifically assigned to arrest these spies once I had found them. I realize that you were here when they passed through, and that it was therefore convenient for you to make the arrest of Miss Brent. However, I was wondering if you might possibly consider allowing me the privilege of taking her back to Charleston with me? This was my first major assignment and I was the one ordered to find them after all."

"Captain Morgan, I appreciate your position, but, as you just stated, I was the one here when the spies were captured, and I am therefore entitled to make Miss Brent my own prisoner. Now that you've seen her, you can understand why any man would be only too happy to take her back to his headquarters, can't you? I mean, she's certainly a tasty morsel, isn't she?" he replied as he chuckled deviously.

Brent fought down his rising fury at the man's insinuating tones and suggested, "I understand, Stephens. But, I was hoping you could make an exception. As an officer and a gentleman," here he paused to make his point even clearer, "I feel that you should transfer the prisoner to my keeping, and then I'll head on back to Charleston and to my superiors." He knew that the man would never agree to it, not the way he had just spoken of Katie. It seemed that Mr. Stephens was very attracted to his beautiful prisoner.

"Sorry, old boy. I can't do such a thing. I think I'll keep her here for another day or so for questioning and see if we can find her friends. Then, I'll take her in myself. Now, Colonel, I'll turn in for the night. Good night, gentlemen." He saluted and sauntered outside.

"Good night, Captain Morgan. Stay around here and maybe the man will change his mind. But, I doubt it. Anyway, I'll see you tomorrow, if you're still here." Brent realized he had been summarily dismissed and saluted the officer as he left the tent. He would fetch his horse and bed down near Katie's tent for the night. He would try and think of a way to get her out of there before morning.

Katie couldn't sleep. She lay awake, wondering when Brent would return to inform her of any plans he had made. It was getting rather late and she became afraid that he wouldn't be able to return again until morning. She knew with a certainty that he had been unable to convince Mr. Stephens to release her into his custody.

She shivered with the cold, wrapping the coarse blanket more securely about her body. She sat down on the cot and waited. When would he come?

Shortly before sunrise the following morning, Brent

was preparing to carry out his plans for Katie's escape. He saddled his horse, packed the saddlebags, then approached Katie's guarded tent. No one was up and about yet; the guards were the only ones awake. He crept through the woods until he was directly behind the tent. Drawing out his sharp knife, he quickly and quietly cut a large hole in the canvas.

Katie perceived movement behind her and heard the soft tearing noise as the knife made contact with the fabric of the tent. She stood with widened eyes and fluttering heartbeat until she could make out Brent's face through the hole.

"Brent!" she whispered with relief. He cautioned her with his lips to remain silent. She embraced him tightly as he crawled through the hole and entered the tent.

"Katie, I've got to check and see if the guards have heard anything. You go on out that hole and wait outside there for me. Go on," he commanded her softly. She nodded and crouched down on her hands and knees to crawl out the hole. He watched her as she disappeared through, then tiptoed to the front of the tent to see if the guards had been disturbed. He slowly peeled back one of the flaps and carefully peered outside. The two guards were no longer at attention, apparently having fallen asleep. Brent deplored the sight of a soldier falling asleep while on duty, but he certainly had no time to stop and reprimand the two young men at this time! He quickly turned and followed Katie out the hole. Once outside, he grasped her hand and pulled her along with him as he ran toward the waiting horse. He lifted her on to its back and then swung up behind her. Gently clicking his tongue, Brent urged the horse to walk softly away and through the thickening woods.

"Now, if only there aren't any lookouts posted in those trees. Katie, don't worry, I think we're safely away. Just hold on, because as soon as we're far enough away from camp, I'm going to ride like the wind," he informed her in an undertone. She inclined her head slightly and smiled in response. He hugged her and then turned his full attention to getting them through the forest without detection.

He glanced up and about in the trees as they rode slowly through the woods. Katie felt almost unable to breathe, so intense was the silence that greeted them in the dark forest. Finally, they were emerging in the clearing and far enough away from the camp to begin the ride to Richmond.

"Oh, Brent, I knew you would come. That horrible Stephens would have taken me with him to his headquarters, somewhere in North Carolina. I don't think I could have stood having him beside me for days at a time! In fact, I don't think I could have withstood his presence for even a few more minutes!" she told him.

"Katie, I could have killed the man with my bare hands whenever I heard him so much as mention your name. I think it best if we don't mention him any more for a while; I need to let my temper cool down a bit. Anyway, darling, you're free now and we'll be in Richmond by tomorrow. I really don't believe they'll think to search for us in that direction. Katie," he said, changing his tone, "I've had just about enough of your running away from me all the time! I think it's high time you started learning to obey your husband's commands!"

"Brent, I explained in the letter why I had to leave Savannah without waiting for your return. And, as far as this last problem is concerned, why, it's really no fault of mine. You see, you were right about my friends after all. Only, they are certainly no longer friends!"

"Katie," he remarked seriously, "Captain Collins won't bother you any more. He's dead." He went on to tell her about what had occurred in the hotel room in Savannah. Katie listened intently, only experiencing a sense of relief and gratitude that her husband hadn't been hurt.

"Brent, I know you didn't mean to kill him, but it's happened and there isn't anything we can do about it now. I just want to be with you forever. I want to feel like a real wife! I think it's about time this war was ended, anyway.

275

Darling," she said, suddenly sobering, "when do you think it will end?"

"Who can say? I'm sorry, but it does appear that the South is doomed. I know how much that means to you, but I'm afraid it was meant to be. The Confederacy won't be able to hold out much longer, and they know it. Can you ever forget that I'm a Yankee and just think of me as a man?" he hopefully asked.

"Yes, I already have. Why, as a matter of fact, I have almost forgotten that you're a soldier at all. Seeing you in those civilian clothes all the time now has helped, also. I have been thinking of you only as a man for a long time."

"So at least the Yankee and his Southern belle have made their peace, haven't they? There'll be no more war between us from now on, Katie."

"Oh, I wouldn't say that, darling. I wouldn't say that at all. With our tempers and uneasy dispositions, I'd say there will be more wars between us. But," she paused here and smiled mischievously, "I think we'll manage to make peace. After all, we'll have one another, and it's very hard to keep a conflict going when you have that particular element of love involved."

Twenty Two

Brent and Katie arrived in Richmond after riding all day and throughout the night. They had stopped only a few times to allow the tiring horse to rest, then were off once more at a swift pace. The day dawned cold and clear, and Katie could see Richmond that afternoon in the distance as they neared its limits. She hoped that Brent's calculation that Stephens or the others wouldn't think to search for them there was correct.

"Brent, isn't it beautiful? Have you ever been to Richmond before?" she asked at a sudden thought.

"Yes, I have. It's been a few years now, though. I came through here just after I came down South. I'm sure it's changed quite a bit since then. We'll be putting up at one of the nicest hotels once we get into the city. I'm sure you'll be ready for a hot bath, some good food, and then a long nap."

"Oh, of course I will. But first," she commented as she giggled, "I want to have a proper reunion with my husband."

"Katie O'Toole Morgan, you're a little vixen! I happen to love you dearly. Now, what do you say we quit gabbing and get on into town?" She laughed and he spurred his mount onward.

They rode through the winding streets of Richmond, noting the great amount of population and its activity. Brent lifted Katie down from the saddle as he drew up before the Grand Hotel.

"Well, this used to be the nicest hotel in the city. I hope

277

it still is. Come on, honey, let's get inside and get that room." He ushered her into the hotel and requested a room of the desk clerk.

The clerk behind the counter took one look at their mud-spattered, dusty clothing and asked arrogantly:

"Sir, are you sure you can afford a room in this hotel? This is one of Richmond's best and most luxurious hotels, you see."

Brent clenched his teeth at the man's pompous impertinence and replied casually, "Yes, my good man. In fact, I can damn well buy this fine hotel if I so choose. Now, I want the bridal suite for myself and my bride, if you please. We don't have any baggage with us. You see," here he paused to wink at his amused wife, "we prefer to purchase all new attire whenever we travel. Now, how about that key?"

The affronted clerk pushed his spectacles farther up on to his pointed nose and turned his back to select the key, which he dangled in front of Brent. Brent jerked the key from his grasp and, taking his wife by the hand, he ran up the long, curved, elegant staircase to the third floor and the bridal suite. He unlocked the door as Katie was still laughing about the scene below. She started to enter the room, only to be halted by the pressure of his hand upon her arm.

"No, darling. This is a bridal suite, remember? I think it's about time we had a proper honeymoon, don't you? A bride is most assuredly supposed to be lifted and carried across the threshold in the arms of her new husband. Up you go, Katie." He lifted her easily in his arms and strode across the threshold, slamming the heavy door shut behind him with the edge of his booted heel. He carried her to the huge, gilded bed and dropped her down into its pillowy softness.

"Oh, Brent, this room is lovely! Why, I've never seen anything like it before. Look at this bed, those chairs, the wallpaper. Why, this is a veritable paradise!"

278

Brent chuckled at her avid description and apparent delight.

"Katie, you are the most enchanting woman I ever have known or ever will know! I think I love you even more now than I did yesterday. How about you, Mrs. Morgan? Do you still love this grubby, unshaven soldier you married so unwillingly?" he asked as his eyes twinkled mischievously down at her.

"Of course I love you, silly. And, as for my 'unwillingness' at our wedding, why, that was your own fault, Captain Morgan! If only you'd been a little more patient and understanding with me for a while longer, instead of so high and mighty, I would have given in eventually! Now, stop being ridiculous and order us some supper. I'm going to have that bath first, after all, just as you promised I could. Since it appears I married a filthy rich man, why don't you get some champagne, also? I've never before tasted the stuff."

"Very well. But, I'm not 'filthy rich' as you call it. I just happen to be independently wealthy! Being the only son of a prosperous banker and the heir to a fortune from my grandfather doesn't make me any less independent, though, I can assure you!" He observed his wife as she scampered off to the bathroom.

"Well, I really don't care if you are as poor as a churchmouse! Now, sir, order me some supper. I'm literally famished! I can tell you, that getting caught and imprisoned as a Confederate spy, then daringly rescued by a handsome knight in shining armor only serves to whet one's appetite!" She closed the door and began to prepare for her bath.

Minutes later, Brent heard her splashing in the tub. He recalled the time, seemingly ages ago, when he had burst in upon her in the bathtub that day up in her room at Corkhaven. She had looked so lovely and alluring then. She was even more so to him now. He smiled wickedly at the memory of her shocked reaction. He tiptoed softly to the bathroom door and gently eased it open.

Katie, seated in the steaming bathtub with her back facing the door, didn't hear or see Brent as he entered the room. She was busily soaping her body with the lavender-scented soap and reveling in the water's soothing warmth.

"My, my what have we here? Mrs. Morgan, it seems that I've had this pleasure before."

Katie jerked her head around and observed her husband, standing a few feet away, wearing a gleeful grin on his handsome face.

"Brent, will you please allow me to finish my bath? I'm almost finished, anyway. Have you ordered supper yet?" she cooly inquired. She found herself blushing furiously before his admiring scrutiny.

"Yes, I've ordered supper. What would you say if I decided to join you in your bath?" he suggested as he began removing his clothing.

"Brent! No! Please, not now, darling. What do you think you're doing? There isn't room enough for the two of us! You're absolutely insane, did you know that?" she squealed as he lowered his naked, muscular body into the tub. He eased down into the water, facing her, and demanded, "Now, dear wife, scrub my back! I expect a wife to be obedient. Do as I say this very instant!" He scowled mockingly. Katie gathered the soapy sponge in her hand and lifted her hand to throw it. He caught it full in the face, while she scrambled from the tub and quickly wrapped her gleaming body in a thick towel.

"There! That's what you get for treating me so shamelessly! I'll be waiting for you, darling. I suppose supper will be coming up very soon now. Enjoy your bath!" She lifted her nose triumphantly and strolled from the room. Brent called out a threat as she glided away, laughing all the while.

Later, after they had both filled their empty stomachs with the delicious supper, Brent rose from his chair and drew Katie to the bed, whisperingly lovingly in her ear,

"Katie, what about that reunion you were talking about earlier? I think it only fair that you fulfill that promise, seeing as how I've chased you all over Dixie ever since I saw fit to marry you! I think it's about time we started getting better acquainted, don't you?"

Katie slowly raised her green eyes to his blue ones and replied in a low, husky undertone, "Brent, I love you so much. Thank you for coming after me. Thank you for loving me, for marrying me. I'll never be able to endure life without you again, my darling husband." She kissed him then, running her long, slender fingers through his thick hair. He moaned and nearly bruised her mouth with his own lips as he felt his passion mounting. He reached over to the table beside the bed and turned out the lamp, then proceeded to undress. Soon, both he and Katie were naked and impatiently waiting for each other's touch.

"Brent, I amost feel as if this is our wedding night, all over again. I'm afraid we haven't had much time to get to know one another. Do you like me, darling? I mean, do I please you?" she asked seriously.

"Yes, I think you're absolutely exquisite. You happen to please me very much. Now, enough of this talk. Let's get on with the reunion. Oh, Katie, I love you so."

Brent lowered his body on top of hers and began to caress her softly curved body with his gentle hands. Katie sighed in surrender and felt the deep fires now growing within the very depths of her being. Soon, the fires had built to a searing flame, and the two of them came together in utmost ecstasy and love.

Much later, Katie began to question Brent about their future, about what his plans were for them now that the spies had escaped and he had allowed her to remain free.

"Katie, I can only try and get permission to travel to Corkhaven and see you home. I haven't really thought it all through that well just yet. I've got to find some way to get you home safely, and it looks as if I'm the only one who will ever be able to get you there! However, I intend for you to stay put this time!" he informed her sternly.

"Brent, you just can't leave without permission. Why, you'd be called a deserter! Darling, I can manage to get home. Until you have to leave Richmond, I'll simply stay here with you. Or, I do suppose we could send a message to Uncle Albert. Come to think of it, did you ever send him word to come and fetch me in Savannah?" she suddenly remembered.

"It's just a little too late to be thinking of that, don't you think? No, honey, I didn't send him the message. I suppose I really didn't want you to go home at all. I thought I'd be staying in Savannah for a while, anyway. Now, though, it's out of the question for you to travel all that way on your own. The war is still going on, no matter how peaceful it may seem here right now. We're here in our own little world, just the escaped Confederate spy and the traitorous Yankee captain!"

"Brent, don't you talk like that! You know that we don't fit those terms. Anyway, we can't worry about what's coming next, can we, darling? When you go and see your contact here, you can find out what your next orders are, can't you? I only wish I hadn't put you to so much trouble. I know I've been nothing but that ever since you first laid eyes on me," she said as she sighed heavily.

"Yes, but you've been the most welcome little bundle of trouble I'll ever have! I'll go and see my contact first thing in the morning and I'll see what I can work out. You'll stay here in the hotel room, and that's an order!"

"Yes, sir, Captain Morgan. By the way, Brent, you needn't worry about hiding your business from me any longer. I've suspected from the very beginning what you have been doing. I mean, it is a bit obvious to your own wife. Are they ever going to let you go back to being a regular soldier?"

"It doesn't look like it. However, since I so badly failed this last mission, they might wish to be rid of me after all! Let's get some sleep now, darling. It may be a long day tomorrow." He kissed her once more and they nestled closer to one another.

The next morning, true to his word, Brent ordered Katie to remain in the hotel room while he made his way across town to speak with his contact. She knew it would be useless to protest, so she merely kissed him goodbye without an argument and sat down to await his return.

Brent located the smithy and the name of the man he had memorized from the list he had previously been given. He entered the smithy and asked for the agent.

"Could you please tell me where to find a Mr. Thomas?" he asked the blacksmith in the building.

"Yes, sir, he's over there, that man in the blue flannel shirt."

Brent thanked the man and approached the agent, who glanced up from his work as he caught sight of Brent.

"Mr. Thomas?"

"Yes, what is it? What do you want, sir?"

"I'm Brent Morgan. I've been referred to you by a mutual friend of ours in Charleston."

"Ah, yes, Mr. Morgan. I've been expecting you. Please step this way, out back with me, so we can talk." He led the way through the back and the two of them emerged out into the sunshine.

"Now, was your mission successful, Morgan? Do you have any details you'd like to discuss?"

"No, the mission wasn't successful, I'm afraid. The spies were captured a couple of days' ride from here, but they managed to escape, all except one. An agent by the name of Stephens has the spy, a woman, under guard, but he refused to release her into my custody. So, consequently, Mr. Thomas, I've come out of this emptyhanded. The spies were headed here, and I'm sure they've already passed their goods. They will more than likely hide out for a while now."

"Yes, I see. Well, I'm sorry, Morgan, that you couldn't have been more successful, but I understand. I haven't always succeeded with all of the assignments I've been handed, either. Don't worry, though, we'll catch them sooner or later. Now, I have here a message for you from

283

Mr. Morrow in Savannah. He instructed me to give it to you when you arrived here. Take this and read it now. If you need to speak with me again, just come to the address I've written on the back of the letter. Remember to burn it after you've read it and are sure you understand its contents. By the way, where can you be reached if I need to get in touch with you?"

"I'm staying at the Grand Hotel. Thank you very much. Good day, Mr. Thomas." He tipped his hat and left the smithy.

He opened the letter on his way back to the hotel. It read,

"Dear Mr. Morgan: I have another assignment for you. I have received word that there is a large gun running operation being run by a dubious character, who is still unknown, to the west of Atlanta, near the border. It's a long trip, but you are to leave Richmond at once and journey to the vicinity due west of Atlanta, and see what you can discover. We already know that the operation is indeed being guided from that area, but we don't know the name of the individual responsible yet. We only know that he has been operating this business for the course of the war, and that this is the first time anyone has seen fit to inform on him. However, they wouldn't reveal any further information.

"Morgan, I wish you success in your mission. Of course, the spies were of primary concern, but the gun running operation is also a major problem. Don't worry, we'll catch the spies sooner or later. If you have any further questions or need to get word to me, please tell Mr. Thomas before you leave Richmond. Good luck. Mr. Morrow."

Brent crumpled the letter in his left hand and entered the hotel, quickly climbing the stairs back to the room where he knew Katie was anxiously awaiting the outcome of his morning visit. He opened the door and faced his wife.

"Katie, my dear, good news! It seems that I'll be able to

take you to Corkhaven myself, after all. Yes, I've just received orders about a mission that will take me in that general area. Isn't that a wonderful coincidence?" Katie smiled in response and threw her arms about his neck.

"Oh, Brent, that is the best news we've had in a long time! Why, we'll have a few more weeks to spend together, and you won't have to worry about my getting back home safely. I suppose you can't tell me what this important mission is, can you? Not even a little bit?" she coaxed.

"No, and you know good and well I can't. Now, we've got to leave as soon as possible. I didn't tell them about your being with me, of course. I can just see their faces now—'gentlemen, I've rescued my wife from our own forces, and she's suspected of being a Confederate spy. I'm going to see that she gets safely away.' I know they weren't too pleased that I failed to bring in those others, but this assignment is almost as important as the last one. Now, come on, we've got to get ready to leave."

"Brent, I haven't got any other clothes, and neither have you. I'm so very tired of traveling in this same dress. Can't we buy a few things before we leave here? We'll have to get supplies, anyway," she pleaded. She deplored always looking like a dirty farm wife!

"All right, I suppose that will be safe enough. I'll go on down and get us some things right now. I'm sorry, honey, but you can't be seen with me," he informed her regretfully.

"Well, just give me some money and I'll go on and get my things myself. I'll meet you back here in the room in an hour."

"Just see that you don't get into any more trouble, will you? And, don't let some man spirit you away!" he joked.

She stuck out her tongue and then whirled from the room, stuffing the money he had handed her into her purse. She hurried across the street and down the boardwalk, where she had recalled seeing a small dress shop when they had ridden through yesterday afternoon. She'd probably have to go to a regular dry goods store to

285

purchase some men's pants to wear on the trip. But, she so wanted some dresses to take with her, also.

An hour and a half later, Katie reappeared at the hotel room, only to be confronted by a very impatient husband.

"Where have you been, woman? I told you to be back in an hour, and I meant it. We've got to leave right away, remember?"

"Brent, don't scold me. It took longer than I thought to get a few things, that's all. Anyway, I think I have sufficient clothing for the trip now. Did you get everything we need?"

"Yes, I purchased some clothing, and then I went on over to the general store and got our supplies. I've got my horse and another one for you waiting downstairs. Come on, let's get going. I don't think it would be too wise to wait around and take the chance on someone finding us together. Who knows, Mr. Stephens may be smarter than I've given him credit." He gathered up the full saddlebags and other bundles and led the way downstairs. He tied the provisions on to the horses and helped Katie to mount. They began to ride to the southwest of the city, away toward Corkhaven.

Katie, occupied with discussing plans for their future together with her husband, didn't at first notice the two couples strolling along the sidewalk, on the opposite side of the street. When she finally did notice their presence and the four pairs of eyes following her, she halted her mount and gasped to Brent, "Brent! That's them! Over there, watching us. Those are the people I was involved with, the despicable characters who left me behind and planted those messages in my bottles. What should I do? I mean, they probably wonder why I'm not still held by the Yankees, and how I got here to Richmond so fast."

Brent laid a soothing hand on her arm and attempted to reassure her.

"Katie, it doesn't matter what they think. I can't do anything about them now, even though I know who they are and what they've done. I can't arrest them, not here in

286

the middle of Richmond. Just turn your head away from them and behave as if they didn't exist. They can't harm you. In fact, I'm sure they're squirming a bit right this very moment, seeing you ride by safe and unharmed," he said as he chuckled. "They're probably scared to death that you were able to give the Union soldiers some information about them that could be their downfall. Come on, let's keep right on going. You can start forgetting about them right now." Katie smiled in gratitude at his words and averted her gaze from the four spies.

"Miranda, can you believe it? Why, there's Katie Brent on that horse over there!" exclaimed Julie in astonishment.

"Yes, it sure is! I wonder how come the Yankees let her go free? Do you suppose they didn't find the bottles or the messages?" Miranda replied.

"It don't matter if they did, you know that. Since we had to worry about her getting caught, it was a good idea to think of planting those dummy messages in those bottles, don't you think?" Jake said, very well pleased with his own cleverness. He grimaced with a sudden pain from his wounded shoulder.

"Well, they simply must not have searched her. But, Jake, what if they did? What if she was able to tell them all about us?" Robert asked at a sudden fear.

"Don't be an idiot, man! She couldn't tell them anything about us that they don't already know for themselves. Anyway, she's apparently all right and has taken up with some man. There, that goes to show you, Miranda, that you were just being silly about making us all be so damned careful not to let her know we weren't what she thought. There she is, bold as brass, latching on to a man while her soldier husband is away fighting for the cause."

"Well, I say the sooner we forget about Miss Katie Brent, or Morgan, or whatever name she goes by now, the better!" Julie remarked derisively.

The four of them continued watching Katie as she rode out of sight beside Brent. She didn't look back at them again, even though her thoughts were occupied with them as she rode.

I wonder what they'll do now? she asked herself. They'll probably do as Brent said; lay low for a while, then resume their activities for the Confederacy. I wonder if what they've accomplished has really been of such a great help to the South. The war isn't going at all well for us. Perhaps Brent was right; perhaps the outcome of the war is already decided.

Twenty Three

"We'll camp here for the night," Brent told Katie as he dismounted in a small clearing of the North Carolina woods.

"I'm so exhausted, I don't care where you choose. I'm awfully chilled, too. Did you have very harsh winters up north, Brent?" she asked conversationally as she dismounted and sat down on the frosty ground to wait for him to build the fire.

"Oh, this isn't anything like our winters at home. You can't even imagine. Why, this is like mere spring to us. It gets extremely cold, snow falls frequently, and one can't even keep one's nose from nearly getting frostbitten. Would you like to see it some day, Katie?" he teasingly asked.

"No, thank you, sir. I despise cold weather, even if it is the 'mild' winters of the South. Darling, while you're building that fire, I think I'll go and wash up. Do you think there's a spring or creek around here somewhere?"

"Yes, of course there is, or I wouldn't have chosen this spot, now, would I? Here, I'll go with you and show you where I saw it. That water's going to be icy cold, you know."

The two of them traipsed off into the trees. In a matter of minutes, they had stumbled upon a narrow, swiftly flowing creek.

"You go on back and start that fire! I'll be along in just a few minutes. I've simply got to wash some of this dust off of me, no matter how cold it is."

Brent turned and walked back through the brush. Katie watched him go, a happy smile on her face. We've been through an awful lot together, she thought. This trip is the best thing that's happened to us, so far. I think I'm finally beginning to know him, and he's finally getting to know me in return. They had come from Richmond to North Carolina so far, making very good time. It was only a matter of weeks now before they reached Corkhaven.

The journey had been, for the most part, uneventful. They had fortunately been able to avoid any troops from either side, nor had they encountered any other difficulties. The route they were traveling kept them away from the towns and most of civilization. They would talk and discuss future plans as they rode, although sometimes they would travel along without saying a word for miles. Katie liked these times, too, for they felt comfortable together, she and Brent, even in silence.

The nights they had shared together were even more rapturous than she could ever have imagined. Who would have believed it? she mused. I entered into this marriage most unwillingly, but I couldn't break the bonds for anything in the world now. I love him more and more each day.

Brent had told her of his childhood, of his adolescence. She had, in return, related to him the details of her own happy past, of her dear father and the lenient hand he had applied to his only, headstrong daughter. They had laughed and talked together for hours about their own future together, about the children she would so gladly bear him. So far, however, they hadn't decided exactly what they would do after the war's end.

Katie shook herself mentally and dipped a cloth into the cold water flowing by. She bathed her dusty face, then her equally dirty neck and arms.

"So, I again have the honor of watching Venus bathing by the water. You are lovelier than when I last saw you, my dear Katie."

Katie whirled around to face the voice's owner. She

experienced a grisly shock at seeing his face, a man she had believed dead, the very man her husband had believed he himself had killed.

"You! I thought you were dead! How did you find me? I believe you must have ties with Satan himself, you fiend!" she managed to blurt out.

"Oh, I told you before, dear Katie, that it was fate for you and I to be together. As for finding you, I have my sources of information, you see. You and I are alone here now. What do you think I'm going to do with you?" he asked tantalizingly.

"Captain Collins, my husband is nearby. If you come near me, I'll scream, and he'll kill you for sure this time, you may depend on that. I don't know how come you weren't killed in Savannah. He told me that you fell out the window and to the street below. How did you manage to survive such a fall? How come you aren't injured?" she inquired cooly, as she desperately stalled for time.

"I wasn't uninjured, my dear. It took several weeks for my body to mend entirely. Luckily, though, I suffered only a small concussion and two sprained ankles, as well as various cuts and bruises. Nothing serious enough to keep me from following my darling Katie, however. I remained in Savannah to recuperate for a while, then set out to find you. You left Savannah rather suddenly, remember? What was the hurry, were you afraid of me, Katie, honey?"

"I don't know why you feel as if you have to acquire some kind of revenge from me! I never did anything to you, sir, other than to defend myself when you attempted to rape me, and then escape when you held me prisoner! You are ruthless, and you are also a coward. I'll kill you myself if you come near me again!" she threatened courageously. Where was Brent? Wouldn't he have become worried about her by now?

"I can see by the expression on your beautiful, deceitful little face that you are expecting your husband to come crashing through those trees to save you. Well, don't. I

291

came upon him back at your camp and incapacitated him before I came down here to deal with you. Oh, he's not dead yet," he assured her as she gasped in horror, "but, he soon will be. After I've finished with you, I'll go back and complete my business with him. For the time being, he's merely unconscious. Enough about him, though, Katie. I promised you that you would pay dearly for the humiliation you've caused me to suffer, the endless searching, the fall from the hotel room. You see, you have been the cause of all my troubles ever since I first laid eyes on your treacherous person at your ball in Atlanta. You were proud and defiant, and you thought yourself too good for me, didn't you? Well, I intend to show you that you're not good enough!" He began to remove his coat and unbuckle his belt. Katie gazed at his actions in horrified fascination, before finally coming to life once again and bolting for the camp. Collins laughed triumphantly and snaked out an arm to catch her roughly about her waist.

"Let me go! I detest you! I'll never give in to you, can't you see that? All this about it being fate, that's just an excuse, and you know it! You and I were never meant to be, and I'll never let you have your way with me. I'll kill myself first, do you hear?" she screamed helplessly as she flailed at him with clenched fists.

"And just how do you intend to go about killing yourself, Katie? I won't let you near my gun, and the water isn't quite deep enough in which to drown yourself, even if you tried. Now that I've got you, I am sure you will enjoy what I'm going to do to you. I'll show you what you've been missing, show you what you could have had if you'd only been reasonable. As for your husband, I am much more of a man that he could ever hope to be. And what's more, you need a real man, sweetheart. You may damn well scream and kick all you like, you can fight me all you want. I will have you, no matter what. I've waited too long for this already, Katie. I've been tormented with the thought of your naked body beneath mine!" He lifted his arm and struck her cruelly across the face with the back of his hand. She reeled beneath the blow and would have staggered and fallen to the ground if he hadn't continued to hold her upright.

He's insane, she thought hysterically, he's crazed with madness and revenge. Oh, Brent, please wake up! Please come before it's too late, too late for both of us. That's what frightened her more than anything Captain Collins could do to her; the thought of her beloved husband being butchered in cold blood afterwards. Oh dear Lord, please help us. Please don't let it be this way. She could no longer think clearly. Perhaps she would faint and rid her mind of this terrible fear.

"I've followed you from outside Atlanta, haven't I? Yes, sir, all over the territory. You didn't think I'd ever be able to find you again. It wasn't easy, but I did. As soon as I could leave Savannah, I went to Charleston after you. I received information about you there, about your heading for Richmond with those friends of yours. I knew where you and your husband were staying. I decided to bide my time and catch you unawares. But, again, you left rather hastily. I've been following you ever since. You've traveled fast, but I've kept up with you, haven't I? Now, do you want to hear what I'm going to do to you now? Do you want me to describe the things I'm going to do?" he suggested as he laughed maliciously.

"No! You'll have to render me unconscious before you'll ever have me! Then, I'll kill myself. No matter how hard you try to prevent me, I'll find a way to do it. I'm not afraid of you any more, Captain Collins. I'm not afraid of what you might do to me. I'm grateful for the time I've had to spend with my husband, for the love the two of us have shared. I'll never be sorry for that. But, you couldn't understand that, could you? You would never understand anything so beautiful. Go ahead and do your worst, sir, but I'll resist. You can kill me afterwards if that's what you want. I don't care any longer. If my husband, the man I love, is going to die, then I want to die, too," she replied.

She meant everything she told him; she didn't want to live without Brent. She didn't want to be raped by this madman, but it didn't really matter any more. She was prepared to die. She prayed fervently then, only that God be merciful and allow her to endure what she must. She steeled herself for the battle ahead.

Captain Richard Collins stared down into the eyes of his intended victim in surprise and acute disappointment. He had wanted her to crawl, to plead and beg! Why wasn't she frightened of him any longer? Didn't she realize the things he could do to her, the terrible, painful way in which he could kill her? What was going wrong? This wasn't the way he had planned it all.

"Katie, you're just bluffing. You think to draw my mind away from you, don't you? You think to postpone what's coming, don't you? Well, it won't work. I'll rape you, and then I will kill you. I can't rest as long as you're still alive. I won't be haunted by your beautiful, disdainful face and your sensuous body any longer!" He pushed her to the hard ground and began tearing away at her clothing. Katie shivered with the shock of the cold that greeted her bare skin. Please Lord, she continued praying, let me pass out now.

"Hold it right there, you bastard! Get away from her right now! Or I'll gladly blow your damned head off where you stand!"

Collins jerked himself upright at the first sound of Brent's voice. He considered going for his gun, but it was too far away.

"So, I thought I left you out cold, Morgan. Ah, yes, I now know what your name is, Captain. A friend of mine knows all about you and your, shall we say, 'secret activities.' I thought that a fine and dandy Yankee soldier such as yourself wouldn't think to shoot an unarmed man," he jeered.

"Well, apparently, you thought wrong, Collins. I could kill you in cold blood and never give it a thought for what you've just done to my wife. I'm only glad I arrived before you could do worse. However, you're going to die for what you've done. I could never let a man live who has done what you have done to her, who had even so much as touched her the way you have. Crawl, you cowardly bastard, crawl and beg me for your life, the way you wanted her to crawl. Come on, crawl or I'll blow you to pieces right now!"

Katie cringed at the terrible fury she saw in Brent's eyes, the cold-hearted desire to kill. She was glad she had never encountered such fury directed at herself. She gave silent thanks that he had arrived in time, that he wasn't dead, as she had begun to fear. She crouched upon the ground, drawing her tattered clothing about her shivering body, intently watching and waiting for what would come next.

"I'll never crawl to any man, much less a Yankee, Morgan. You are an officer in the Union Army, while I am an officer of the Confederacy. You can't shoot me down in cold blood, for it's decidedly not in a soldier's style, now, is it? Why don't you quit quibbling and gabbing about my being a coward and prove yourself worthy of your rank, Captain? Let's make it a fair fight. Drop your gun and fight like a man." He smiled tauntingly and awaited Brent's response.

"Brent, don't listen to him! He's insane! He's got some trick worked out in his devious mind, I'm sure, or he wouldn't even suggest it! You don't have to shoot him, though. You can take him prisoner and . . ." Katie began.

"No, Katie, that won't serve. He can't be allowed to terrorize you and possibly some other poor soul any longer. He can't be allowed to go free. All right, Collins," Brent said as he turned back to the man held at gunpoint, "let's make it a fair fight. What do you say we use knives in a fight to the death?"

"That's quite satisfactory, Morgan. And, whoever emerges victorious may have the pleasure of your wife's charms and company, right?" he taunted further.

Brent ground his teeth in anger at the man's insolent

suggestion and approached Katie for a last word with her before the fight.

"Katie, take my gun and shoot him if he comes near you again. If I do happen to lose, which I won't, don't wait around; take the horses and ride as quickly as possible in that direction, understand? Don't worry, honey, I won't lose," he informed her in an undertone. She nodded, wide-eyed and fearful for him.

"Collins, get ready to die." He removed his coat and drew out his long knife. Collins took one last ogling look at Katie, designed to further enrage his opponent, then also grasped his knife in his hand and the two men faced each other across a mere two yards of space.

"Brent, be careful! Collins," she yelled at the other man, "this isn't a fair fight, and you know it! Why, you've knocked him over the head and he's still bleeding!" The two opponents ignored her protests and commenced fighting.

They circled one another in the twilight of the winter evening, each breathing slowly and evenly in anticipation. Collins attacked first, swiping at Brent's muscular chest with his knife. Brent jumped out of the knife's reach and managed to direct a well-aimed kick at Collins' right knee. Collins grimaced with pain and cursed, then viciously attacked once more. Brent again agilely defended himself and brought his own knife slashing down into Collins' left forearm. The Confederate deserter grunted as the knife made contact with his flesh and he staggered backwards.

Katie watched with dreaded expectancy as Brent wielded his knife and fought with cunning cruelty. He knew what he was doing, he meant to kill Collins, that was evident. Collins also appeared to be knowledgeable about such warfare, but he didn't possess the strength or agility of the younger man.

Finally, Collins lashed out at his opponent with all his might, slashing Brent across the chest, but failing to lodge the blade within his flesh. Brent brought his knife up into

296

the other man's chest, burying its sharpness deep within his heart. Collins gave one last grunt of pain, then collapsed, lifeless, to the ground.

"Oh, Brent, you're bleeding something awful!" was all Katie could manage to comment at the time. She ran to his aid and helped him over to sit on a large rock by the stream.

"It's over now, Katie," Brent gasped as he caught his breath. "I thought I killed him the last time, but I now have for sure. I don't know how he survived that fall in Savannah. I should have made certain of his death and then you would have been spared such torment."

"You couldn't have known he wasn't dead before, since he apparently appeared to be so. Oh, darling, he's dead now, and we needn't ever think of him again. You didn't murder him, you killed him in a fair fight. Now, come on and let me see to those cuts. Oh, your head is bleeding even more than before. Brent, I'm so glad you weren't killed! I didn't want to go on living without you. When I thought he was going to murder you, I told him to kill me, too. I threatened to kill myself if he didn't. He was going to do terrible things to me, but I could only think of you. I love you so much," she brokenly told him, tearful now at the release of all anxieties. Now that it was all over with, she needed the release of tears. She put her head wearily down between her hands and began to cry.

"Katie, don't think about it any longer. I can't stand to see you cry this way. It's all right, darling, I'll never let anything happen to you again. I would give my very life to protect you from harm. I love you more than life itself." He drew her painfully into his embrace and cradled her head on to his shoulder. He winced from the pain in the cut on his chest, but he held her tightly in his arms and sought to comfort her.

As her wrenching tears began to cease, Katie pulled away gently and apologized, "Oh, I'm sorry! Your chest must hurt you terribly. Your head isn't feeling too well, either, I'm sure. Here, you sit there and I'll see to fixing you up, all right?" She sniffed one last time and set about to work on his wounds.

He watched her lovingly and knew that she'd be all right now and that she'd had a good cry. She had been through so much, been forced to endure so much more than most women. And, she was so young.

Several days later, they came upon a small troop of Confederates while they were riding through South Carolina. They rode within the army camp and paused to speak with a few of the men.

"Howdy! What are you folks doing way out here in the middle of nowhere?" one of the soldiers asked with a friendly grin.

"We're going home, west of Atlanta," replied Katie, She noted the poor man's bare feet, his faded and patched uniform.

"Have you got any news of the war?" asked Brent.

"Well, depends on what you heard last, don't it? Where you coming from, anyhow?" another of the men said.

"Richmond. We've been traveling for a while now and haven't heard anything since we left," replied Brent.

"Well, then you probably ain't heard that Savannah's been captured by Sherman, have you? Yep, and the Yankees got Nashville, too. Things ain't going too well elsewhere, either, from what I heard. We've had several deserters from our outfit the last couple of weeks. Come to think of it, mister, how come you ain't in uniform?"

"Well, I was wounded and discharged. I'm much obliged to you all for the information. Sorry we can't stop to chat any longer. We've got to hurry up and get on home. Good luck, men," Brent remarked as he and Katie left the camp and continued on their way.

"Brent, Savannah and Nashville lost. I'm afraid you were right. It doesn't sound as if there's much hope left now, does it?" she sadly remarked.

"No, honey, it doesn't. I'm sorry. I know we'll neve fully agree about this war, and what we've fought for o against, but I don't suppose we have to. It doesn't matter between us, Katie, don't you see? What happens was meant to be, and we can't change it."

"I suppose you're right," she answered with a resigned sigh. "Well, I won't argue with you about the war just yet. I promised myself that I wouldn't do that until after it's over!"

"That's fine. I suppose we'll have more warfare between us after it's ended, then, is that it?" he teased.

She laughed at him in return and then turned her attention once more to her riding. They were now well within the boundaries of South Carolina. Before too much longer, they would be in Georgia again. They had already been traveling for a couple of weeks, but they were swiftly nearing their destination.

They camped one last night several miles west of Atlanta, excited at being so near to home. Brent's mind began to concentrate on his assignment, the reason he'd been allowed to make this journey in the first place. Gun-running. Surely a profitable business, but certainly not a very safe one. How could anyone get away with it, especially in this area? he wondered. Now, he had set about gathering information about the operation's leader. All he'd been told was that they operated the business near the border, west of Atlanta. That didn't tell him too much. Suddenly, a growing suspicion lodged itself in his brain. It might very well be someone Katie knew, since he was in the same general area as her home, at least as had last been reported. Oh, that's all he needed, to be forced to arrest one of his wife's own friends! Perhaps it wasn't anyone she knew, though, just someone hiding out near Corkhaven.

"Brent, what on earth are you thinking about? You look so stern and forbidding."

"Oh, just thinking about my mission, darling. It isn't anything I can tell you yet. How about us getting some sleep?" he suggested, changing the subject. "It's been a long and hard journey, but we're almost there. I can't think of anything I'd rather do than be with you, and I've certainly had that opportunity for the past few weeks, haven't I?"

"Yes, I feel like we've finally gotten acquainted. I'm kind of sorry to be going home, I mean, after all we've been through together. It's all been so exciting, hasn't it? I'm afraid I'll be bored silly with all the uneventful days at Corkhaven. Oh, Brent, I can hardly wait till this war's over with and we can live together as a man and wife should. I want to start a family, build a home. I want to be like other married couples. At least, before the war came along, that is."

"Well, we haven't yet decided where we're going to build that home, have we? And, as for starting a family, what would you say if I wanted to start one right now?" he suggested with a meaningful expression on his handsome face and a decided glint in his blue eyes.

"I'd say that I think that's a wonderful idea," she replied. He grasped her tightly against his hard leanness and then lowered her gently to the blanket spread upon the ground below.

"I once heard that if you make love with your husband in the evening, you'll have a girl, and if you make love in the morning, it will be a boy. Which do you want, darling? Because, if you want a boy first, perhaps we should wait until morning . . ."

"How about a girl tonight and a boy in the morning?" he interrupted teasingly as he kissed her into silence.

Late the next afternoon, they finally rode within sight of Corkhaven. They had traveled across much war-torn and scarred countryside, but Corkhaven and the surrounding lands had remained untouched. They were still lovely in their splendor, even in the winter.

"There it is! I can't wait to see Mama and the boys again. Oh, do hurry, darling, we've got to hurry. Come on!" She spurred her horse onward and left an amused and chuckling Brent behind her. He waited a moment, then slowly guided his horse after her. He wanted to allow her time to be warmly greeted by her loving family. He still believed that they didn't know of his marriage to Katie. He believed he would be looked upon as the intruder, still the enemy.

"Mama! James! John! Where is everybody? It's me, Katie!" she shouted with excitement. Soon, the front doors flew open and her own dear mother appeared on the veranda, looking very puzzled at all the noise and commotion outside.

"Who in the world . . ." she started to say, then paused to stare incredulously at the disheveled, suntanned creature dismounting from the dusty, sweating horse. "Katie, could that possibly be you?"

"Oh, yes, Mama, it's me! I've come home! Where is everyone?" she answered as she bounded up the steps to embrace her mother.

"Katie, my own darling daughter! So, you've finally decided to let us know you're alive, young lady! James! John! Jenny and Albert! Everyone, Katie's come home! Hurry up!" she called toward the house. Katie's two energetic young brothers ran down the steps and launched themselves at her. Aunt Jenny and Uncle Albert hurried down the steps to welcome her home, also.

"Brent is behind me. I guess he wanted to let me say hello to you first, and maybe to explain things . . ." she began hesitantly.

"Katie, we know all about your marriage to him," her mother broke in. "Esther and Sarah told us all about it. Now, I can't say that I approve of your marrying a Yankee, and in such a shameful fashion, but what's done is done. I suppose we'll simply have to let him stay, since he is, after all, your husband."

Katie opened her mouth in astonishment at her mother's news and subsequent acquiescence. So, they had told! Well, she didn't care, she was glad her family knew the truth. This way, it would be much easier for Brent.

Brent rode into the yard and slowly dismounted, observing the reactions of Katie's family to his presence.

Seeing no hostile opposition, at least not outwardly, he supposed that Katie must not have told them yet about his being her husband. Either that, or they already knew. Sarah! he remembered suddenly. Sarah must have told them. He strolled up to James and John, who playfully punched him in the stomach. He laughed and ruffled the hair of each boy, then they jumped back up the steps and ran into the house.

"Young man, I presume you are Katie's husband. Captain Morgan, how do you do? I'm her Uncle Albert, and this is my wife, Jenny. I'm pleased to meet you. We've been looking forward to the pleasure of meeting the fortunate young man who has been able to tame our wayward niece."

"How do you do?" He glanced over at his wife's face, which was positively glowing with merriment. He grinned and was led inside by his wife's Aunt Jenny and Amelia, who had graciously welcomed him to her home. Katie followed with Uncle Albert.

As they sat down to supper that evening, there were hundreds of questions that the family wished Katie and Brent to answer, and she was forced to put an end to their curiosity, at least for the time being.

"Enough, everyone! We've been traveling for several weeks, and we're both exhausted! We'll be only too happy to answer your questions tomorrow!" she informed them, then laughed to soften her words.

"Very well, dear. James and John, you two go on up to bed now, you hear? Katie, Brent, please excuse us. I'm afraid that it's time for us all to turn in. Albert, Jenny, are you coming?" Amelia inclined her head toward them meaningfully. She recalled how it was when she and her own dear husband were still newlyweds.

"Ah, yes, Amelia, we're coming," Albert replied. He urged his wife from her seat and the three of them climbed the stairs just behind the two boys.

"Oh, Brent, it's so very good to see them all again. But I must confess, I'd much rather still be out in the wilderness along with my husband! I'm sure I'm going to miss our privacy, aren't you?"

"Yes, I can see that I am. However, I do still have an assignment I've got to work on while I'm here. Why don't you go on up to bed and I'll join you in a little while? I'd like to go into the library and do some work there." He had to sit down and think about the information he'd been given, about the possibility of the leader being someone known to the O'Tooles of Corkhaven. He also wanted to have a few moments in which to ponder his and Katie's future, about where they would settle after the war. There was so very much planning to do.

"If you wish, darling. Don't be long, though. We haven't spent the night in a real bed in a long time!" she commented as she left the dining room.

Brent rose from his seat and strode across the hall to the library. He tried opening the door, but it was locked. Now, why would anyone want to lock up the library? he asked himself. It had never been kept locked before. Before Katie's aunt and uncle had come to live at Corkhaven that is. Katie had told him that her uncle operated some mysterious business, something he wouldn't ever discuss with her when she was visiting him in Atlanta. Maybe this had something to do with his business. She assumed he was some sort of loan shark or something, but Brent began to doubt her conclusions.

He reached into his pocket and drew out his pocket knife. He inserted the tip of the smallest blade into the lock, and after jiggling and turning, the door opened. He peered into the darkness of the room. He knew where the desk was, so he walked straight across the room and lit the lamp sitting upon it. Holding the light high, he then set about searching the library to determine exactly why anyone would have wanted it locked.

He rifled through the drawers of the desk, but found nothing he considered to be out of the ordinary. Just some papers concerning the plantation, and the thick accounts book. His fingers then closed on another book, a smaller

303

one hidden inside the larger one, a book which had fallen out of the larger book's pages. It had nothing stamped on its leather cover, and he opened it carefully.

Written on the inside cover was the name of Katie's uncle, Albert O'Toole. Brent flipped through the pages, noting the various names of cities and individuals. There were lines of figures beside them. What could this possibly mean? Why would a loan shark be doing business all over the countryside? It suddenly dawned on him then.

Albert O'Toole must certainly be the man he had been sent to find, the mastermind of the gun-running operation. What a coincidence if it were indeed true. Or was it a coincidence, he wondered.

His superiors had known of his marriage to a Southerner, so why wouldn't they have known her name, and also where her home was? They had probably suspected her uncle for some time, had probably known about him long before he fled Atlanta. Why hadn't they seen fit to tell him about it, though, and why hadn't they told him his name? Probably because they were afraid I wouldn't accept the assignment, not if I had known it involved my own wife's uncle. And yet, they had sent him on this mission, knowing full well, that if he was successful, he would discover the man's identity for himself. Now, Brent realized that he was faced with a dreadful dilemma.

Reading the book further, he soon became convinced of Albert O'Toole's guilt. It all fit together too well. This general vicinity was known as the man's location, Albert's book had the important cities and figures, and there were the names of other individuals within the pages that confirmed his involvement with known criminals. Now, what was he to do about it?

He knew that his superiors waited for him to prove himself, for him to find and arrest his own wife's uncle. How could he do that to Katie, though? Perhaps he could think of another way out of this situation. Only, what other alternative was there?

Twenty Four

"Sir, would you mind stepping into the library with me for a few minutes? I have some matters I'd like to discuss with you, privately," Brent requested of Albert the next morning as the breakfast dishes were being cleared away.

"Sure, Captain. You womenfolk go into the parlour and have your little chit-chat. I know you've got so much to discuss and ask Katie that you're all about to bust!" Albert told the women. Katie, Amelia, and Jenny nodded their heads and chuckled in agreement, then took his suggestion and left the dining room to sit in the parlour, where it was true they would have much to talk about.

"What's this all about, Brent? I suppose, that as Katie's only adult male relative, you'd like to have my final blessings on your marriage. Well, I give you that, my boy. Now, is there anything else on your mind?" he asked Brent as he continued to lead the way into the library.

"Thank you for the blessing, sir, but that wasn't quite what I had in mind. Now, if you'll please be seated, sir, I'll get down to business." He'd been awake half the night, trying valiantly to think of a way out of the predicament that had arisen with his knowledge of Albert's guilt. He had finally hit on a plan, a solution that should work, at least he hoped so.

"Now, Mr. O'Toole, I'll begin," here he received a confused nod of agreement from the older man. "I was here in the library last night after the rest of you had retired upstairs. I can see that you are a bit surprised at finding it unlocked this morning, aren't you? Well, I just

305

happened to be curious, so I managed to unlock it and came inside to discover precisely why anyone would have wanted it locked in the first place. I found such a reason."

"Yes, I only locked it to keep the boys from playing in here, though. You see, there are some important papers contained within the desk drawers, and they are forever getting into things they shouldn't," he lied smoothly.

"Yes, well, please allow me to continue, sir. As I said, I discovered why you had locked the door. I found the book, Albert, the secret book in which you kept the accounts of your business. I also happen to know which business that is. I am a Union officer, remember? Why do you think I was allowed to travel all the way to Corkhaven? I have the complete authority to place you under arrest for being the leader of an illegal gun-running operation."

Albert's face betrayed his surprise and trepidation at Brent's commanding words. He sought to control his expression, but it was too late.

"Well, young man. It appears that you are not only a Yankee, but a spy as well! We all wondered exactly why you were no longer in uniform. What right had you to break into this room and rifle through the desk? What right had you to come into this house and spy into my personal belongings?" he blustered, knowing full well that he had finally and irrevocably been caught.

"Don't speak to me of rights, Mr. O'Toole! What right had you to supply both sides of a war with weapons? You employed various criminals and known outlaws, and you sold stolen goods, goods that should have been returned to their rightful owners. Now, if you're willing to cooperate with me, we might be able to work out a deal," Brent suggested reasonably.

"What kind of deal?" Albert replied as he narrowed his eyes suspiciously. It wouldn't do him any good to deny his guilt, he realized, so he might as well try and bargain with the man. The young fellow was just too crafty for him to get around.

"Well, let's say that you receive amnesty from any arrest and prosecution by my government. In return, you must be willing to supply me with full details of your business and the complete list of names and cities. Are you agreeable?"

"I'll have to think about it for a while," he stalled, "but, if I do agree, my life would be in even greater danger. Those whom I revealed to you would surely seek my life in retribution. Think of it, man, I'm your wife's own flesh and blood. Why, she could even have her own life threatened as a result!"

"I'll take care of those particular details, sir. Well, either you agree or you don't. Which is it to be?" he demanded, becoming a bit impatient.

Albert calculated the risks, weighing them against possible prosecution and imprisonment by the Yankees. He decided to choose the former.

"All right, Captain Morgan, I'll tell you whatever you wish to know. But, understand, I have complete amnesty. And, you'll see to it that I nor my family come to any personal harm?"

"Yes, I can take care of that. Now, first off, I need a complete list of the names. Then, a list of the cities still involved in your operation. This book isn't evidence enough. I need a statement signed by you. By the way," Brent paused to ask, "why did you get involved in such a dangerous business in the first place? Weren't you afraid of retribution at the beginning? How did you manage to elude the authorities on both sides for so long?"

"I have my ways, Captain. Yes, I've been afraid for my life and the life of my dear wife, but there was such a huge profit to be made, I couldn't seem to stop the dealings. Later, when I actually did contemplate getting out, I was in over my head. I was informed that I could never get out, that, if I tried, I would surely be killed. These are the type of men I've been in business with, you see. However, you wouldn't have been sent to apprehend me at all if it hadn't been for the fact that more guns are being sold to the

Confederacy right now than the Federalist officials can tolerate! It takes weapons to keep a war going, my boy, no matter where or how those weapons are acquired. I supplied your own troops with many guns and cannon, not just the Confederacy. How do you think you Yankees could have fought the war in the South without them? Where else were you to get the necessary weapons and ammunition? Now, though, I've simply made the higher Yankee officials angry, and they have decided to do something about it. They feel betrayed, perhaps, but I operate my business for profit, not for ideals. I took no side in this war, and I do not still. The South is losing, Captain, and you are well aware of that fact. Therefore, they are the most desperate to purchase my guns, and they are willing to pay the higher prices. I've been sending couriers with the necessary instructions to my various contacts ever since I was forced to flee Atlanta. Now, I'll see about writing that statement. By the way," here he ceased his discourse regarding his business and inquired anxiously, "you're not going to tell my niece about all this, are you? You're not going to tell the rest of the family?"

"No, sir, I am not. Oh, I'll have to tell Katie something, but I won't supply her with the full details, I promise you. It wouldn't serve for anything but to make her unhappy if I did. Now, start writing, Albert. I'm sure I can work out the bargain with my commanding officer. There's no reason to arrest you if there is no longer any gun-running operation, now, is there?" Brent asked with a twinkle. He'd decided that Katie's uncle wasn't all bad: just misguided and rather spineless.

"Captain," Albert replied companionably, "I do believe I both like and admire you, sir, even if you are a Yankee."

Later that night, up in their bedroom, Katie happened to mention Brent's request to speak privately with her uncle.

"Brent, why did you have to talk to Uncle Albert so privately? What on earth could you have had to say?"

"Oh, I had some private matters to discuss with him,

that's all. However, I see that I'm going to have to tell you a bit more about it, or I won't have any peace tonight!" he mocked.

"Well, I am your wife, remember? And, he is my own uncle. Is he in trouble or something?"

"What makes you say that?" he replied noncommittally.

"Oh, I just happen to know that he's involved in something that isn't very good for him, that's all. Well, am I right? Is that it? Is he in some kind of trouble because of his mysterious business?" she demanded to know.

"Yes, as a matter of fact, he is. But, it's all been cleared up now. In fact, he was an important part of the assignment I was sent here on. He was involved with some criminals we're anxious to find, and he was able to give me some valuable information. But, he's no longer in trouble. He's no longer connected with the whole affair so you can just rest easy about him. He didn't want you to know anything about it, but I told him that I would have to tell you something. You are much too quick to catch anything out of the ordinary in the air!"

"Well, I'm glad it's all right now. I won't press you for the whole story. I hope you weren't too harsh on him, though. Poor Uncle Albert, I can't say that I admire or even respect him much, but I do still care for him. After all, he was Papa's only brother. Are you completely finished with your mission, then?" she asked, hoping that there was still something to keep him at Corkhaven for a while longer.

"Katie, I can't stay any longer. Don't get your hopes up about that. Darling, I'm sorry, but I'll head on to Savannah tomorrow." He hated leaving her again, but there was still a war being fought and Mr. Morrow would want a full report. He couldn't postpone it any longer. They probably hadn't expected that he would complete his business so soon, he began to rationalize, but he would still have to get on back. He was, after all, a soldier in wartime.

"Brent! So soon? Oh, I don't know what I'll do after

you've gone. I've become so accustomed to having you with me every day. I can't bear the thought of your returning to the war, of being caught up in the battles, of possibly being wounded, or killed. I can't let you go back!" she cried. He came to her and drew her into his arms, saying:

"Katie, I've got to go. But, I'll be back, I promise you. After the war, just like we planned before. We've been very lucky and you know it. We've had a lot more time together than a lot of couples during the war. I won't get killed, honey. I'll hurry on back here to you as soon as I can. Now, don't cry. This is our last night together before I leave. Let's end it on a happy note. Let me carry a happy memory of this night with me. I don't even know if I'll be reassigned again, and I may not be in a location where I can send you letters, but I'll try. It will be over soon, I know it. The time will pass quickly if we know we'll be together afterwards."

"I don't think the time will pass quickly for me, Brent. I'll be sitting here at home, waiting for any word from you, waiting for you to come home. Oh, darling, how can I bear it?" She clutched him frantically to her and hugged him as if she would never again release him.

"Katie, let's simply not think about tomorrow yet. Let's think only about this very minute, about our time together tonight. I'll have to get an early start, so you will have to explain everything to your family after I've gone. I know you'll be in good hands until I return. This time, I won't have to worry about where you are and who the devil's chasing you!" Brent lovingly teased her. She managed a tremulous, teary smile in return and led him slowly toward the bed.

She would do as he wanted: make this a night to carry with him in his memory, through the fighting and danger of war, through the sleepless, lonely nights. She would have such nights, also, only she would be safely at home in a real bed, while there was no telling where he would be forced to spend his nights.

"Brent," she breathed softly as they undressed, "I love you so very much."

"And I love you, Katie O'Toole Morgan," he whispered in reply as he turned out the lamp.

Early the following morning, Katie stood upon the veranda to say her last goodbye. She held back her tears. She wouldn't cry; he wouldn't want to remember her crying. She smiled brightly at him as he left his saddled, impatiently waiting horse to kiss her once again.

"Katie, I'll carry all the wonderful memories of you throughout the next weeks, months, however long it takes to end the war. I'll never forget last night, nor all of the other splendid nights I've spent in your arms. Now, kiss me goodbye, sweetheart, for I really must leave you now."

"I know. I'll remember, too, Brent, as long as I live. When you come back, we'll speak some more about where we're going to build that home and raise our family, won't we? Oh, I love you so much!" she blurted out as she wrapped her arms tightly about him. He kissed her, gently moving his warm lips caressingly over her own. He then tore himself away from her clinging grasp and mounted his horse. Waving goodbye, he kicked the horse into a gallop and rode away, back to the war.

Katie stood waving until he was out of sight. He was gone now. She'd have to face that fact. She didn't know when or if he would return, but she would pray for his safekeeping. She would manage to pass the time until he came back. There still was an enormous amount of work to be done at Corkhaven, and she could certainly occupy her time with that alone. Oh yes, she would be ready when he came home, to go wherever he wanted, to follow him anywhere.

Part 4

Homecoming

Twenty Five

Richmond, the capital of the Confederacy, fell to the Yankees in April of 1865, and with it fell the last vestiges of hope for a Southern victory. The limit of endurance had finally and irrevocably been reached. The remaining Confederate Army had no food and tattered uniforms, while the citizens of Richmond were also starving. As the Confederates fled and the city was evacuated, the flames of huge fires began.

The President of the Confederacy, Jefferson Davis, also fled its capital, only to be captured and imprisoned later. As Lee met with Grant at Appomattox in April of 1865, it was apparent that the end had arrived.

President Abraham Lincoln visited the remains of Richmond, only to be struck down ten days later by an assassin's bullet. The entire country grieved; he had been the hope for the future, the only remaining encouragement for the fallen South.

Katie had done as she had resolved that day Brent had ridden away from her and back to the war; she had occupied her time with the reconstruction of Corkhaven. Although the slaves were now legally free, the few at Corkhaven refused to leave. Uncle Albert had indeed turned over a new leaf; he had invested his fortune into bringing the plantation back to life and prosperity.

Brent had been able to write only once, at least that was all Katie had received. He had been in Nashville at the time, working on another secret mission. He couldn't give her the details, he only said he would again journey to

Virginia. She memorized every word of his letter, after repeatedly drawing it from her apron pocket many times to read it again and again.

Oh, Brent, when will you come home to me? They had heard the astounding news of Lee's surrender only yesterday. Surely he could come home now. But, no, he'd have to remain in the army until they would allow him to resign his commission, until all the loose ends had been taken care of. Simply because the war had finally ended didn't mean an end to the struggle; there were still those who would never surrender, never give in.

Now four months pregnant, Katie was finding it more and more difficult to work hours at a time without tiring. She knew exactly when this precious baby had been conceived; the night in the woods near Atlanta, their last night alone together before coming home to Corkhaven. They had jokingly talked about starting a family that night. Well, it was certainly no joke now! She would bear him a son, or daughter, she didn't care which. He would be so ecstatically happy when he found out. She hadn't been able to write him about the baby, as she didn't have any way of knowing where to send a letter.

She gently slid her hand over her still slender stomach. Her mother had said that she had carried Katie the same way, not showing her condition until well into her fifth month. Katie sighed. She wanted to show now, she wanted to feel the baby's movements and be able to see its evidence. She would love this baby so much, this child of hers and Brent's. If only he would be able to return soon, if only he hadn't been wounded or killed as she had endlessly feared.

"Mama, I think I'll go on outside and see what those two brothers of mine are up to," she remarked to her mother, who sat across from her.

"Very well, dear. You know, I still can't believe the war is over with, can you? Don't worry, child, your husband will come home to you. I don't see how he can very well help it, with your tireless prayers for his safe return! Now, you go on out and get some sunshine. Your Uncle Albert and Aunt Jenny are busy going over some of the accounts. I do believe, Katie, that Albert is really going to put this place to rights again. He's invested quite a sum of money into it. I'll be eternally grateful to him if he can preserve it for your brothers."

Katie strolled out of the parlour and onto the veranda outside. She took a deep breath, drinking in the fresh, fragrant spring air and warm sunshine. Her two brothers were absorbed in building a treehouse in the big oak tree standing in the front yard. Tom was lending them some assistance with their project.

She sat down upon a bench and watched the workers in the nearby fields. Uncle Albert had hired some additional hands to help with this year's crops. Whatever shady business dealings he had been involved in, he certainly changed. She knew that Brent had been directly responsible for that change, for her Uncle Albert had eventually told her more about that morning in the library and of Brent's generosity to him. Here she was, back to thinking of her husband once again. Oh well, he was constantly in her thoughts, no matter how hard she tried to concentrate on other matters. She loved him even more now than when he had gone away.

"James, John, you two be careful up there! You might very well fall and bust your little heads!" she yelled to her brothers, who were, by now, high up in the tree's branches.

"Aw, Katie, don't be a spoilsport! We won't fall. You're only a girl, but boys don't fall out of trees!" they replied. She smiled at the memory of that day, long ago, when she had fallen from that very same tree. Her brothers had been much too young to remember the event, but their father had delighted them with stories of their older sister's precarious childhood.

She leaned comfortably back against the front wall of the house and dreamily closed her eyes. She was so tired of waiting, so tired of trying to fill her days and night with other thoughts. Dear Lord, let him come soon.

"Katie! Look, Katie, someone's coming! And, he's wearing a Yankee uniform! Is he still the enemy? Has he come to take over the house, like the others did that time?" James and John excitedly asked. She opened her eyes and slowly stood upright.

A Yankee, coming to Corkhaven? Why, the war was over, so why would a Yankee be coming here? Of course, there had been several Southern men who had fought on the North's side. Perhaps this was one of them, traveling past on his way home. Well, no matter which side he had fought on, the least they could do was to offer him something to eat and drink.

"I see him, you don't have to holler any longer! You two just stay put, and I'll take care of this," she called in return. She slowly approached the front steps of the veranda and awaited the stranger's arrival.

Suddenly, she gasped with excitement, unable to breathe for a moment. That wasn't just a Yankee, that was her husband, in uniform once again! She clutched her skirts in her hands and flew down the steps as he rode within the front gates of Corkhaven.

"Brent! Brent, it's really you! Oh, Brent, you've come home!" she shouted as she ran toward him. He dismounted and quickly ran to meet her with outstretched arms.

"Katie! Katie, I told you I'd come home, didn't I? It's over now, darling, the war's over with. I'm only in uniform because I didn't wait to buy other clothing. I wanted to come to you as soon as I could!" he told her as he crushed her into his loving embrace. They kissed hungrily and passionately, oblivious to the amused stares and giggles of the various onlookers. Her mother, aunt, and uncle were now standing out on the veranda. James and John were scurrying down from the tree.

"Brent, are you really out of the army now? Are we going to be able to be together now? For good?" she demanded breathlessly.

"Yes, darling, I'm out for good. I'll tell you all about the past few months later. How have you been? Have you been busy? I see you haven't wasted away from missing me!" he said as he laughed happily.

"Oh, Brent, I've got so much to tell you, too! But, come on in the house. Everyone's going to want to welcome you home. I'm so very glad you've come home, Brent!" she repeated. They walked toward the house and to her waiting family, arm in arm, unable to keep their eyes from straying to one another as they walked.

Later, up in the privacy of their bedroom, Katie listened as Brent told her of his plans for their life together.

"Katie, I think I've decided where we'll build our home. I think we should head for Texas, maybe even California. I know that's a very long way from here, but the war hasn't touched it like it's touched everything here. There was some fighting in Texas, of course, but nothing that would affect it too much. As for California, why, it's a whole new territory. What do you say, sweetheart, would you like to head west?" Brent anxiously asked her, intently watching her face for any sign that she disapproved of his suggestions.

"Brent, I don't care where we go, as long as it's what you want and we're together. Texas sounds fine, so does California, whatever you choose. I know we can't stay here, we can't remain in the South, so I know you nor I wants to go up north. So, I think heading west is the perfect solution," she told him approvingly. Should she tell him about the baby now? Would he demand that they remain in Corkhaven until it was born? She didn't want to stay here, she wanted to go away with him right away, she wanted them to start a new life together, just the two of them.

"Brent," she hesitantly began, "about that family we were talking of starting before you went away..."

"Oh, yes, our family. Well, I think it would be best to wait until we're settled, don't you? Of course, if it happens

316

before then, I'd be mightily pleased, you know that. Why, is there something you wanted to say on the subject?'' he inquired casually as he began removing his boots and clothing.

"No, nothing, darling. I just want to start one as soon as we can, that's all." She would tell him about the baby later, once they were well on their way. If she told him now, he probably would refuse to allow her to make the trip. It wouldn't hurt for him to know a little later. Besides, she didn't know if he was one of those men who was afraid to make love to his wife after hearing of her condition. And, she certainly didn't want him to react that way! Not when she needed him so badly, after she had yearned for him so much.

"Brent, I do love you. Thank the Lord you've returned to me safe and sound. I don't want to ever be parted from you again."

"Me, neither, darling. I won't let you out of my sight ever again, that's for sure. I can't trust you to keep out of trouble if I do!"

They faced each other from either side of the canopied bed, each of them smiling at the thoughts of now and the future. The Yankee and the belle were no more; they were now simply Brent and Katie Morgan, pioneers, settlers, the hope for the future.